Reel and Rout

Reel and Rout

Robert A. G. Monks

brook street press
SAINT SIMONS ISLAND

Brook Street Press
www.brookstreetpress.com

Brook Street Press is a trademark of Brook Street Press LLC

First Edition

Library of Congress Cataloging-in-Publication Data

Monks, Robert A. G.
Reel and rout / Robert A. G. Monks
p. cm.
ISBN 0-9724295-2-2
1. Consolidation and merger of corporations—Fiction. 2.
Periodicals—Publishing—Fiction. 3. Chief executive officers—Fiction.
4. Mass media—Ownership—Fiction. 5. Corporate culture—Fiction. 6.
Business ethics—Fiction. I. Title.
PS3613.0536R44 2004
813'.6—dc22   2003023670

Jacket and interior design by David Baldeosingh Rotstein

Printed in the United States of America

10 9 8 7 6 5 4 3 2 1

To

GAG
George Herrick
Gardner Monks

Prologue

Saturday, August 1, 1998

Blue Wave, World Publications' Gulfstream IV, circled over New York City on a clear and cool late July evening, twinkling in iridescent purple and gold, in the light of the full moon. A controversial gift from the board of directors, it was designed personally for CEO Cedric Rhodes, known throughout the world as Drive, his wife, and staff. Drive always occupied a special Pullman seat on the left side of the cabin so he could follow any conversation with his good ear, and with a customized desk in front of him, piled with the latest editions of the day's newspapers from major cities in the States and around the world, he had plenty to do and could prevent anyone from annoying him needlessly during the flight.

Drive relished that moment in the jet's descent when he could see the company's longtime New York home and the apartment exclusively reserved for him and his family in the Sherry Netherland Tower at the southeast corner of Central Park.

The Assyrian came down like the wolf on the fold,

And his cohorts were gleaming in purple and gold;

And the sheen of their spears was like stars on the sea,

When the blue wave rolls nightly on deep Galilee.

While the plane made its approach to Teterboro, he smiled broadly at the prospect of the new adventure. Drive was given to flights of self-reflection. Like many colonials, he took great pleasure in the imagery of British romantic poets. He knew them all, but Byron's *Destruction of the Sennacherib* had been a personal favorite since childhood. He had aways enjoyed feeling like the ancient Assyrian and that is why his plane's colors were purple and gold. He could hardly wait to assemble his cohorts and unleash them on the campaign he had planned so carefully for so long. *The gods are clearly on my side*, he thought as he glanced at the headlines on the different newspapers sprawled on the desk before him. The *New York Times* was his favorite of the lot: CLINTON VOWS "COMPLETE AND TRUTHFUL" TESTIMONY. The first line said it all. WASHINGTON, July 31—"President Clinton declared today that he would testify 'completely and truthfully' in the Monica S. Lewinsky investigation on August 17 but said that until then he would have no public comment on the matter." It sang like sweet music to Drive. Even he could never have dreamt up a more perfect distraction for the ever-shrinking American public's attention span, and he had been doing it for four decades. He liked the headline so much he superstitiously rolled it up and took it with him, once the taxiing jet came to a stop.

Limos were waiting. Drive and his wife were met on the runway; bags and staff of three to follow. Saturday night summer traffic was light and they were quickly home to the studied lobby, the magnificently painted elevators, and the superb apartment that Drive had World Publications purchase some twenty years ago and had been modernizing and redecorating ever since. The elevators rattled a bit, but there was a unique feeling of privacy overlooking the park and Hudson River from high above. With his staff and wife installed, Drive stepped outside, all alone on the west-facing balcony. With a specialized, bulky cell phone, only ten feet removed from his wife, he closed the sliding glass door and began an intimate conversation with another woman, a younger woman, his right hand and second in command of the new team he would assemble. He spoke softly, with a boyish eagerness, into the device, betraying his more-than-professional interest in his secret partner.

"Hello." Drive wondered if she would be as excited as he was.

"You're here and ready to go." She was happy sounding, he was pleased.

"Like never before. This is the big one and no mistakes will be made." He felt compelled to sound authoritative now, even though he wanted to share something more personal. He didn't want to disappoint her.

"You've worked so hard, so many false starts. This time, we've got the target, the credit, the right people. We've got a winning strategy. I don't think we've overlooked anything. The right company; and the price…getting better every day."

"And with the eternally vigilant press having all eyes on the President's crotch, it really is the perfect time to make our run. My only regret is not being able to see each other for the duration."

"It's for the best. No one will be able to put us together, that's a certainty. It'll be a long month, but then we'll have some time for ourselves."

"Yes, the *rest* of our lives. Have you really got all of our dominoes in line?"

"I think so. You'll build the team there and for now, some timely press. The investigator's work and the shareholder suit are on schedule. And we're almost there with the attorney general."

"Dear girl. And that favor?"

"At least one of the Big Three will feature our version."

"Which one? *Fortune, Forbes,* or *Business Week?*"

"You'll just have to wait and see."

"Oh, will I? My minx. Look, I've got to go. Good work."

"Don't thank me, thank Bill Clinton. He'll keep peoples' minds busy for several more weeks, I'm sure. Just enough time. Sweet dreams, my prince."

Chapter 1

Drive had arranged two meetings at World Publications' offices in the Chrysler Building. A great conceit of the Art Deco splurge of the late 1920s, the imposing edifice towered above Forty-second Street and Lexington, across the street from Grand Central Station. Drive was proud of his foresight to enter into a long-term lease for the entire forty-second floor during the doldrums of the early 1970s.

During thirty years of occupancy the building had endured decline and then enjoyed revival, thanks in part to Drive. Armed with options to renew his rent at a fixed price well into the twenty-first century, he had spent lavishly. An exclusive elevator, the first one on the third bank, went directly to his floor. The exit doors opened right into the office lobby and reception area that said it all: magnificent flowers, fresh every day, a splendid-looking receptionist behind a custom-designed white desk, and a floor-to-ceiling glass view of the United Nations Building, the East River, and the morning sun. Only a business owned by a family, that confidently expected to exist forever, would tolerate such luxe. Each of the four corners comprised a single office, with the one on the southwest corner permanently reserved for Drive, no matter where in the world he was actually located. Next to Drive's office, along the southern face of the building, was a boardroom that also served as a dining room for the splendid catered affairs the firm sponsored. The workers were huddled along the west face in eight-by-ten-foot spaces; the managers of the local businesses and their support staff each had a corner. Somebody's wife had done the decorating. It was a scandal at the time, too much money and too French, but as is usually the case with such things, nobody today could remember the details.

Whenever he arrived at one of the company's principal offices, Drive followed the same routine. Invariably, he awoke around five o'clock, stopped at whatever delicatessen was serving something he could eat for breakfast, and using his master key, arrived in his own office before six. Staff around the world would have prepared summaries and his top lieutenants expected his call. Everyone knew his schedule and so adapted their own, knowing that Drive would ignore the fact that it was a Sunday and that the local time was inconvenient for mere mortals. There was a one-page up-to-date summary of the company's cash position and usual stack of latest editions hot off the world presses, identical to the stack back at the apartment, refreshed twice a day. Drive had been involved for too many years in the vagaries of accounting to believe anything other than the real balance in the bank. His computer was on, but being Sunday there was no happy ticker tape crawling relentlessly along the bottom. It was the computer's sole contribution to his office because he hated reading newspapers on-line, absurd, and e-mail was for pikers who couldn't afford a secretary. Somehow, this routine was less comforting than it usually was. His mind really wasn't on World Publications business, Drive confessed to himself.

He began his morning ritual, laying out his papers on his great desk, and like a conductor with his score, he tracked his favorite "melodies." The domestic papers aped themselves, striving to seem unique as they feature local dustups and recite the same national litany. Television had made him very rich but he never respected the medium. Too superficial, one giant advert from beginning to end, and television "news" was laughable. Misleading coverage, talking heads, and images based on where the light was better for the shot, with trained monkeys reading the headlines and very little else. Not much would be learned from television except what people were being sold, one way or another. Drive liked playing detective with his papers. Eager for a fresh take, or a new voice, but finding them fewer and fewer as American democracy settled for "freedom from choice," Drive assuaged his usual disappointment with the knowledge that this thundering monotony would make his great challenge that much easier. But it really didn't seem like a fair fight anymore. Clinton had reduced every inch of every national paper to a scandal-rag tabloid and no real news for pages. Like a Torah of Idiocy, each paper was padded with column after column of commentary on the commentary. The European papers were bemused and snide about the Yankee teapot tempest and the Pacific Rim reported dry facts like a fastidious anthropologist. He was bored with his papers.

He went into his private bathroom and briefly wondered about the different kinds of water flow and drying apparatus that were in use in various parts of the world. Drive was abruptly pulled out of his musing when he caught sight of his father's face in one of the several mirrors. He blinked and remembered the old saying, "When you see your father's face in the mirror, you are no longer young." With a twinge of pain, the memories of a lifetime, and the fear of not quite measuring up to the old man, came flooding in.

Drive was walking around in his shirtsleeves with a piece of the *New York Times* in hand. EAST HAMPTON, N.Y., August 1—"The Hamptons didn't exactly offer President Clinton a red carpet and a clamorous ovation this weekend. The greeting was more confused than that, more complicated, muted." The elevator chimed. It was just seven o'clock when the elevator door opened, revealing his long-time lawyer, Spencer Sherman, impeccably tied and black suited.

"What's a guy like you doing in a place like this on a day like today?" Spencer was the managing partner of one of the largest and oldest law firms in the city, well accustomed to the idiosyncrasies that wealth and power permitted his principal clients. He had a good sense of humor and dressed the part of a Wall Street lawyer on a Sunday in August because it amused him to humor his clients. He had also found that his uniform protected him. People thought they knew what to expect. This gave his subtle mind and keen intellect extra leverage, which accounted for his huge success in a most competitive profession. Meetings in mid-Manhattan on an August Sunday were a metaphor for big-firm law practice, limitless money in exchange for total commitment.

He had done legal work for Drive for thirty years. Now he eyed him ironically. "What's with the clothes? I never thought I'd see the day, my favorite Kaffir wandering around in silk shirts and Italian slacks. You look pretty fit for an old man."

Drive declined the bait and led Spencer back to his office. "We need to talk privately, old friend. I need your advice." *Into my parlor, little fly*, thought Drive.

Spencer had heard this before. "I'm glad to give it. You rarely follow it. And you are the most powerful press magnate in the world and I am still a wage slave."

Drive's laugh was hearty, and showed he was ready to listen to the tailored aristocrat before him.

"To the point. You asked me to find a lawyer, a lone wolf without big-firm connections who could personally handle a financial transaction on your scale. Should I be grateful our firm couldn't do the job?"

Drive laughed again, cut with a tad less sincerity, and a bit more diplomacy. "I need to talk to you as a friend as well as a lawyer, I feel the same as I did twenty years ago, but everybody else is getting older. My kids and the board are all talking about succession; the executives glance past me now when someone else comes into the room. They act as if they don't have to relate to me any more. I'm history...without a retirement policy. Why should I leave? For God's sake, I own this company!"

Drive's appeal to friendship seemed out of character; Sherman wondered what might be wrong with his most lucrative of clients. "Slow down, old buddy, you don't own the company. You and your family are the beneficial owners of trusts, which have 30 percent of the voting stock. You are the biggest holder, by far, of the voting stock, but your percentage of the total invested capital is closer to 3 percent." Spencer pinched his finger and thumb together to emphasize the point but wondered to himself, Drive knew all this. Was he getting senile?

"The same 3 percent that calls every shot that keeps us here, but thanks, counselor, that's just what I need, a touch of the legalities in the midst of my tantrum. I can create value as well as I ever could. Retirement? I intend to run this company as long as I live. In the meantime, I am sixty-seven and I want to prove I'm not just another old fart, coasting on the momentum. I am going to do a deal, by myself, outside of the company."

"Suffering from a delayed midlife crisis? Is there a girlfriend in the wings?" Sherman regretted the words before they had passed his teeth, even before he saw the look on his client's face.

Drive was caught by surprise by the question. *Does it show?* he wondered.

"No, I'm still a young man and I want to do deals. I hope I'm never too old to hold the attention of a beautiful woman."

That's a "yes," thought Sherman. Change the subject. "Well, your employment contract states that you are entitled, after age sixty-five, to devote whatever time you want on matters outside of the company that do not interfere with your functioning as chairman and do not conflict with company operations. You are entitled to use company facilities, like the GIV, the apartment, condos, and various offices, but you are not entitled to use company personnel."

"Wait a minute, this is my place, all $450 million in after-tax profits this year. I made it." Drive was pacing but Spencer kept his poise. "Three percent. Absurd," grumbled Drive. He enjoyed this little drama that he was acting out on his lawyer of many years.

"Every once in a while, I get to act like a lawyer. You need to know this. I thought you did. When you first took money from the public, the nature of your enterprise changed. Sure, you control it, but, being a public company, you are exposed to a well-established battery of rules and traditions. You cannot use World Publications' personnel to make money for anybody other than all the shareholders of World Publications. You cannot induce people to do things for your new venture with a wink and a nod and then they will be taken care of by World Publications. No matter what. Now, what's this deal?"

Drive's tone was testy. "Yes. Yes. I see. I see. Are you sure you want to know? Wouldn't that give you a conflict of interest?"

The two stared silently at each other, like poker players who knew each other's game too well. But finally, thirty years of mutually beneficial business prevailed.

"I am going to buy the *American Observer* magazine."

Sherman was struck dumb for a moment and Drive found that moment exquisite. The *American Observer* was a national treasure found in every library, every doctor's and dentist's office in the nation. It was required reading in every public school system. For previous generations it had been America's greatest literary ambassador, translated into more languages than the Bible.

"Are you kidding? It's not for sale. I know, everything is for sale, but these guys, these guys are welded in place. They own voting stock, not just a little like you," again, pinching his finger and thumb together to make his point, "an absolute majority. They are trustees for every charity in New York." Sherman wondered if Drive was really serious, the partners at the firm would hate this deal on sight. Who would dare fund it? "You won't get help on this one. But, I'll say this. I have got you the perfect lawyer."

"Sometimes, the impossible is easy precisely because nobody has imagined it yet. No one ever figured that I would build this enterprise from a family newspaper in South Africa. Speed will be critical. We have the money. We know the law. From beginning to end, we can get this done in one month—August."

"This August?!?" Sherman could argue with Drive's logic but not his track record.

"That's right." Drive said, beaming, "So tell me about this lawyer."

"Marty Beal expects your call. I told him you wanted full-time, immediate services. The single best corporate lawyer in the country, with none of the conflicts of interest of an establishment firm. He likes that "best lawyer" stuff. He's local, a great rabbinical family. Father wrote books on holy ritual. The Gold Medal for being Number

One at Brooklyn, Yale Law School, and out to the Coast. First Jewish employee of one of the big firms, first Jewish partner. Shame on us. Our loss."

Drive settled in as Spencer took a breath and continued. "Colossal law practice. He personally represents the biggest money manager in California and the largest conglomerate. Brought those clients with him when he came back to New York. Says he couldn't stand working in a place where you couldn't get a bagel after midnight! The late eighties takeover boom in New York City made lawyers royalty."

"His Majesty Martin," mused Drive.

"That's right," laughed Spencer. "Nobody can be his partner. He works too hard; too demanding. He became 'of counsel' to a well-established firm. He hates bureaucracy. The firm gives him office space and bodies to do the bulk of the work he brings in, but he still likes to do the work himself. Do you remember the deal when that guy tried to take over Chemical Bank by himself? Marty did all that *personally*, drafting, pleading."

"Am I going to like him?"

"All that, and you want someone to make nice, too? Can't think of guys like him in terms of likability. You deserve each other. Do you want to get out of here and get a bite?" Sherman had only just realized, now that the element of surprise had worn off, that Drive had just played him. Had him come over, and talk himself out of the deal of a lifetime...if he's got the funding?

"No, I've got to call my new lawyer and do a little work." Drive rose and Sherman took his cue but made a final pitch as he got up to leave.

"I'll forgive you, but you are going to need a fairness opinion and counsel. Keep that slot open for us."

As he led him to the open elevator, Drive noticed that his trusted associate of many years was losing some of his spark, and there was no room for old friends on his new team.

"Spencer! I can't believe that your firm actually could be involved here. What about a conflict of interest with all of the other business we do?"

"Conflict of interest, what's that?" Spencer chuckled. "That's one of the good things about being a lawyer. We're the ones who get to decide what *is* a conflict of interest. This situation isn't even close." Sherman gave Drive a parting Cheshire cat smile, but Drive was already halfway to his office.

Drive sat down and punched the newest number on his speed dial.

"Martin van Buren Beal?"

"Yeah?"

"This is Drive. Spencer Sherman told me about you."

"Yeah?"

"Can we talk?"

"When?"

"Tomorrow first thing"

"I'll be at your office at nine o'clock."

Drive got up and stretched his lean five-foot ten-inch-tall frame against the bookcase beside his desk, pulled his fingers through his thinning sandy hair and smiled in anticipation of the rest of the day. He lost himself in the view of the empty streets below. Why couldn't the city be this peaceful every day? Ah well, back to work. He actuated the speed dial on his mobile phone and without ado said, "Scottie, my boy, do come up!"

"Coming."

With the ding of the elevator, there he was, a welcome sight, one Drive could easily read. From a distance, Scott Moffie looked, in middle age, exactly like the Ivy League linebacker he once was. The Sunday pullover and slacks seemed tailored to advertise the classic triangle between his shoulders and waist. As he came closer, the years of resentment for slights real and imagined, stamped on his face, advertised an angry intensity. Things had happened as this golden boy aged. He wanted to be somebody. Lawyers, once his partners, were judges; political activists he used to mentor, cabinet officers; and some of his old ne'er-do-well clients were now the richest people in the world. He made a good living, but *he* wasn't somebody. Drive couldn't help but be fascinated.

Scott had waited downstairs for the summoning call. He had been a financial gumshoe long enough to understand his clients did not want their relationship with a "peeper" to be public, and wouldn't make a formal appointment where they might bump into somebody. Scott was used to meetings at odd times and places, and he didn't like it. Drive, however, was different. He treated Moffie with the deference he craved. So Moffie settled down to act like a professional. He eyed the available seating and chose one of the two plush white sofas facing each other in the vast office, now flooded with mid-morning light. Coffee was waiting in a silver pot, between two porcelain cups. Moffie grabbed his and served himself.

No small talk. "Hey D. Welcome back. You asked me to look into three matters. First, you want to know about Martin van Buren Beal, 'Marty.' He's sixty, runs marathons, and should live to be a hundred. Ever since his divorce twenty years ago, he's been chasing women, and catching them. Attractive ones, too. The word 'relationship' doesn't apply to this guy. He is a loner. Totally, completely, 100 percent his own person. Honest. He really doesn't care that nobody likes him. Plenty genuinely hate him! Whatever is going on for him, it's going on inside." Moffie walked toward the window, glancing out on the view of the southern end of Manhattan. Nice fucking view. "Rich as Croesus, and you'd never know it. Never buys a thing. Can't drive, doesn't own a television, and he rents. So where does his money go? Clients. They have some very imaginative off-shore investment vehicles."

Nothing like a cook who likes his own cooking, thought Drive. He was curious. "What's his connection to Atco International?"

"He was the CEO. The rest just worked for him. He has a lot of stock. There is no reason for this guy to work. During the eighties, he showed everybody that he was the best. Either he is going to like you and your deal, or he isn't. It's in your favor you're South African. He likes outsiders, and considers himself one, being Jewish. He's not proud or ashamed. He's just pragmatic."

"He sounds like my kind of guy."

"You never can tell, but he is worth a try."

"What about Stillman? I'm thinking of him as the lead banker for this deal."

Drive was a man of action, and had pretty much made up his mind, but he'd paid his money and so he sat back to listen. His mind wandered a bit as he thought about his new life.

"Vernon Stillman, CEO of Universal Bank, is a WASP Sammy Glick."

"Listen, Moffie, I need a translator for all this Manhattan *shtick*, did I say it right?"

"You said it right. Sammy Glick was the hero of Budd Schulberg's book about a West Side rag trader who makes it big in Hollywood. Vernon Stillman, the name says it all. You didn't ask for family background, so I'll start when he got out of Harvard Business School and came to work for Universal. Apparently, the guy is a world-class accountant. Assistant professor at Harvard, before graduating. Came into the bank as its *first* internal auditor. That sounds like a pretty dreadful place for a future CEO."

Wrong, thought Drive. Scott Moffie liked to get to the bottom of things, but either he doesn't do the math or he just doesn't get it. Drive poured himself some more coffee and settled into his spot on the sofa while Moffie continued. "Well, there was a Harvard Business School professor who was a director of Universal. He had been a mentor. Then a scandal. So many outrageous losses in loans that the professor came up with creating a permanent internal audit department and he persuaded the board to come up with some guidelines. Clear and public. He wanted to make his internal audit the fast track with a double promotion at the end."

"Result?" Drive was curious because Stillman himself had told him the same story, ambitious goal and all.

"The board wanted to send a message and they did. Apparently Stillman did a brilliant job. They liked him so much they elected him assistant secretary so he could continue going to the board meetings."

"What kind of style does he have?" The more Moffie talked about Stillman the more it confirmed the opinion Drive already had, but it pays to check. Moffie added more sugar to his coffee and sipped it. "He doesn't waste time with subordinates or claw at the back of his competitors. He knows what has to be done and does it.

"In 1992 he became CEO. Several national business groups. All those years, he'd been networking. His geekiness is part of his charm. An odd duck who makes everybody feel better about themselves. It was easy to make fun of this guy when he first came to New York. Now, everybody works for him."

"Any watersheds?" One of Drive's favorite words.

Moffie squinted thoughtfully as he sipped. "Vern's got a lot of markers out there. Oh, yes. He went to battle a while back for the Business Roundtable, the D.C.-based group of CEOs. They have a formula, only CEOs at meetings, no deputies, no permanent staff. After Vern was made CEO, some big boys came to him and said, 'We've got something really important for a New York City bank guy.' Vern was the man. He went out for a year or so and beat accountants over the head about the proposed rule to expense options. Vern handled it really well, and no Roundtable fingerprints. The talk was all about 'entrepreneurship'. Joe Lieberman, Connecticut's friend of small business in the Senate, sponsored the bill. Options went to the CEOs. And that's how these guys have been able to make so much money for themselves."

"Yes. Thank you, Mr. Stillman." Drive blurted out and then refocused. "Any other markers?" Drive was already sold on Stillman, but he wanted to know the full story.

"He engineered Universal's takeover of New York Safe Deposit & Trust Company. Nobody had ever thought of pulling those sleepy trust companies into the twentieth century. He took a chance on that one. The conventional wisdom was the company was a cultural institution beyond assault. But, day of the deal, everybody tendered."

Drive shook his head, he knew what that meant. Despite talk of a merger of equals, all it took was a few early retirements and the old NYSD&T would be gone.

"People always invest once *someone else* gets the bandwagon rolling. His personal life? Wives, children?"

"His first wife was beautiful, rich, and smart. The perfect calculated choice. He had her money when everyone else was struggling to pay the rent and the kids' school tuition. When people met her, all class, they looked at him a second time."

"What happened?"

"One of those career things. She put up with his never being home, but the word got out that he'd discovered women. He rediscovered Henry Kissinger's maxim that power is the greatest aphrodisiac. No scandal; apparently, one day she told him the marriage was over. He's on good terms with her and with their two daughters, who now have professional careers. She continued her legal career, got involved with the Clintons, and is running some agency in the Labor Department down in Washington."

"Did he remarry?"

"Oh, yeah. A trophy who understands the big picture."

"Do you trust him?" Drive knew he could count on Moffie to be frank, and he was.

"I do. He knows there's a financial services revolution going on, and he wants his bank to survive it. You can rely on him to do everything possible to outlast his competition. You can always tell where he is coming from." Moffie paused and looked pointedly at Drive. "Why Stillman now? You've never done any business with Universal."

Drive let out a small laugh. Maybe Scottie-boy's spying goes two ways. "You may remember, about ten years ago when I had a bad case of the shorts."

Moffie laughed outright. "How could I ever forget? You persuaded all those guys their only chance of getting paid back was to loan you *more* money and back your next deal. Sweet."

Drive smiled with self satisfaction and walked toward his desk. "I learned a few things then. Some golden rules. Never talk at a meeting until there is silence, let everyone else say what they want. Creditors like to feel that it is their meeting. Never leave one of those meetings for any reason. Don't even leave the room. Just be there. Just be quiet. Sooner or later, there is no other answer than you." Drive sat in his large desk chair, swiveling as he spoke, and silence filled the room as both men nodded reflectively. It was a very fond memory. Drive continued. "That's how I met Vern. At one of those meetings, I looked around the table and it was empty. Everyone else had gone somewhere. There was only this strange guy sitting there. He was new; Universal was not in on the credit. We started talking and I realized that he was quite an innovator. He'd dabbled in new kinds of mortgages, then credit-card debt. In this deal, he had the idea for bundling subscription renewals in order to raise quick cash. The worst idea in the world; as the money I took today to pay down debt would be earnings I wouldn't get in the future, ensuring that I would spend the rest of my life shoveling manure out of the barn. I said no. It was a matter of leverage. But, if I had to get some more cash right away, this would do it. With that card up my sleeve, I was a lot more comfortable carrying on the negotiations. Finally, they agreed to do it my way. But I remembered Vern."

Now it was Moffie's turn to absorb a good story. He put his cold coffee down while Drive continued.

"He is some kind of Rolodex freak. I kept getting calls from him at exactly three-month intervals. Flowers for my birthday, wherever I was. Frankly, a little weird. He knew he had no social skills so the only possible market for him was with foreigners who might not know the difference. Whenever I passed through New York, I gave him a call. He was CEO by this time. He had spent his whole life knowing that he wanted to be CEO of a big bank; he had spent no time thinking about what he would do when he got the job. Maybe he was a one-act play, but I could feel the hunger, so we built a relationship, kind of an informal understanding that I would do a big deal and he would be the banker."

Drive had to ask. "What do others on the street say about him?"

"I gotta tell you, people say to know Vern Stillman is to hate him. He's clean, but he isn't quite human. Never takes time off. He's one of those guys who learned how to play tennis and golf as an adult. You can see the money in his swing. He gets the job done, but it's no thing of beauty. Now, he beats the guys who were college champions. He's not malicious, but people have lost jobs and money, as well as tennis and golf games, because of him. Just as long as it is clear you're going to help him and his bank. Bring your own life raft!"

Drive got up from his desk and motioned Moffie to follow him through the concealed door connecting his office to the boardroom. Laid out elegantly at the end of the table were two place settings and a formally clad waiter, with a towel over his forearm, hovering expectantly for their choice of drinks. Moffie marveled. Once again, Drive made plain why he was one of the leading businessmen in the world. He instinctively realized that Moffie would be flattered by a splendid luncheon on an August Sunday afternoon, while Spencer Sherman preferred to go home. Drive motioned for Moffie to sit on his right. Lunch was one of the ways he built loyalty.

Drive liked Moffie, which was a considerable accomplishment when one reckoned that Moffie didn't like himself. Moffie was extremely good at his work but he took no pleasure in it; indeed, he felt demeaned by it, because of its stigma. Political candidates would lose the race if hiring him became public knowledge. And business leaders, even Drive, hid him behind elegant closed doors.

Moffie followed Drive's taste for a Campari and soda before their simple but elegant meal of cold asparagus, Dover sole, exquisite frites, plain lettuce salad with oil and vinegar, a superb orange soufflé, and Pouilly-Fuissé to drink. Fine food and atmosphere calm the spirit and encourage creative reflection. They talked about the *American Observer* magazine, the way old friends would reminisce about fishing trips or a vacation cruise. Not a word was said to suggest that the proposition was impossible.

Drive spun the fascinating history of Randy and Shelley Porter and their joint creation of the hugely successful *American Observer*, listed on the New York Stock Exchange as AOM. The company was like a child to them, literally, as they had no children. They had built a legacy, and they wanted it to continue forever. They would accomplish this in two ways. They would give the entire ownership to the finest charities in the land and they would give complete management authority to self-selecting trustees in perpetuity. Ironically, this well-intentioned combination failed. "A formula for disaster," noted Drive as the two worked on their salads. The governance structure of the company, Drive understood, sapped it of the vitality it needed to produce wealth. Nobody *had* to perform. Its share price was declining, creating woes for the company and the perfect opportunity for Drive.

"Institutions have short memories and no gratitude," reflected Drive as he sipped his Campari. As the two men dug into their fish, his thoughts ranged wide. The Porter gifts were the largest single element of the endowment of half a dozen of the greatest American charities. Those charities quickly became accustomed to their new assets and adjusted their operating style and expenses accordingly. Colonial Williamsburg, the Metropolitan Museum, Sloan-Kettering, the New York Zoo, Hudson Highlands, Lincoln Center, MacAlaster College collectively held some $2 billion worth of AOM stock. The dividends had always been modest, in the range of 3 percent, but in recent years the company hadn't earned enough to cover the dividend.

Drive polished off his last bit of soufflé and began, "What are the charities thinking, feeling, about the sacred behemoth?" Moffie confirmed Drive's other sources. No surprises. The institutions felt on the edge of a precipice; they needed the money; they were entitled to the money; they wanted someone to get them the money. Their own trustees watched the stock markets in the late nineties escalate while their AOM values melted away. The trusts were controlled by those loyal to AOM management, but the beneficiaries would welcome any newcomers, provided they would offer cash and the possibility of a diversified portfolio.

"It's time for a white knight," declared Moffie solemnly.

"From your lips, my friend. How *would* the employees feel about a new owner?" Drive really wanted to finish lunch, but he did like the white knight image. At some point in the game he might try to feed it to the press.

Moffie had picked up conflicting reports of employee attitude. Workers were united in their dislike of the current management but many continued to feel as if they worked at a "special" place and that the gospel of pure Americana associated with the *Observer* was needed more than ever in the twenty-first century. Some would welcome any change. The Employees' Stock Option Plan was emerging as a real force in the future of the enterprise. The ESOP owned twenty percent of the voting stock. Moffie suggested an alliance with them might make the acquisition simpler. A flicker of impatience crossed Drive's forehead reminding Moffie that he was a paid employee, not a partner in the proposed venture. Drive would make up his own mind, thank you very much, about who was going to participate in this venture, his grand vision.

"OK, Moffie, now I know what they're saying, but what are they feeling? I need more, how can we get into their heads? Who is their guru? Can we get to him, to her? I'm counting on you."

"We'll push hard. We've already done a lot of work with the list that we bought from those shareholder activists at LENS."

As he got up and moved toward the elevator lobby, Drive said, "We need to find the chink in the trustees' armor. Dig down deep, I don't know what you're going to have to do, but this one is for real." He stopped right in front of Moffie and poked his forefinger in the middle of the investigator's chest for emphasis. "I've got a start. When I meet them personally, they will quickly understand 'he wins who endures the most pain.' We have to find out what kind of pain they feel."

Chapter 2

August 2, p.m.

Drive was smiling as he walked up Fifth Avenue on this lovely Sunday afternoon in high summer. *How many Sundays have I meandered up the great commercial streets of the world, reveling in the special pleasure of plans carefully conceived, fascinating people to work with, and the operatic composition of bold and ambitious projects? Sundays are timeless. No phones, nobody claiming the right to my time. I feel like a great chef. I am creating something new, something that wouldn't exist unless I willed it so. The best ingredients. Careful preparation. Contemplation of the process about to unfold is very bliss. I live to work. This is what I am. I have special talent. I was placed on earth for this.*

Drive passed the facade of Saint Patrick's Cathedral on his right. *If ever I were tempted to be religious I would be a Catholic. One of my wives took it very seriously, but I could never be persuaded to accept an intermediary priest between me and my creator.* Drive could never find the words for his personal form of faith. At the core, he was a Cartesian, convinced of the relevance of his existence and the worth of his effort. This, in turn, led to acknowledgement of some kind of Supreme Being. The outside world usually saw Drive as "homo economicus," the incarnation of globalization; universally admired for generating value, but he was well read, too. Passing Rockefeller Center, the old man in Drive grew increasingly uncomfortable, silencing the inner voices of emotional discontent with larger deals, more violent timetables, and more reckless relationships. An inner emptiness was unignorable, but the beauty of the day made his forced distraction easier.

As Drive's gaze extended to the leafy southeastern corner of Central Park, he felt that special frisson of pleasure revealed to the world by Marcel Proust as the recollection of time recaptured. Whether it was the espaliered trees surrounding the gardens of the Royal Palace in Brussels, the dotted evergreens around the moat of the Imperial Palace in Tokyo, Boston's Public Garden with its swan boats, the impeccable pebbled walks of the Tuilleries, the grandeur of the San Francisco and Singapore botanical gardens or Stanley Park in Vancouver, the marvel and beauty of nature always uplifted Drive, especially in the midst of the complex urban environment his world was now made of, so far from his South African childhood.

As he neared Fifty-seventh Street, his mood changed. Drive indulged in an old man's contempt for modern times in the form of the glitzy Trump Tower on his right and the absence of his beloved Doubleday Bookstore on the left. *How do I find myself here, this day, walking this street that I have walked a thousand times before? I am not like other people. Will I always be looking? Will I find it this time?*

It all started with Drive's patrilineal grandfather who left the West Midlands of England as a young man in the 1870s with a group of Wesleyan Methodists to do good and to do well in the burgeoning Cape Colony of South Africa. John Rhodes was a product of dissenter England, and regretted being no relation to the Great Cecil. This was a remarkable two-hundred-year-old country within a country, and the inhabitants were conspicuously restricted with no access to the professions, forbidden to live in large cities, no admission to Oxford or Cambridge, and not allowed to stand for Parliament. This community, quite naturally, looked within itself for its values, largely expressed through religious worship, and so, turned its energies to where there were no restrictions. The dissenters implemented the industrial revolution in Britain and the Quaker names from the West Midlands are prominent even today as leaders of UK business, Clark and Cadbury among them.

While deprived of university education, John had highly developed accounting skills and a pronounced aptitude for business. The change in continent agreed with the Rhodes family. There is romance in the experience of these "second-class" citizens leaving the dark and wet midlands of Britain for the glorious openness of the southern African veldt. The wealth of the continent at that time, diamonds from Kimberley mines in the north, flowed through Cape Town. As Cecil Rhodes acquired full ownership of the diamond workings as DeBeers Consolidated in 1889, John diligently provided accounting services and patiently acquired, for himself, interests in all manner of business. Twenty years later, the extent of his investments, in finance, banking, and newspapers, became evident with the cessation of the Boer war. Cecil Rhodes died in 1902 just as the British Colonial Secretary Joseph Chamberlain came to visit the newly pacified colonies. It was noted that Chamberlain and his young and beautiful American wife, Mary Endicott, spent several weeks at the Cape Town estate of John Rhodes. There was a new baby in the house. John had married in his forty-fifth year a dissenter originally from Birmingham, and their son, also named John, was born in 1898. Mary Endicott, who had no children of her own, delighted in the little boy and, on her departure, left a silver christening mug, with the letter C, as a memento.

By any standard John was a very rich man, but he maintained the modest manner of the dissenters. Life in Cape Town at the end of the nineteenth century was free of the military skirmishes with the local Xhosa tribes or with the Dutch nationalists that plagued the rest of the British presence in South Africa. Blacks were segregated early into their own living areas, it was said on account of health concerns, and, yet, they were formally involved in political life on a restricted basis rather along the lines of the United States Constitution. Slavery had been outlawed in 1834 and the missionary efforts had been successful in spreading Christianity.

Two-thirds of the Cape white population was Afrikaners and there was always concern that Boer military units would overrun the Colony during the hostilities of 1899. As a consequence of the peace negotiations, the Cape Colony was granted self-governing status within the British Empire. The High Commissioner, Lord Milner, contrived all manner of structure, called gerrymander in the United States, to assure the continued British character of the colony, but there were too few immigrants. Demography prevailed in the 1905 elections and the party of the non-English Jan Christian Smuts and Louis Botha was elected for almost half a century. Ironically, the Cambridge-educated Smuts traveled the world as an imperial statesman and brought South Africa into war twice on the British side.

The wealthy English population near Cape Town enjoyed a standard of living hard to describe and impossible to replicate. There was an abundance of help; everyone had an estate that resembled a medieval palace with every want provided for. There was political "peace" amidst a rather precarious balance, and, always, there was the beautiful countryside. The mineral resource base assured constant wealth and, for the white rich, Cape Town was an ideal combination of the twentieth century and the feudal age.

The second John Rhodes was just the product so desperately sought by the advocates of hereditary monarchies. An only child, due to his parents' late marriage, he was brought up as the young prince. Through some combination of the "soul" of the young blacks with whom he grew up and the omnipresence of nature, John's disposition was singularly devoid of envy, pride, or the desire to be anything other than what he was. And what he was, in the eyes of the traditional English, was formidable. He had a fine mind that tested well, and he graduated from the Diocesan College with highest honors in his entry papers for Cambridge. More important to the English mentality, he could run, really run, and with a rugby ball in his hands he could run better than anyone. Not particularly tall, he had immense upper body strength on top of two legs that seemed never to stop. He arrived in Cambridge just as the First World War came to an end, the spirit of release and joy almost covered over the decimation of those who would have been expected to fill the newly emptied places. At his father's urging, he stayed in the Northern Hemisphere for much of the next five years, twice traveling to the United States. Playing rugby for Emmanuel College and for Cambridge University provided entrée to all circles of British society. He graduated with first-class honors in law in the same month he was invited to play rugby for England. In view of the fact that both his parents were born British, he was deemed, by that logic so beloved of athletic qualifiers, to be himself, a British citizen. He earned his cap and then regretfully resigned himself to the responsibilities of his inheritance. His father's business interests had worldwide implications and the young man needed to learn the trade of a modern economic prince.

At some point in the glamour of being an authentic undergraduate hero, John found himself very much in demand by the young ladies of society. Serious athletic involvement requires much dedication; it means one is not free for weekend dalliances. Parties are difficult and fixed commitments claims one's energies. These constraints serve to intensify the urgencies of marriageable young men and women. *Les jeunes filles en fleur* display unexpected depths of imagination in conquering the barriers to love. They have so little time; there is no leisure for the traditional courtships. Indeed, John's family was thousands of miles away.

John acquired the habit of taking young ladies to tea in London at the Lenox Gardens home of Mary Endicott Chamberlain Carnegie (who had remarried Reverend Carnegie, a Canon of Westminster Cathedral following the death of Joseph Chamberlain). Mary had been thrilled when her butler, Pink, came into the drawing room with a silver christening cup marked with a C and said, "Madame, a young gentleman gave me this and said it would serve as a proper introduction." She enjoyed acting in loco parentis for this extraordinary being, whom she had not seen since his first days. Her credentials as matchmaker were unrivaled. Did not her own charm and beauty, some thirty years earlier, secure the personal blessing of Queen Victoria to her own unusual union?

From the covey of potential suitors, Henrietta Gould emerged as the one most determined to marry this South African nobleman. She came from a recently wealthy investment banking family with very high expectations for performance in all spheres of life, which translated for daughters at that time into "good marriages." In later years, Henrietta would carry on about the dukes whom she had passed up in order to "bury myself" in the prison of South Africa. Had psychiatry been more advanced or had Henrietta's family been a touch more forthcoming, the young couple could have had some warning of the emotional traumas to come. There was little to warn the open and optimistic John Rhodes about the problems of mental instability. He never really processed Mary Carnegie's tactful hesitation about Henrietta. Indeed, for many years, neither he nor his parents had any conception of the nature of the obvious problems of their daughter-in-law.

In 1925, the elder Rhodes took the long boat ride to England to be present at the Wedding of the Year of their brilliant son to the acclaimed and beautiful daughter of the Gould banking family. There were those who said that the wedding preparations were a bit excessive, but there always are. From their country mansion in Gloucestershire, the Goulds had emptied greenhouses of flowers to decorate the old church and the tents in Bibury. This was quite a homecoming, a little more than a half century in actual time, for the Birmingham dissenters. While the patriarch was in good health, he had already passed his seventieth year and he needed his only son at home to pass on responsibility and wisdom.

But first, John Rhodes the younger and his new wife took a wedding trip through Africa, choreographed as the return of the beloved son to the southernmost tip of this least known but most romantic continent. At the high tide of the empire, it could be traversed without ever leaving British soil. When they finally arrived in Cape Town, John and Henrietta might well have gotten out of a space capsule on the surface of the moon. Everything was so new to Henrietta and John had been away for most of six years. And what was new was exciting; new house, new family, new responsibilities. Even Henrietta was impressed by the availability of help for every possible need, and the scope of her authority in running a household estate. No one in England had anything like it. John began, naturally and respectfully, to take his father's place in the political and economic leadership of the colony.

A son, the third John, was born in 1927 and another son, Cedric, was born in 1931 on the family estate in the pine forests overlooking Cape Town just adjacent to the imperial properties, Groote Shuur, from which the great Cecil had run his colony, his company, and, indeed, his continent. In his eightieth and last year, the elder John seemed obsessed with the need for his family to understand that change is the only constant in the world. It seemed the height of incongruity that this hugely successful man warned again and again that no one should take his circumstances for granted. The dissenter boy had come so far that he wanted to be sure that his descendants could survive a trip in the other direction. Attributing much of his success to luck, he realized that same lady could turn her charms in other directions. And so, in 1933 the founder was gone.

South Africa was, in many ways, the best place in the world to live during the decades of the 1930s and 1940s. Worldwide depression had less impact on an economy based on diamonds and gold. South Africa had little direct involvement in the World War. The boys had an idyllic upbringing, surrounded by supportive servants and friends. Both excelled in school, although not like their father. From the beginning, they were the best of friends. Cedric, as a little boy, desperately tried to keep up with everything his brother John did. Far from being irritated at having to share attention in the family, John welcomed his brother's company and spent their earliest years together teaching Cedric, helping him to acquire adult skills. They made common cause against the world. In the years to come, customarily half a world removed from each other, their trust and clarity of communication would remain undiluted. John was gregarious, uxorious, community oriented, and a natural leader. Cedric was always called Drive because, according to family legend, this was his first word on seeing John with the reigns in his hands "driving" the horse pulling their wagon. The name seemed to fit his omnipresent energy, like a flower seeking the sun. Cedric was comfortable alone, but had many female friends, and was loyal to none. He appeared driven by an inner compulsion, always changing, always moving, always acquiring new things, new enthusiasms. His pleasures were insular: music, reading, strategizing.

John, their father, became aware of Henrietta's profound discomfort shortly after their return to South Africa. She blamed him for every element in her life that was not pleasing, how boring his family was, how unglamourous the society was, how inadequate he was to abandon a wife in a place like Cape Town. After Cedric's birth, she said "Thank God, an heir and a spare; that's over, we're not going to do that again." She had little interest in being a mother and even less in being a wife. For most months, she invited friends from England to spend long and luxurious visits. They were glad to accept; the weather was good, the game parks fantastic, and the Depression, so omnipresent at home, was never in evidence in the Rhodes's South Africa. These professional guests bored John, so he simply left his wife to pass her time as she saw fit. Colonial life has often been characterized as boring, and bringing out the worst in people in their efforts to alleviate their own dullness. Henrietta, like the wives of other British proconsuls, didn't hesitate to become intimate with any male she chose, whether or not they were married to friends. The more promiscuously she behaved, the greater her contempt for her husband. In the midst of this destructive psychological descent she discovered an unexpected bulwark in her eldest son. For some reason, she felt less alienated from him.

Mental illness in rich families doesn't impact the rest of the world to the extent that money and loyal servants allow the illnesses to be contained. Within the family, however, sickness is the dominant theme. It is the energy from which all have the greatest difficulty in escaping. Henrietta expressed her misery in a variety of ways; the worst was by self-mutilation, cutting herself, usually around the wrists and forearms.

One day in 1943 when sixteen-year-old John returned home early from school, he heard cries for help that could only be coming from a terrified Cedric. He ran through the house, past silent and frightened servants, upstairs to a scene of absolute horror. In her bedroom, his mother was standing with a straight razor in her right hand, holding her bleeding left arm up in defiance. In a hypnotic chant, she demanded of the skies that her misery be witnessed and all her wishes be granted or she would next draw blood from her throat. Twelve-year-old Cedric, who had merely passed by his mother's room on the way to his own, was now held at bay by his mother's violence and the threatening blade. He had shrieked his vocal chords raw and was now soaked with tears, wracked with sobs, and hissing prayers for deliverance from his mother's fit.

John very calmly approached his mother, who seemed pacified by his presence. He said evenly, "Mother, this really isn't a good day for it. I think you had best let me help you lie down and get some rest." Almost like the cobra in the thrall of the mongoose, Henrietta was induced to follow her eldest son. She dropped the razor idly and picked up a cloth to shield her carpets from the dripping blood. John told Cedric to sit down for a minute.

When John came back, he held Cedric in his arms for what seemed like hours, but no amount of time was long enough for the horror of the experience to work through the conscious and unconscious sensibilities of the young boy. They never spoke of the experience to their father, who had his own catalog of the horrors of living with madness. The shared experience bonded their psyches and nervous systems to such an extent that each brother would be attuned to the other's feelings at critical times during the rest of their long lives. Allied in this most primal comradeship, the struggle for survival within the sickness of the family, the brothers grew up to become very different people, but their utter devotion to each other was more perfect than any diamond.

The impact of Henrietta's sickness defined the lives of the three males in the Rhodes family. John, her husband felt personally at fault, guilty that his son had to bear responsibility that should have been his alone. John, her son, understood the world of demons that his mother inhabited. His father's excellence was so pervasive that he was relieved, finally to able to be helpful to the family. For the rest of his mother's never happy and brief life, he was her connection to reality. In simple terms, she had no use for Cedric and so he developed insulation protecting him against emotional involvement with women. He gave himself lifelong permission to make use of women with no consideration or remorse. The psychological dynamics of the Rhodes household were soon to be importantly affected by an unexpected political development.

On May 26, 1948, the Nationalist Party, led by Dr. Malan, defeated the regime led by Jan Smuts. It had required half a century, but finally the Boers won the war. From this time forward, the English residents of the Cape Colony would have to contemplate minority status in a white government that, in its turn, was trying to maintain political control over the black majority. Was this the change that the first John foresaw in his final days? The second John, now fifty years old, decided quickly that the family must prepare once again to be ready to move.

John III, now twenty-one-years-old, and a senior at the University of South Africa, would gradually take over the family businesses. Most importantly, he would take care of what was becoming the family's most intrusive problem, his mother's health. His father would move into political life where his personal skills and integrity enabled him to deal effectively in the troubled society. Cedric would enroll at his father's old Cambridge College, Emmanuel. Cedric was expected to develop property outside of South Africa as insurance against the day they all might have to depart. In some profound place in his psyche, Cedric acclimated himself to a life in which adaptation to change was the most important factor. Indeed, in psychological terms, most of what was considered important had already been taken away from him. He was to develop skills and resources to be able, always, to create new realities, personal and economic. Because Cedric lost, at an early age, that which mortals prize the most, he became insensitive to risk. What was there left to lose? This manifested itself in certain recklessness, not so much in the fashionable manner of pursuing physical danger, but in personal relationships. It also manifested itself in business; he had no concept of losing.

The Emmanuel College, "Emma," where Cedric arrived in the fall of 1949, bore little resemblance to the joyful place his father had embellished in the early 1920s. Everywhere, there were the ruins of war: rationing, socialist government, cold, rain, multiple London deaths caused by a combination of coal fires and fog. If a person wanted heat, he had to plug a shilling into a heater placed in front of a false fireplace. There was only one thing that these heaters could do well, toast crumpets. Human beings either stayed cold or toasted whichever part of their body seemed to need heat the most. If one went to the Pitt Club, home of the legendary Cambridge grandees, one had to plug in a shilling in order to turn on the phosphorescent lights over the snooker table. As for food, all that could be said was thank goodness for the Indian immigrants, who managed to provide about the only edible fare. Cedric played rugby, but only for the college; he read law, went down with only a 2.2 gentleman's pass degree. His mind was in a different place. He spent much of his university time in London. The trains worked and he could read the business news going back and forth to Liverpool Street. His father's correspondents were assiduous in their efforts to accommodate the new merchant prince. He was polite, diligent, and silent. There was something depressing in the universal enthusiasm that all manner of English people, tutors, business people, and sportsmen had for his father. With every introduction, people would automatically say "son of?" and smile as if in recollection of a more joyful time, and, Drive feared, of a more exciting person. Even Mary Carnegie's stories of the war, such as when Pink told the firemen they could not use the water taps to put out bomb fires because that would disturb Mrs. Carnegie's bath and of the early days in the Cape Colony when she first stayed with his grandparents, could not lift the sense of gloom.

The Rhodes family had long had an interest in the *Cape Times* and had come to the conclusion that communications was one of the industries that would increase in importance during the postwar years, as the world grew smaller. The one thing that the allies indisputably won from World War II was the establishment of English as the global business language, so Cedric started at the business desk. Family friends were glad to take on the inheritor, so the young graduate found himself on Fleet Street in the autumn of 1952. This was a time when press lords had names. They were frequent visitors of prime ministers. Indeed, the most celebrated of prime ministers had himself started off his civilian life as a journalist, most famously in the Boer War. In London, each paper had an admitted political bias and rose and fell with its party's fortunes. London papers had the largest circulation of any in the world, but there were too many of them. Embedded in the London newspaper world was a crazy mélange of craft unions. There were unions for virtually every function involved in producing the finished newspaper. These unions had many demands, which were frequently incompatible with the demands of other unions and always irrelevant to the continued prosperity of the publication. It all finally came to a head on Boat Race Day, March 28, 1955. On that day, London went blind, so to speak. No newspapers were published. Not on the Sunday, not on the Monday. Indeed, not for some forty days. From this experience, Cedric derived a lifelong hatred for socialism, unions, and the opinions of the "best people." He saw for himself how the union questions were resolved, not at the bargaining table, but in the halls outside with direct payments of cash to union officials.

Cedric never again was astonished at the corruptibility of mankind; the only surprise was in how low the price was. On the other side, he appreciated how powerful press lords could be in a democratic society. All the while candidates for Parliament were virtually forbidden to spend any money in aid of their own campaigns, the newspapers were free to espouse any views they wanted, at any length and frequency, and to support candidates openly. He began to realize that all of the codswallop he had been taught about freedom of the press could be looked at another way. The press was accorded by society vast power over the political process, which in turn set the rules within which everyone lived and the chance to make a great deal of money in the process. How else could power and profit be better combined? Cedric had absorbed a great deal from six years in the suffocating atmosphere of his motherland, but it was clear that England was no place to build meaningful wealth for his family.

At Emma, he had met a succession of Americans who were sent over as an annual expression of thanks to the alma mater of John Harvard for the gift of his library and the use of his name. Through them, Cedric became acquainted with the other Cambridge and with the extraordinary jewel of urban mass centered in Boston, Massachusetts. Dissenters, of course, founded Boston some two hundred years before his own family had left for South Africa. This quality of being English, and, yet, also dissenters to the point of successful rebellion, made him feel that New England would be a good center for the next stage of his life. While his family had always spoken English, his experience as a colonial at Oxford had not entirely prepared him for an utterly new culture in America. He realized that it would take time to become fluent in the idiom of a new land, but, at the same time, he also had determined that this was where he would build.

His father had made the acquaintance of Robert "Beanie" Choate, the longtime publisher of the *Herald Traveler* newspapers, some thirty years earlier, when the Cambridge rugby side visited Boston. Cedric's call to Choate in late 1955 was timely. The newspaper had just begun a long and expensive process of setting up a television station and, because Choate's stock position in the publicly traded stock of the company was relatively small, he was pleased at the prospect of a private placement of a new stock to a friendly holder. Early in 1956, Cedric as Drive, accompanied by wife number one, arrived in Boston to take up his position as assistant with the publisher. He became immediately involved in the brouhaha accompanying the effort to be awarded a television franchise, Channel 5, from the Federal Communications Commission or FCC. The *Herald Traveler*, as WHDH, had filed an application in 1947. The Commission promptly imposed a seven-year moratorium on granting new licenses. Shortly after Drive's arrival in Boston, the hearing examiner awarded the franchise to someone else. Drive was part of the ferocious scheming that ensued. Indeed, he was one of the guests at the luncheon with FCC Chairman

McConnaughey on April 2, 1956 that would be styled by history as the "Hundred-Million-Dollar Lunch."

During his first year with Choate, Drive acquired an expertise in dealing with federal regulatory agencies that would stand him in good stead around the world for the rest of his life. This was the "Whorehouse Era" of the FCC, when matters were arranged and not adjudicated. And as a later commissioner put it, "This was the era when the Commission lost its virginity, and liked it so much, it turned pro." However, it was accomplished, the hearing examiner was reversed by the full Commission on April 24, 1957, and eight months later Channel 5 signed on with the call letters, WHDH-TV, owned and operated by the Boston Herald Traveler Corporation. The losers filed a desperate appeal. To the surprise of all, on July 31, 1958, the U.S. Court of Appeals acted; it ordered the whole matter reopened and on December 4 the FCC began, again, a process that was to last another fourteen years. The famous luncheon and the possibility of improper influence were one of the principal grounds on which the appeal had been granted. One of the first lessons learned during Drive's months in Boston was the requirement that television franchises are awarded only to American citizens. The birth of a daughter at the Boston Lying-In Infirmary in June 1957 assured that there would be an eligible American on whose behalf the Rhodes family could seek any licenses.

Drive learned the TV business. Everybody made a lot of money. The easy part was programming and relationships with the networks. From the start, independent television stations were money machines. The explanation was, very simply, that they made free use of the public airways. Because access was limited to a very few parties, monopoly pricing was the rule. In contrast to the UK, the United States had a system that wasn't government controlled and financed. The hard part was how to influence the several parties in the U.S. governmental framework who had some piece of the allocative power for TV franchises. Among them were the White House, the Congress, the U.S. Senate (from which base Majority Leader Lyndon B. Johnson built quite a communications empire in the name of his wife), and the FCC itself. After the tower is built and the transmitters set up, there is little operating cost beyond electric power. The networks provide programming. Local news and advertising sales are about the only controllable costs. The real expense is maintaining a favorable political position. This is a matter requiring great subtlety and patience.

During the Channel 5 fiasco Drive had met with the Republican White House staff and the Democratic leadership in both Senate and House Committees. That began his lifelong pattern of keeping track of the careers of key people in all positions. He quickly became a foreign affiliate, because of family holdings in the South African press, of the National Association of Broadcasters. Particularly, he studied the flow of money between business and politics. American naivety was extraordinary. Everybody knows that you have to pay something to get something, but America insisted on the continuing pretense that the governmental process of deciding who is going to be bestowed vast riches is conducted according to some constitutional notion of legitimacy. Within this hypocrisy, great care has to be exercised so that favorable positions are secured in ways that are not offensive to public sensitivity. Drive learned that the publication and broadcast businesses provided vast opportunities to do "favors" that were highly valued. He was an apt student and spent a large part of his life understanding what was important to whom and how to get it. He figured correctly that if he took care of the right people they would take care of him. He was a wise young man when it came to such things.

Drive had learned of the great power newspapers had in British politics; now he learned there could be a very tangible quid for this pro quo in the United States. Power could be converted into money and a lot of it. Support of the right candidates and causes has yielded some extraordinary rewards. The only public obligation imposed on recipients of television licenses in exchange for the free use of the airwaves was to operate in the public interest. A succession of Commission decisions, court interpretations, and legislative hearings over the decades has insured that these words are a nullity. The United States

Supreme Court, through some appalling aberration, was moved to decide that "commercial speech" is protected by the Constitution. Nor are the slander and libel laws of any moment, what a contrast with the UK! What this means is that anything can be published by anybody without cost or risk. What a splendid climate for publishers and broadcasters. Television is where the power is.

Henceforth, Drive commited his principal energy and the family money to television, although certain newspapers and publishing properties were useful for favors. Newspapers could publish Op-Ed pieces at convenient times; they could set the tone before elections, they could endorse candidates. The power was almost worth the cost.

Choate fell on evil times at the newspaper. He lost his job as chief executive officer in 1963 and died shortly thereafter. With his mentor gone, Drive had little reason to stay. Aside from this, the huge television profits had vastly increased the value of his family's original investment from seven years earlier. He was anxious to use the money and his experience to greater personal advantage. This would be the last time in his life that Drive ever worked for someone else.

During his Boston days, Drive established what would become his own very particular style of life. With variations, he would continue this same style in every city, in Europe and in Asia as well as on the West Coast of the United States, through all of the deals, and with whatever wife, over the next forty years. The first thing he did was to buy the biggest house in a formerly fashionable part of town and fix it up to its former splendor. He did this for a reason. The fine mansions of the late nineteenth and early twentieth centuries had been built by people who wanted to be able to walk to the best stores, the museums, the theatres, and even, as time passed, to the small elite office buildings. The problem that Americans had after World War II was the disappearance of servants, and these mansions required a lot of live-in help. Drive seemed to move about with a private coterie of a dozen or so helpers from the family properties in South Africa. All spoke perfectly accented English; all were professional either as household servants, chauffeurs, shortly to become pilots, and office assistants. So he was able to buy splendid properties that everyone else wanted to sell, which had a favorable effect on price.

During the winter months of 1956 when he first arrived in Boston, Drive stayed in a suite in the Ritz-Carlton Hotel overlooking the public gardens. The offices were just a short walk away and all variety of entertainment people used the hotel as a refuge before trying out theater performances on the discriminating Boston stages. He fell in love with Back Bay and when a double house on the water side of Commonwealth Avenue between Berkeley and Clarendon Streets became available next to the statue of Alexander Hamilton in the mall, he was glad to buy it. Boston's rich merchants had built these magnificent structures after the land was filled in following the Civil War. The architects had created back streets with stables for the horses. These were easily converted into automobile garages. Elevator shafts could accommodate modern shafts and cabs. Rewiring and re-plumbing were small problems in houses with crawl spaces between rooms and floors. The fact that most of the neighborhood was now occupied by schools and clubs, and that it was no longer considered a stylish place to live, made little difference. The location was supreme and the parking accommodations a rare jewel. The openness created by the mall and proximity of the Public Garden gave the property a park-like elegance, removed from the usual crowding and dirt of cities. Indeed, on the occasions when they entertained, it was obvious to Drive and his wife that their invitees, all, would like to live in such a house but they could not master the logistics of household help. Being a foreigner and speaking Cambridge English, Drive appealed to all of the most pervasive of Boston snobberies. He was invited to join every club and was very much lionized by the best people in society.

As a foreigner, Drive was aware of the extraordinary draw exercised by Harvard and MIT on the best minds from all over the world. Notwithstanding his relative youth, he made it a point to invite as many of these people to his home as possible. He learned about medicine, electronics, and communications technologies. Again, everything went onto his lists; he kept track. He made a few political contributions. Not many people did, so his gifts were remembered. Young Senator Kennedy was in the process of running unsuccessfully for the Democratic Party nomination for vice president. "Tip" O'Neil had taken his place in Congress. This fortuity equipped the young Drive with a lifetime friendship with a future president, his brothers, future senators both, and the most powerful Speaker of the House of Representatives in modern times.

Fortune magazine published its first list of America's Richest Men. To his surprise, Drive read that a quiet unassuming man living in Cambridge was high on the list with a net worth approaching $400 million. He took it on himself to visit the Central Square offices of Polaroid Corporation and to make himself known to Edwin Land. Land ultimately would be awarded more patents than any American other than Thomas Edison. What struck Drive was that all this wealth had been generated so quickly and that it was based not on decades of established technology and proven markets, but on new inventions and the hope that consumers would buy the product. The facility with which Americans, and not just establishment Americans, could move into public markets for new money for an unproven venture was a revelation. Two MIT graduates of Greek ethnicity, the Bakalars, founded Transitron. The public offering of its stock made them centi-millionaires overnight.

The last five years of the sixties were a time of trauma in the United States. The assassination of John Kennedy in November of 1963 and the progressive failure of the war in Vietnam transformed postwar optimism into a time of violence. The only aspect of this violence that affected Drive personally was the turbulence of the stock markets. He was not eligible for the draft and therefore immune from the omnipresent pressure of the war. At some point he moved his base of operations to Los Angeles. Neither his daughter nor his wife accompanied him, but the usual confusion that surrounds any account of Drive's personal life exists as to whether they stayed in Boston or returned to wherever their home was. Again, he bought a magnificent home in a traditional area, Hancock Park, which was close, in Los Angeles terms, to downtown, the beach, and the movie studios. He didn't feel ready yet for New York. Many Bostonians had said to him, "You know how the Brits think of all of us as foreigners, well, that's how we think of the Californians." Drive figured that he had best get himself involved in that creative energy while he was still young enough to adapt once again. As usual, his staff provided the basis for splendid entertainment and there was no shortage of honorary hostesses. Specifically, he came to Los Angeles because a network affiliate television station was available. The price, $100 million, was the highest ever asked for a single station, befitting the size of the market and the glamour of Tinseltown. Drive had banked substantial profits from his *Herald Traveler* stake. He had put family money into several of the new technology ventures growing up on Route 128 around greater Boston. In the late 1960s the values in these holdings literally skyrocketed. After he sold them all, he had about $25 million to invest.

This brought Drive to his first publicly held corporation. He remembered the Polaroid experience and turned to their investment bankers, Kuhn Loeb. He liked this firm. It reminded him of Cape Town and London. When he went into their offices in downtown Manhattan, he was introduced to one of the Messrs. Warburg, who appeared ubiquitously to be the senior partners of several of the London and New York branches. Drive didn't feel that the meeting would last very long. He couldn't imagine that this famous old investment-banking house would back someone who had never run a business and was trying to buy into the newest industry at the highest price in history. But this was the sixties and there was an inexhaustible appetite for the new common stocks, particularly in the areas identified with growth in the twentieth century. For a firm like Kuhn Loeb, to have a client walk in the door, an old-world person, a Cambridge man no less, with $25 million of his own to invest, was manna from heaven. They would have underwritten virtually anything he wanted. There would be two classes of stock, Class A, all of which was to be owned by the Rhodes family with 100 votes per share, and Class B, which would be sold to the public and would have one vote per share. Kuhn Loeb advised that this might in time inhibit the New York Stock Exchange from listing the stock, but experience with the Ford Motor Company indicated that if the float was big enough the Exchange could bend its principles. There were a couple of other fillips. The Rhodes family contributed some of their interests in UK media properties to the new corporation rather than cash, and the majority owner of the A shares was the Rhodes family trust, cunningly crafted around the beneficial entitlement of Drive's eight-year-old daughter, Sis, so as to qualify the corporation as American for purposes of U.S. laws regarding the ownership of television franchises. Finally, the question of the name, and World Publications and Broadcasting, known by its ticker symbol WPB, was born. Kuhn Loeb undertook to raise $40 million in Class B common stock. Drive worked out of New York and as Kuhn Loeb organized the selling syndicate, he came to know an entire generation of Wall Street leaders. They planned a massive road show. Traveling by private jet, they hit fifteen cities in the United States. The indications were so favorable that they went over to London and Paris and Frankfurt.

The lore of this offering created Drive's global reputation. This pleasant, quiet chap with a British accent leavened by Boston and Los Angeles turned out to be just about the best salesman anybody could remember. The word got out after the first couple of cities, and crowds of brokers pressed to attend the selling sessions. Finally, these sessions were held in public halls. Every time Drive allowed that he had no experience running television stations but that he had a bit of common sense, the crowd's empathy was palpable. They loved him. They wanted him to win. This may have been the single offering that would be remembered by history as the froth on the '60s stock market boom. The offering was oversubscribed by more than 100 percent. The underwriters could not believe their good luck and urged Drive to accept the new money. Mr. Warburg called him in and said, "These things are beyond understanding. Sometimes, people will give you their money. Other times you cannot sell them a U.S. government bond. My advice to you is, take the money. You have no problem with control and you look like a young man who can put that money to good use pretty quickly." So, when the largest destruction of equity values in the history of the New York Stock Exchange occurred in 1972 and 1973, WPB was sitting fat with a rapidly growing debt-free television station, cash in the bank, and bank credit unimpaired.

What changed Drive's life was the perception by the financiers that he was a hot property. You could sell a Rhodes issue. He was a "bankable property" in the terminology of his new home, Hollywood. People brought him every imaginable kind of proposition. Indeed, nothing in his field was ever sold without someone showing it to Drive. Because he could use stock as currency ("Super Money" according to the contemporary author styled Adam Smith), there were no limits on the size of properties he could buy. Having invested such a large amount of the original equity, which multiplied in value with the TV station's success and the bottom fishing from 1972 to 1973, there really was no concern with dilution. The Class A stock voting provisions guaranteed control. The pattern of Drive's adult life was molded out of his two great aptitudes, the ability to "sell" ideas and securities to whomever he needed and the temperament for the endless pursuit of ideal women.

Drive was a visionary and a player. He never took the chance of losing a deal because someone else offered more money. He figured that he could always find a way to pay for it. As he built up his networks in Asia and Europe, he came to understand the opportunities presented by what, he had always thought, was the absurdity of accounting rules. Because there were no global principles of accounting, a company like WPB could pretty much take its pick of which was most favorable. It all boiled down to the auditor. Drive was one of the first to appreciate that the Big Seven, as they then were, were very much in the business of offering consulting services. He quickly became the best consulting customer of his audit firm and held them to the mark in giving him the benefit of the most aggressive practices. Occasionally, during economic lulls, Drive would suffer a shortage of cash. No matter what his fancy accounting firm had been paid to report, there was an ultimate reality, cash could not be simulated. On those occasions Drive would patiently meet with the creditors who would sooner or later come to the conclusion that their only chance of being paid at all was in backing Drive to do the job. And so he did. He invested in all the newest technologies, he owned production facilities, a movie studio in Burbank; he had vast cable interests in the United States and the United Kingdom and he was the largest satellite broadcaster in Asia. There were also several high-visibility newspapers and a couple of publishing companies.

All this time, he kept score. He did favors. He used the leverage of his properties to advance the causes of those who could be of some benefit to him. The single largest asset of WPB was the List, who owed, who was owed, what was the quality of the obligation. This, and not his balance sheet, was what made Drive a candidate for the principal businessman of the twenty-first century.

The 1980s came and like Ronald Reagan Drive moved east, although to a different city, New York, where the money was, in time for a drab business and investment market. He had improved on the occasion by having the company buy him the Chrysler Building suite of offices at the lowest cost since the Depression. Drive found it impossible to wait out the cycle until boom time multiples would return and again give him the value and currency to expand his business globally.

He was in the right city, the city that doesn't sleep. When there's no business to be done, New York is full of imaginative people who'll conjure up opportunities for profit. The city's motto should have been taken from a post–Civil War banker: "To sell somebody something they want at a price they can afford, that's not business. To sell somebody something they don't want at a price they can't afford, *that's business.*" In recent times, refined by business schools, dressed by fashionable tailors with the most expensive accoutrements like cuff links and fancy watches, and generally cloaked with the patina of respectability, that spirit lives on. Like well-upholstered piranha, these dealmakers rip unimaginable fees out of the commercial world.

Under normal conditions, Drive's contempt for investment bankers was so palpable that even with the protection of their alligator carapaces, most demurred from risking an appointment. So it was a bit unusual to find Drive, on a rainy April day in 1984, sitting at his conference table across from four exquisitely attired minions of the firm Silverman Seligman. The most senior, George Rubel by name, spoke of his affection for the Jerome Kern song "Look for the Silver Lining." Drive didn't drum his fingers on the table, but his body language indicated that his attention was rapidly waning. Rubel turned to one of his colleagues who produced an easel with a large pad with an empty cover sheet. On a wave from the master, the sheet was turned to show a large solid red caption, OPERATION CRAB. That got Drive's attention. A lifetime of being sold can't-miss concepts by the sleaze masters of the Western World had not conditioned him for such a thoroughly disagreeable verbal introduction. The page was turned again and Rubel whispered, "The outside shell is shed and a vital new life inside is revealed." Feeling a bit pink and unprotected himself, Drive began to scowl as Rubel keened, "When the price is high, sell stock; when the price is low, buy the stock back." The new sheet said Management Buy In. The next several pages were straightforward arithmetic Drive could recite with his eyes shut. Borrow, tender for the outstanding shares at a price close to the current market value. Drive picked up the phone and discovered that the stock had sunk even a bit below the figure used for the calculations. More sheets described High Yield Bonds that apparently were going to be subscribed to by somebody to provide the cash for the stock buyback. So far, it was just a shell game. Finally, neat pro forma statements illumined the extraordinary increase in value for the surviving stockholders when the market turned and multiples returned to traditional levels.

Drive asked simply, "What assumptions have you cranked in about business growth during this period?" Rubel pointed to one of his silent colleagues, who nervously said, "We're using current figures with a cost-of-living inflator, no real growth." Drive nodded. "No real growth? Are we talking straight debt here, no conversion, no equity?" There was silence, broken by Rubel. "There may be some warrants in connection with the expenses of the underwriting, but otherwise, *No*, straight debt, no conversion." Drive pressed on, "This is quite a difficult package of financing to assemble. I know that Mike Milken can do it; I didn't know that the 'best people on Wall Street' were in the junk business." The reference was to a particularly unfortunate advertising campaign that haunted Silverman Seligman. Rubel gave a token lecture on the obligations of investment banking firms to serve the needs of their customers, all of which Drive readily translated to mean they couldn't stand losing out any more on the fees that Milken was rumored to be amassing.

Michael Milken changed the world and, like most messiahs, was crucified for his success. Companies like WPB had traditionally been limited, in times of low stock values, by the amount of money they could borrow from banks. Only the most reliable and established firms could meet the requirements of the rating agencies, and secure a rating that would permit institutions to invest. For the firms below investment grade the only debt source was the restrictive and expensive private placement from insurance companies. Milken did what economists have prayed for since the beginning of time; he discovered an inefficiency. Many companies who couldn't tick the boxes of nominal compliance were, in fact, excellent credit risks. With persistence, energy, and verve, Milken created the junk bond world, or what his Drexel colleagues insisted on referring to as the high-yield bond world. Junk sold and Milken's personal success was so extraordinary that the traditional Wall Street investment houses not only paid him the ultimate compliment of damning him and copying him, but they used all manner of political connection to destroy him.

Drive got up, walked around the office for a long minute, turned, and, with a smile began, "Have I got this right? Let's assume the company is worth $5 billion, we own 20 percent and no debt, and we earn, before taxes, a billion and a quarter. OK. We successfully tender for the four billion, What's the ticket?"

Rubel blinked, not sure whether he was being asked a question or even what the question was. Drive answered his own question. "What's the interest rate? Give or take 10 percent." Rubel nodded. "OK, so we'll have earnings of $850 million, all for us. Right? And when the cycle turns, as we all know it will, and the multiples get back to customary levels, rather than just doubling my money, I'll go from one to six billion." Rubel began to speak, but Drive went on pleasantly, "Now, I realize you fellows have to make a living so what do we put in here for you?"

Amazingly, Rubel took this moment to consult with his colleagues before speaking very quickly: "There aren't many places where you can get this kind of money. We think it's reasonable to be well paid. The Lehman Brothers standard..." At this point, Drive couldn't resist, "Wait a minute, mate! Either this is a unique service or it's standard with a street rate. Which is it?"

"We'll need something in the area of 5 percent and some warrants for, maybe, 10 percent of the company." A smile crept across Drive's face. "So, you get the $200 million, come hell or high water. And you think there's inefficiency in the market so you can charge me a higher price than your investors are going to insist on. Are you going to pay extra for these warrants?" Rubel just shook his head at this rhetorical question. Drive now knew the salesman's deal better than the salesman. "You'll have 'free warrants' to buy 10 percent, now is that 10 percent before the financing or after?" "Oh, after, of course," assured Rubel, as if to dismiss the very idea that he could have proposed a fee that would give him a third of the company. "So," persisted Drive, "if the market returns to normal, you'll be able to buy $600 million worth of my stock for $100 million, a profit of half a billion dollars?" Rubel did not reply but he did smile.

Drive just stared into space for a short time and slowly in a quiet voice, almost as if to himself, said, "I don't mind you guys getting rich. I'm trying to figure out what's really happening here. I wouldn't sell my own stock at this price. Indeed, I would advise anybody else not to, if they asked me. I know the company is doing well. The public

investors don't know any of this and yet they've trusted me by investing. I'm selling their participation in their investment out from under
them. As I see it, this deal is lose/lose for me. Either I pay too much
for the outside stock, in which case I'll lose a lot of money, or I paid
too little, and screwed a lot of people who invested in me. That I
couldn't live with. I want to make real money for my investors as well."

Rubel took another swing at it. "I understand, and your concern
does you credit. The beauty of the market is, it provides an impartial
fair value all the time." To which Drive said, "How can the market
value what it doesn't know? The market doesn't know what I'm going
to do, and that's a big factor in the value of this stock. My shareholders
have invested in Cedric Rhodes, not a mathematical projection. This
transaction isn't making a *better* company. I don't need the money, I
need more patience and vision. Am I just screwing my investors to
make a fee?"

As Rubel got up to go, his professional poise briefly deserted him,
"I'm sorry to have wasted your time. I thought we all wanted to make
money." Drive let that remark go unanswered.

Drive walked back towards his office, bemoaning the wasted morning. "Snake-oil bastards," he muttered as he winced at the fumes from
fresh varnish. The renovations never stop when period office space is to
be maintained. The floor was empty as people escaped the fumes for
lunch. In front of his office, his secretary was on holiday and the temp
was nowhere in sight. All that remained of her was an overturned copy
of *How to Prepare for Your Series 7 Broker's Qualifying Exam. A
petty ambition*, thought Drive. Who would fetch his lunch since there
was no one to have lunch with? He entered his office and was startled
by the temp, who was sitting on the sofa across from his desk, reading
the *Journal* next to a stack of his morning papers, all neatly refolded.
Startled, and guilty, she leapt to her feet, upsetting the pile and the
pile's original owner. She was unseemingly tall, with freckles and a
mass of red curls on her head that bounced as she jumped. *She is very
young and more than fit enough to fetch lunch*, Drive thought, as she
stooped to gather the papers from around the world.

"I'm sorry. I thought I should tidy..."

"There is *no* tidy, *ever*, till after my departure each day," Drive explained. She smelled sweet, like a summer garden. He stooped to help her with the papers and to steal another sniff.

"I'll need some food brought up to me." He picked up the open *Wall Street Journal* off the sofa. Following the honey versus vinegar adage, he decided to turn on the charm for the sweet-smelling giraffe, who did seem graceful in her slender way.

"Did you find anything in my copy of the *Journal* of interest?" He felt sort of grand. He always did with young women. He believed they all found him cute.

She was recomposed and so was her pile. She turned to face Drive, looking him in the eye, and he felt a tingle somewhere way down deep. He barely noticed. She said, "I was looking up some of the other Silverman clients 'cause the office gossip is you're shopping for junkers, and I was curious how they had done for other companies."

Drive was surprised and a little impressed. But he was hungry, so speaking over his growling stomach he said, "My, well, tell you what. Ring downstairs for a pastrami on rye with mustard, a cream soda, a whole pickle, and whatever you'd like. When it arrives, you come back in here and I'll tell you all about the slippery services of Silverman Seligman. Deal?" She had pale blue eyes and a tendency to furrow her brows.

"Oh, sir, yes, that would be great, I mean, nice." The temp was flummoxed and he felt a decade younger.

"Call me Drive," he said as he crossed to his desk, to seem very busy and speed up his sandwich.

She turned back in the doorway, spoiling his view. Never to be one caught looking, she caught him. She was trying to introduce herself, "I'm..."

"My dear, with all that lovely hair, I shall call you Rose." he said as he looked down at his desk, hoping to hasten her mission with the sandwich that would bring her back soon.

Shortly after Drive had dismissed the imitation Milkens with their contemptible proposal to transfer his shareholders' money to themselves, he went out of his way to meet the Man himself. No matter how many words were written about Milken, none communicated the evangelical fervor of the man, whether at his wheel in the Santa Monica trading room at 4:00 a.m. or speaking to the institutional investors by the sea later that same day. He knew everything, he spoke softly. When he was finished, you didn't know what he was selling, you only knew you wanted to buy it. Even Drive, disgusted by the Wall Streeters, was taken in by Milken's charm. For Milken, Drive was very much heaven; a real company, with real cash flow and a real owner. God, he'd been doing it for years with none of those essentials. So the two of them sat down, very quietly, and figured out how they could buy up the world. Drive never intuited whatever it was about Milken that subsequently got him in jail and Drexel bankrupt. For him, the man was the energy necessary to fulfill his dream of a global communications empire.

The excitement was too intense. Judgment weakens on the upside. Maybe, just this once, things will go up forever; well, if not forever, at least for another few days. So, Drive got caught at the end of the 1980s with a bad case of the shorts. All of his properties were promising, but the cash requirements to service his debts were not immediately to hand. This was the beginning of the limitless days and nights of sitting patiently through meetings until the debtors came to the always obvious, if a bit irritating, conclusion that they had no choice but to finance Drive further to get them out of the mess. The decade was a mixed bag for Drive but he found in "Rose" an eager student whom he would ultimately trust with many of his hopes and dreams. He taught her everything he knew and she had an instinct for power, how to recognize it, parlay it, and keep it, that Drive would grow to depend on. Starting in one of the many reserved corporate suites in the city, eventually she would run an entire separate office, equipped and staffed by World, but devoted to Drive personally. On the books, it was all one big company, in reality it was a secret to

everyone but Drive and Rose. When Rose returned with his sandwich
that day, for the first time in years, as Drive held court impressing the
bright young girl, he felt a little less lonely, a little less restless.

Chapter 3

Monday, August 3, 1998

Up with the sun, Drive bathed, dressed, and wolfed down a dainty bowl of sliced fruit set out for him, on doctor's orders, and cheerfully slipped away to the office. The city seemed to Drive to be alive like never before and the newsstands were filled with the presidential soap opera. At one of his favorite delis, while ordering his forbidden bacon, egg, and bagel sandwich, he had to browse one of the *Times*es scattered on the counter as the life's blood of the city ebbed in and out of the place. LAWMAKERS CALL FOR EXPLANATION IN LEWINSKY CASE. Drive was giddy with the thought of how this tale would spin on, filling column after column. He popped two pink tablets in anticipation of his second breakfast of the morning and munched them while he read. WASHINGTON, August 2—"Senator Orrin G. Hatch, the chairman of the Senate Judiciary Committee, said today that President Clinton should 'pour his heart out' to the American people about his relationship with Monica S. Lewinsky, and that by doing so he could take the steam out of any possible drive to impeach him." He stopped reading. While his adopted country had been very good to him, it had not been very good to itself over the decades. It was all so formulaic and predictable. A nonstory that would write itself. A great nation had lost its way. With that the counter bell rang and Drive's order was up.

In his office, deep in his papers, Drive thought he was beyond being surprised by anything, but when a whippet-thin figure with an apparent age anywhere from thirty-five to fifty (he was, in fact, sixty), with big hair, an Afro, came into his office, he was dumfounded. Marty didn't say hello and didn't hold out a hand for shaking, he sat down at the desk. He didn't have a briefcase, a pen, or a pad of paper. Forget Yale and the West Coast, the voice was all Manhattan.

"You want me to drop everything I am doing and do a deal for you? What's in the deal for me?"

So much for small talk. "I want to make a hostile tender offer this month for the *American Observer* magazine." Drive could play the short, sweet, and direct game with anybody. Silence.

"All I can tell you now is, you came to the right guy. Anybody else would have walked out the door by now. Do you want me to tell you what's wrong with the deal?" Drive knew a rhetorical question when he heard one. "Give it a shot, mate," and was pleased to prod Marty into a reaction. "Number 1: Nobody ever does anything in this town in the month of August. Number 2: Every law firm, every accounting firm, every bank, every investment house is making a fortune out of the situation the way it is today. Nobody wants it changed. Number 3: The insiders have this thing welded tight. They can tie any effort up in the courts forever. Number 4: This is an American institution. You're a foreigner. Why don't we make an offer for Mount Vernon or the Washington Monument?"

"I didn't get where I am by doing things that *other* people can do."

"OK, OK. Fair enough. You're real. Let's see. It's $1 million for me to drop everything I am doing and figure out how to do it. You're out the million no matter what. I may decide it can't be done. If I decide to do it, which I will do by the close of business tomorrow night, it'll cost you another $4 million for me to work out the detailed plan by the weekend and to pay for the necessary arrangements. When I pull off the deal, I'll expect an additional fee according to the investment bankers' schedule. You need to understand something. This deal is going to close a lot of doors to me in this town. I have to be paid enough to retire. So what's the deal?"

Drive decided this was no time for subtlety, so he didn't even comment on the fee. "This is a deal for me personally, not for World Publications, and I do not propose to put in any equity. I've got a financier but we still need to firm up the arrangements. I want to do it in August because that's when it will be hardest to mobilize effective opposition in the press and the government. My plan is to do this in two steps. First, offer for the voting stock only. That will get everybody's eye off of the ball. They will all protest that the nonvoting stock, which is owned by the public, is somehow being trashed. I want them to focus on that and not that some foreigner is buying up a national treasure. Do you remember when Mitsubishi bought Rockefeller Center? What I am counting on is that the largest holders of the A are huge respected charities. They're suffering under the present arrangements, and will do anything to get cash and liquidity for their endowments. After a week's firestorm, we offer for *all* of the stock. At this point, we should get support from the charities. They will have to be careful, and so will we. We choreograph that. When these high-type people connected with the Met, Sloan-Kettering, and Lincoln Center come out enthusiastically for the deal, can the trustees who are also executives of the company refuse to deal? Their conflict of interest is too big to be ignored. You're the lawyer, but it seems to me that trustees, no matter what the instrument purports to permit, can't refuse to consider an offer to sell, it's in the best interests of the trust. The law can't ignore their conflict of interest."

While talking, Drive wondered at the unflappable demeanor of his $5 million lawyer. How does a person get to be so good that they ask and get $1 million just to consider a proposition? He liked his cool. He isn't hearing anything yet that he can't do with his left hand. Marty broke in with a note of reality.

"If this deal depends on the courts, it will never happen. These guys can buy half of the bar association and most of the judiciary. Look at it this way, if the deal goes through, they are still trustees, they are still big men. They simply have different assets. In many ways, the assets are more attractive. The most popular people in town and they'll have less headaches. I can tell you right now. We are going to need the best public relations talent in this town. For this deal, at this time of year, you can't even think about cost. Money is the only way we're going to be able to get the talent. Have you got the money? My check had better clear!!"

Many years had past since anybody had questioned whether Drive could pay his bills. It was not a nice feeling, particularly since he never had money in his own name when he controlled World Publications and used it to pay for all his expenses, hobbies, and occasional needs. He realized that he would have to make a few calls to move the money around so that he could meet Marty's initial requirements. The thought of having to juggle some personal funding was irksome but this was no time to show any lack of confidence about the chicken feed at the beginning of the deal. He remembered the friendly caution he had received. "When Marty is hired to do a deal, the deal is easy, Marty isn't."

"Look, if we're going to work together, let's be clear that I am the client and you're the lawyer."

"I'm not your lawyer yet and I'm not coming unless I feel that busting my backside and using up all my brownie points in this town is going to result in success. I am not in the business of nice tries and brilliant failures. When I take this on, it'll get done. Right now, I haven't made up my mind. Now what's the deal?"

Drive didn't like the feeling that he had to audition his deal, but hadn't he come to town to build a new team all his own? The biggest and the baddest? Maybe this ferocious Hebrew had some lessons to teach him about his grand scheme. He took a deep breath and began, "This is the greatest communications property in the world that is not owned by a conglomerate. The magazine has the largest paid subscription level, 28 million, of any publication in the world. Its database has 100 million names. The stock price is the lowest it's ever been since the public offering in 1990, about half of its high. They have cut the dividend to less than a quarter of its former level. Since 1995 cash flow has been negative. When you have charities as shareholders, that dividend is really important.

"Look at this report on last week's meeting between the new CEO and the analysts; 'earnings and cash flow performance are unacceptable' and are 'disappointing, embarrassing, and scaring employees.' The company took a big restructuring in 1996 that was supposed to hard wire profits, they cut a quarter of the jobs, new CEO. Then they fired the guy, the old guard took it back, and now they got this new guy in May from Citibank. He announces his 'Global Reorganization' last week and the stock tanks." Marty fidgeted politely in his seat. He knew all this. *Tell me something the rest of the world doesn't know already*, he thought.

"With all this, the company has virtually no debt, a lot of art, and the best part of $100 million in cash." *This should hold your attention*, thought Drive. "The market values the company around $2.5 billion. My valuation is $4 billion based on its long-term cash flow. That's what's important to me, as that's what will persuade the lenders to put up all the money.

"The greatest franchise in the world is available for purchase with its own cash. That's what I like about this deal. Right now, today is one of the few times that the financial markets are bulging with money. They can't get the money out the door fast enough. How many times could you borrow 100 percent with no personal recourse? When you can get money on those terms, it doesn't make much difference what you buy."

Marty couldn't restrain himself, "If this is such a great deal, how come these local deal guys have given it a pass? There must be a dozen buyout funds with the smartest, most aggressive acquirers in the world within ten blocks of here. Have they suddenly turned stupid?"

"My edge is being a foreigner. The American Observer supports most of the best-known charities in this area. Everyone who is anybody wants to be on the board of the Metropolitan Museum or Sloan-Kettering or you name it. AOM is the great earth mother. Nobody wants to get crosswise with this organization. Think of the legal fees for the charities, to say nothing of the investment banking and management fees. Look, if it was just money, it would have gone already. There is a matter of community prestige. Everyone has always thought it's impossible with the voting stock being held by the self-perpetuating former management."

Marty wanted to hate the deal, but he just couldn't. It was a sexy long shot and they could make one for the business history books. He popped up out of his seat, surprising Drive. "I didn't waste my morning. You know, compared to this, the first chapter of Genesis was a bowl of cherries. But I think you've got a real bargain. This is a project worthy of my attention." Marty shook Drive's hand, at last, and walked out. The meeting was over. Marty was out the door long before Drive started to smile realizing he had passed his first audition in a very long time. He felt it boded well.

"Moffie, this is Drive, I need a couple of more bits of information." Drive was interrupting his scheduled phone list for the day to follow up on a tip from an early call. Ultimately he had been impressed with Beal and the day was flying by. "On the board of our favorite company, a guy resigned. He is president of one of the big banks here in town. Bank presidents just don't resign from the board of companies with all the deposit and trust arrangements that AOM has. Can you find out what happened? While you're at it, there is a rumor that the chairman of one of those foundations, who has written a book about corporate governance, tried to get the rest of the board to agree to value the company, and hire Goldman Sachs. They wouldn't do it so he quit, at least that's the story."

"I'm on it." Moffie hung up and Drive rose to stretch and pace and savor his good fortune as he stood in front of the best view in the city. He watched the traffic as his secretary brought in the latest editions from the world press at large. The rule was never to disturb his desk until he had left for the day, so she placed the stack on the table by the sofa.

"Here's the latest, Drive," said the sweetest voice that ever came out of Human Resources.

"Yes. Thank you, dear." He watched her reflection in the window, so as not to be caught looking. He waited for her to turn, but he was defied as she raised her hand pointing, "You've got a fax in your machine, sir." He looked over, too quickly, but said, "Yes, thank you. I heard it." She turned and walked out, but he missed her turn and exit, distracted by the fax machine being on the side of his bad ear.

Damn stupid thing. But then he remembered it was his very private fax and today would be a good day for a very private fax. He leapt across his office. He couldn't read it fast enough.

CAN ANYBODY BE TOO GENEROUS?

August 4—That is a question that a lot of people are asking about Randy and Shelley Porter. Over the last years of their lives, they created massive charitable trusts containing virtually all of the equity of the *American Observer* with a value of several billions of dollars. The stock was divided into two classes, voting and non-voting. The trustees holding the voting stock make extensive grants largely to educational and cultural institutions. There are also several trusts for the benefit of some of the most beloved and important charities in the country: Sloan-Kettering, The Metropolitan Museum of Art, Lincoln Center, Colonial Williamsburg, Hudson Highlands, and the New York Zoological Society. The Porters' contributions were valued at levels close to those of the Rockefeller family, who have long been associated with these great national institutions.

Over the years, since the death of the Porters, the value of the *American Observer* has plummeted. This is tragedy enough for those directly involved, for the jobs lost, for the impact on the community, for opportunities destroyed. It is disaster for the shareholders. These great charities have come to depend on support from the Porters' trusts. Annual distributions are an essential part of their working capital. AOM hasn't earned its dividend since 1995. If it were not for the Internal Revenue Service rules requiring that trusts annually distribute at least 5 percent of the value of the trust, there would already have been a serious shortfall in payments. The trusts have to sell their principal in order to make payments. That is a road with a predictable end.

Persons close to several of the key trustees of these institutions have, for the first time, been willing to air their concerns publicly. There is a very real loss of confidence in the management and trusteeship of the Porters' interests. It is felt that too much was given to people not able to meet the responsibilities. There is real concern about the viability of the enterprise. Individuals having knowledge of the events disclose that conversations have been held between certain trustees of the beneficiary organizations and the trustees of the voting trusts. It is reliably reported that the beneficiary trustees have insisted, in the face of marked opposition, that sale of the enterprise be considered. These conversations went so far as to contrast the situation of all the trustees if they held a portfolio of marketable securities (which one hesitates to mention have been going up at a rate in excess of 20 percent per year) rather than continuing to bear the risk of AOM's uncertain future.

The Porters gave so much to the trusts that the trustees are now obligated to press to change the arrangements for AOM's continued management in order to be able to continue to carry out the Porters' intent. As one trustee put it: "Would the Porters have preferred to have the company broke and the trusts unable to fund their worthy causes, or would they have preferred the company sold, presumably to someone who knows how to take advantage of its still superb assets, and the trust beneficiaries fully supported?"

Handwritten at the bottom, with some flair, was the note "Arriving on newsstands today, thank you very much." Drive was pleased and started whistling to himself, as he slipped on his jacket and then picked three late editions from the stack on the table and headed out of his office. "Goodnight, Drive," chimed his secretary. "It *is* a good night, my dear Cynthia, very good." She pushed the button for his car and got up to clean his desk, check for filing, and shred his Out basket.

Drive went down in the elevator to the ground floor and went out of the Forty-third Street exit. He got into the waiting limousine for the short ride back to the Sherry Netherland. He opened the slender briefcase that he always carried and took out his unconventional cellular phone. On closer inspection, it was slightly larger and substantially heavier than the usual phone in order to accommodate the sophisticated encryption attachments. Drive had registered his phone and its frequencies worldwide in order to avoid creating anxiety by the security personnel of his host country with the simple explanation that it was designed for keeping business secrets. He pressed the only preprogrammed number in its state-of-the-art memory bank.

"Thank you very much, indeed. The article was perfect. I won't even ask."

"We owe a few friends. There's another one coming out tomorrow. A London financial paper asking, 'Does everybody have to sit around and watch a great institution destroy itself? Can't somebody help?'"

"I'm glad you're on my side."

"I'm looking forward to the day when I can be there all the time. How's our lawyer?"

"No mere lawyer, my dear, more like a force of nature, and a pricey one, at that."

"They say the street loves him."

"I just hope Vern loves him. We audition him at the bank tomorrow." He yawned, "Pardon me."

"You've had a big day. It's still a new time zone for you."

"So it is," looking at his watch. "Well then, good night, my love."

"Good night, my lover."

Chapter 4

In the middle of the financial district, Universal is the unabashed, most ambitious bank in town. That ambition was apparent in the tasteful yet opulent office where Drive, Marty, and the bank's President and CEO, Vernon Stillman, were about to meet.

"Vern, I don't know if you are acquainted with Martin van Buren Beal, who is going to do my legal work on this deal?"

"Marty, nice to meet you. I know your reputation. It's all good. What's that firm you are with?"

"Brandeis, Breyer, and Ginsburg."

"Oh, goodness. First-rate people. If you don't mind my asking, Drive, why aren't you using Spencer Sherman on this one? He's been your lawyer for longer than I can remember." Vernon Stillman's life was an unending chain of transactions and he had charm in abundance for every one of them. His southern gentility was as apparent as his southern accent was absent. There was a lilt, but Vern banished his native inflection long ago, and now it was like a jack-in-the-box, bursting out whenever Vern might lose control, which wasn't very often.

"Vern, this is a personal deal and Sherman advised me in the clearest possible language that I may not use World Publications' personnel or professional advisors. We are determined to avoid any conflict of interest here. As you know, Citicorp has been our bankers for generations. I would certainly start with them on any company deal, Vern. It's only that you and I have developed a relationship over the years and that's what brings this business to Universal."

"Well, I sure do appreciate that, Drive. Yes, I certainly do. With your permission, over the last several months, I explored your plan with my key people on a strictly confidential, no-names basis. We've done a lot of work. I don't mind telling you that this is one big fish. Nobody wants to put themselves on the other side of AOM. They've been a very lucrative client for a lot of people. However, we've never had any of their business so we have nothing to lose. We agree with your analysis. This company can be bought for less than it's worth, with you running it, of course, and we ought to have sufficient cash flow to back up our loans."

No outsider could detect a change in Drive's appearance, but some fundamental signal in his nervous system shifted into racing mode. He could feel it, he could smell it. *This is the time to make the deal. This is the moment when I can extract the final critical elements in the negotiation. There are times when the other party will accept anything; there are times when they will accept nothing. Does he want it more than I do? It all comes down to that. This is the time to push, and here goes. Give me this deal for free*, he thought.

"It is important to understand that I, personally, am not going to co-sign the note and that your entire security will be 100 percent of the stock and assets of AOM. Aside from having to preside at World Publications board meetings, I intend to give my full time and attention to AOM, but I do not want my time to be legally committed. You know that I will remember my friends. You and I have been talking about this deal for months, and the timing is now. The stock is at rock bottom, the new management hasn't really taken over and disparaged the situation, and the shareholders are very restless. We need to move, right now. Are you able to do that? You and I both know that this is a very different kind of deal for Universal. You are the traditional commercial bank. I am asking you to line up permanent financing as well as the bridge to get the initial tender done. Are you comfortable that you can do this big new controversial deal quickly?"

The master was drawing the dry fly along the surface of the tranquil water. He had chosen his lure with care, new bank, speed, new image, professionalism, and he had cast it so as to distract attention from his own, admittedly aggressive, conditions of no personal commitment of time or credit. Marty watched with interest as hungry

Vern gulped down the bait, hook and all, while the stone-faced Drive couldn't stop his own eyes from twinkling with greed.

"Drive, you and I have shared a lot of thoughts over the years. You know that I feel that Universal's future lies in being a global full-service bank. We want to earn the reputation of being a one-stop shop, where anybody from any country can come to get the appropriate financing for any kind of deal. I don't mind telling you that the reluctance my people would usually have to get involved with AOM has been overcome by their lousy performance and management turnover. The guys at the top are locked in, so they do not seem to understand that public shareholders have expectations and sensitivities. This is the time to go and we're ready. Let's you and I go out and have a little luncheon and I'll let Marty get together with our people to work up a term sheet."

Bankers' luncheons in Manhattan follow a predictable pattern. Take an elevator to the top of the building, walk down a corridor lined with large oak doors, push one open, and admire the full bar, the waiter, the view, and the elegantly set table. Vern did it differently. He simply pushed a button. His bookcase moved over to reveal the entrance to a small glass-sided dining area with a view of Park Avenue, only three stories below. Vern knew what the CEO of a bank was supposed to do. He was supposed to schmooze with big clients. Here he was with one of the biggest accounts in the world, about to do the biggest deal in New York and he had no idea what to say. Drive, on the other hand, had been borrowing and scheming with the greatest energies in the world for most of the last forty years. He fully realized that none of them had anything to say worth listening to and it didn't bother him in the least. If both of them could have had their druthers, there would be no luncheon, no obligation to take the time to pretend to a civil relationship, and more time to get on with the deals. They were trapped.

One subject that was safe with close friends was the state of their nonexistent marriages. Vern was on his second wife, who understood entirely that what she got was a charge account and what he got was a trouble-free decorative escort. Drive had been married four times, but his current marriage had lasted almost thirty years and three children. The children were all involved in the business and Drive had no compunction about using his voting shares to insure that they were in positions of executive leadership. Drive's wife constantly asked him why he didn't take it easy, why as one of the most accomplished and wealthiest men in the world, he didn't simply enjoy the fruits of his accomplishments? She asked him so many times, "Why don't you stop and smell the roses?" that Drive was forced to admit into his consciousness the reality that he was bored with his wife. He had no interest whatsoever in doing anything other than new deals in order to build his personal and corporate empires. He hadn't consciously sought out new female company, he kept telling himself, but he seemed to need confirmation that he could deal with the best of them and his best years were ahead of him. His hearing was going, but the rest worked just fine. The fiction of a business marriage was compounded with the fiction of a business social life. The wives of CEOs were expected to like, or at least to put up with, each other. After all, they had a lot in common. So Vern and Drive proceeded to organize the choreography by which their secretaries would enlist their wives to agree on a dinner date in the near future.

Maybe I can learn something, mused Drive to himself, as he started off the conversation. "Vern, you having any fun?"

A pained contraction of facial muscles was witness to Vern's difficulty in trying to process this question. Was it serious? At what level should he respond? He decided on a Manhattan trick, always answer a question with a question. "Am I having fun?"

"You know, is all of this," Drive extended both arms to indicate the whole world encompassed within their view, "the wife, the family, the bank, is it working for you?"

Vern, who had never permitted himself to consider fun beyond his professional status and his bank account, dug down deep and honestly said, "You know, sir, I've never really thought much about fun."

"Let an old man tell you something. If you're not having fun, all you're doing with life is dying a little early. I'm not the final authority on any of this, ol' buddy, but you have to find some way to allow joy into your life."

Vern wanted to ask if Drive could recommend a course or even a guru, they could talk about people like Peter Drucker as gurus, from whom he could learn. But just in time, he figured that was not the right way to go. He realized that Drive was interested in something inside himself that was quite different from reading other people's wisdom. Vern's discomfort with this line of conversation was apparent, "I'll have all the joy in the world when we get this deal all tied up. That's right."

Sports were always a helpful topic, but what could an American and a South African do? No baseball in one place, no cricket or rugby in the other. As usual, business considerations came to the rescue. Drive was buying an American basketball team in order to have filler for his European and Asian TV stations. Basketball was beginning to possibly be the international sport. Golf was always there to talk about. Tiger Woods ought to get a licensing fee for the conversational use of his name. He had given more people something to talk about than anything since Edward VIII gave up the throne of Great Britain. Actually, most of the lunch was consumed with talk of their visit to The Country Club in Brookline, Massachusetts, that next weekend. Drive had asked to play there because the Ryder Cup would be held there in 1999 and he had worked closely with the promising golfers from South Africa. After a lot of playful haggling, they agreed that each had a legitimate handicap of six; that Vern would bring a partner who was an officer in their trust company and would arrange for the club pro to play with Drive. Vern did not mention the coincidence that he had learned how to play golf at The Country Club and that his familiarity with the course was worth at least a couple of strokes off his nominal handicap nor did Drive mention that he had maintained his nonresident membership there since his Boston days. They enjoyed the big boy talk. The partnerships would play straight low ball. For stakes, they choked; both of them were beyond money. Probably, what they really wanted was to be able to tell the whole world how they had beaten the other guy, but they needed something specific. Hey, even Tiger takes the trophies home, when he could buy them in gold with the cash prizes. Something distinctive, how about ten krugerrands to the winner? Or a case of wine, of the winner's choice?

Somehow, luncheon was survived.

People in the financial public relations business came to believe that only God and themselves could make market value. They were descendents of the company called Crosby Kelly, and California magic of the 1960s, when a beautiful story yielded a superb price earnings multiple. Business changed forever when Crosby Kelly created business glamour. Annual reports and shareholder meetings became marketing events that made boardrooms sexy. There would be no going back. Drive knew the breed, like most modern industries, good was great and bad was death to any project. So much of modern media lived and died by them; there was a level of excellence possible but rare. Marty's recommendation was with the caveat to Drive, "Yeah, he's family, but he *is* the best man for this job." Marty made it clear, "In our family, we've a rule about business. I'm a runner, so the rule is, when a runner stumbles, everyone else jumps over the body and keeps running. No looking back. Not a problem, cuz we don't ever stumble." Drive respected family loyalty and with Marty's reputation riding on the recommendation, he was eager to audition a new and crucial team member.

Joey Jones never doubted for a second that he was a genius and didn't stop talking for five minutes after entering Drive's office. Even Marty was silent and with good reason. Joey was his sister's boy and Marty was giving the kid the break of his professional life. Hey, what's an uncle for? What did he say? Who knows? What was being communicated? He was the key to the success of this venture; with him is great success, without him, certain failure. Jones wore no necktie and was otherwise the picture of California casual, perhaps in continuing homage to the industry founders. If this was Marty's candidate for the team, Drive would indulge him.

"I gotta tell you, I like the deal. Things are slow in August. Everybody is thinking about President Clinton and those Nobel geniuses screwing up long-term capital management. We can get a few people seeing things our way and nobody is going to bother to challenge us. We're just a little summer deal. We need a few key people; the right article at the right time and this thing can happen. I got to say, Mr. Rhodes, I don't know how you did it but that article today, pure gold."

Drive piped up, "Wait a minute, mate. A lot of people are seeing the same problems we do, I wouldn't want you to draw any improper conclusions about our influence."

"Yeah yeah, sure sure, you've got to say that, I guess. I'll only tell you, in my line of work, there are no coincidences, know what I mean?"

Drive was back to business. "So, if it were up to you, how would we get this deal done?"

"I'm not the business genius in this room but I know my spin. This calls for a dual tender strategy. First, tender *only* for voting stock. The public rage will focus on the fate of the nonvoting shareholders being squeezed, not on the foreigner taking over a Great American Institution. Only then, extend the tender *same terms* to *all* shareholders. The American public will make you do the full tender, Brer Rabbit and the briar patch." Joey continued. "We gotta feed 'em some bait. Offering for the voting stock will provide a simple reason for everybody to hate the deal. They'll hate it so much, they'll forget why they hate it. But right now, the stock is at an all-time low and all the fancy shareholders are incontinent wondering where those fat dividends are going to come from. The stink is so bad, nobody can really get upset about somebody coming in, offering a ton of money, bailing them out, and taking the risk of running this dinosaur. This is a disaster waiting for a place to happen. Hey, you ought to get a medal for taking this one on." Joey could feel his heart pounding. His job was to dance as fast as he could and he was dancing so fast, he was out of breath. This was a really big fish. He could spend his whole career and never get this close again to clients like these. God bless his uncle.

What he knew about business, he could put in a shot glass. He prayed it didn't show.

Drive finally got a word in edgewise. "Joey, you're OK, we've got a lot to do quickly. Marty, do I take it that all this means you're going to do the deal?"

"Do you think I'd sit here and listen to this crap if I wasn't? I'm going to do the deal. I'll have the full plan by the end of the week. Meanwhile, we've got to tie down the money." Before Marty leapt out of his chair, he gave Joey a secret smile and a wink. Joey's day was made, and if he didn't stumble, maybe even his career was too.

Back at Universal, only a few blocks away, Vern went upstairs to meet with his full loan committee and legal staff who had finished preliminary meetings with Marty earlier that day.

A senior bank officer, acting as the institutional conscience, said, "Vern, you have to be careful of this deal."

"What are you talking about? This is the most exciting piece of new business that this bank has had in the last ten years."

"Vern, you want the deal *too* much. We're reaching here. Yes, the cash flows are there, just, but we have no personal guarantee. We have no idea whether we will ever see Drive after the ink dries on this one. If AOM continues to go downhill, we won't get out whole. We're bankers, not speculators."

"Son, listen here, this is just the problem I am trying to deal with in this bank. If you're a banker, big deal, best case you get your money back plus interest a point over the prime. How do you make any money that way? You don't. We have to go into investment banking, where the real fees are and the real rewards are. Big fish. Goldman made five times as much money last year as we did and they have less capital."

"I understand what you are trying to do, Vern, and I understand that there is no such thing as the perfect deal, but I am worried. We can do the initial loan for closing the tender offer for the voting stock ourselves, but we need partners for the balance of the loan for the entire stock and for the long-term credit taking out our advance. We have to get other people to believe in this deal and to come along with us. We're forbidden to talk with anyone else except on a no-names basis."

"What feedback are you getting from the no-names inquiries?"

"Marginal deal. We need some sweeteners, we need some signatures, we need to have the person responsible on the line."

"Well, that ain't happening. You understand that I'm trying to get this client away from Citicorp. Citicorp, you hear? He has a thousand ways of financing this deal. I have worked for years to get him to come here and be the shine on our new Universal Bank. We can't go out and shop this loan. If word gets out, the AOM supporters' association will make our lives shit before we get to the plate. Suppose I get a commitment for the permanent financing, would you have any trouble filling in the balance of the closing credit? You like that any better?"

"Hell, yes, boss. If you can do that, Vern, I'll hand it to you. How do you figure on finding that piece of money?"

"You just worry about getting our job done on time. I'll get me that piece of the pie."

Chapter 5

Vernon Rogers Stillman

Vernon Stillman was born in Woodbine, Georgia, early in the war year 1943, the only child of a Scots Presbyterian clergyman and his wife. His father was a chaplain in the Army, who, they later learned, landed in North Africa at the exact time of his son's birth. Vern's earliest months were spent with his mother's large and devout family.

The Scots Irish settled southeastern Georgia during the eighteenth century and established a life pattern that was little changed by the time of Vern's birth. With rice and cotton, shellfish and ocean catch, game and domestic animals, subsistence was relatively easy. Locked in the maws of puritan religion and racial segregation, Woodbine, with its dusty square, antebellum courthouse, Camden County government buildings, and huge live oak shade trees, was south of William Tecumseh Sherman's March to the Sea and west of the great trunk railway lines that brought money and crowds to south Florida. Nor did industry locate in this rather inaccessible inland town, 250 miles, as the crow flies, from the state capital. In a place advertised as having the best climate in the world, the sameness of days was most rudely changed with the coastal wind-borne smell of the sulphate-process paper mills in Brunswick.

Vern's first ten years could have been his father's or grandfathers'. The children of pastoral families were always a little different. They helped with church. They spent a lot of time with books in their hands, bibles, hymnals, and the Book of Common Order. They were not wealthy in the world's possessions and got by through a practice of time-honored homilies of rural poverty, "save, repair, and do not waste." It would be difficult for Vern to explain in his adult years the quality of friendship that he had with Negro children during his childhood years. His father's church was open to all races, although, to be honest, they did not sit together. The children played together, hunted together, and fought together. At some point short of adolescence, this idyllic communion quite naturally faded away and the separate rest rooms for Whites and Coloreds were an accurate measure of the divided society.

Great changes came while Vern was in his early teens. *Brown v. Board of Education* was pronounced by the Supreme Court of the United States in the spring of 1954. Separate but equal was no longer the law of the land. The next decades would witness, one hundred years after Lincoln's Emancipation Proclamation, the commitment of a proud country to live up to its own principles. The surge of industrial development following the end of World War II was hardly interrupted by a war in Korea and electric generating plants were built and high-tension wires were strung across the land, bringing the energy of many to do what individuals had had to do for themselves since the first settlement. By the time Vern finished high school, many public places, and a few homes, were air-conditioned, liberating the people from the tyranny of heat and humidity. The rewards from committee chairmanships in the federal Congress had brought huge military expenditures to the South, and many industries seeking relief from unions were glad of a social and political environment that welcomed them. The South was finally to arise from the post–Civil War torpor. But before that, something quite remarkable happened in Vern's life.

The public school system in Camden County, even for white children, had never achieved the level of the North, but the bookish tendency of the only child, in the tight world of the church, was encouraged and stimulated by the parishioners. Nobody in Vern's family, indeed nobody in Woodbine or, for that matter, in all of Georgia, knew what to do when it was announced that one Vernon Stillman had achieved the highest mathematics aptitude test score in the United States for sixteen-year-olds. There was no old boy network to enable Vern to attend private school, where it was felt he could get the best education. The church was poor, its parishioners had no extra funds, and there was literally no money for Vern's education.

It was an old-world custom for young men to go to work as apprentices at age sixteen, so Vern became articled to a firm of certified public accountants in nearby Brunswick, one of the boomtowns of the South. He lived with relatives and came home by bus on weekends. There wasn't much fun in Vern's life after his first ten carefree years. As he experienced the optimism and prosperity of the Eisenhower years, the contrast with his own circumstances created some core elements of character. Never, never as long as he lived was Vern going to permit an absence of money to constrain his opportunities. As the clergyman's son, he had accepted the slight condescension of wealthier parishioners who took it for granted that he would work harder and be paid less than their children. Increasingly, Vern came to resent his seeming helplessness and, ultimately, those who could not help him, including his parents. As he tossed restlessly on the cot bed in the kitchen of his cousin's Brunswick house, with the flickering of the fluorescent lights from the signs advertising cars across the street, a sense of himself bitterly emerged. He could rely only on himself. Psychologically he had left home. While this seemed, at the time, only to be release from the burdens of the past, Vern would, in later years, impress others as having no roots, no values, no sustaining principles.

Vern was a brilliant accountant. As the Kennedy years brought in all manner of legislation and regulation to "get America going again," the partners in the firm became used to Vern being the firm's authority on the new tax incentives. By this time, Vern had physically matured into a lean, attractive man appearing somewhat older than his eighteen years. He was able to explain all the new wonders in the tax codes with such simplicity and clarity that the partners began taking him to client meetings. He became something of a celebrity and clients specifically asked for him. At this point events began to cascade. He was the youngest CPA in the history of the state, had the highest grades in the high school equivalency tests, and steady salary increases. Vern got his own apartment. He learned to drive and purchased a car. Talent, at least talent at Vern's level, attracts. Several of the firm's clients invited Vern to their homes. Without any conscious intent, many felt Vern would be an ideal son-in-law or even a surrogate son. They were struck by his good manners, his appearance, and, above all, his extraordinary intelligence. It was quite a shock for Vern to come to appreciate that people really liked him. He wasn't yet liberated from the spell of the Puritan God who reminds constantly of our failings.

Vern liked girls and girls liked Vern. At age eighteen Vern was a grown man. He supported himself, he was in a position to make decisions and commitments, and he was a far cry from the high school seniors and college freshmen. He never groped or grabbed. He was earnest. But his grip on prosperity was too fragile to permit emotional exploration and risk; he was too close to home to test his sexuality.

The good news was the bad news in the accounting firm. That Vern could add and subtract was undoubted. What was off-putting was that he could quite accurately calculate his value to the firm and understand that he was being paid only a pittance of it. After all, he was still a minor under Georgia law, and, therefore, legally incompetent to enter into contracts, among other things. It was a sign of how far Vern had come that he realized that this firm would never pay him what he was worth. He turned his attention to the next step. During his countless meetings and meals, he had kept his eyes and ears open and his mouth shut. He learned how to tell who were the real players in the game.

The gentrification of the Sea Islands south of Charleston, South Carolina, was in full stride. Charles Fraser had developed Hilton Head close to the Georgia border and had turned his attention to Cumberland Island in Camden County on the border with Florida. One of those extraordinary coincidences that punctuate most lives, was the presence of a boy from Woodbine, the seat of Camden County, in a Brunswick accounting firm at just the time that some of Fraser's smart boys were beginning to develop plans for Cumberland. Charles Fraser had achieved the distinction, in one year, of having hired the largest number of graduates of the Harvard Business School by a single employer. This level of sophistication was new to South Georgia real estate development. It is not surprising that Fraser's team latched on to Vern and he became their guide and interpreter of the intricacies of the county.

Cumberland Island is a legendary property; its magnificence has attracted explorers since the beginning of time, beyond the dreams of even the most megalomaniacal real estate developer. Over twenty miles of beach, half a mile wide; beautiful dunes, live oaks, meadows, forests, slews, wild life, shrimp, oysters. It possessed all the glories of the earth. The Carnegie family had acquired one of the great American fortunes after the Civil War and created an impressive existence on Cumberland. The span of grandeur was relatively short. Thomas Carnegie died in his forties leaving Lucy Coleman Carnegie with nine children. She proved capable of running both the family and the island. It was estimated that some 300 servants maintained the principal residence at Dungeness, complete with gardens, pools, gymnasia, and all the accoutrements for luxurious living. Smaller mansions were built for her children elsewhere on the island. Dungeness was shut in the early 1920s, at the time of her death.

In 1968, Fraser was able to buy two large tracts from one family member and set about trying to work out a modus vivendi with his new neighbors. They were not amused. Without lingering overlong on the peregrinations of Charles Fraser and the Carnegies, one barely noticed consequence was the growing respect and affection of the Fraser team for Vern Stillman.

Who thought up the idea? Nobody really knows, but everyone there now takes credit. Somebody went to the dean of the Harvard Business School and said there was a boy he should look at. Vern had never spent a day in college, but he had the best instincts and experience for someone his age that they had ever met. They arranged for Vern to take all manner of aptitude tests and his scores were close to the top levels ever recorded. The dean listened to people who employed large numbers of his graduates, and a meeting with Vern was soon arranged.

Vern had literally never been outside of the state of Georgia, so his plane trip to Boston and subway rides to the Brighton campus of the Harvard Business School were one amazement after another. He wasn't afraid, he wasn't even apprehensive, he was leaving his past behind and that made him very happy indeed.

By this time in his life, Vern had mastered the role of surrogate son. He had learned how much people, usually men with important jobs, enjoy acting as mentors for younger people who were respectful, attractive, and bright. Having no real relationship with his own father, he had mastered being a son for others. The dean was one of the few to intuit the first suggestions of manipulation. Their conversation went well, *maybe too well*, ruminated the dean. It made him nervous to have *his* rough edges smoothed over. By the end of the day, Vern had a job as teaching assistant in an introductory accounting course, which, truth be told, most HBS faculty considered beneath them. This would provide him with money to live on, while basic expenses and tuition were covered by a scholarship fund set up by the Fraser Company.

Harvard Business School—or simply the "B School" as it is known by its intimates—had not yet become the destination of choice for the most accomplished graduates of the best colleges that it was to become in later years. The first top talent came from overseas. The outstanding Australian businessmen of their generation came to HBS at this time. It was large, it had been in existence for a long time, and it had substantial endowment and a varied roster of professors, some of great distinction. Business in America fell into disrepute with the Depression of the 1930s. The war changed much of this as American business responded with model efficiency to the need for more and more sophisticated military apparatus. Some considerable part of this was attributable to Harvard Business School. It was Professors "Tex" Thornton and Robert McNamara who worked with the training programs at the school during the war and then afterwards became heads of Litton and Ford respectively. They can be thought of as the proconsuls of the world of the technocrats. HBS's Class of 1949 was the Class of the CEOs. From that point on, the B School increasingly attracted the brightest and the best.

Perhaps the tone was best set by the colorful professor of small business, the French-born General Georges Doriot. It is history that the General created the first venture capital firm, American Research & Development, and invested in the founding stock of Digital Equipment Company. Everybody made a great deal of money, including the General and his protégés from Harvard Business School who served for him on the board. As the alumni became the CEOs of major companies and the professors were the energizers of emerging firms, HBS took on the character of a commercial mixing valve, the place where important things came together. One professor would start a consulting firm, other professors were on the boards of directors of the most prestigious companies in the land, and many professors were co-opted on a part-time basis from successful businesses in the Boston area.

For Vern, the terrible consequences of getting what he wished for weren't that terrible. He had gotten out of Georgia. He could create a geological biographical layer that would be the base for all subsequent consideration of him. He would forget the poverty, the meanness, the humiliation. He would put his origins and his parents behind him. The wise man said: "He who knows what he knows, knows; he who knows not what he knows, knows not." Vern was in the maelstrom of keeping up his public appearance on the one hand while trying to scramble to fill in the private gaps.

For the first time in his life, he was not the best student in the class. He was probably the best accountant and was outstanding in classes in which numerical skills were essential. He had so little experience with the kinds of people whom B-School students rather grandly, if accurately, assumed they would be managing, that he had trouble following the conversations in class. Real life for his colleagues involved sports, vacations, travel, and shared college experiences. All of this was a blank for Vern. He had no major in college, he had no college. His job experience was limited to the rather feudal earning of his accounting certification. Vern, having cast off the baggage from the past, was the quickest learner there ever was. He listened, he made notes, he went home and studied the notes. He learned what he didn't know and made effective plans to learn more.

After his first year at the Business School, the dean himself helped Vern to a summer internship with McKinsey & Company. The remarkable Marvin Bower, a graduate and benefactor of HBS, ran McKinsey. Bower, who had also graduated from Harvard Law School, created a new profession or, to put it more accurately, he so changed the existing notion of management consulting as to create a new category. McKinsey and its alumni would be one of the dominant forces in the world economy during the last decades of the twentieth century. Bower had an almost legendary insight into the capability of young people. He quickly concluded that Vern would not be a good consultant. His drives were so strong, his self-referential nature was too pronounced. He would never credibly persuade clients that his interest in their affairs was more important than his interest in his own. The question then was, what line of business would be best for Vern? It was Marvin who latched on to commercial banking. It had always been a fool's game, loan someone money. If you are successful, you get paid back; if you are unsuccessful, you lose everything. Hardly an attractive proposition and yet banks enjoyed a central position in America's economy. So long as an individual can be fulfilled by the utmost care in lending and the utmost attention to collecting, banking is a perfect business. Whatever happened to the economy, banks would be important. Vern's numerical skills would give him instant credibility in banks. He could rise to the top. He had become too big for Charles Fraser.

During his last year at Harvard Business School, Vern was sufficiently relaxed to observe and take advantage of some of its fringe benefits. B-School graduates were aware of sharing a helpful distinction and, in an informal way, went out of their way to assure that other graduates did well. They wanted their equity in the HBS degree to be embellished and they would welcome return favors. Many graduates found it hard, for years, to engage in more than ten sentences of conversation without anyone dropping the name Harvard. This was

Vern's *real* family, a family not by blood but by bloodlessness. And that was fine with him. *Just let me in*, was Vern's unconscious prayer. He discovered that the school had hired an assistant dean whose job was to monitor the progress of the sons of the rich and powerful who were attending the school. It was important that these individuals have a positive experience during their time there. Rather than resenting this blatant favoritism that would normally exacerbate his own disadvantages, Vern took it as one of the keys to his new world. It was important to know who counted. He began compiling a Rolodex during that second year, a modern office innovation that had worked well for the secretaries at Fraser, and Vern thought would be the perfect device for organizing his personal data. Whenever he went out to a social occasion, he would debrief himself and write down the salient characteristics of the people he could remember meeting. So many of the professors had aspirations beyond the limits imposed by their academic roots. Vern began to find time to analyze materials that had been sent to them in advance of their board meetings and to do research on the articles they wanted to publish. His genius with numbers illumined many important board meetings, without, of course, any attribution. Vern was looked on as a promising addition to every occasion, and that was fine with him.

Professor Chamberlain, in particular, picked out Vern. He was the professor of a new course called Organizational Dynamics. This was a rather novel concept, which looked at all organizations, not simply business corporations, with an effort to identify those structural characteristics that were commonly correlated with achieving the mission. Vern was given the very prestigious job, unheard of for anyone other than a Ph.D. candidate, of being Chamberlain's assistant in the course. The course involved law and psychology, ethics and cultural anthropology, so admission was open to all students of Harvard College and the graduate schools. During the fall of 1966, Vern's last year, there were some thirty-five attendees at the lectures. Again and again, the strikingly attractive, simply dressed young woman who sat in the second row raised questions. She processed the lecture and reading materials so as to conclude that ownership by participants was essential to the success of any enterprise. Pleasant, unassuming, and patient, she effortlessly dominated the classes because she appeared to have a core belief and could organize the class material to support it. If the truth were told, Vern fell in love with her voice, the tone that F. Scott Fitzgerald called "the sound of money," and her apparent comfort, which so contrasted with his own unease. When he got to know her better, he asked how she was so comfortable in engaging Chamberlain so consistently and directly. She said simply, "He is an old friend of the family and we have been talking about this since my grandfather's time." After one class, he went directly up to her and said, "I'd like to see more of you." She replied, "Go outside, cross Storrow Drive, and look around you for a few minutes." This rather Delphic answer only whetted Vern's curiosity. He did what he was told and while wandering around the banking of the Charles River looking at the Memorial Bridge, Eliot House, Winthrop, Dunster, and the married student housing in front of the Weeks bridge, he heard a clear voice, "Over here, dummy." He still kept looking until one of the slender crafts gracefully moving up and down the river from the Weld Boathouse across the river pulled up alongside him. There, in rowing togs, was the beautiful Molly Munro. He knew nothing about rowing, but he knew class when it was in front of him. He never imagined being in love with a girl in a shell. This was their first date.

Chapter 6

The ESOP

Charles Hill "Horse" Bowditch IV was meeting with seven employee representatives of the company profit sharing plan, which owns 20 percent of the voting stock of the *American Observer* magazine. Bowditch is very tall, six feet six inches, lean, early fifties, and is wearing the traditional blue uniform of the midtown trust bankers. Notwithstanding his formal city clothing, he was very much at home in this meeting. Over the years, the membership teased Horse that he was the man who put the "trust" in "trustee" for them. His response was always the same, "Hey, it's my job."

The meeting was taking place in one of the conference rooms of the campus-like office complex of the American Observer headquarters in Tarrytown, New York. The lavish landscaping and the generous open spaces between buildings communicated a strong impression of leisured excellence beyond the stress of the marketplace. In reality, the meeting over which Horse was presiding was a battle: the worry of middle-aged professionals fearing that their skills were no longer needed versus the hostility that employee organizers instinctively feel for company executives. There was an air of frustration. If Horse could take the time to reflect on his situation he would probably be quite proud. These men and women were exercising a right they never really believed they had before Horse came into their lives. As their representative, he helped them organize and take an interest in the management of their own company's future. He explained that they had a voice and at this moment that voice was deafening. This was his calling and he was good at it. The AOM group was his special cause because they had an uphill fight. The employees owned 20 percent of the voting stock, a percentage large enough in any company to give effective control. In AOM, the reality was that the self-perpetuating management trustees owned 50 percent.

Many employees of AOM were desperate about the company's decline and about the quality, indeed, the continued existence, of their jobs. Every reform targeted at persuading the stock market of the company's new commitment to profits had started with statistics of layoffs and recitations of continued unacceptable employee costs. This extended to a series of meannesses from cancelled magazine subscriptions to reduced quality of food in the cafeteria. More importantly, the sense that this was a company with an exciting future with an important role had disappeared. The *American Observer* magazine no longer stood as a voice for American values, it was an anachronism being allowed, gradually, to self-liquidate. There was vast distrust of senior management. "People who the Porters would never have invited to their own house" were now treating the company as if it were theirs. The real insult being that cutbacks on expenses only started below a certain level in the corporate hierarchy.

Bowditch, Senior Vice President of the New York Safe Deposit & Trust (NYSD&T) Company in charge of employee benefit plans, had been the official responsible for the American Observer plan for the last ten years. Over this period of time, he had become the personal friend of everyone in the room, all of whom knew him as Horse. They had worked together towards the objective of making employee participation as owners of AOM as meaningful as possible. This had involved a succession of very simple steps: informing employees of the existence of a collective to which most of them belonged; newsletters about company affairs; notice of meetings; the development of a constitution and rules of procedure for the group; the scheduling and conduct of periodic meetings, notices, and votes; and formal actions authorized. By this time, the AOM employees were comfortably working through the duly elected officials and procedures of the employee benefit plan, the ESOP. In a time of demoralization, the ESOP provided a focus for protest and for alternative action.

Management really took little notice of the ESOP. So long as voting control was permanently vested in the self-perpetuating senior management trustees, there was no reason to notice minority shareholders. At its last meeting in June, the ESOP council received overwhelming support from the participating beneficiaries, their fellow employees, to investigate borrowing money against the collateral of the existing shares to purchase more of AOM Class B voting stock in the open market. At that meeting, there was a sense of urgency. The membership felt that top management turmoil (three CEOs in two years, with the newest one coming on board in May) created a buying opportunity. The shares were close to a low since the stock was publicly offered in 1990, almost 50 percent below their highs. These employees had quite a bit of experience with new management. They knew that the first steps would be to denigrate the present situation, blame it on prior managements, to incur large charge-offs and to accept a drubbing in the stock market, and finally, a more favorable platform for hoped-for future improvement and personal stock options. So, they wanted to buy now. Horse was concerned about their morale, he knew they would rise to meet his expectations for them, he just wanted to be sure he wasn't setting those expectations too low.

Horse had just finished explaining his frustrations with Universal, the parent company of his employer, the plan trustee, NYSD&T. He detected for the first time an atmosphere of suspicion and discomfort. For a number of years, NYSD&T had been successful in being named trustee of the employee benefit plans for many of the Fortune 100 companies. NYSD&T's appeal simply was that they were unaffiliated with any of the large financial conglomerates and, therefore, particularly attractive for their independence. With the acquisition by Universal, this advantage disappeared, but NYSD&T built on its existing competitive position. While the issue rarely came up, it was tacitly understood that the trustee would do nothing except at the express request of management. It's an embarrassing but practical point of fact that the fiduciary duties to employees had never been enforced by the U.S. Department of Labor or by the courts, so the trustee was running no practical risk in ignoring them. The AOM ESOP was fortunate to have Charles Bowditch as their representative and mentor because he knew, better than most, the letter and, more importantly to him, the spirit of the law.

Horse worked for NYSD&T for twenty-eight years, his entire business life. Few college hotshots went to work for banks, fewer still went to work for trust companies, almost no one went to work for NYSD&T unless they had a family connection. The bank was run more like a private club. Working there was considered to be a social distinction by some. Horse had no particular connections and initially no real commitment to his work. The job was the minimum that was expected of him by his mother, his wife, and his community. The nature of the work was undemanding. A polite nature and a certain care with details was all that was necessary. There was no accounta-bility for poor performance in an account; there was only risk for those willing to take a chance. Otherwise, the bank carried on, with its annual income largely provided by fees from accounts created by those long dead. They couldn't lose the business. The bank had only a nom-inal value in the market and its voting shares were closely held by friends of the management so as to forestall takeover.

Almost in spite of himself, Horse Bowditch developed into a superb trust officer. What he cared about was helping the beneficiaries to make the best possible use of their assets. While his contempo-raries were busily being promoted and moving on to grander things, Horse insisted on keeping a position that allowed him free access to real people. It was this hands-on expertise with trust beneficiaries that made Horse the logical person to work with the new employee benefit plans. The fact that he cared very much for his new clients was, for them, an utter surprise, indeed a joy. They had always been the neg-lected stepchildren in the corporate finance departments of the huge institutions that usually acted as trustee.

Horse became involved in employee benefit plans in the early 1970s. Banks were slow to understand that all of the long-term capital of the country would, by the end of the century, reside in the pension systems for which they were the most logical trustees. This single fact would change the face of business forever. The amount of money involved was so great that it attracted its own breed of entrepreneurial money managers with a commitment to superior performance. Traditional banks have trouble with marketing, particularly to the new "masters," trustees of union and public pension funds. But some of the "Biggest Lump of Money in the World" began to rub off and the rapidly rising fee income indicated, by the 1980s, that NYSD&T could not avoid income growth despite its aspirations for a more genteel life. The stock price advanced very smartly.

Horse was drawn from the beginning to the notion of employee ownership. It accorded with his own sense of America, a rather Jeffersonian ideal of individual laborers closely associated with the management and ownership of the means of production. Nobody really could have predicted the enthusiasm of corporate America's top management for the kind of legitimate protection that ESOPs provided. Management appointed the trustees who then became the largest shareholders and were better able to fend off unwelcome initiatives. Major commercial banks were not particularly well staffed for this kind of work and their conflicts of interest were immediately apparent. There were bigger fish to fry and so NYSD&T became the referral bank of choice and Horse's operation became a significant contributor to the earnings of this relatively small and unleveraged trust company.

Horse played a cameo role in the stately negotiations that preceded Universal's acquisition of NYSD&T in 1996. He was invited to play in a foursome with his own company's chairman, and with Vernon Stillman, CEO of Universal, and a Universal senior executive. Horse played his usual par round and contributed little to the conversation. On the one occasion that he found his ball next to Vern Stillman's, he was speechless when Vern said, "You know, to get a player like you as a partner makes this whole deal worthwhile." In the locker room after the match, when Horse was putting his suit coat back on, Vern noticed the little gray-colored rosette in his left buttonhole.

"What's that?"

"Oh, it's just a family thing."

With his mania for constructing a new personal identity, it was predictable that Vern would not rest until he discovered that it was the indicia of membership in the Society of the Cincinnati, restricted to the eldest male descendant of Revolutionary War officers.

Horse had built the ESOP business because he believed in it. He was close to many employee groups and had been a leader in developing procedures. Nowhere had he progressed so far as in the American Observer organization, where the employees' group actually proposed, without reference to management, to take steps of its own. It wasn't clear yet whether management would object to a live ESOP, and, if they did, what Universal's response would be. Horse's difficulty in obtaining a commitment for the loan from Universal reflected more the novelty of the request in a bureaucratic organization than any institutionalized opposition. But the result was the same; he didn't get the money.

He told the meeting of the success with both the Internal Revenue Service and the Pension and Welfare Benefits Agency of the Department of Labor in changing the classification of their plan to a leveraged ESOP, which permitted very substantial tax benefits and subsidies for financing, if only he could find the financing.

There was never any question who was the moving energy in the AOM ESOP. Louis Skapinsky was Horse's first convert and now had grown into a true leader within the group. He had immigrated to the United States as a small child from a displaced persons camp in the ravaged Baltic States. He embraced the ideologies of his new mother country with a fervor that those accustomed to its practicalities could rarely match. He found in the concept of employee ownership, and the structure of the ESOP, an ideal blending of the virtues of capitalism and democracy. His enthusiasm developed into a religious faith and he required all who dealt with the ESOP to treat it as holy.

"Horse, looka here. You, we know well. You are friend to us, always, but we're getting to the rock and the hard place, no? After all these years, finally, our act is together and we're *entitled* to backing of our trustee, this is correct? From now on, must we go to somebody else for the help?" Louis and Horse were brothers in their cause but Louis had learned from Horse himself that everyone's worst fears should be the first thing they addressed in all their meetings. Horse would say, "Right between the eyes cuz life is too short."

Horse took this as a sign to bolster morale with hard facts. Fear comes from not understanding the lay of the land. "I'm not telling any secrets out of school. The only thing that has kept me at the bank all these years has been working with groups like yours. I believe in what you are doing and I am going to fight for it all the way to the top of my shop. I can't give either you or myself any assurances because I really am only socially acquainted with the Universal people. We have had a kind of Chinese wall between our operations since the acquisition. Notice, I included myself along with you. I figure that my future with the bank requires that I get the right answer. You know that I am very close to the assistant secretary of Labor; I've kept her up to date with what we are doing. She is a true believer. If necessary, my next step may be in D.C. with a request for a formal opinion of the Department of Labor advising me as the corporate officer, responsible for your trustee, what my real obligations are." He never wanted to be patronizing so he always just broke it down for them. He could tell they were following him. They had come a long way together to get here.

Skapinsky, again, doing his job of being a pitbull with a bone in his unyielding jaw. "No time, we have *no* time. The heart of this organization is being emptied of blood every day, drop by drop, you see. We need voting strength, then we are not going to be ignored. We must, you know, to name at least one of the directors to the board. To defend ourselves and make them listen. If we do nothing, our stock will keep sinking like a rock and it never comes back. We have to fight for our savings and jobs. You see?"

Listening to Louis always got Horse fired up. He could not let him down. He always spoke for everyone in the room. "I've made that argument to the assistant secretary. The trustee here is on notice that the current management arrangement has resulted, over this decade, with massive destruction of employee savings." Horse had come a long way too. There was no turning back for him. "The bank as trustee has no choice but to intercede in order to reverse this trend."

Chapter 7
Charles Hill Bowditch IV

"We came over on *that boat*. Never forget it." The only time that Charles Hill Bowditch IV remembered his mother slapping him was after he had gone to the local library and couldn't find the name of his reputed ancestor on the manifest of the *Mayflower*. Whichever boat had delivered their forefather to this shore did not derogate from the grandeur of the Bowditch name. There had always been Bowditches in important places in American history. Charles grew up with his mother in, what else, the Bowditch House on the green, one of the "musts" in the historical tours of Colonial Lakeville. Charles's sense of belonging was so strong that few questions more pressing than the *Mayflower* manifest haunted his childhood. There was, however, the question of his father. His mother's father CHB II was well remembered in the town. She was quite vague, irritatingly so, about the details of marriage, conception, divorce, and name, but in any event Charles was accepted quite naturally as his maternal grandfather's grandson and namesake. From childhood, he had the ability to accept events as they were with little discomfort. It was only after college that he checked the registry of births, not for Litchfield County where Lakeville is located, but for New York City, where a chance comment by his uncommunicative mother indicated he had been born. After returning from Vietnam, Charles hired an investigative firm and discovered that his biological father actually lived in a retirement community near Sarasota, Florida. He wrote once, the letter was returned unopened. Such pristine organizations as the Social Register and the Society of the Cincinnati were pleased to accept him as the legitimate Bowditch heir, so his life went on undisturbed albeit under an incorrect name.

Charles had a natural feel for the earth and all living things. As a young man, his hero was Paul Siple, the sixteen-year-old Boy Scout who accompanied Admiral Byrd to the South Pole in the 1930s. Scouting revealed several curious aspects of Charles's nature. He wasn't interested in merit badges and yet he was the perennial leader of the troop. Ultimately, he became an Eagle Scout as the result of maternal nagging and a fine scoutmaster's tutelage. What really happened is that the world gave a good name to what he wanted to do more than anything. Living in the rural northwest corner of Connecticut he was a part of the changing seasons. There were rivers, small mountains, many trails, parkland, and all manner of wildlife. He had a feel for the land. When an early grade school spring vacation expedition took him to Gettysburg, he was able to point out the strategic implications of the positions of the various armies. He knew where the snipers would locate, he could feel the cover where others saw only a field, and he could interpret the bird noises, announcing the presence of human beings. There were no merit badges or grand awards for what Charles could do better than any Scout, or adult for that matter, but Charles had no choice. He simply had to do what he was comfortable doing. He could not make himself different to accommodate the priorities of others, including admissions officers for college, superior officers in the military, or hiring partners in business firms.

Charles went to the local high school. Bowditches had always gone to it and felt that the public school system was an element essential to being American. It was one of the few experiences that all, irrespective of religion, race, and wealth, shared and, thus, did much to create the values underlying nationhood. He was a good student but left teachers feeling that there were depths in the young boy that they had been unable to explore. Notwithstanding his size, he was a poor athlete in the ways in which society measures. He could match the speed and stamina of any walker on the Appalachian Trail, but he could not bring himself to run across a field to catch a piece of leather or to race around a track. During high school his appeal to women was strongly evidenced. He combined gentleness and kindness, a sense of being comfortable with women, as with other living things. One thing that the world treasured, where Charles excelled, was golf.

Money was a subject that was not discussed. In later years, as Charles acquired an expertise in the management of people's resources, he could not imagine how his mother had done it. To be sure, the house was a little threadbare and there was precious little maintenance beyond what Charles himself could do. They had enough to eat, but Charles always preferred fruits and vegetables, which were locally grown, because he said it made him feel like an Indian. From late boyhood, around the age of twelve, Charles had a job, after school and then all summer, working to maintain the golf course owned by Hotchkiss, the local preparatory school. This kept him out-of-doors and provided a splendid education in landscaping, which became a lifelong enthusiasm. Charles, who never felt deprived of anything, did not pause to wonder why he was shoveling manure while his contemporaries at Hotchkiss were lining up putts. He never acquired the vocabulary of class warfare. He never felt that anyone was better than he was, not that he lingered on how he felt about himself much at all. Indeed, the groundskeeping staff was given a schedule when they could play, early and late when the owners preferred to do other things. Probably two hundred days a year, for eight years, Charles played golf. The professional was a local man who took a real interest in this young boy. The result was Charles had a flawless swing, superb coordination, and could read greens. He was a throwback to the pre–country club days of golf, when Scottish youths from a rural environment, not very different from his own, dominated the game and it was an accoutrement of country living and not, as now, a badge of social success for the accomplishers. The work allowed him to contribute steadily to the household budget. He did this because it pleased him to be self-reliant, not because he thought that his mother needed the money. In fact, his mite was very useful.

The image of this boy achieving maturity in the company of his dotty mother and relatives, with less money than other children, in a house that resembled an exhibition in a poorly endowed museum, impresses as a case study for modern psychotherapeutic help. There must have been something in the genes, as Charles grew up in the innocent small town mode so beloved by chroniclers of early American life. Beyond his regular job at the golf course, he occasionally delivered newspapers, cut neighbors' grass, helped at the supermarket during school vacations, and achieved a boyhood that he always recalled with affection. Charles was sustained by many of his mother's tales and myths of the country and his family's days of glory. He was energized by his origins, real and imagined.

Lakeville, Connecticut, like many of the pre–Revolutionary War towns scattered around New England, still had a volunteer fire department in the 1960s. Traditionally, the department had a professional chief and the squad was composed of paid volunteers. Like many local boys, Charles joined up when he was sixteen. That was the end of a formal high school athletic career. Instead, he learned early of violence and death and developed a keen sensitivity to people in distress.

The idea that citizens would contribute some of their own time, to say nothing of risking their bodies, to maintaining public order was part of the core of ideas that informed Charles Bowditch for the rest of his life. It can be no surprise to learn that after being married, when he moved to a more fashionable portion of the state, he nonetheless continued regular service on the Darien Voluntary Fire Department.

A lot of people would scratch their heads when conversation turned to Charles Bowditch. The tall nice-looking boy was widely admired for his devotion to his mother and his hard work. But there was always something. Charles would mow lawns, with no apparent concern as to when or how much he would be paid. He would stay outdoors after recess watching a particular bird simply because it was so beautiful. When the class began having outdoor outings, Charles would always disappear, sometimes for hours, once for days, in search of some plant or animal or vista. He was an excellent student, but he could not be interested in studying things that would be good for his future. It wasn't that he didn't care; he simply did not understand the concern.

He was, to be sure, always different from other children. First there was his mother; then, there was the absence of a father; and there was no way to reconcile the obvious marginality of their current living: pass-me-down clothes, no travel, no car, no TV with the advertised grandeur of yesteryear. With this level of familial confusion and the cruelty of small towns, it is a wonder that Charles graduated from high school with no worse damage than the lifetime nickname of "Horse," awarded him at a nude swimming party after his senior prom when his awed classmates viewed his male member. In later years, while everyone used it, no one in the cities and towns where he lived and worked really knew how he came by the name. Those men who knew the explanation repeated it in envious whispers. The women were apt to giggle, but there were always those of both sexes who wanted to find out for themselves.

Horse and his mother agreed on his college education. He would go to West Point, a place with traditions congenial to the Bowditch family. Admission was no longer exclusively in the gift of the local congressman, the procedure had become bureaucratized. Horse's academic grades were adequate, but his strength was in the humanities, history, and philosophy, rather than the sciences favored by the service academies. One day in early autumn of 1961, his senior year in high school, Horse went to be interviewed by a panel of West Point admissions officials in a room in the Morgan Library in Hartford. The questions were friendly and the responses seemed at first highly satisfactory. Yes, Horse could play golf and enjoyed a handicap of zero; yes, he had hiked an average of thirty-five miles a day for two weeks over the most difficult portions of the Appalachian Trail; no, he didn't smoke or drink. As Horse talked, his interviewers came to understand that his love of golf was based in the joy of the out-of-doors and the marvelous symmetry of the parabolas sketched against the sky by a properly hit shot and not by a killer's instinct to win. His hiking was part of his love of nature. He knew the names of the birds, the flowers, and the trees. He was a believer in the most hallowed of American traditions. With that iron logic of bureaucracies, it is almost redundant to recite that a man who would have been a star in every army since Julius Caesar's failed to be admitted to the United States Military Academy.

Horse managed to be admitted to Williams College, then as now considered one of the most difficult institutions to enter. What appealed to the admissions and scholarship offices was that he was an old-family Yankee boy from a small New England town who had not gone to private preparatory school. He evoked the image of a past that brought pleasure to the imagination of others.

Horse never really felt comfortable at Williams. It seemed like a place where everybody but he was member of a club and knew languages that he could not understand. Horse actually struggled to keep up. By great good fortune, he got a part-time job as caretaker and resident pro for a local golf course. By that wisdom then prevailing for amateur sports, this meant that he was disqualified from competing in golf for the college. The college and its museum specialized in American history and particularly in the origins and development of the European settlement of Berkshire County. Horse became immersed in the library accounts of the lives of the earliest settlers. What they had to do was what he loved to do. What they felt was important, freedom for themselves and their children and the chance to participate in the process under which they were governed, was what he felt. The "secular religion" of America is the continuing commitment by the citizenry to inform and involve themselves in the conditions of their state. Coming from the tradition of New England town meetings and volunteer fire departments, this was Horse's personal religion.

Horse got by but he didn't really believe in his better instincts. Maybe the childhood fantasy of famous family and the reality of a missing father had created a problem that a more secure person could have treated with psychiatric help. His appearance and his name got him through; he was unignorable at six feet six inches, good posture, an open appearance, that splendid name, and the ever-disarming nickname. Also, his patriotism was a striking flash from the past. He had been an Eagle Scout and was a model regimental officer in the college ROTC program, although typically someone else held the position of commanding officer.

While Horse could not elicit an effective response to all the challenges for competitive success in the classroom and on the sporting fields, he changed character when the national interest was involved. At a time when graduates of the finest colleges and graduate schools were scrambling for appointments to the National Guard and dodging any commitment to Vietnam through every means, legal or illegal, Charles Hill Bowditch IV graduated Williams in June and found himself with a two-year hitch in Vietnam in July. Like many ROTC officers, he was a company commander. This involved lengthy patrols through areas where one never knew ally from enemy and where the natural conditions of humidity, heat, tropical growth, insects, reptiles, and animals were always menacing. Morale at this time was still fair in the country.

Horse, of course, loved the countryside and its people. He had spent a fair amount of time during his last semester at Williams learning about the land and all its inhabitants. He learned what was poisonous and what could be eaten. The times that he liked most in his early life were those living on the hard in the mountains of Appalachia. The circumstances were different in Vietnam but the essence was the same. The land is hospitable to those who take the trouble to learn its secrets and accommodate its demands. Being an officer in the Army put Horse into a new and not entirely welcome position. He did not like the distinction between enlisted and commissioned personnel. Yet, he was very comfortable being responsible for the welfare of his company. He had no particular interest in the rest and recreation orgies that were the dream of most troops. He had no interest in the company of fellow officers; the thought of promotion never occurred to him. He saw himself as an American with responsibility and he willingly took on the burden.

For the men in his company, Horse was an enigma. He was an officer, yes, but he had no airs. He wanted to carry out assignments well, but he was scrupulous about not exposing the men to needless danger. Before starting a day's patrol, Horse would study the maps with such intensity that he could not hear people asking him questions. As he walked, he would stop frequently to listen to a bird or animal sound, to taste a bud on a shrub, and to inspect the contours of the land. The men came to understand that Horse had an instinct for safe ground. Booby traps were almost an amusement for Horse as he was able to figure out where he would have put them, and there they were. He had an acute sensitivity for how each of his men was feeling. He could feel psychological distress without seeing or hearing of it. He was responsive to their unexpressed needs. Horse was capable, after one of his map inspection séances, of going back to headquarters with requests for different routes. Although the army does not easily tolerate such requests, traditions empowering the officer in the field meant that Horse was able, over time, to acquire full authority to determine how missions were to be accomplished. Sometimes men were lost. Such is the nature of war. But Horse's men were not lost stupidly. There were few officers who really liked being in the field. Most officers put in their time and then joyfully accepted other assignments. After his first year "in country," Horse became quite well known at headquarters. Although twice wounded himself, he had managed his patrols with such care for life and success in accomplishing the missions that he was repeatedly recommended for decorations. Not a political man, Horse ignored the process. Eventually, his superiors suggested that he take a larger command and a more executive role. Politely, Horse demurred. The requests were repeated in a less suggestive way. Again Horse demurred. These demurrals ultimately ruffled the bureaucratic feathers. "Does this guy think he is bigger than the United States Army? Does he think we can't win the war without him?"

Helicopters changed the nature of command. It was not unusual for even the top-ranking American generals to descend from the skies and inspect the field units. William Westmoreland, the Supreme Commander, had enjoyed a dream career in the army, always the youngest man in the most prestigious post. He was the Commandant of West Point when General McArthur returned to deliver his famous "old soldiers never die" speech in 1951. He truly loved the army and was unspoiled by his successes. The tension between headquarters and Horse had reached an impasse on the day in late 1968, just prior to the Tet Offensive, when General Westmoreland made a regular inspection of his unit and asked to meet Horse. His physical appearance was startling to an unprepared visitor. Having been up country for virtually two years, often preferring to eat local food, Horse weighed barely 175 pounds, which left no fat on his long frame. He was tanned from the sun and his eyes had the kind of focused hardness acquired only from days of squinting and peering in the effort to avoid dangers. He looked like nothing so much as a frontiersman fighting Indians on the Western frontiers of the Republic just prior to the Revolution. If someone had asked him, Horse would have said that he was a happy man. Being of puritanical background, happiness was associated with a sense of fulfilling his obligations, of doing his duty. He was mildly aware of the discomfort of field quarters, but had recently re-upped for another year in the field.

Westmoreland had a gentleman's feel for the troops. He liked them. They knew he liked them; they could talk to him. The general addressed Horse.

"Captain (Horse had been promoted), what am I going to do about you?"

"Let me keep leading the company in the field. The men will follow me. We're getting good. We can win the war."

That was the first time anybody who was physically in danger from the Vietcong had ever said that to Westmoreland, who asked, "How do you figure that, Captain?"

"We know how they do it. We can do it better, and we have better equipment and better backup."

"How can we help you?" Small wonder that Westmoreland was a great commander.

"For starters, let me stay here. I know we can produce the results you need."

"I wish I could stay here with you."

"General, I really believe you would."

Westmoreland came to the point. "Captain, I cannot have my command disrupted because you will not obey army orders. Therefore, I take it on myself this day to issue a new transcending order. You will continue in the command of this company, so long as such is agreeable to both of us." Westmoreland returned to headquarters, dictated an extensive memorandum to the secretary of Defense and the superintendent of West Point saying that the best officer in his command had been denied admission to the Military Academy and formally recommended that Horse be given the Silver Star for Gallantry in Action.

Several companies, totaling approximately four hundred men, were bivouacked in tents in the area where Westmoreland had visited. Officers and men dined under the same canvas, albeit in different areas. Word spreads fast in close communities and the fact that Horse, a junior officer, had spent over an hour with the Supreme Commander was incredible. It was known Horse had refused to leave his company and accept assignment in a less exposed command. The rumors started. Horse was to be court marshaled, he was to be moved to Westmoreland's staff, his two-year contract had expired and his option to stay an extra year had been turned down. Just before dinner, one of the officers who had a copy of Westmoreland's handwritten transcending order was passing it around to other officers and finally to the senior noncoms. The word spread like a fog so quickly that there was a ground swell of noise when Horse entered the dining area. The officers didn't know what to make of it. The enlisted men, many of whom felt they owed their lives to Horse, said with love and respect, "That crazy bastard, that crazy bastard, he has taken on the whole fucking U.S. Army and beaten them." Out of all their frustration and all their fear, several hundred men collectively voiced their joy in deliverance from the horrors of their present situation. This wild euphoria spiraled into a spontaneous demonstration of affection, black and white, Hispanic and Anglo, stoned and drunk, demoralized and hating, all found in Horse's conduct something that made them feel better about themselves and their fates. The applause started as a thunderclap and drowned out the talk, it endured like a great wave. A minute is a long time for people to applaud. After fifteen minutes Horse was finally allowed to sit down in quiet and eat his meal. Virtually no living person has had the experience of being the object of such public affection. Marilyn Monroe, coming back from entertaining the troops in Korea, said to husband Joe DiMaggio impatiently waiting in Tokyo, "Joe, you cannot believe the applause." As it happened, DiMaggio was one of the few human beings who could. There wasn't an officer in the American army who would not have traded his rank and privileges to be accorded such a personal honor by his command. Typically of Horse, he served out his year, surviving Tet, and continuing to patrol effectively with his men. Westmoreland's order made it clear that he had no future in an army where idiosyncrasy was not tolerated. He had neither World War II maverick hero General George C. Patton's wealth nor seniority. The demoralization of the command was pervasive by 1969. Typical of Horse, he never mentioned the incident of the mess tent to another human being for fifteen years, and, then, only once.

Horse returned to an America tired of the war and disgusted with those associated with its conduct. He expected no plaudits but he was perplexed by the dichotomy between what was asked of the men in the field and the attitude of the people at home. His mother had not been idle. In towns like Lakeville, where the Civil War monuments are well maintained and parades are a joy to the whole town on Memorial Day, word of Horse's wounds, decorations, and promotions (he was discharged a major) were faithfully recorded in the local weekly. He was twenty-five-years-old, a college graduate, and a war hero with medals to prove it. That was enough to interest the younger daughter of one of the ruling industrial families of the Housatonic Valley. Industry was attracted early here by the availability of water power. Before the Civil War, fortunes had been made and many of them kept for the next century. Gloria Cunningham was a modern iteration of this industrial aristocracy. Private school was followed by two years of junior college, still called finishing schools. Some girls wanted careers, most wanted to be married. Gloria was a fine tennis player and had won several singles and mixed doubles tournaments on the national tour and was considered promising. Professional tennis meant going south in the winters and world travel year round. Gloria was a seemingly uncomplicated girl who was sustained through the socially accepted expression of her physical energies. The serious career men would wonder whether Gloria, heiress or not, would be able to help them as much as they wanted. Horse had no particular forethought about an ideal spouse.

He was utterly directionless off of the battlefield. It seemed sensible to accept his mother's definition, marriage to a pleasant heiress, a home in Westchester, and a bank job in the city. In the fall of 1969, Gloria and Charles were married at the church constructed on the grounds of her industrial ancestor's model community built for workers at his first great plant.

The marriage was based on making the minimum demands on each other. They were both decent people and went out of their ways to avoid creating needless difficulty. To their credit, both Horse and Gloria tacitly agreed that their commitment to marriage and to each other was too tenuous to start a family. Early on, in light of the predictable consequences of Gloria's frequent trips away in mixed athletic company, they agreed to have an open marriage in the sense that either was permitted to choose other sexual partners. Horse often flew to wherever she was playing, so they could spend weekends together. As a result, none of their dalliances with other people became serious. In hindsight, it's clear that this soulless vacuum was very destructive to both, but we are not given the gift of seeing the future.

For fifteen years, life was commuter train schedules, tee-off times and Saturday nights at the club, too much to drink and casual, and not so casual, gropings that seemed more persistent because of interest in Horse's apparatus.

"Hey, Horse, how do you keep those honeys happy?"

"Horsie, don't you ever get enough?"

"Hey, man, leave some for the rest of us."

The golf was joy, the sex a narcotic, the job barely registered, and Horse was aware of a coarsening of his sensitivities. He wasn't sure what he was anymore.

Horse's professional life, increasingly, was outside of the bank. He was either at the employees' meetings or chairing one of the committees for the professional associations. The acquisition by Universal in 1996 had relatively little immediate impact on Horse's work. Two things were to cause that to change; first, his golf game. As an effortless scratch golfer, Horse became an invaluable partner for his parent company executives in the new banking world, where golf was an indispensable element of business promotion. Second, Horse's book of business included the greatest names in American industry and the Universal marketers wanted access. During this evolution, it never occurred to anyone in NYSD&T or Universal that they had lost Horse. He was personally and profoundly committed to advancing employee participation in corporate management. His clients loved him. He had retrained himself to be an expert in fiduciary law. He knew all the industry leaders and government officials. They knew him as the much-respected senior official of the principal industry associations. "A prophet is not without honor save in his own home." It would be a surprise to many of his powerful colleagues to discover that Horse had become a committed person. His personal life was adrift but his work, with and for other people, was his redemption. He was a respected expert in a field, the existence of which they barely suspected, and the importance of which would be one of the most powerful commercial forces of the next several decades.

Chapter 8
Wednesday, August 5, 1998

Drive awoke with a start. Haunted by dreams beyond his recall, he rallied and got out of bed and into the shower without disturbing his wife. He chalked up the nightmares to the stress of carrying so much of the planning in his own head. It'd been years since he had to sweat out his own deal. He briefly wondered if it would be worth it. He remembered all too well, years ago, when he made peace with delegating the sleepless nights to a handful of long-trusted underlings. He really didn't have to do everything for everybody so long as he could keep his foot on a few key throats. As a boy, he reveled in the tales of the great tribal kings who ruled his dark continent, long before his ancestors arrived. He always thought of the king who ruled by having his foot on his people's throat. It was years before he would realize it was merely a metaphor, and now he laughed to himself because he knew it really wasn't a metaphor after all.

Yesterday had brought a memo that there would be an adjustment in the market today. The international banking bailout for Thailand and Indonesia was going to have to be paid for, with one of those unsettling ripples on Wall Street. International companies, like his own, followed the world markets on a twenty-four-hour basis and the experts agreed, now was the time. It would be a dip and would hopefully make the *Observer* even more attractive. He wouldn't know for sure for several hours into the market day, he would have to remember to check. The day was full of meetings. Hopefully no surprises just foregone conclusions and confirmations. He'd run every scenario he could imagine for months; now he was building something real at last brick by brick. He was excited again and it had only taken fifteen minutes in the shower to bring the old enthusiasm back.

At 8:00 a.m., the senior officers of Universal Bank, several having been summoned back from vacation, together with a battery of lawyers, crowded into one of the bank's conference rooms awaiting the arrival of Vernon Stillman. It is not the usual practice in large international banks for the Chief Executive Officer to concern himself with the details of a financing, but, as everybody in the room sputtered, "It's *his* deal." The fact is closing this deal would be impossible. The timing, the credit, the financing itself, all impossible and Marty is beyond impossible. Complaints about the other side's lawyers are one way the aggression involved in accommodating very smart and determined advocates of incompatible positions is harmlessly channeled. But this went further.

With a mixture of admiration and exasperation they complained about Marty, "There we are, 8:00 p.m. on Monday night, with preliminary documents. Barely had the chance to proof them. The five of us, and *him*. He has one sheet of yellow paper and a couple of notes. Over the next two hours, he just stands us on our heads. It's the goddamn bar exam all over again. Finally we begin to list the open issues for the closing documents, around 10:30 we start to move for the door to go home, but the prick won't budge. He just sits there and starts writing. So we ask, Is there a mistake, we finished listing what has to be done. Is there something else?

"He doesn't even look up and says, 'No mistake, I'm just doing it. I need to begin drafting now.'

"So help me God, that is what he does. One of our guys has to stay to shut the place up. By 1:00 a.m., he wants to review the document with our guy, some junior schmuck, who's never heard of half the concepts. Absolutely inhuman. I wish he was working for our side."

At 8:30 a.m., Vern Stillman walked into the musky room, already rancid despite the arctic air conditioning. He's heard the stories from his secretary, whose principal job is to be his ear for all things. Ever efficient, not one to let feelings get in the way of progress, Vern came right to the point.

"Gentlemen, I appreciate you putting a little back into it last night. This is the most important transaction this bank has ever done. We're going to be one of the major players in international finance. We can be on the short list. This is what makes fees, makes relationships, and this is what makes earnings." Nervous about the lack of response, he increases his energy and resolves to go "preacher" on them.

"Look here, people, I don't want any naysayers on this one. We're dealing with one of the most respected, wealthiest businessmen in the world. He has paid back a dozen times as much debt as we're proposing. When his back was to the wall ten years ago, he sat down with the lenders and worked it out. I was there. Everybody got paid. It's taken me more than five years to develop this relationship." Vern was evangelizing now, and his drawl was seeping in, from his countless boyhood hours pew-side.

"There is good work to be done here, people. We have to move fast. We have to lock up commitments so that we can close within the next two weeks."

"Boss, listen, Goldman Sachs, Merrill Lynch, Morgan Stanley, and the whole Swiss banking system couldn't produce a long-term commitment to finance this deal in two weeks. Find me the takeout and we can have short-term money by noon today. The guy is giving us nothing we can work with, no credit, no personal signature. The cash flows from American Observer look like a toboggan slide. Sure, the guy is smart and tough, but this is a very tired old business and there just ain't that much coverage for the debt. We have to have the takeout."

Relieved at getting some response, Vern wondered if that "ain't" was supposed to be patronizing. Tempers were high, and people were tired. Screw it, just get the job done. He eyeballed every man in the room and concluded before walking out, "I have given this a great deal of thought. We are righteous in our cause, brothers. I think that I can produce the permanent financing. We know he ain't giving up any equity, but he's going to have to budge some on the upside. He can keep the whole company, but the people putting up the money, all the money, are going to need some very fancy returns to make this duck quack. You all settle down and get this job done, I've got to make some calls."

"That son of a bitch! Can you beat that?" Andy Jones, CEO of Texaco Chevron, shouted to his tablemates as they watched the helicopter, with prominent Chrysler Corporation markings, gently lower onto a flat pitch near the old croquet courts. The other three CEOs knew just what was on his mind.

CEOs are known by the planes they fly. That was always a problem coming to a meeting at The Greenbrier in White Sulphur Springs, West Virginia, because the local airport had runways too short for the *really* big corporate aircraft, so they all had to take their number two or spare planes. The sixty-eight-year-old "Tex" Symonds, famous for his chutzpah, apparently had done it again, flown the big one, the Gv, into Roanoke and then had a corporate helicopter waiting for him. Somehow, Tex had made a deal with old Sam Sneed that he could land his chopper right next to the golf course, Sam's private domain for a half century. So while the rest of the committee had driven simple limos from the airport, and walked down to the elaborate golf house overlooking the first tee of Old White, one of three eighteen-hole courses where their private meeting was scheduled, the chairman arrived on time from the sky.

Vern knew he was on another planet with a whole new atmosphere. He couldn't learn about it fast enough. It was May of 1997 and he had really arrived. He had backpeddled his way into moving where the movers and shakers shook. He knew them, but did they really know him? He wondered if he was there just to fetch their firewood, but then, that didn't really matter, so long as he could keep getting invitations like this one.

Tex came into the meeting room at the golf house and said, "Why walk when you can fly?" The Business Roundtable doesn't have private meetings. The executive committee authorizes certain projects and appoints a CEO, who, with his own corporate staff, takes charge. Symonds was in charge of politics. This was one of the most senior and circumspect committees of the Roundtable. To be a member was the highest honor. Vern could still remember a year earlier when Tex had summoned him to one corner of a cocktail party to say, "Vern, boy, you did us all proud with that options accounting business. We noticed there were no BRT fingerprints on the deal, and we want you to be with us on the political committee." No request, no answer needed, nobody ever declined. This was Vern's third meeting, always in a place with golf, always on a weekend so that everyone could come and go without causing comment, always with the wives to create the impression of naturalness. The other three participants were among the most senior of Roundtable CEOs: Bruce Atwind of General Mills, Bill Durant of Tenneco, as well as Andy Jones.

Tex started. "The way I see it, this president just can't keep his pecker in his pants and that's going to get his party into a lot of trouble. Al Gore will have to figure out how to run with him and how to run against him. Hubert Humphrey failed trying to do that; Gerry Ford never had a chance. So, it looks like we got us a Republican for 2000, unless, as usual, they screw up. We're here to make sure that doesn't happen. Bruce, what do you fellows up there in darkest Minnesota think?"

"Tex, we've got a whole bunch of folks who want to run. The one guy who could give us a lot of grief is that John McCain. He really means to have campaign finance reform and God knows what else. He is a hero, primary voters will love him, but he's not our man."

"Whatever happened to him? He was with us on that savings and loan stuff," this from Andy Jones. Durant chimed in, "I talked with him about that, he feels ashamed of himself. He wants to make up for it. The worst kind, a real reformer." Tex asked, "Is there anybody else? There's always a senator or two who jumps up and salutes when they play 'Hail to the Chief.'" Andy Jones chuckled, "Bob Dole's making too much money out selling Viagra, so we don't have to go over the falls with him again." The discussion went on for an hour or so to no consequence. Vern's only contribution was what you'd expect from a banker. "A guy with the most money can lose, look at John Connolly.

But nobody can win without money up front, money for emergencies, and money at the end."

Tex pulled it all together. "We're gonna have to come to some kind of conclusion, or all hell will break loose if our wives have to wait for their cocktails. I think we can agree with our banker friend," a nod to Vern, "money's the thing. That little George W. has done a great job in Texas, he's gonna get reelected big next fall. You can rely on him. He's a patriot, he's a friend of business. There may be some rough spots, but he'll be our guy. Now the thing we have to do is to make sure we can put together a pile of money and commitments that'll make it clear to everybody else that they don't have a chance." Almost as a way of passing the mantle, Tex pointed to Vern and said, "You guys better talk with young Vern here. He knows how to get something done without everybody knowing who did it." Vern was beside himself.

As they were walking up the path to the main hotel building, Bruce Atwind said to Vern, "It doesn't get any better than that, old buddy. I have to tell you, I would personally have given my left nut if Tex had said about me what he said about you." Vern felt an involuntary frisson. From somewhere there intruded in his consciousness the words his father had said at his wedding. "He who availeth himself of the whole world and loseth his own soul availeth himself of nothing." Vern impatiently shook his head and the thought disappeared. They weren't his friends, he knew that, and if they were only using him, well, yes, please, use away. He was helping to make a man president, without an electorate, and that was fine with him. It was his fondest memory to date.

Back in his office, Vern closed the door, giving his secretary a nod. She understood. Hell or high water, no one gets in until he himself opens the door. Those glory days at The Greenbrier should count for something, and this was just such an occasion. He sat down and took a list that he had prepared over the previous several days with his secretary's help. He's a miner, been digging for years, and this was his gold. It was the names of the chief executive officers from the Business Roundtable, the companies with the largest internally managed pension funds, the phone number where each could be reached at the time indicated, and a few pertinent and important facts about their funds and their personal lives, just in case. He took a deep breath, hit the speed dial, and thought to himself, *Float like a butterfly, sting like a bee.*

Most of the long-term capital in the country is in the pension fund system. The public plans, being governmental, are very bureaucratic and none of them could make a deal as quickly as this deal needed. That leaves the private pension plans. Several of the largest pension funds administer substantial assets in-house. The category "private equity" has become popular. This is where annual returns over 20 percent have been achieved. By going to the corporate CEO, rather than CEO or CIO of the pension fund, Vern was sending a subtle message. "I need your *personal* help." And they did owe him, everyone he was calling swore they would make it up to him; he had carried their water on that option accounting deal with the Senate. The total wealth of CEOs had moved over one decimal point to the right as a result of that arrogant, but successful, use of power. They owed him all right, and now he was coming to collect.

Each of the four calls was approximately, "Hey, Tex, how're ya doing...ole buddy. Sorry to catch you on vacation, but I need a favor, and you're the kind of friend who would not forgive me if I didn't ask. I'm trying to put together a really exciting deal, a big takeover, great entrepreneur, one of the best names in the world, a truly great property that is run down badly. We need a chunk of long-term debt with participation in upside cash flows. I'd sure appreciate it if you could give the private equity people in your pension fund a heads up on this one. We're looking at a great return, but I really need top attention and quick authority. We want to get more guys like you, make the decision, and move. Hey, save me a slot in your foursome at the Homestead next month. Thanks a ton, Tex. I'll remember this one and so will you."

The calls were made and the deals were committed. Nobody plays the old-boy game like a Southern good old boy but Vern would never want to admit it to himself. So, Vern had the money. CEO-level commitments made over the phone in minutes involving hundreds of millions of dollars were as binding as the most lawyered written agreements. He didn't want to think about the agony that the lawyers and accountants would have to go through for the next two weeks to get the paperwork done. They could slave for a hundred years and never move as much money as he just did with his first-name-basis, personal relationships with some of the most powerful business leaders in the world. Vern figured, this is as good as it gets. All the silly stuff, private elevators, fancy cars, office accoutrements to try and keep up with Sandy Weill's 106th-floor wood-burning fireplace, the jets, and compensation consultants, is all just for show. This is the real thing. Billions of dollars moved around on a phone call, no lawyers, no bureaucrats, no hesitation. *Personal relationships and earned loyalty at the top level; this is what I've wanted all my life.* He felt his whole body relax and he pulled, from the cabinet behind his desk, a laundered shirt from his supply, and went to freshen up in his private bathroom, hidden behind the bookshelves.

At 10:00 a.m. Drive and Marty were in the Chrysler Building. Marty showed no sign of wear from the drafting session of the night before. The running pays off. In his laconic way, he said, "Look, you'll get the money. I don't know from where, but those guys know their boss is committed, so they'll find it. That's their problem. You are going to have to give up a lot on the fees. Commit, at least, to a very fancy return on the upside. They'll take the chance, but if you are going to make billions, they'll want their rates of return at the top of the scale. These guys are trying to think of themselves as investment bankers and the first way to do that is to get paid like investment bankers. The fact is they're providing that service for you, but it will cost big bucks.

"I haven't finished the whole plan; I've got till Friday. You have to go, no later than Monday, to meet the trustees of the Porter trusts, that's 50 percent of the vote, then the trustees of the ESOP, and that's another 20 percent. You might want to leave the ESOP in the deal. They'll think they can help us. In my opinion, they're very good at helping themselves; altruism is not a highly developed trait, so I'd leave them alone. At this point, they can only help the deal."

Drive snorted. "No equity partners, no employees or anyone else. If we can get the financing with $10 million, or however much I have invested in stock purchases to date, there is no reason to take anybody else in. I need the flexibility. Minority shareholders would be a disadvantage. I simply must have this flexibility."

"Just think about it a little. Their 20 percent is already in the deal as equity. It could make it a lot easier for us in the negotiations. With that percentage of ownership, they can't get in your way, and you may have an easy way of rewarding executives without hurting your cash flow or your reported earnings."

"Drop it, OK? I want it all."

Marty pushed his point hoping that Drive might hear him. "Look, boss, I have got to give you your money's worth. My experience is you best leave something on the table, do you know what I mean?" Drive was in full sail. "I've waited years for this deal. The timing is right. The bankers are throwing money around. Call it an old man's conceit. This time, I want it all." Marty usually began negotiations when others thought they were finished. "You know, bulls get rich; bears get rich; pigs get eaten," Drive was getting a little red around the edges. "OK. OK. We'll leave it for now." Marty recognized this issue was going to be a blind spot for Drive. A bad sign if there were going to be any more of them. He had spent much of his professional life listening to grown men whine "I want, I want," and he usually got them to see the light. He knew he'd have to bring it up again, if only to watch Drive turn red again, so he turned back to the business at hand, for the moment.

"We have to get these trustees off balance. A two-stage approach. When you see them Wednesday, they can be defending the rights of the investment community, the integrity of international capitalism, all without having to stand up themselves and say No because they like the power and they want to keep it. We want to keep the discussion limited to the fairness of offering to the shareholders. No talk of price, no talk of whether they will even consent to do the deal. We do this one by doing an end run. We get the trustees of the nonvoting stock trusts so hot that a momentum for the deal sweeps the voting stock trustees along. How can they stand up to the reasoned wishes of the 'great and the good,' all the trustees and supporters, all of the lawyers, money managers, and service providers for the greatest institutions in New York?"

It was 4:00 p.m. and Vern was back in the conference room with the team. When he turned the big wheels, they turned fast. He was preaching to the converted now, as the room was filled with true believers. "Have you been to see those pension fund guys?" It was a rhetorical question, the answer was apparent in the new happy buzz of activity surrounding him. He had to bask in the moment a little longer, " I'll bet they took your calls and were glad to hear from you. Think you can get verbal commitment by the end of the week?" Few things pleased him more than knocking a roomful of Yankee know-it-alls on their asses.

Crossing back into his office and picking up messages, Vern said to his secretary, "Tell that tall golfer fella, Horse, I can't see him. I just cannot see him right now." He took his messages with him.

It was the end of the day at the Department of Labor and Molly Munro was sitting in her spacious offices on the second floor of the Frances Perkins Building on Constitution Avenue in Washington, D.C. Across from her were her two most trusted associates, David Klebowitch, the deputy assistant secretary, and Bernie Levin, the general counsel to the Pension and Welfare Benefits Agency, also known as the pension agency. She started every day meeting with them; she closed every day meeting with them. They had been with the department since authority over the national pension system came into the Department of Labor in the early 1970s. They were knowledgeable, levelheaded, and absolutely incorruptible.

After finishing with their concerns for the day, she leaned back, looked them in the eye and started, "I think I need some very straight advice. This is official, but, if we weren't friends, I would never bring it up. My friend, Charles Bowditch, the senior man at NYSD&T on employee benefit plans, called earlier. We've worked on industry committees together. We had a relationship for a while. I like him. I realized when I took this job that we would be dealing with Charles, so I fully disclosed the facts of our relationship and received the opinion of the department's conflict counsel that I am not obligated to recuse myself in matters involving Charles or his bank. Well, now he has a well-established ESOP, deciding to borrow money to buy additional employer stock to become more activist in the company. The company has been grossly neglected and the employees are losing their jobs and their savings. As you know, Universal bought NYSD&T a couple of years ago and my former husband, Vernon, is CEO of Universal. Charles is worried that Universal will not want to go along with the beneficiaries' activist program. He has been the bank officer on the account for the last ten years. He is concerned that the Universal people will tell him not to use his discretion as trustee in the activist direction. He is sending us a fax tonight outlining his situation and asking for our advice."

Levin responded first. "Well, technically, there's nothing in the Federal Register that restricts a federal officer from dealing with a former spouse or someone with whom they have had a relationship in the past."

Klebowitch said, "Cut it out. The press will just love this one. Employee benefit fund triangle right in the middle of the federal triangle. Ho, ho, ho."

They all looked at each other, a raised eyebrow here, a shrugging of shoulders there. It was complicated. Molly created a team atmosphere and she knew she could count on their advice and support, and so with the kind of trenchant insight that had endeared him to a quarter century of employees, bosses, and constituents, Levin concluded simply, "Look, it's a no-win situation. Just do what you think is right and let the PR fall where it may. No offense, boss, but it looks like the president has got a much juicier scandal. Hell, we're only Labor."

Back in Manhattan, Drive was sitting in traffic in the back of his limo. He took his shoes off and was flexing his toes. On his lap was the *New York Times*. The headline confirmed the overseas prediction, BIG SELLOFF SENDS DOW PLUMMETING NEARLY 300 POINTS. "The President was no longer the lead story temporarily. The Dow Jones industrial average plummeted 299.43 points, or 3.41 percent to 8,487.31, and other market gauges were down even more sharply. While up 7.32 percent since the beginning of the year, the Dow is now down 9.1 percent from its peak on July 17." The Observer stock held. *Go figure*, thought Drive. *All those vested interests cannot be ignored. This really is a complex deal like no other.* He felt a chill but it had nothing to do with the perfectly climate-controlled limo, one of four available to Drive worldwide, courtesy of the shareholders. But it was a chill, nonetheless, and so he reached for his cell phone, his lifeline.

Drive was eager to report to Rose. "Vern came through big today. He called in some favors and got commitments for the financing."

"We've worked so hard; we deserve some luck. The stock continues to tank. We hit a time when all the stars are aligned and you can get financing for a deal like this. How are we going to 'roll' the trustees?" Rose was his compass, always pointing true north.

"We can embarrass them, but, at the end of the day, they've got the power. We've got two great follow-up articles, one in the British press, raising the question whether society, employees, charity stock owners, and customers have to let a management destroy a company, and then a local tabloid quoting an 'unnamed trustee' saying, 'We're all praying for a takeover, but don't hold your breath.'"

"Nice, we've got a few others in place, once we see which way the wind is blowing. Are you doing your exercises? You've got to stay in shape for our long campaign here."

"Yes, yes. Don't worry, there's plenty of life in the old dog. I'm on my way to the Racquet Club for a massage and a workout."

"Isn't that backwards?"

"Yes," Drive lied, "quite right."

"When do we get the plans from our expensive genius? I am dying to hear."

"Tomorrow!" Drive was annoyed and feeling a bit nagged about his club time. Really. "I'll keep you informed."

Drive had developed a million ways to communicate when he was finished with a conversation. After years of feeling hounded by a world of people always wanting something from him, he was no longer conscious of it. But that really wasn't the point, everyone else was conscious of it and that was all that really mattered to him.

"Well, good night, sweet prince."

"Yes. Good night, my dear."

Chapter 9

Molly Munro

To Vernon Stillman, Molly Munro was a low-maintenance wife, who did, however, insist on keeping her maiden name. She had a very uncomplicated and clear view of life. She had a plan. She would raise two children, graduate from law school, and begin to practice. She had plenty of money for nannies and household help, but she was always at home when the children got back from school. When her children had successfully made the transition from adolescence, she would turn to her legal and public service career full time. Vern wasn't home much. Vern wasn't much help. He was caught up in the endless networking that is the warp and woof of a banker's life. Because his wife was so self-sufficient and seemingly content to spend long school holidays in the traditional homes owned by her family, he was apt to spend his time at places like the Bohemian Grove making more invaluable contacts.

Molly had a great deal to do and given the circumstances felt she could do it best if left alone, so the marriage proceeded like a successful partnership. Neither seemed to stray. Vern contented himself with a kind of WASP prurience, making halfhearted passes at stewardesses on long flights. Rituals were observed, birthdays remembered, anniversaries celebrated. For the first fifteen years, it was marriage by the numbers; exactly what would have been taught if HBS had a course in executive matrimony.

Molly Munro never had any doubt about her place in the world. She was the third and last child, the much-wanted only daughter in a professional family. Her father was an aesthete who served as curator of nineteenth-century French painting for The Art Institute of Chicago. When Molly was ten the family spent an entire year in southern France where her father could better study the genius of Chagall,

Matisse, and others. Her mother ran the family and her own considerable assets. Her paternal grandfather and one of her older brothers
were doctors of medicine. The other brother, her favorite, was a
painter. Money was not discussed in the Munro household. Her
mother's great uncle was Owen Young, the Chief Executive Officer of
General Electric Company between the World Wars. His nephew,
Molly's grandfather, was one of the high-ranking GE executives, so her
mother's early life had been spent as one of the aristocrats in a series
of company towns in Upstate New York. Young, known by his descendents simply as the Ancestor, had been generous and insistent. His
nephew and the whole family always participated in rights offerings
and never sold any shares of GE, which were instead routinely transferred between generations in amounts calculated to avoid inheritance
taxes. The result was a comfortable environment during the balance
of the twentieth century that allowed the family's energies to be
devoted to nonmonetary concerns. The Munro family always formally
celebrated the Ancestor's birthday, October 27.

It was a tradition in the Munro family that each child received at
birth an allocation of 5,000 shares of GE stock within the family trust.
When Molly was born on January 2, 1940, her birthright of shares was
valued at $233,500. Those same shares in 1998 had multiplied to
1,440,000 and were valued at $62,431,250. The last half-century had
been very good to GE.

Those who knew the family when Molly was young always com-
mented on this youngest child who sat by late at night quietly listening to every guest. She appeared comfortable and undemanding,
so the full conversational flow of a generation of self-confident and
verbal, creative people passed through her consciousness. The Munros
were an artistically talented family. Summertime musicals at their
cottage on Racquet Lake in the Adirondacks were punctuated by
family creations. Both parents could play instruments and sing; their
sons were musically gifted. Molly was tone deaf. Nor could she draw.
Notwithstanding the patient tutelage of her beloved brother, she
proved incapable of putting paint to canvas to any pleasant or satis-

fying effect. And she had an eye, which made her lack of any gift more obvious, so she was more than content to collect art in the years to come. We can't all be artists, she would say, who would be left to admire the art? The Munro family was saddened by Molly's absence of expressive artistic talent, but they were very sophisticated people who realized that there were gaps in everyone's aptitudes. Molly lived in her own world and didn't feel diminished because there were things she couldn't do. She focused on what she could do. Racquet Lake was a paradise for boats. There were the wonderful old Adirondack League Club shallow-bottomed rowing boats. The Munro family also kept a collection of modern single racing sculls. The Aesthete, Mr. Munro, and his sons were accomplished rowers and distinguished themselves in school and college competitions. Oftentimes people don't notice how fast the youngest child in a family grows. The marks on the door frames, showing year-to-year increases, lose their excitement as the older children achieve maturity, duly surpass their parents, and the game is over. By the time Molly was sixteen she had achieved her full height of five feet nine inches and she could beat both her brothers in the single scull over any distance on the lake.

Women's competitive rowing was not well organized, but Molly got in the habit of taking a single with her most places she went. It was relatively simple. Mount a ski rack on any car, strap on the single and its oars, and stop at any stream. With great charm and tact, Molly managed to inveigle regatta organizers to let her participate in the boys' events. She was not listed as official winner, she didn't keep the medals, but she was rarely beaten. The Munros played all the conventional sports. Molly played tennis well enough to be on the varsity team for New Trier High School. It should come as no surprise that as Molly matured into her high school years, she made up her own sense of direction quietly but firmly. Her father and brothers were enthusiastic graduates of Harvard, so she too would go to Cambridge for college.

She always dressed simply and appeared elegant. While not stylish, her clothes had about them the sense of comfort and appropriateness. Her splendid figure, a revelation in a bathing suit, was usually shrouded in the loose-fitting, loosely belted sheaths that she preferred, with curves flattened by the kind of bras she always wore. Women liked her; she never showed any interest in taking men away from them. As the younger sister, she grew up with her brothers' friends and, while never naïve about the impact of testosterone, regarded men as a potentially educable species. It was this belief which made her mother maintain that her only daughter was a dreamer. Men liked her, indeed, many lusted for her, but like many of the most attractive girls, she seemed quite unaware of her impact. As for sex, in an older time, it might have been said, "She isn't that kind of girl." It wasn't that she lacked appeal or instinct, but rather, she defined relationships in open and energetic enthusiasm. What she was prepared to give was so appealing that very few pushed the line to her discomfort. By the time she reached college, her intellectual interests had blossomed to the point that she could not contemplate a relationship with anyone unless she found him interesting.

Molly listened well. She always seemed to make sense, to be the person to whom others turned when they most needed help. She seemed sure and confident in ways that did not threaten others. Lacking the facility with expressive arts enjoyed by the rest of her family, Molly was more interested in what made the world go round. She was fascinated by the career of the Ancestor, not so much in his role as corporate CEO, not even as a world-recognized statesman and author of the Young Plan for refinancing German World War I reparations debts, but for his transcending view of the role of working people. In a 1927 speech at the dedication of the George P. Baker Building at the Harvard Business School, he articulated this vision: "I hope the day may come when these great business organizations will truly belong to the men who are giving their lives and their efforts to them....Then, in a word, men will be as free in cooperative undertakings and subject only to the same limitations and chances as men in individual businesses. Then we shall have no hired men."

The words had an almost mesmerizing impact on Molly, even though there was no mention of women. Stemming as she did from a family of self-employed entrepreneurs in medical and artistic endeavors, it seemed to her that a job, no matter how well paid, could be a form of slavery unless it was somehow linked to ownership. It intrigued her that the Ancestor saw that even as he was bound in golden shackles himself.

To the horror of her mother and father, who had never guessed at the possible limits of independence, Molly went as far towards majoring in business as was then permitted of Harvard undergraduates. The university was a feast for someone as intellectually courageous and hungry. She took courses in four of the graduate schools: Law, Kennedy, Divinity, and Business, as well as the college requirements for her major in economics. She had a lot of energy and money was not a problem, so she took a fifth course each semester, one semester she even took six, which gave her a chance to study fine arts and further stir the collector's passion she had started as a child. Ultimately, she wrote her college thesis on the Ancestor's concept of employee ownership and was preparing for a career in law.

Molly was not so much a liberated woman or a product of women's lib as she was a member of a very singular class that was comprised of independent women with graduate degrees and careers. Her mother came from the managerial aristocracy and, although not interested in the professions, enjoyed her own ability to run things. Rather than participating in the proper and fashionable charities of Chicago, Molly's mother started and financed a home for aged women. She argued with mayors, congressmen, and governors about the needs of the elderly. At irregular intervals she would leave the family house and spend whatever time was necessary at the home. Once when Molly was with her, an aged woman appeared to be choking to death. Her mother grabbed her, and in a personalized version of the Heimlich maneuver, managed to clear the terrified woman's airway and restore her breathing. It was a moment of simple heroism that the young and impressionable Molly would never forget. Her mother took care of people. At times, their guest rooms were packed with needy relatives and friends. She did what she thought was right without the need or desire for confirmation by anyone else. Molly never imagined there was any other way to be.

Molly was a species of American aristocrat. In a naïve way, she was content with a simple conception of her post-college life; marriage to a competent professional, two children as soon as possible, graduate school at night followed by professional work compatible with child rearing. She always assumed that she would do something important and whatever it was would make itself known in due time. There was no hurry. It wasn't that Molly was dull, she unconsciously accommodated to whatever standards a particular group might require. She devoted no energy to examining her own life. Life and Molly had a deal. They wouldn't crowd each other. So long as Molly stayed in the groove created by money and meritocracy, reality would never rear its ugly head; any real questions would be stifled long before entering her consciousness.

In later years she asked herself how she could possibly have gotten married to Vernon Stillman, but, at the time, there seemed no other choice. Vern turned an intensity of focus, concern, and raw attention to the lovely aristocrat with independent wealth that would never have been experienced in the home of the aesthetes. He simply paid court with such a vigor and determination that Molly was bowled over. His energy was not prurient. He made it clear that he wanted to marry her. Molly, coming from a century of family security, found it fascinating that Vern was in the process of creating himself from scratch.

After only one year at HBS, he had come to realize the importance of certain athletic skills for the life he intended. Somehow, he had managed to barter with the golf professional at The Country Club and the famous tennis and squash coach for the Harvard College teams to give him some instruction. Molly later learned that he had told both men the same thing: "Someday I am going to be in a position to make some serious money for you. I am asking you to take a chance on me today." Vern had a clear idea of what he wanted. This was not some nice college boy with vague ideas about a future. He was so different. It was exciting.

One thing about Vern, he could learn. Someone once said in his presence that Oscar Wilde boasted that he could seduce any woman in a night's time so long as he first let her talk as long as she wanted. So Vern always listened. Never a prude, but always careful, Molly found Vern's basic animal energy more sexually attractive than that of those careful and thoughtful boys with whom she was brought up. He called once, and then he'd call again. He sent flowers. He even endured the humiliation of meeting with her father and mother, whose sensitivities were jarred by the ambition and energy of this success machine. Her father bleated, "I can stand anything except that little-boy look of coming down the stairs on Christmas morning." This was what the psychologists would call transference. While the Aesthete was very conscious of what surroundings his wife's money had provided, Vern was quite impervious to it. He was smiling because there was so much to learn. He was a primal force. Maybe Molly needed such a shock to move beyond the security of childhood. But Vern's drive for self-creation had its limits; he simply could not enjoy being with Molly's family. Homes, where the familiarity and love of things past suffused the atmosphere and the athletic graces, acquired in youth, elude even the most determined efforts to compete, and so, he never really tried.

Vern insisted that the wedding be in June at the Harvard Chapel in the middle of Harvard Yard. With typical persistence, he had managed to secure one of the dates that are usually reserved months, if not years, in advance, during the traditional June reunion and graduation celebrations when it would be possible to have his classmates serve as ushers and attend the ceremony. In no other place, at no other time, could Vern Stillman have produced a single wedding guest, beyond the loyal Charles Fraser, on his side of the aisle. Once Molly had made up her mind, around Christmas, that she would marry Vern, there was nothing more to be said. Her parents knew their daughter and knew the limits of their influence. Wedding preparations were vastly simplified. Harvard could provide the place for the reception, so all was quickly arranged. Vern had persuaded the Harvard Chaplain to conduct the service. When he sat down with Molly that night to tell her this exciting news, she was shocked to realize that Vern either didn't intend to invite his own parents or that he had forgotten that his father was a clergyman. She asked. Vern, ever the quick learner, immediately realized that he had gone too far in his effort to create, in his HBS incarnation, an impenetrable biographical beginning. He quickly added that he intended to ask his father to participate in the service and hoped to phone him that very evening.

Vern had not been home during the eighteen months since being accepted at HBS. He had written briefly but in a desultory tone. He called on occasion, but no longer considered himself part of the family or community of Woodbine, Georgia. His accent had adjusted to the cosmopolitan strains of HBS and in many ways Vern had succeeded in blotting out his origins and his past. He did call that night and spoke with his mother and father, neither of whom had any inclination that their only child was contemplating matrimony, or that he intended to marry a Chicago heiress on a specific day in June in Cambridge, Massachusetts. During the uneasy conversation, Vern's father asked, "And what is her religion?" This was not a question that had come up between Vern and Molly so he literally did not know the answer. Vern was so angry at the implied need to satisfy an ancestral demand that he almost hung up. He paused, however, and said simply, "She is a Christian, Father." For a Scots' preacher, aware of the centuries of blood that had been spilled over the niceties distinguishing the Church of England, Episcopalians, Presbyterians, Congregationalists, and Baptists, North and South, to say nothing of the Catholics, this answer was almost a sacrilege. But the tone improved and the senior Stillman agreed to participate in the ceremony if there were no intervening doctrinal problems.

If Vern had been the worrying type, he would have been concerned about the fact that the only two persons, in the church holding several hundred, having anything to do with his past, were strangers, not only to him, but also to the entire world out of priestly South Georgia. He didn't know what to expect of his parents. He need not have worried. He had forgotten that in a world of homogenized people with fashionable tastes in hair and clothing and behavior, simple integrity would make an enormously positive impact. Vern did not come by his pleasing country boy looks by accident. His father stood tall, a little taller than Vern, in a dark suit with a couple of military decorations in the buttonhole of his jacket. His mother looked like she had walked out of a Grant Wood painting. In passing, Vern learned for the first time that his father had been wounded in action during World War II and had served during five separate campaigns. They were polite but not forthcoming. Molly's mother broke the ice. She said that she had no formal religious affiliation but that she felt, in the grace of the senior Stillmans, the presence of something that she wanted in her own life. She volunteered stories of her home in Chicago for needy women. The Reverend Stillman listened attentively and said simply, "You have nothing of which to reproach yourself. The spirit of God is in you."

Just before the marriage service, the Reverend had a minute alone with his son. "You are a good boy and I am proud of what you have accomplished. You must not be ashamed of your background. You must never forget that you are a child of God and that your life is sacred and not profane. Never forget, my boy, the words of the Gospel, Matthew, Book XVI, Verse 26, 'For what is a man profited if he shall gain the whole world, and lose his own soul?'" Vern was moved and, spontaneously, embraced his father; this was to be the only occasion of harmony between Vern's past and future lives, from this day forward, forever separate. Everything happened according to plan. Molly finished her last year at Radcliffe commuting from an apartment in New York City, largely made possible by her GE dividends. Her degree, magna cum laude, thank you very much, and first child arrived during the same week and a second daughter a year later. Molly was excited by the new lives for whom she was responsible and easily organized a Manhattan life with principal attention to the growing children but ample opportunity for her to graduate from law school over five years. She was busy, but it was fortunate because Vern was incessantly preoccupied with making new contacts and was rarely home. Their marriage was a partnership where each member could accommodate his or her own interests. Vern counted on it and Molly never really gave it much thought. She just kept busy, moving forward on other fronts.

Molly had been admitted to Harvard Law School but Vern's self-reinvention energy was infectious and Molly decided to consider the local schools. She didn't choose Columbia, but picked New York University Law School instead. She planned to practice law in Manhattan, so it seemed sensible to learn the local customs. NYU was something different. There were a lot of students, most of them were in a hurry. Most of them had too little money to meet all their commitments and were convinced that only good grades in law school would liberate them from a marginal existence. There was little choice in courses; the school taught what the bar examiners tested. The professors usually had been the best students and were glad to continue to focus on areas where they had demonstrated excellence. Legal education in the early 1970s had a learn by rote traditional core. Law students hardly reflected the national malaise of the late '60s. These were people who saw, in the existing system, opportunity. They did not want to change society or to blow it up. What other young people were doing, at the Chicago Democratic convention in 1968 or on college campuses, was beyond the concern of this urban graduate school.

Molly's wedding ring insulated her from all but the most insistent male intention. Once it was understood that she was not available, she began to make friends. Never a snob, Molly found that just by listening she could learn much of the modern history of New York City. There were the driven second-generation immigrants of every race, hoping to reward their parents' endless sacrifices with good grades. There were the Orthodox Jews, who seemed a race apart, not only from her but also from everyone else. There weren't many women, but those who braved it through, wore their degrees like medals and their experience created a lifelong sorority. Molly worked hard in law school. She wasn't as good a student as she had been in college, but she was in the top half of the class, and passed the dreaded New York State bar exams on her first try.

Vern discovered early that Molly's intelligent independence was much admired by his colleagues and customers, but even more so by their wives. Business rivals and professional acquaintances pigeon-holed Vern as another driven bright young man. When they met Molly, they thought again. He must have more depth. As business couples gathered and came to know each other, spouses would patiently explain that Molly was something genuine and exceptional. If Molly had been anything other than modest, responsive, and a bit under-dressed, she would have been envied. As it was, she loaned a touch of class to every gathering. Vern couldn't have been more pleased. He never anticipated her value in these circumstances and to his discredit, never really understood what all the fuss was about. He assumed they all just smelled her family money.

A year after Molly's graduation from law school, Congress passed the omnibus retirement statute that would change her life forever. The Employee Retirement Income Security Act of 1974 (ERISA) provided a framework within which employers and employees could confidently make provision for retirement, profit sharing, and employee ownership. It was the final result of a vision that had been formed over the eleven years since John Kennedy had created the original study commission, as one of his last acts before flying to Dallas.

Molly was not at all diminished by specializing in the area that, she liked to think, had been invented by her great uncle, and young lawyers suffer no disadvantage from lack of experience in practicing an utterly new branch of the law created by a complicated and comprehensive statute like ERISA. Molly very quickly became her firm's ERISA specialist, which ultimately solved two difficult problems: how to get anybody to take the trouble to learn what one author called "Every Rotten Idea Since Adam" and how to make a woman a partner in the firm without threatening the males who might have felt passed over. By the mid 1980s she had developed a substantial law practice and was regarded as one of the principal authorities in the country on ERISA law.

Chapter 10

Spring 1984

In the darkness, the phone rang at some indeterminate hour. Horse was alone. His wife was gone for two weeks at a time because this was tennis season. Hung over and stinking from his usual weekend sex, Horse grabbed his gear and raced to the firehouse. Volunteer firemen don't get speeding tickets. They usually didn't call the volunteers unless the fire was out of control. He was glad to be up and out, the night air was helping to clear his head. Most people would say it was freezing, even though the snow for the season was gone for good. Horse craved that bone-chilling cold tonight. He had hit bottom. The separated wife of a man he knew. Not a friend, but he might have been. He seemed like a decent guy. They were just bored with each other. So much of Horse's time was spent drifting these days. He pulled up, and like clockwork, within minutes of each other, the brotherhood was assembled. Everyone knew his job and they were rolling in two minutes flat. When their old truck pulled up near a neighborhood of triple-decker wooden dwelling units, everybody could see from the intensity of light and heat that it would be a miracle if this fire could be put out before everything was destroyed.

Horse followed his part of his unit to one of the high-pressure hoses aimed at the heart of the blaze. For minutes at a time, the only impact of all this effort was to create a lot of steam. It was futile. Horse first sensed, then he saw, human figures moving in one of the structures, obscured by the fire, smoke, and steam. He shouted to rotate his position off the hose with another volunteer and went in. He walked forward and into it. He kept track of his footing and watched for anything falling from above. People panic and would run in circles in the space of ten feet in a fire. All he had to do was get to them and take them out the way he came in. Nobody can be confident who issued what orders, who took what initiative, but those who were there clearly remembered that Horse, wrapped in his insulated coat, returned three times to the inhabited house and three times returned with somebody under his coat. No one else could bear the heat; no one could understand how this middle-aged man was able to hold his breath against the smoke. Horse was, at the core, a creature of the elements. He could survive the wind and the fire, as well as the bullets and mines. This is when he was alive. Spray from the hose knocked him over once, but he kept going. He had to align himself with the basic human elements of survival: respect for nature, respect for fellow human beings, deep distrust of institutions.

The sun had been up for an hour. Two of the three structures were gone. It was probably a cigarette in a bedroom; it usually was at that time of night. No lives lost. His hip was sore and would be purple for a while. The hangover was gone and all he could smell now was smoke, but he couldn't shake how bad he had felt when he woke up to the call that morning. He wiped his filthy face and spoke to the men but all he thought about was how empty his life had become. On the ride to the firehouse, the countryside was so beautiful and he thought about how the war had broken his heart. So much waste, more than a decade with no direction. He guessed he'd been settling for less, ever since he got home. The morning light glinting on the wet truck made him feel like he was waking up. It was warm and he was occasionally blinded in the sun. He wanted to wake up, at last. He had picked up some bad habits that were going to be hard to shake but all he had to do was figure out where the hell he was and walk out the way he came in.

There's a dreary sameness to trade association conventions. Banking meetings are, if anything, at the more boring end of the spectrum. As for employee benefit plan fiduciary gatherings, simply hearing the title of the association conveys dehumanizing concern with actuarial, legal, and economic niceties, far from the mainstream of life and joy. And so the Annual Meeting of the National Association of Employee Stock Ownership Plans in May 1984, notwithstanding the grandeur of the

Gotham Hotel on Fifth Avenue, impressed as being an occasion that only those who had no choice would attend. This included the responsible officers of the Association, those who wanted to be officers, speakers, panelists, occasional spouses, and all manner of service providers.

The one redeeming feature, for Horse's enforced evening presence at the current dreary gathering, was the availability, for the night, of the newly decorated apartment, several floors above. The suite was maintained by New York Safe Deposit & Trust Company at the Gotham for favored officers and customers. Horse, who rarely got any of the fringe benefits customarily available to senior officers, was already comfortably installed in the splendid suite. The current reception held none of that charm. There was elevator music, a bar, the usual hors d'oeuvres, and a general emptiness in the room in which twice the 150 or so people present would be needed to create a sense of warmth or hospitality. Horse finished his first drink and was content to munch from his fist full of carrot sticks before committing, if he must, to a second drink. Because it was Stanley Cup time and the local Rangers were, for a change, still involved in the play-offs, there were large TV screens in two corners of the room, which had the effect of utterly destroying any sense of community or collegiality that this gathering might otherwise have achieved.

Molly Munro, one of the better-known younger lawyers in this field, entered the reception late and wondered with growing exasperation why she had chosen to organize her life and her time in such a way, bringing her to such a dull place. Once again, Vern was not at her side. Molly ruefully considered whether she would feel better if Vern had reciprocated for the literally dozens of bank functions she had embellished for him or whether the anticipated dreadfulness of this reception was best borne alone. She had not bothered to change for the occasion and was dressed in her customary dark unisex uniform.

As Molly became aware of the television sets blaring over the conversations, the thought flashed through her mind that her husband was going to be entertaining customers in the bank's box seats, right behind the Rangers' bench. In that same instant the television cameras panned the sidelines as the players change on the fly and there was the image of Vernon himself, with his arm draped in an unmistakably proprietary way around the lightly clad shoulders of the most beautiful girl Molly had ever seen, whom she recognized as one of the stewardesses on the bank's GIV. The fast-moving camera, the noise of both crowds, the TV and conference, and the almost hallucinogenic image on her retina, combined to knock Molly right out of the world of the living. Rather than feeling shock or rage, she lost any sense of self and place. She was shattered and the beliefs she clung to were in pieces, on the ground, all around her.

Horse always took refuge at cocktail parties by looking over everyone's head to see if he was missing something. He could literally feel shock from the young woman who was just turning away from the television screen. He was familiar with this visceral response in others but it was the last thing anyone experienced at this kind of gathering. He vaguely knew who she was but had never met her and her appearance made no particular impression. What was unmistakable was that she had experienced something that caused her body to spasm in an uncontrolled way, in the mindless processing of some horror. He had a great deal of experience with traumatized men. She was disoriented and Horse moved towards her.

As Molly came out of her momentary oblivion, the first impression was of the large and approaching form of Horse. They shared the instant, but unexpressed, intimacy of two strangers creating a private moment. The existence of this enveloping canopy around Molly and Horse was so palpable it caused the people around them to speak more quietly and to glance in their direction. Who spoke first or who said what was never clear, Molly needed to relate to the physical presence of a flesh and blood human being. Horse was caught up in the force of her feelings that was so intense it permitted no time for analysis or consideration.

Horse took Molly by the arm and swept her out of the room and into the quiet calm of the empty elevator bank. The door behind them clicked shut and they were enveloped in sepulchral silence. Horse's look of genuine concern comforted her but as her control returned in the cool antiseptic hallway, they could feel the edge of embarrassment encroaching. Horse wouldn't be able to be of any help to her here and so he spoke without thinking, "We have an apartment in this hotel." From somewhere inside of her, a place she barely knew existed, the words came out, "I need something." They must have gotten into an elevator cab and pushed a button. The doors opened onto a small private lobby. Without hesitation, Horse crossed the lobby, unlocked the door to Universal's suite and held it open for Molly to enter. He suddenly realized he was acting by instinct and became aware that he didn't know what to do or what to say. He felt that something precious was involved and he knew he didn't want to ruin it.

What else? A ritual response, a comforting gesture? A tour of the apartment. The large living room, followed by a sitting room, framed by floor-to-ceiling glass doors facing Central Park. An open bar next to the door giving access to a dressing room, a grand bath suite, and a master bedroom with a huge king-size bed with the covers already drawn for the night. Molly sat down tentatively in one of the straight chairs next to the table and Horse went to the bar, opened a bottle of champagne, and poured each of them a glass. Neither of them said a word, neither lifted the glass to their lips. It wasn't a time for eating or drinking; it wasn't a time for talking. It was a moment made on instinct, a natural human response that he could feel deeply.

Horse stood up and went into the dressing room where he had earlier unpacked and said he would be back in a moment. No reply. He took off all his clothes and neatly folded and put them away, pulled a silk dressing gown over his naked body, and in bare feet, walked back into the living room. Molly was sitting straight in the chair with a hand placed precisely on each arm, staring out of the glass doors. Horse came around to the front of the chair, looked down, and helped her to rise. He held her closely and carefully placed his lips on hers and kissed her gently. He looked down, turned her slightly by the shoulders and handily unzipped her simple black dress so that she could step out of it. She pulled her slip off over her head. No matter how many times he experiences it, the first sight of a woman getting ready for him stirs and impresses a man's nervous system like nothing else ever will.

He guided her to the bedroom and, exercising all the restraint of which he was capable, held her closely while they were standing at the side of the bed. Her heart was still racing and he held her tight. Eventually, she sat down at the edge of the bed and he unpeeled her pantyhose. She raised herself up to make it easier for him and then she leaned forward on her bare legs. Horse reached behind her. Gently unfastening the clasps on the elastic sheath, he lifted off the material that appeared to have been designed to flatten and conceal the size of her breasts, which spilled out of their confinement. He encouraged her to lay her upper body flat on the bed with her legs loose and her feet on the floor. Horse knelt on the floor, between her legs and reached under her, each hand now, flat under her buttocks. He gently pushed her further up on the bed so that her knees were at its edge. She was lying expectantly with her head on one side and her breath catching in excited rhythm. He pushed his arms under each thigh to massage her breasts, at the same time beginning to tease with his tongue and lips the flesh around her lower body. Her body began to shake and he detected a pleasant astringent odor. With only the gentlest contact from his tongue, he traced a course around her until her first orgasm was unmistakably begun. A guttural sound, quick, shrill cries and her body was convulsed.

When her rate of breathing subsided and the pulse on the side of her neck regained its normal rhythm, he turned back to renewing her pleasure, in confidence that her body was properly tuned. Horse's height gave the impression of size when he was standing up, but when those arms were wrapped under her thighs with his hands encasing most of her breasts, she felt herself in a trap of sinew and muscle and man, a fleshly trap.

He got up and gently turned her lengthwise and moved her to the middle of the bed. Before Molly could more than fleetingly wonder how she could possibly contain him, Horse was on the bed again kneeling between her outspread legs. He put his hands under each of her buttocks, lifted her and put pillows under his hands so that she would have a comfortable resting posture. He inclined gently forward so as to bring them to center stage of the oldest and most pleasurable choreography of human existence. Molly grasped immediately that Horse was leaving to her the choice of how to proceed. Rather than being made love to, she was given the gift of being an equal participant. This license stimulated Molly to an enthusiasm, inventiveness and carnal hunger that she had never before experienced. With the help of his hands, she scissored her body until his entire length was encased. From someplace deep in her cortex, Molly found the controls to cause the right muscles to contract. Whether it was her state of joyful discovery, his thoughtfulness, his pure physicality, or all of them combined, Molly became feral, constantly inventing and reinventing modes of satisfying her wants and her needs. Her sense of flesh and the need to gnaw was so intense; she actually caused herself sharp pain. She uttered noises of a timbre and fervency, so new, as to make Molly wonder from whence they came.

Horse responded with the energies damned up by a decade of deterioration, self-disgust, and the absence of a real passion. This was demanding more than just the skills honed by the suburban weekend couplings of the open marriage. The fleshly dance improvised its own movements and its own rhythms with intervals of rest and resurgence until the darkness passed and they awoke, finally slaked, at ten o'clock in the morning.

"I'm Molly Munro."

"Everybody calls me Horse."

Molly thought about that for a minute, smiled, blushed and asked, "But how do they know?"

"They don't, it's just something that started in high school."

There was no sense of "morning after," no disgust after the indulgence. There was innocence about it, as if it were intended. They had shared an experience that few humans had enjoyed. After the fire and the wind and the noise, there was a place of supreme joy in being alive. This was something that they had experienced together. It belonged to them for as long as they lived. It was not something they deserved; it was not something shameful. It was akin to a natural disaster that they had the good fortune to survive, and to relish the memories. They talked for hours. They could talk with a freedom and a naturalness that neither had experienced before; whatever they were, they wanted to share. Molly explained what had happened on the television screen and blamed herself for not acting sooner to do something about her failed marriage. Horse said that he was ashamed of himself, not caring enough for his marriage; he just let the relationship drift. He determined either to make something of it or to stop the mutual destruction. Molly asked if Horse had ever experienced anything like their night together. Thinking of occurrences that seemed like an act of God and not related to his own desserts, he told her of the mess tent in Vietnam, almost as if it had happened to another person in a different time. When he finished, he looked up and tears covered her face. This was probably the first time Horse appreciated the enormity of what had happened in the jungle, so long ago.

"The hell of it is, like they say in the movies, I am not this kind of girl. I have never done this kind of thing before. All I can say is I considered myself divorced the moment I saw that TV screen."

Molly said that she would end her marriage immediately, and, that settled, she looked forward to being with Horse as much as possible. Horse told her about his own "open" marriage. He was never under any confusion; Molly was not a potential wife for him. The love he felt for her was not the love for a spouse, but both of them felt that they could help each other. They both recognized that this could quickly become a convenient self-deception to enable them to continue to enjoy sex together. With a laugh they agreed on a bit more self-deception. Neither of them wanted to destroy or dilute the wondrous gift they had been given. In hindsight, it was absolutely clear that they did each other a world of good at a time both needed help.

During the minuets of giving and receiving, of limbs and organs finding impossible postures and new resting places, apparently there was a time when the second joint on Molly's forefinger and her mouth were not otherwise in use, because she noted to her amazement that she had bitten her finger clear down to the bone. There was no bleeding, but there would always be a scar to remind her. It was a fair commentary on the current state of both their lives that when they arrived at offices and homes in late afternoon, nobody had noticed that they had been gone.

Horse took from the magic at the Gotham and a few more interludes with Molly over the next several weeks, a desire to make his life more meaningful. Like Molly, he started at home. But he went in a different direction; he asked his wife to forgive his inattention and to help him make their marriage work. His new devotion made it easier for her to make peace with leaving the circuit before it left her. They made time for each other now, and found they had a love for each other that they previously never bothered to express. It was a new kind of romance for each of them, truly a gift they never expected, but gratefully received. Everything happened quite quickly and by New Year's Day 1987, two sons had been born to a newly happy, middle-aged couple who were anxious to reclaim together the life they had so nearly frittered away.

Molly's immediate reaction to the night at the Gotham Hotel was to face up to the hollowness of her marriage. She needed to start again. She calmly confronted Vern. She did not carry on about the woman next to him at the hockey game; she simply announced the conclusion of their marriage. Over the next five years, both her daughters graduated from college and were pleased and well equipped to pursue their own kind of happiness, well endowed with GE shares. Molly's professional reputation grew and her job was very satisfying. Both of her parents died and she was astonished that the combination of the aesthetes' restrained living style and the continued success of the General Electric Company resulted in her enjoying the fruits of serious eight-figure capital.

Awareness of her sexuality did not make Molly promiscuous, but it made her miss consistent male company. In 1989, she met and married Judd Hagan, a sculptor some ten years her junior, a man of great kindness, adored by her daughters, who wanted to stay home, do his work, and be there for her. He was a sexual athlete who could never satisfy his hunger for Molly and was utterly unthreatened to live in a world provided for by her money.

Like many American professional women in the late 1980s, Molly became acquainted with Hillary Rodham Clinton and was immediately attracted to her. They worked on a number of commissions and boards together and Molly took a leave of absence to work on Bill Clinton's successful presidential campaign in 1992. With her children independent, herself wealthy beyond any possible need, and Judd content to live in Georgetown, Molly went to work at 1600 Pennsylvania Avenue, basically as friend, confidant, and trusted advisor to the First Lady. By 1992, Molly concluded that the vision of her great uncle was possible and asked to be appointed assistant secretary of Labor in charge of the Pension and Welfare Benefits Agency, to participate in the realization of her ancestor's vision.

Two years into her appointment, Molly's phone rang. It was the detested voice of the president's general counsel. "Molly, my love, why don't we just celebrate this Christmas season with a long luncheon at the Hay Adams?" Hitting on women was one of the prerequisites of high government males, and some females, who vigorously enacted and enforced sexual harassment laws on the rest of the citizenry. The general counsel was the epitome of official Washington. He was the son of a great man, rich, tall, member of all the clubs, including the handy Metropolitan, tennis partner for important White House events when the boss couldn't lose, a mixture of southern charm and northern efficiency and the impenetrable conviction that he was God's gift to women. Answering back just encouraged him, so Molly was silent. "OK, roll call on the securities litigation reform legislation and you are penciled against. We're seriously thinking about a veto. What say you?"

"We say veto."

"I think that's the way it's going, too. Now, don't forget our little date tonight." Counsel's prurient mind never forgot little details, like the obligatory, yet intimate, "senior staff only" Christmas party in the residency part of the White House.

Molly was uneasy with Christmas in the White House. The trees, the decorations, even sometimes the snow were only token ornaments for the ongoing business of government. During her first two years, Molly was amazed by the corporate domination of the government agenda. She was astonished when the president said in jest he would like to be reincarnated as a bond trader, and then he made his principal economic advisor the former managing partner of Goldman Sachs. Again and again, public policy issues came up against the reality of business power. Two years of promoting health service reform had been thwarted by skillful and persistent lobbyists. Molly had to ask herself, *What am I doing here that has to do with the public interest?* The kind of law that Molly practiced had nothing to do with the flamboyant controversial and lucrative class-action lawyers' bar. America, uniquely in the world, provided a mechanism whereby lawyers could become entrepreneurs and finance class-action litigation against a whole host of societal wrongs: asbestos, silicone injections, securities frauds. The good news was that many important issues were effectively raised; the bad news was that lawyers became obscenely rich and powerful. As she prepared for the Christmas party on this twentieth day of December 1995, Molly was proud and pleased that the president would deliver his first veto. He was certain to be overridden by the Congress and castigated by the press for paying his debts to campaign financiers, but this veto was a statement that her president was prepared to stand up for the public good. Molly felt good about her job today.

As she got off of the elevator in the residency, Molly was struck again by the utter lack of charm in holiday Washington. Tinsel and poinsettias, wreaths and trees, it all seemed like department-store décor and not a family-inspired holiday, in the least. Her elbow was grabbed a little bit too familiarly and she turned to look up into the smiling face of the general counsel. "I was standing here all alone, worried that my pussycat wasn't going to make my evening." The president himself was circulating, so Molly easily drifted over to be in his aura, which he liked to be populated by attractive women. The GC didn't have a chance. She caught the president's eye, she always could.

"I hope you approved of my veto today."

"Mr. President, I am proud to be part of your administration today."

"Aren't you proud every day?"

"Of course, but today is special because your government is insisting the citizens be empowered to challenge wrongs." She didn't mean to make a speech.

"The worst thing about this job is the amount of time and energy you have to devote to those who don't need it. The real challenge is to find some way for people, who *are* doing what is right, to make some money. That's about as good as it gets in our capitalist system." He drifted off, like he did with so many people, all eager for a tenth of the attention that Molly just got. That night Molly learned something about herself. Thirty seconds of face time and a substantive discussion with the president had given her more pleasure than any other professional accomplishment in her life.

Chapter 11

Thursday, August 6, 1998

Drive and Marty took the limo to the offices of Georgeson & Company, America's premier proxy solicitation firm. They had decided to engage the firm to loan credence to the reasonability of the offer to the trustees. This deal was going to make Caesar's wife look like a junk bond broker, in Marty's words. Marty was marveling at Drive's selection of newspapers he brought with him. He guessed they weren't going to chat, so he picked up the discarded *Times*, whose headline was LEWINSKY SET TO TESTIFY BEFORE GRAND JURY TODAY. Marty got a tingle. He loved the prurience in the process. The leader of the free world got a little too free with himself. Just how out of touch was that guy? His mother was right, they're all going to hell in a handbasket and everyone is fighting over the best seat. WASHINGTON, August 5—"Ms. Lewinsky is expected to tell grand jurors that she had a sexual relationship with Mr. Clinton, flatly contradicting his finger-pointing denial to the American people last January, as well as his denial in a sworn deposition in the Paula Corbin Jones sexual-misconduct lawsuit, lawyers familiar with her account said." At least the stock was holding at next to nothing. From this point on, the word would be out. There was too much money to be made, up or down. They would have to move fast even if most of the city was out at the Hamptons.

Georgeson had prepared a listing of the major AOM shareholders. There were no surprises beyond Georgeson's recent advice that Shark Capital had been amassing a large position in recent weeks. *Shit*, thought Drive. "Shit," said Marty, "looks like we're doing business with the 'King.'" At least they wouldn't be required to disclose the holdings until the end of the quarter. That kind of news could ruin the tender. If word gets out that Shark thinks there are values in AOM at its current lows, the thinly traded stock will shoot up and the indicated premium in the tender offer will appear less attractive.

"Do you think word is out?" Drive looked past the experts, to Marty. Marty was a little embarrassed but he was touched too. He had Drive's trust in this room.

"No, that bastard can afford to have a chip on every number." Trying not to seem irrelevant, one of the experts spoke up.

"That's why they call him the King." Drive didn't hear it, and he just responded to Marty.

"Well, those are my kind of odds." Marty was pretty sure they just thought Drive was being rude. Marty wanted to make sure everybody would save face, so he raised his voice just enough, for them to realize, and then said, "At some point, we will have to cross paths with this bastard they call the King."

The story for the street would be that Drive's offer was the last best chance the shareholders have to get out from under. Not only should they tender their shares, they should do everything imaginable to persuade the Porter trustees to do the same. Georgeson agreed to act as a neutral information center for discussions with the trustees of the trusts for the New York charities. Marty said again and again, "We need to know what everybody is thinking all the time. We love them and they must love us," and then he figured it was time to crawl out on a branch in front of witnesses. "Can we solicit directly the employees who own shares in the ESOP or are we restricted to soliciting the trustees?"

One of the suits responded, "That's a very interesting question. There's been a lot of pushing and shoving about that, I think the law now requires the information about the tender be given to all participants and the trustees are obligated to follow instructions."

Marty, with the smell of a little blood, said, "Hey, you know, we're going to need an answer to these questions." *Some experts*, thought Marty. Now he was going to have to bring it up privately with Drive because it had to be resolved if he was going to deliver a final plan tomorrow and he still hoped Drive would listen to reason.

They agreed to break while Joey was let in and prepared for his presentation. The room emptied. Everyone was hopefully running to get Marty's question answered. Joey was at one end of the room, busy, so Marty turned gently to Drive, emboldened by his show of trust earlier.

"You know, it would be a lot easier here if we made some arrangement with the ESOP people. They might be able to help us, and I wouldn't have such a miserable time negotiating the financing. It would give us a little flexibility. We can always change our minds in the end."

Drive was getting irritated. When he was angry, he was curt, "That's a dead subject." *There he goes, red like a South African lobster, except that he has claws*, thought Marty.

"Listen, we're in this together. I mean, I get the big sugar only if you win, so we're like partners, yeah! I just have to keep telling you. Something always happens. We need a little slack somewhere. We ought to give where we don't need it. My people say, don't be a *chazzar*." *Damn*, thought Marty. Twice the work, twice the risk. Joey very efficiently finished shuffling his paperwork for the third time, never looking up. It was an accurate measure of Drive's irritation that he didn't ask for his usual translation. That was lucky for everybody; he was in no mood to be called a pig by his lawyer.

The experts were back and Joey decided to tend to his client before he began to outline a press strategy. He figured a nice ass-lathering would cheer the old guy up. "Before I get started, I gotta know how many more rabbits you are going to pull out of the hat. I love those pieces you got on the nonvoting stock trustees' situation and the question of liability. Frankly, I am not modest, but I couldn't have done that. I never had a world-famous press baron as a PR client before. What next?" Nothing cheers a spirit like praise before strangers.

Drive was pleased. "If we need 'em, there are a lot of people around the world with whom we've swapped over the years. We've got a few things up our sleeve. They won't get in your way. The only thing coming up is a piece in one of the local tabloids speculating about the need for the attorney general of the state of New York to get involved here. The article picks up from the British piece and concludes that, at some point, the state of New York has a responsibility to assure that charitable status is not being abused to the detriment of the public good. They may even get some quotes."

Joey was impressed and charged ahead. "The attorney general's office. Sweet! That's great. It will fit in really well." There, now we're all friends again. He took a deep breath and saw the smile on his uncle's face. "We've got two problems. First, we have to persuade a few individuals who are rich and powerful that they want to do something they are not obligated to do and we want them to do it in a hurry," This half of the meeting was for Georgeson's benefit so Drive thought about what a clever boy that Joey was and Marty thought the kid was doing alright.

Seven minutes into his presentation, Joey passed out an elaborate schedule to everyone at the table individually, while walking around them and never pausing for a breath. "We have deliberately made a lot of mistakes. We have taken a bad situation and described it as being even worse. The numbers are almost right, but they are always worse than the real ones. I don't have to tell you, this isn't rocket science, we're trying to create a situation where the trustees can't say a thing. They have to speak up and we're giving them the perfect opportunity to correct the 'scurrilous and irresponsible articles.' Maybe they'll be tempted to say more than they should. Who can tell? We will certainly demand a press conference if they try to issue a press release, and we will be sure to have people at that press conference prepared to ask the right questions. If they don't take the bait, we've got a guy who will write the article "The Trustees Reply," setting forth the corrections that they should have made." *That kid sure can talk, and classy presentation*, thought Marty, the proud uncle. Joey knew his job. He gave Drive a gracious nod and continued.

"That's it on the attack. We start with a couple of interviews for Drive tomorrow with the *Wall Street Journal* and, a lucky break, for Bob Gwirtzman to get a last-minute exclusive into *Forbes* scheduled for next Wednesday. I've got to tell ya, we expect everybody to go crazy. Even though the $30 is 60 percent over the current market, it was selling at or near $30 three months ago. Everybody will say we're trying to steal it and we're only offering to buy 20 percent of the total equity. Drive is one of the most distinguished publishers in the world. He is the kind of person whom the Porters would've wanted to carry on with their life's work. He has made an offer, simple as that; nobody is obligated to accept it. If it looks appropriate, he will modify that offer and buy more stock, but he doesn't see why he should disturb the capital arrangements made by the Porters with their own company. If there's a problem, it is with the current management."

Finally, Joey stopped. Marty complimented him. "I like it. It sounds good. But let me tell you, once this baby is on the street, there's no telling what is going to happen. What are you doing with the television and the Web? There's tremendous opportunity with those chat rooms to create a new 'reality' for the trustees to have to react to."

"Yeah, well, we've got Drive on "Bloomberg" whenever the deal breaks."

Drive got into the act. "When are we going to make this first offer anyway?"

Marty looked a little askance, showing some wear from days and nights without sleep. "If nobody screws up, we could go close of business next Wednesday, August 12. We can, by that time, at least, button up the $600 million for the voting stock tender. But, you and I have got to spend time going over the final plan, which is due tomorrow. This will be the fastest turnaround on record. Approve the plan and execute the first step, all in ten days after the idea first came up. I love Manhattan in the summer."

"Joey, I want to be sure that you have the LENS people all prepped to write in letters to the weekly and daily print press. That creates a record for the big-foot journalists to discover." The meeting was over. Drive thanked everyone as they rose and moved away from the table. Joey collected the schedules and Drive made a point of shaking his hand. "Nice job, Joseph. Not too painful at all."

"Thanks, Drive, satisfaction guaranteed." Marty snorted audibly at that comment.

"Can we drop you?" Drive started walking to the door.

"Gee..." Joey always had somewhere to be but this was the Big Kahuna talking.

Marty pushed Joey towards Drive with his shoulder, and said, "Move it. 'Gee?' What's with this 'Gee'?" And they both followed Drive out of the room. They left the Georgeson offices, got into the waiting limo and headed for the Chrysler Building.

Marty shook his head and said, "I don't know how I ever got myself committed into moving this thing along so fast, but there seems no reason not to push. Plenty will come up to slow us down later, you can be sure. I have a couple of important things to talk with you about. Fees and expenses."

Drive was not put out. "Hey, there are always fees. In a deal of this size, they're just parsley on the fish."

Marty smiled. "Welcome to Manhattan, boss. In a deal of this kind, like impossible, you are going to need some partners."

Drive didn't understand Marty. He wasn't letting anybody in on his deal. "I have told you. No partners."

"Call it what you want. Let me introduce you to Mr. O'Neil. He'll get 1 percent of the total financing proceeds in cash at the closing."

"My God, that could be $30 million..."

Joey really hadn't understood the significance of the deal until this moment. He didn't know where to look so he just remained invisible and listened in shocked silence trying to sink deeper into the black leather interior.

"But only if the deal closes."

"Only if? Who is Mr. O'Neil?" managed Drive.

"He is the trusted friend of some top pension officers. He serviced their accounts for Bankers' Trust for years. When Bankers' couldn't understand how much he was contributing, he went into business for himself. The American Way."

"What does Mr. O'Neil do for his money, contribute to the retirement fund for Bankers' Trust executives?"

If he can joke about it, it's OK, thought Marty. "Listen, I haven't
got the time right now for the full story, so let's just say, he's a finder.
This isn't the first time you've paid a finder's fee to someone you had
to introduce to the deal, is it?"

"OK, finder's fees are acceptable graft. What next?"

"The word is that we should use Morgan for the fairness opinion."

Drive remembered Sherman's last-ditch effort for a fairness opinion and Marty was a good teacher, expensive, but good, so he didn't
cut him off.

"Every time you are dealing with trusts or people to whom you
owe a fiduciary duty, you have to get an independent person to review
the transaction and give their opinion that it is fair."

"What do they know about the deal?"

"It doesn't make any difference. Hey, they use their best judgment. They consult with whomever you have to consult with, and
prayerfully come up with this answer. I can give you cases where the
best names in commercial America gave fairness opinions to selling
shareholders, where the management was buying out all the outsiders,
that the stock was worth X amount of dollars and within a year it was
worth more than ten times that amount on the market. Fairness opinions have been the basis for a lot of the fortunes around here."

"It sounds like legalized theft to me."

"Don't knock it. It's going to make you a lot of money."

"How much do I have to pay for this extraordinary service?"

"It all comes out of the loan proceeds, so don't sweat it. We can
probably get it for under ten million."

"Jesus wept, and why, if I may ask, are we giving this business to
Morgan?"

"Good name. Gives the deal some balance, some weight, you
know, some gravitas. Just look at the 13f, the public filing required
by the SEC which shows the institutional ownership in public companies. Who are the largest shareholders? They all use the custodian

banks. We need to be sure that they have some incentive to actually tender all the shares under their control. Also, there's a lot of work that has to be done here and we want the right people to pitch in. No deal, no fee. The more people who have something riding on this, the better chance you have of pulling it off."

"I don't want to sound like your country cousin, but isn't this a classic conflict of interest? We know that these big custodial organizations have money management subsidiaries, all with AOM stock. I don't mind buying the shares you know; I just don't want any kickback."

"In the good old US of A, we believe in the Chinese wall. An organization gets its lawyers to publish a policy that solemnly decrees one department will not talk to another and everybody is cool. Look, there is something else; those guys with the pension money are getting hot for the deal. We need to put out a little more sugar."

"Why, if they want it so much, do I have to spend more money to make it attractive to them?"

Marty ignored the question. "Also, we need the arbs in the deal. The arbs bid up the price; the trustees ask their lawyers what their fiduciary duty is. If their lawyers know them well enough, they ask, 'What do you want it to be?' But it all boils down to the lawyers telling the trustees that they have an absolute obligation to maximize their beneficiary value and that they must tender, in the reality of a $30 price. That gets them off the hook."

Drive was fascinated. "Why don't we give the business to Vern? Maybe I'll get a discount."

"This is a deal that can't be done. Those trustees at AOM control the luxurious living style of half the trustees and lawyers in New York City. They can make everybody's pet charity a winner; you want money for the Central Park Conservancy? Who is your best friend? Nobody wants to get caught kicking these guys too hard. Nobody can afford to get on their shit list. We need friends.

"People need to understand that the trustees are still big men after your deal goes through. The only thing is that from now on they are trustees of a portfolio of stocks and bonds, lots of brokerage, much more secure income stream for the charities, and chance of capital growth in a market like this one. Hey, they are even bigger men. Everybody wins, but we have to get over the hurdle. Carrot and stick. The carrot, they don't lose a thing and somebody else takes over that nightmare up in Tarrytown. The stick, that's where the extra vig is needed. We got to get the arbs into this deal."

"What does that mean, if I need to know?"

"It's your money, I am your lawyer, you need to know from me, but you do not discuss this with anyone else, OK?"

Both men looked at Joey at the same time. His big eyes and sheepish smile made them both burst out laughing. Drive deadpanned, "Should we kill him?"

"No, but I know where he lives, just in case," was Marty's answer and then Joey was invisible to them again and he was relieved.

Drive picked up where they left off.

"I thought I could just borrow some money at a good time in the market and buy a mismanaged faded treasure at a good price. Is nothing simple?"

"Listen, I hate to keep making long speeches, but you are paying big bucks for the education. Nothing is simple if you want to buy something from somebody who doesn't want to sell and doesn't have to sell; arbitrageurs make money by buying in situations where they know something that gives them an edge. Now, in our deal, the edge is that you will make a second offer at a higher price for the nonvoting. They are going to the banks to borrow a ton of dough to buy AOM nonvoting. They need to know that the offer is really going to happen, then they need to know the deal is going to happen. That's where we get ours. All that greed and energy is going to be devoted to them putting pressure on the trustees. Do you have the trustees' home phone numbers, even the unlisted ones? Do you know some of the trustees have had bad habits in the past, nothing criminal you know, but not nice stuff? We wouldn't be comfortable doing anything with information like that, even if we had it, but the arbs will do anything to see that the deal goes through, they pay back the banks and they make themselves a nice bit of change in a short time with no risk. We've got to get some of your money in the system to prime that pump and to give the arbs confidence. With any luck you'll get it back.

"One of the things you need in a deal like this is class-action litigation. The arbs work with these guys. They have a tremendous record of going into court, citing statements that the managements have said in the past, and claiming that they were misled and damaged. This is a big industry now. Whether they win or lose, the company and the trustees have a nightmare when one of these guys gets involved. There are only two or three of them, like bankable Hollywood stars, and the arbs have to get them committed to this deal quickly. That takes a lot of doing, because the lawyers can't afford to get into a deal where they fail to show big results. That would kill their reputation and that would kill their income. So, somebody has to do a lot of work seeing all that works, see what I mean?"

"Yes. I have it. So, tomorrow morning, first thing, we're on for your plan and then, we go public Wednesday. Don't worry about the shareholder litigation. I have been working with Bill Pomerantz's people for several months. That bomb will drop next week."

They pulled up to Marty's stop. Marty turned to his nephew, "Kid, that's your free MBA. We're getting out now."

"Joseph, you're the best kind of company. Thanks for this morning."

"You're very welcome," Joey was clearly awestruck by his inside look at the big picture, and almost as an afterthought he added, "My office will call with your schedule." Drive opened the door for him and said, "Lovely," and shared a smile with Marty as the neophyte stepped out, stunned. Marty waited for Joey to get to the sidewalk, out of earshot.

"Don't forget, with the plan comes the bill for four big ones. A lot of that is for expenses. It has been a tough week. Just give me some notice if you're going to open up a path in the Red Sea again."

Drive held the door open for Marty, with a gracious and silencing smile, but Marty was never silenced.

"A pleasure to do business with you."

"Yeah. Likewise." Marty got out with a wave, closed the door, and the limo pulled back into traffic.

Joey turned to his uncle with a whole new world of appreciation. "Holy shit!"

Marty looked Joey in the face and said "Gee," as he started walking. "Come on, nudge, it's time to nosh. You're looking at a condemned man and this'll be my last real meal, for a while."

Vern met with his loan team in two adjoining conference rooms at Universal, seventeen of the most qualified professionals at the bank and, to a man, bone tired. Each had a secretary or assistant next to them running back and forth from the different offices and departments.

"Boss, what gives, all of a sudden everybody wants to do this deal."

Vern smiled. "I wish I could claim credit. We're witnessing genuine momentum. In this market, the chance to put a lot of money into a pretty safe deal, with a marquis manager, world reputation, and good upsides, *is* pretty attractive." He made it sound obvious, because he could take credit and they knew it.

"The pension boys want to increase the amount of the loan. They want him to take on some extra money. Maybe invest it, maybe use it to buy back stock, but they are pushing hard for us to take on more than we asked for. Technically, the deal is tight. The cash flows are OK historically, but in the last months, they have dried down to a trickle. But, if they want to give us more money, they won't have to ask twice."

"Let's get Drive on the speaker phone. Did you notice, he carries a secure phone with him all the time? I don't have that number."

"Who does?"

"Hush...Hey, Drive, Vern here. Our team and I just want you to know that it's 'all systems go' on this end. The only problem we have is the pension funds want to give you *more* money than we asked for. Can you believe it?"

"It's not the first time. With all the fees in this deal, I'm going to need it. You're worrying me. It looks like I am going to be a janitor for those pension funds. Thanks for the news."

Later that day, Drive was moving down the street talking into a cell phone, making Manhattan look like the urban hub it was. "I'm just walking up the street to the Racquet Club. Got to keep fit. The deal is going like a bomb."

"Everyone here is waiting on the latest gossip about that girl and Clinton. Men can be utterly ridiculous. We are going to have to fight for room in the media if it comes to that. What's the latest there?"

"No news is good news for us right now." Drive was feeling reproached, never quite confident in the appropriateness of their relationship. The Clinton scandal was like salt in the wound. He continued, hoping to ignore the imagined slight. "You know those pension fund guys want to stuff more money into this deal. It's like the Milkin days, the next thing you know, they'll be telling me what to buy with the money they made me borrow. This pension surplus is like nothing in the history of the world. A couple of guys can do what they want with billions. In this city at this time, that's dangerous."

"We've got some more 'news' coming out from our friends. I hope you'll be pleased."

"I hope I'm not being utterly ridiculous. You've done a brilliant job creating this deal. All these guys can't believe how smart I seem to be. I owe you."

"I wasn't referring to you. You don't owe me anything but your good health and honesty. You're not the president of the United States halting the nation with your bad judgment and bold-faced lies. Just stay fit and don't overstress yourself. Yours aren't the only shoulders, spread the weight around. We're a team, love."

"Well, here I am. Don't worry about me. I can do this, I've been doing it my whole life and if anyone should know that, it should be you. Bye for now."

"But, Drive, honey..."

But the line had gone dead.

Chapter 12
Friday, August 7, 1998

The day started in Marty's office, which was on Third Avenue only four blocks east of the Sherry Netherland. It was a working office, not a show office. You couldn't tell whether Marty spent the nights here, whether anyone ever cleaned up the papers or, indeed, whether anybody but he could ever find anything. There was vast evidence of work done and to be done and Marty started right in. Drive had never really known anyone quite like Marty and he was grateful they were on the same side.

"You want a plan today. You've got more than a plan. You've got a program in the process of being implemented. The plan itself is not complicated. We have a Bermuda corporation that will offer to buy no less than 50 percent but up to all of the Class B common shares of American Observer, the voting shares, at a price, I suggest $29. We can return to that in a minute. That makes a total price of something around $600 million. If you acquire control of AOM and are subsequently able to merge it into your Bermuda corporation, you will change the nature of the company's cash flow. Henceforth, you are not taxed in the United States on earnings outside the country except and unless you repatriate them. This increases significantly the amount of cash available to amortize debt, an important consideration to the pension fund investors.

"We have a critical element still open in the negotiations with the pension funds. They have come to really like this deal and they would give up a lot in terms of current interest rates, amortization requirements, and restrictive covenants in exchange for some convertibility. They would really like some equity in the deal. Otherwise, it is high interest rates, fast repayment, and extensive restrictive covenants with provisions for sharing profits over five years up to their target rate of

19 percent." Marty's eyebrows danced as he spoke, heightening the drama of everything he said.

"I want to keep the equity. So long as you can get me the right to prepay the loans without penalty, I will take my chances at being able to refinance one way or another and keep the entire upside." Drive felt like a broken record. This was his deal, why wouldn't Marty accept that, and give it a rest.

"Normally, there would be no thought of being able to prepay. When they are getting a locked-in return like this, they want to keep the money at work. But the market now is soft and they may not insist. If they do, what are my limits?"

"Full prepayment without penalty after three years. Before that, an initial 3 percent penalty declining 0.5 percent every six months." Drive said it by rote because these terms worked for him in the past, but on a much smaller scale.

Marty conceded. "You've thought about this. OK, that's fair enough."

"I presume that you have already bought as much as you want for yourself. I need to know the exact numbers as we have to file with the public authorities based on our offer later today."

"There are a few honest people in the world. I have made substantial purchases and the price only continues to drop. Well, it will pay some of my expenses."

Drive wondered whether Marty would ever expense some competent assistant or was he just a full-on control freak.

Marty went on. "Listen. I have taken out an insurance policy here. Too many loose ends. Nobody knows what we have to say now about the possibility of another tender; nobody knows what your filing requirements are for each class of AOM stock."

Drive chimed in, "Yeah, my own lawyers had the same questions. How do we buy insurance?"

"When you have a problem with the SEC, you hire one of those firms, with the names of defeated candidates for President, Dewey, Nixon, Davis, Wilkie, Hughes. They always hire former SEC commissioners and directors of the big divisions such as Corporate Finance. It's kind of like an alumni association. We put their name on the tender documents, pay their bill, and forget about it." *This is what you get with a $5-million lawyer,* Drive marveled. *Worth every penny, so far.*

Marty actually sat down and indicated to Drive that he should listen carefully to the nuances of the detailed plan.

"The critical moments will come next week with the firestorm of criticism. You will be accused of everything from theft to committing indecent acts on the Statue of Liberty. Remember, no matter what anybody says, we have one object and that is to persuade the trustees to sell. You will have a meeting with them personally on Wednesday at a private room in the Brook. No lawyers, just principals." Marty leaned forward for emphasis. "This meeting is the key. There is nothing to counteract a wrong reaction. No anti-venom. Let's review a careful strategy. You don't personally know any of these gentlemen. They will outnumber you so they will be dealing from a position of strength." Drive thought, *here's Marty's feet of clay—people.* If you can charm one, you can charm twenty. It's the herd mentality. Drive knew people. "They'll associate recent unpleasantness with your arrival on the scene. They are accustomed to being treated by one and all as superior human beings; they are not accustomed to the challenge of having to respond. Think entitlement. From an American's point of view, you talk like a Brit. You have a civilized old-world air about you and the story of your creating World is well known. They know that you are out of their leagues. They really don't belong at lunch with you or at the Brook for that matter. They are lucky guys, there when the music stopped for the Porters and everybody grabbed a chair. You need to communicate infinite patience and conviction that you can fulfill the Porters' mission. They should come out of the room convinced that you are determined to be their beloved partner. You can say, after the initial emotions are spent, that the trusteeship is a tragic mistake for running an active business. It is not their fault. It is nobody's fault. That's just the way it works. One needs hands-on

energy in the ownership management of communications companies."
Drive had already been through much of this strategy but he was
grateful to hear it all scripted out. His brilliant lawyer confirmed
much of what had been anticipated by Drive's home team, weeks ago.
"If possible, you want to focus on your offer being only for the voting
stock. A red herring, but it is a critical bit of bait. This is one that they
can win. You can let them publicly have the credit for persuading you
to give all the shareholders the same opportunity they have. Winning
may assuage their fundamental frustration in being maneuvered by
you into doing something they do not want to do." Marty spoke with
an air of inevitability that Drive always found persuasive.

"You're talking to the *Times* on Monday. "Bloomberg" will broadcast over the weekend. Then, in the middle of next week, Gwirtzman's piece will come out in *Forbes*. These are probably the only
communications that you will be able to spin. Everything else will be
a reaction. For the *Times*, you are one of the world leaders who has
decided to spend a great deal of time and personal resources in New
York, the capital of the world. For "Bloomberg," you are making a
serious offer to acquire stock at a price 60 percent over its close. For
Forbes, it's big boy time, AOM's a great property. The New York community is shut out from buying it. If Kravis went for it, Icahn would
be offended; if *Forbes* went for it Time Warner would be affronted; if
NBC tried then Disney would want in. As a foreigner, with an English
education and background, you are the only person with the stature,
the energy, and the vision to take on a quality property and improve
it. You have the record. This is what we want in the public mind, full
price, fair offer, the best guy in the world to preserve what is, face it,
otherwise a disaster in the making." *Yes, yes. The white knight*,
thought Drive. "Your acting gets a lot of people off the hook. A lot of
those nonvoting trustees are sweating bullets because the endowments
are incredibly important to their institutions, much too important to
suffer the decline in market value and cash flows that have characterized the last several years of AOM. The community is suffering, the
employees are beyond comfort, and the government is beginning to

understand that it may have an obligation to come in if there is no improvement.

"I can only sketch the outline for the balance of the plan. We want to appear to be persuaded by the 'good' people to extend the offer, even to increase it a tad, to all the shareholders of AOM. We need to choreograph your increasing your personal commitment, perhaps beyond reason, but that may be too much."

Marty took a breath and adjusted himself in his chair and his tone became more intimate. Drive grew wary.

"At some point, you're going to have to decide whether you trust me enough in this deal to share the colleagues who have informed and backed your plays here. There is some genius here, beyond what you personally can claim. The targeting, the timing, the nerve, absolutely world-class. You know with Clinton getting deeper into trouble every day, we may keep this whole deal off the front pages. I know what we're buying with O'Neil and with the arbs. They will take care of the politicians. Obviously, you have a myriad of contacts and I imagine that you have made arrangements to use them as necessary. I will just say once, I am paid well to do the job and I will do it, but it would be easier if I had access to all the resources at your disposal."

"I take your point. Let me think on it." But there was something about Marty that made Drive uncomfortable. He was too damn fascinating. He was funny looking, yes, but driven, with a good sense of humor, and damnably younger. He trusted him with business but with affairs of the heart, Drive was insecure. Unconsciously, something he could never admit to, a fear most profound, that Marty might be a better man. A better match for his beloved protégé.

Robert Gwirtzman, senior editor for *Forbes* magazine, is a friendly lumbering man. His office communicates a kind of chaos. The combination is most disarming, as Gwirtzman is extremely well informed and underneath the cloak of bonhomie very insightful. Drive enjoyed the compulsory tour of the Forbes family's office building on lower Fifth Avenue; the toy soldiers, the various collections all confirmed his view that publishers were a breed apart. It pleased him to see these manifestations of idiosyncrasy spread so proudly and publicly. He made a resolution to do something to relieve the tedium of his own offices.

There were no Forbeses in town, so they proceeded directly to business. Gwirtzman had agreed to hold out some last-minute space that had to be locked up by Monday evening in order to make the Thursday edition. Notwithstanding Gwirtzman's particular style, *Forbes* magazine rarely said anything uncomplimentary about advertisers or potential advertisers; a kind of professional courtesy. Drive felt that he should stress the success of his existing businesses in this interview with the hope that *Forbes* would welcome such an addition to the New York scene.

All went well until Gwirtzman asked, "Who is doing the buying? You or World Publications?" *It had to start, let it start now*, thought Drive. *We really don't have much time.*

"Actually, I will be making this acquisition on my own. At age sixty-seven, my contractual responsibilities have been reduced and I am anxious to bring along the next generation of executives. I have three kids in the business, you know. Also, frankly I think that I can personally do something here and I am looking forward to the challenge."

Gwirtzman detected a new slant for the story. "Is it fair to say that mere mortals live only once, but that Drive is going to go around the track a second time?"

"I do not consider myself a geriatric case study if that's your slant. Like a lot of company builders, I find myself in a position where conventional retirement really isn't appealing and I have to find a way to channel my energies for my family and my existing businesses."

Gwirtzman smelled a rat. That was just a little too pat. "If you don't want to retire, you don't have to retire. You *are* World Publications. Legally, you control the voting stock. You don't have the AIG problem where the great man's sons decided to leave, or do you?"

"No, nothing like that."

Gwirtzman didn't press the point any further, but made a mental note to revisit that question in the days to come. He already had his story and there were absolute space limitations due to the printing deadlines, so he left it alone.

Drive rode home in a cab, shoes off, rubbing his feet. He decided to check in and get it out of the way. "Our boy isn't bad. He's figured out that there *is* a you in this deal. He asked me straight on to share you with him."

"What do you think? We could be the perfect team."

Drive was stung. He thought *they* were the perfect team; a secret to the world and under everyone's noses. It was childish, he knew it, but it hurt all the same.

"I hate to share you with anyone. This guy is as straight as they come and really smart. I'm glad he's on the team. It seems stupid not to put all of our resources where they will help us the most."

"I'm only another resource?" There was no response so she confessed, "I'm kidding, my prince. Decide soon before we get too far along. A girl gets lonely in her ivory tower."

Chapter 13
Saturday, August 8, 1998

The bank's limousine picked up Drive and Vern early and arrived at Teterboro right at 7:30 a.m. Horse had driven to the airport directly from home on the other side of the Hudson River. The beginnings of the day were surprisingly cool. There were no clouds in the sky and the air was dry. The big car drove right onto the taxiway and discharged its passengers at the steps of the modest GII, where Horse was standing awaiting their arrival. Introductions were made all around and then they started the journey that would take them to Hanscom field in Lexington, Massachusetts, where another limo would pick them up for the half-hour drive, a helicopter was too noisy and pretentious, to The Country Club in Brookline.

Only sheltered international corporate executives could contemplate scheduling a private golf game on five days notice at one of the premier clubs in the country on a Saturday afternoon in the middle of the summer. Drive felt giddy as a schoolboy and ignored his morning papers like so much homework. It would be a perfect day of golf. Usually club tournaments would claim every minute of daylight to complete the elimination rituals of the multiflite competitions. This outing was meant to happen. At TCC, as The Country Club is sometimes referred to, most of the members went away in August to vacation homes and, accordingly, the club was not too busy. Beyond that, extensive renovations were in progress to prepare the grounds for the Ryder Cup tournament in a year's time. There was always a war between those members who wanted to play and the groundskeepers and financial types who wanted to keep the turf safe for the tournament and the club's reputation, to say nothing of the enormous bonanza that such a tournament means for the club's finances. As the date of the tournament got closer, play would be severely curtailed, but Vern, based on his many years' relationship with the club pro, had easily arranged a good starting time and the company of one of the younger pros as a playing partner for Drive.

Vern was always excited when his company jet took off and he was particularly pleased in contemplation of a day at the club where he had learned the sport so many years ago. He paid a lot of attention to his golf and always had the latest in playing paraphernalia. It was virtually an obsession. So today, he counted on picking up the Callaway Big Bertha E.R.C. II, the most recent addition to the technological innovations that have given much greater length to the ball-carrying capacity of golfers. This particular club was very controversial. The U.S.P.G.A., in an utterly unprecedented challenge to the commercial free market instincts of its members, declared the club to be illegal for tournament use with all kinds of sanctions threatened against anyone or any club that ignored this diktat. Arnold Palmer endorsed it. Vern was exactly the person whom the manufacturers had in mind, a little more length off the tee. The trouble is that this new factor has ruinously altered the careful geography of the traditional golf courses. Even the famed Masters course in Augusta, laid out by Bobby Jones and sanctified by three-quarters of a century of the best players in the world, had to be changed to accommodate the vastly increased length off the tee, attributable to clubs and balls of new materials.

The Country Club insists on continuing with the diminutive as part of its proper name because it was, in fact, *the* first such organization in the United States. The golf course was the site for the famous U.S. Open in 1913, when the local caddy Francis Ouimet, one of the handful of honorary members in the club's history, defeated the famed British professionals, Vardon and Ray. The course is short and tight. Actually, the championship course is an amalgam of the two club courses, the basic eighteen and the Primrose nine. When Jack Nicklaus was just at the beginning of his remarkable career, as the reigning U.S. Open champion in 1962, he played a practice round at TCC, where the next year's championship would be held. At that time, he was among the longest hitters in golf. The course did not suit his style. Indeed, he failed to make the cut in the 1963 championships, which ended in a three-way tie with the winners scoring over 300, an unimaginable total in modern times. Even though Arnold Palmer tied for the four rounds' lead, he never played Primrose 1 to Primrose 2's green in less than seven strokes. However, Vern was going to need a lot more than a fancy new driver to make his length off the tee a threat to the integrity of the course.

Golfers feel that one can tell a great deal about a person from their choice of equipment. Horse carried his rather modest bag onto the plane and stowed it in the rear of the cabin. These were the same clubs that he had earned as a professional during his time at Williams College. He knew all about the new equipment. It had nothing to do with his feelings about golf. Golf was a gift of nature, a walk in the field. Swinging a club and following the ball's trajectory was as natural for Horse as skipping stones on the flat surface of a pond or throwing a baseball. When people asked him if he minded being out-driven by players who lacked his skill, he seemed not to understand what they were talking about. Golf was a personal thing, a private pleasure. What other people did was their business. Much like the old Scots, Horse understood what was right, what was the right club for a hole. The human characteristics that emerged from dissecting Horse's golf equipment were the peace within him and the capacity to enjoy the pleasure of simple things.

Drive understood this immediately. As a collector of talented human beings, he looked forward to learning more about Horse. After the three of them were seated in the comfortable Pullman chairs, and the plane had achieved its cruising altitude, a steward passed around incredibly fresh croissants and French roast coffee. Drive had to say it, "I cannot imagine what someone with the taste for those golf clubs is doing working in Vern's bank." Vern, ever nervous, missed the point, "Wait till you see him swing 'em and then you'll get the message." Drive, himself one of a few foreign members of the Augusta National Golf Club, simply left it to the resident pro to make sure he had the best set of golf clubs available each year. They lacked the fetishistic character of Vern's clubs, no big Berthas for Drive, but he wasn't giving anything away in terms of having equipment that could help his game.

The match would be Vern and Horse against Drive and the pro, with full handicaps. That meant that they would play with Vern and Drive getting extra strokes on the six hardest holes. Arriving at this result consumed all of the flight and most of the driving time to TCC. It's a part of the modern game of business executives' playing golf, that everyone's handicap is suspect. Vern had actually made some calls to check out Drive's recent play. His six seemed reasonable; Vern had a six at his local club in Long Island, but no one appreciated that having learned the game at TCC was probably worth a couple of extra strokes to him. Somehow everybody missed the fact that Drive not only knew the course, he was a member of the club. Horse was a scratch player and so, they assumed, was the club pro. This is where Horse's old equipment becomes a factor. He could expect to play from tee to green in regulation figures, but the pro would always outdrive him and would be able to play to the green with a more steeply pitched club and could get his ball closer to the hole. Over the course of eighteen holes, he would probably be able to putt for a birdie more often than Horse. There didn't seem any solution to that problem, so they went on to the terms of the match. All of a sudden this seemed pretty serious. Drive said, "I really like a man who is willing to compete on every hole." When all was said and done, he was the customer and the customer is always right. So the decision was for match play, that means who won the holes, in contrast to medal, who got the lowest score. Even normally sane mature men like Vern and Drive really got into all the details; this rite was an essential commercial bonding experience.

Driving through the main gates of TCC is a thrilling experience. The driveway crosses the fifteenth fairway, but too far away for anybody, except Tiger Woods with a Big Bertha, to do serious harm to a car. On this day in August, the air was still, the sky was clear, and the place was deserted. All kinds of earth-moving equipment dotted the landscape, evidence of the cosmetic cleaning up for next year's Ryder

Cup and a worldwide TV audience. Drive owned the rights to it in seven different markets. The course was remarkably green. Usually, at this time of year, even with heavy sprinkling, the feeling was of dry grass and burned-over roughs. The limo dropped them off at the clubhouse, where they changed into game clothes and put on their cleats. They all took some practice swings, tried a few out of the practice sand trap, some putts and they were ready to go.

The first hole is always important. It creates an impression both in the player's mind and in the minds of the other players. Vern and Drive bantered around a bit and finally Drive was given the honor in view of his age. Drive had a simple compact swing that bespoke a lifetime of playing good club golf. He would never win a lot of tournaments, but he would never lose a lot of money. He would be straight, not too long, and probably very skillful with the putter. Vern would never look like anything other than what he was. If he had known, he probably would have given up the game. Every motion, every movement of the club, advertised someone who has learned the game as an adult, an excellent student with no natural talent. Watching Vern swing was like watching a drunk walking home along the sidewalk. You were relieved when he made it. However, never let it be said that Vern did not get his money's worth. The ball went down the fairway. The problem with Vern's scoring is that every so often he would strike the ball in a way that would produce an unimaginable result. He didn't miss by a little bit; it was as if he were playing a different sport. The ball could go straight up in the air, it could go behind him. Keeping his game together was an obvious strain for Vern, but he was used to strain. The pro was just that, a pro. He hit an easy drive that bounced almost three hundred yards down the fairway. The showstopper was Horse. At his six feet six and with long arms, his natural swing had a huge trajectory. As he approached the ball and took a full practice swing, even the pro stopped to acknowledge that he was in the presence of something quite unusual. Horse, that underemployed gawky bank underling, was a magician with a golf club in his hand. He played without a glove as if to emphasize the fusion of his body with the shaft. His body coordination was so perfect that you felt like applauding every shot. His play more closely resembled ballet than hitting a stationary object. Horse striking the ball was an object of wonder, and so it went on, hole after hole.

The pro would hit it out three hundred yards; Horse was out two hundred and fifty. The pro would hit a nine or eight iron right at the flag with plenty of backspin, leaving relatively short birdie putts; Horse would hit a longer iron and would be on the green but further away. Gradually, Drive and Vern eroded into irrelevancy. The careful guarding of strokes that supported their optimistic handicaps simply faded away in the presence of the superb golf of their partners. Horse got a rare birdie three on three to give his side a genuine one-stroke lead. Quickly though the pro got back one with a birdie on four and another with a birdie on five. Both the pro and Horse got birdies on six. An elderly female club member had advised Jack Nicklaus in 1962, when he failed with repeated shots to the par-three seventh, that he should play it short. America's longest hitter had never thought of that as a viable strategy for par threes. Drive actually put his tee shot three feet from the hole and sank his putt. Nobody could match this birdie. So two up for Drive and the pro.

The eighth was very mean. Nobody was on the fairway with his drive. Horse was right up against a tree, having pulled his drive into a lie where a right-handed shot was impossible. He took out his wedge, inverted it so that the blade headed straight down and stroked it cleanly, left-handed, so that it landed five feet from the hole. Vern was so upset that he forgot that it was his partner's shot. His grasp of the game required a literal understanding of all of the rules and Horse's shot wasn't in any of the books he had read. Vern asked the pro in a loud voice whether such a shot was legal. The pro slipped and said simply, "They don't teach that kind of shot in school." So Horse sank the putt for a birdie, got one hole back, and they were one down looking into the Himalayas, the first of the par fives. The pro simply tore the cover off the ball and was within an easy iron shot of the green for a gimme birdie, a likely eagle, and a possible double eagle. Even Vern, with the super metal of his new driver, was near the green in two. Drive earned his handicap by dribbling off into the water and was never in the hole. Horse hit a superb drive two hundred and seventy-five yards and then a three wood, which would have warmed the heart of Bobby Jones, to be on the green in two, within thirteen feet to the cup. The pro hit one of those shots that separate the pros from the rest of the field. His eight iron landed nine feet beyond the cup and then the backspin brought it back so precisely, it raised the possibility of a double eagle. He tapped in for a three and Horse missed the eagle putt. So down two and on to the back nine.

Much of the appeal of golf to businessmen is the opportunity to talk business. Somewhere between the fourth and the ninth holes, when they were out of the serious competition, Drive and Vern found themselves walking together down the fairway. Vern raised the question, "You know, I really need to have you take over as chairman of my foreign advisory board. No heavy lifting. Two meetings a year. One in New York, the other at some attractive foreign city. We'll send our jet for you or pay you for coming in your own. We want to send the signal that we're in the first rank. You can do that for us." *Damn it*, thought Drive, *the piper must be paid.*

"You know we've done business with Citicorp since old Stillman Rockefeller was CEO and I was a kid. Sandy Weill has asked me to be on their advisory board and I've turned it down every time."

Vernon Stillman was probably the first banker to ever voluntarily go out on a limb for Drive. It was appreciated. "I don't mind telling you, I've had to call in some serious favors to get the financing for you on this deal, so I don't mind asking you to do this for me."

"You're right, but it's going to raise hell with my own folks. You've agreed not to require my personal time in AOM, so, OK, I'll do this."

"There was no way that you could do this deal the way you want to, in your own name, without recourse, without leaving a few corpses on the battlefield."

What is it with Southerners and battlefields? Drive was starting to feel a little tired. *We're playing golf; I don't need to hear about corpses now.* And so he said with some heat, "Some eggs must be broken. When would we announce this?"

Vern felt the old man's fatigue and stopped to let him catch his breath by pretending to drop his ball. "Sorry," he chased it a few feet, clumsily. This was the real game, and he was winning, "No great hurry. After the deal is done, sometime this fall should be time enough." He grabbed the ball and straightened up, smiling.

The conversation then turned in a direction that is very rare for top people. Usually they have subordinates who protect them, who preserve their deniability, but Drive was genuinely upset.

"What is it with these goddamned fees? I don't mind paying for my money but these intermediaries with the pension funds are something else. I have never seen such greed."

"What do you object to?"

"Well, I don't mind paying this guy O'Neil 1 percent because I understand, a competitive price to get this money quickly and on my terms. I do not like being asked to risk now another 1 percent with the arbs, whatever the hell they are."

Vern started them walking again, a little slower than before. "I know what you mean. You have a very, very tough sell here. The trustees can turn you down. You *are* trying to change the laws of gravity, my friend. The money becomes its own energy. They can all smell the fast buck, but they won't make nickel one unless the deal goes through. Insurance. These guys are going to make sure your deal happens. They are going to make the trustees understand that this is a proposition they can't afford to turn down."

"How are they going to do that?"

"You don't really want an answer to that question. You never asked it and we never mentioned arbs."

Drive wondered just how much more venal business had become since he last spent some time in the trenches. Flying the plane is very different from getting one off the ground and now the ground, in recent decades, has grown dark, and truly evil.

"You're right, old man. I'm a little out of my element."

"And out of mine too, I hasten to add. We've now gotten into the area where the enormity of the fees is going to drive this deal, whatever we may want."

The eleventh hole, Arnold Palmer's nightmare in 1963, was the first place where the pro lost his touch. Like the immortal Arnold, he was in the trees on the left from his drive and two shots later, he was still there. Horse went out straight, across the water with a beautiful long iron and the margin was down to one. Twelve was impossible for someone playing the course for the first time, because the green was small and blind. No matter where the drive went, you couldn't see the green. It was behind a hill, so the distances on the card were deceptive. Horse climbed the hill before taking his second shot. He was glad that he did, because the shot was in fact a lot shorter than it looked. He was on in two and had a rare birdie putt for the hole and to halve the match.

Horse really needed to talk with Vern. It looked like Drive and Vern were done chatting, drifting apart. He caught up with him walking down the fairway next to the pond.

"I really need to talk with you about the situation at AOM. We need to deal with their request for financing."

Finally, as the British would say, the penny dropped. Vern understood that he was working on one deal for AOM and Horse was working on another. A chill shot through him. The probability was that the two efforts were incompatible. He did not want to share this insight with Horse right then and there. He simply couldn't believe that anything the trust department was doing could possibly have an impact on his big deal but it almost ruined his game to consider the alternatives.

"Why certainly, we'll definitely get together at the beginning of the week. Yes, son, you've got yourself that meeting, at last. I've been hoping to squeeze you in sooner but we've been going like a house on fire. Not your typical August, that's for sure."

"Great. I appreciate your time. It's important."

Horse wondered why it took a game of golf to get a meeting with his own employer, but then golf was magic and Horse would never question that.

No blood on thirteen. Fourteen, the second par five, was the pro all the way. Horse couldn't make his birdie putt. The pro tapped in his and so one up, going across the road on to fifteen. Routine fours and then the par-three sixteenth. Both Drive and Vern were on the green with their tee shots and, mirabile dictu, they both sank their putts, to redeem their honor and bragging rights for the next umpteen years. Seventeen was the surprise crescendo. With handicap strokes counted, all of the players were on the green in regulation. The problem was that the hole was in the bottom shelf of the treacherous two-level green, hiding right behind the Vardon Bunker, where the English professional had lost the championship some three-quarters of a century ago. Only Horse had gone for the hole and he had a level eight-foot putt for birdie. Vern putted first. Even with the utmost care, the putt got away from him, picking up speed as it went careening off of the green and into the Vardon trap. Drive was warned. He hit it more gently. His ball only went off the green on to the light rough some twenty feet from the pin. The pro, exasperated because he had been shown up by Horse's skill in making the correct approach shot, read the green perfectly for the double break and had to watch his ball roll right over the cup at about three times the speed that could have let it drop. Fifteen feet away. All played the next putt and the next. Horse had two shots for the hole. He made the birdie.

Drive had taken the opportunity to talk with Horse as they walked down the fairway on seventeen. Vern quickly joined them, worried his prize customer not be bored by a mere employee or worse, a fanatic. Drive waved him off. Vern was a little crushed for a moment, and fell back behind them.

"Playing like this, you should be chairman of the bank." And that was not an old man's flattering but an observation based on a lifetime's experience.

"I like what I do now."

"Tell me about your job."

"I am in charge of the employee benefit plan investments. We have major positions in most of the large American companies and I am working with the investor/employees to develop an ownership culture. It's very exciting. Frankly, the reason why a company like yours is successful is because it's run by owners. The modern American corporation with the split between management and ownership produces an inferior product. I'm really enthusiastic about employee involvement giving us better companies."

Drive was skeptical, "It certainly seems sound. How does that work?"

Horse was on a roll. He never spoke much and he never spoke at all in these customer golf situations. But Drive seemed genuinely curious and the sheer joy of playing wonderful golf on this, the queen of golf courses, opened his mouth. "It's simple. The top management has to be accountable to someone real, someone who knows the company and has a stake, and won't accept stupid answers. The same with a private company like yours. The genius of America has always been based on respect for each individual's talent and their effective organization in the project, whether it is writing the Constitution, waging a war, or transacting business."

Quite the patriot, marveled Drive. "That's quite a statement, mate. Do the CEOs of this country know what's happening?"

"I haven't thought about that much. I've been too busy getting something healthy and productive going with all of these companies."

"Off the record, we're friends here. Give me an example of a company you are working with right now." Drive envied the younger man's passion and caught a glimmer of something he never had and never would; selflessness, that patriotism, something intangible to Drive.

"Well, confidentially, we're pretty far along at the *American Observer* magazine ESOP with a scheme for the employees to increase their percentage ownership up to 50 percent." Drive was thunderstruck. He stopped walking and looked Horse in the eyes, nothing, no recognition, no giveaway reaction. He immediately thought that Vern was playing some sort of game. Fortunately this conversation took place on the seventeenth fairway or the game would never have finished. Drive kept his peace, and began walking and listened carefully to the excited Horse share his passion. There were serious problems to be dealt with. Horse had no idea.

All even at eighteen. Anticlimax. The pro's massive drive and nine iron to three feet could not be matched and Drive had the victory, on the golf course. He extracted payment in full by choosing a case of a legendary South African Stellenzicht Syrah 1994 red. Simply making Vern find it would be reward enough.

Flying home with a couple of drinks, Horse suddenly realized that on one of the great competition golf courses in the world he had played virtually a perfect round, no bogies and six birdies for a 66. It was one of those unique moments when all of the joy that golf had brought him since childhood was suffused in the pleasure of the moment. Drive and Vern were deep into the details of the Universal Bank's Foreign Advisory Board and were swapping Rolodexes to determine who they could get and who would bring them the most prestige.

Drive got to the point. "You know, Vern, we're all alike. All these guys, no matter how rich, want to feel special. They want something nobody else has got. You should offer a compensation plan based on stock options in some tax haven like Bermuda. My guys can help you with that. We use different accounting and tax systems in countries around the world. You'd be amazed. If we offer something unusual and special, you'll get everybody." Vern wrote that down in his omnipresent notebook. "I am an accountant by training and I always appreciate a bit of extra imagination. Thanks, chairman, you can count on it."

There were fresh copies of the *Times* by every seat and Drive was tired of eager, pushy Vern. He had certainly gotten his money's worth out of Vern this day. Drive picked up a paper for the first time all day, hoping to be left in peace. But it was not to be.

"Bloody bastards," Drive's outburst frightened everyone on the plane. He realized he had accidentally demanded everyone's attention and so he held the headline up for them to see. BOMBS RIP APART 2 U.S. EMBASSIES IN AFRICA; SCORES KILLED; NO FIRM MOTIVE OR SUSPECTS. NAIROBI, Kenya, August 7—"Two powerful bombs exploded minutes apart outside the United States Embassies in Kenya and Tanzania this morning, killing at least 80 people, 8 of them Americans, in what officials said were coordinated terrorist attacks."

"The world is a messy place." Vern felt he had to respond for Drive's sake but it was so far away. These things happen all the time. There was no point in letting it ruin their day, but the remaining flight was somber as everyone read his own copy of the paper.

The sun had set for all but the topmost floors of the city. Red and orange highlights against the cloudless sky, and below, the dim city prematurely had started to turn her lights on. Drive, blind to the spectacular view, was back on his balcony at the Sherry Netherland, on his cell, an informal dinner party going on inside without him.

"Hey, Moffie. Did I get you on your cell phone? This is Drive." Drive really needed to know that people on his payroll were there waiting for him, all the time. "Listen, I need to know about a guy named Charles Bowditch who works for Universal. He's their employee benefits guy and they are doing something with AOM. We need some face to face time early in the week. You've got to educate me about the arbs."

Drive was so eager to get to his next call; he didn't realize he'd hung up on Moffie. He'd been waiting to make this call ever since he left the plane.

He started out, directly. "Hey. He's got me running his advisory board. That's going to raise hell."

"Fair's fair. So long as he comes through on his end." She was ever practical.

"Did I tell you about this guy from the bank? He played the best golf of anybody I've ever seen with old clubs. Even the pros were watching him. He works with employee benefit plans and said that he was doing a lot with AOM. He has no idea."

"Vern has got himself quite the oversized octopus. How embarrassing. What did Vern say?"

"Didn't bring it up. We need to get a little more information before I take him to task for it. This golfer is quite the zealot. Dangerously persuasive."

"Do you know anything about him other than his golf swing?"

"No...good idea. I have already put Moffie on to it. Say, what do arbs have to do with this deal?"

"If they get committed to the deal happening, they'll raise heaven and earth. We should be so lucky."

"I'm not sure any more that it's a matter of luck. Things have changed, changed for the worse. Everything is an act of terrorism or cowardice. Craven and mean. No one wants to fight a fair fight."

"Shh...shh, you're just tired, my sweet."

"Yes, I suppose I am, but I can't help but worry about these changes I've noticed in the world. You're far too young to understand, I have seen and known a very different world from this one and I believe that something has been lost."

"I *am* young, that's true but, Drive, you're not responsible for the world. Just your own actions. Let's get this deal done, build a future, and leave the world to fend for itself.

"You have a point. It's late. They're waiting for me inside. Good night."

"Good night, Drive."

But Drive did not go inside for quite awhile. The sky had grown dark and the streets were bright with lights. He wondered how many years he had left until he wouldn't be able to see those lights anymore. In the biggest city in the world, ten feet from people he has known for years, he felt very much alone.

Chapter 14

Drive was particularly pleased with the quality of the gardenia he'd bought from the sidewalk vendor outside the entrance to the Chrysler Building. It pleased him to be able to thread its stem through the hole in his lapel and in back of the restraining cord thoughtfully placed there by the best of London tailors. There were compensations to working in the city in the summer, cool in the morning and much less crowded. No one else in the elevator and a beautiful morning light through the entrance hall made him feel utterly gratified about the decision to own this property. A day off, lazing with his wife after the golf on Saturday, had made for the perfect weekend, particularly in light of what looked to be the most significant week of his life. Questioning the significance of his own life was best left for another time.

His longtime secretary was still on holiday so a temp had just stacked all of his messages on his desk. There seemed to be a lot of them, and it had been rather quiet since he'd been here. He pulled out his chair and glanced at the top message, in huge scrawling print, "CALL IMMEDIATELY, Scott Moffie." As he dialed the number, he looked down at twenty-five prior messages from Scott.

"Hey, mate, what's up?"

"You sure know how to pick 'em is all I can say."

Too early for drama. Drive felt his peaceful morning evaporate around him.

"Do you want to tell me what you have found out or are we going to play guessing games?"

"I think for this, maybe, I had better come over."

Nothing could be this important. "Listen, I am always glad to see you, but I have a whole agenda today. Can you give me some idea over the phone?"

"How did you happen to get to know this guy, Charles Hill Bowditch IV, anyway?"

"I was playing golf with him on Saturday. Vern brought him along as a partner. The guy is one of the most beautiful golfers I have ever seen. He played 66 on his own ball on the Ryder Cup course with thirty-year-old clubs. Even the pros were applauding him."

Moffie asked, "Why did you call me on a nice Saturday evening in the summertime and ask me to find out all about this guy?"

This is the last question you'll get from me, Mr. Moffie. For a moment, Drive wanted to go back outside and not come in at all. "He told me that he was the guy in the trust company that they own in charge of employee benefit trusts. The more I asked him about it, the more enthusiastic he became. I didn't know what he was talking about and was just making conversation. This guy loved what he did and was very committed. Anybody who can play golf like he does, you want to be sure he is going the same way you are."

Moffie interrupted, "Wait a minute. I missed something in this conversation. What about what he does? What's that got to do with you?"

The thought of the passionate Horse rallied Drive's spirit and he explained, "I asked him for an example of what he did and he began to tell me about this group of employees who had a 20-percent stake in their company. The company had been doing very badly and they had just gotten their act together and were going to do something about it. I don't know how it happened, but it came out it's the same company I am buying this week, the American Observer!"

"Oh, my God. Look, Sunday I couldn't find out too much, other than he has never been one of the top people in that bank. But, I found out two things that just about blew my mind. Number one: This guy is an authentic war hero. He is one of the only guys in America who came through the Vietnam experience cleaner than he went in. He won every medal. He personally persuaded General Westmoreland to let him stay in the front lines and continue to lead his company on patrols. My God, people would pay millions to avoid getting anywhere near that. I ran down a guy who was there the day that Westmoreland came in, he told me what happened. Do you remember that scene in that movie about the bridge on the River Kwai when the uptight British colonel is let out of the hot box and the whole camp just goes berserk? They jumped, shrieked, hollered, and screamed till they were hoarse. That's what happened to this guy. Nobody knows he's a bona fide hero, like a Gary Cooper character or something. Your instinct is right. This is a serious person and we've got to find out immediately what he is doing."

"Well, that's one to start Monday morning with. The good news is that we're going for the company; the bad news is that Napoléon Bonaparte is leading the opposition."

"Wait a minute. We don't know anything yet. It'll take me a day or so to get fully informed."

"I had better get on to Vern in a hurry about this. He is..."

Moffie cut him off. "Look, that's the other thing that I found out."

"What do you mean?" Drive was up to speed now. Ready to go. He always liked it when he knew the competition, a face to visualize. This was real sport.

"How well do you know Vern? Like do you know his wife, his kids? Are you social friends or is this just a business thing?"

Drive admitted, "I don't know him very well. We've had dinner a number of times with his wife. I didn't even know he had kids until you told me. Look, it's like everything else, we know enough about each other to maximize the value of the relationship."

"I told you that he was first married to a goddess, right?"

"Right."

"Well, it so happens that at just about the time that she gave Vern his walking papers, she was, as they say, intimate with...Charles Hill Bowditch IV, who is known by his friends, for good and sufficient reason I am told, as Horse. It didn't last. They're both happily married, and remain close friends."

Drive exploded, "Christ on a bicycle. Does Vern know this?" The last thing Drive wanted was a distracted banker. This soap-opera crap could ruin everything.

"I have no way of knowing, but the strong impression is negative."

"Hell! How did you find out in two nights and a day what he doesn't know?"

"I got lucky. I looked up our friend Horse and it seems he belongs to every association having to do with employee benefit plans in the world and is president of most of them. I have a friend who is a lawyer in the ERISA field, so I called her. You know, summer weekend, unwinding, she may have had a few pops, she said, 'You called me to ask about Horse?' I said, 'Yes, that's about the size of it.' Long silence. 'What do you want to know?' By this time, I wonder if I am in cuckoo land, all I am trying to do is find out about some low-level bank officer and this lady, known to me as not only sane, but beautiful and charming, is treating me as if I have asked for the combination to her chastity belt. All I can do is hold on. She says, 'You'll have to hold on for a minute until I get to another phone.' What do I do? I hold on. Five minutes, she's on the line and very straight and clear. It turns out that our boy Charles was for many years, although not lately, a real stud. That horse business is for real. Apparently, my informant was involved with Charles. After about half an hour, when we got out from under who had ditched who, it turns out, my lucky night, that the lady was present at a certain professional association reception a few years back when something happened to startle the usually cooler than cool Mrs. Stillman. The lady seemed in a state of shock when who else but the Horse comes up, takes her by the arm, leads her out the door to the elevator, and they are not seen again that day or the next." Drive was intrigued about what made Horse tick. Everybody's got his or her price, what would his be? It couldn't be women, could it? "Now normally, I would discount a lot of this, but, in light of the abrupt end to the Stillman marriage, and the unusual interest of my lady in the sexual possibilities of her former lover, it rings true. She wanted to talk. Everything seemed to click. I knew it would be important."

"You are so right. Thank you for an extraordinary piece of work. This is really helpful."

"Do you want me to keep digging on Bowditch and the former Mrs. Stillman?"

"Dig, Dig, Dig!" said Drive like he was waking up at last. "Wait a minute. Didn't you tell me that she has some federal job now? What is it?"

"Don't know. I'll find out."

"I just gotta tell you. It turns out that our friend Horse was bopping the former Mrs. Stillman and good ole sensitive Vern hasn't a clue. And, Horse, that's the golfer's nickname, is some kind of war hero, so he better be on our side."

"When the boy-girl thing gets involved, everybody starts to behave in stupid ways. I think I'd better not be in direct communication with Marty until something really critical happens."

"You're great. Well, I'm off to see Vern. We'll clear the air and keep on track."

"Good luck! I don't envy you your mission."

Within ten minutes, while washing his hands in his private bath, he saw himself in the mirror and Drive wondered why he didn't pick up the gratuitous mention of Marty.

Bankers' hours are getting earlier every year, thought Vern, as he reached for a phone call his secretary had put through. *It must be important*, thought Vern. Straight on, it was Drive. "Vern, I need a minute with you. Can I come right over?"

"Sure, you know what kind of day it is going to be and you know why, but, what the hell, it's all on account of you, so, brother, come on over."

"Do you have an office or a spare room where we could be sure of some privacy and not be interrupted?"

"No problem, I have a sanctum. Just walk on over here. My secretary will meet you at the elevator and lead you to me."

During the entire limo ride, Drive relived every moment he had spent in Vern's company. He was certain that Stillman was made of the right stuff and would keep sight of their higher purpose. The secretary met him at the curb. Less than a minute and he and Vern were face to face.

Drive recounted the story of his brief conversation with Horse during the golf game and his concern that this highly competent man might not be headed in the same direction. Vern listened, irritated at Horse for mentioning anything about a client to a stranger, but increasingly concerned that he had frustrated Horse's efforts to talk with him for weeks. *I'll set that straight in a hurry*, he thought.

Giving his most winning smile to Drive he said, "Oh, don't be concerned, we're all one team here and Horse is a team player. There will be no difficulty. If that's all you're worried about, thank God, because this is going to be the week to end all weeks."

Drive sat down, in one of the two overstuffed leather sofas in the tiny room. Vern sat, too, relieved that the fire was out, or at least contained. "Vern, listen we've been good business friends. I like you. People like us, we don't have many *real* friends, we have business relationships. I've come across some information that I feel you need to know. It's none of my business, but it may become important to what we're trying to do."

"Drive, I really appreciate this. If there's something I need to know, I would be grateful for your telling me." Vern thought of every fiscal vulnerability his new deal with Drive exposed him to. Nothing career threatening but Drive was in a state, for sure. Vern, looking back on that awkward moment, had no idea what he was anticipating, but he wasn't anticipating what he got.

"Your first wife was Molly, correct?"

"What about Molly?" Where is this going? Vern felt off center.

"She has a job in the federal government. What is the job?"

"Oh, I don't know. One of those assistant secretaryships that get handed around to political friends."

"You really don't know?"

"I think she is an assistant secretary of Labor in charge of one of the agencies. Why?" Vern thought Drive looked like he had eaten a sour pickle.

"Vern, look, I'm sorry that something like this has to come up in our relationship, but I guess I feel I am doing the right thing. I don't know how to say this but I am told that Charles Bowditch, our golfing buddy, the Horse, was, in times past, intimate with your former wife."

A look of such horror passed over Vern's face that Drive, utterly out of character, got up, sat down next to him, and put his arm on his shoulder. Vern had been so consumed with guilt about his own stupid infidelities that the thought of the perfect Molly being with anybody else had never crossed his mind. And now that it did, he didn't like it. A shudder passed through his body as the memory of Horse in The Country Club shower, only two days prior, passed through his mind. Even now, he was embarrassed by his prurience, but you didn't have to be prurient to notice the Horse, you just had to not be blind.

Vern was not known for social sensitivity and had never been thought approachable on a personal basis. Drive was a little more experienced, so these two leaders of commerce just sat in the misery of not having any idea what to say to each other for a time longer than either would care to remember. Neither of them had any sense of how to end the misery.

Vern recovered, "Thanks, Drive. I think I'd better find out about Molly's job."

Horse came directly from home to the Tarrytown Conference Center of the *American Observer*'s headquarters with the vague hope that after a morning's work, he would be able to drive home for an afternoon of golf with his nine- and ten-year-old sons. With their mother having been a tennis professional, he was going to have to devote some extra energy to get those boys started right with golf. He was dressed casually in a sports coat, striped shirt, white and cerulean blue and open at the neck, khaki slacks, and loafers. As he got out of his car to head into the Center, he became aware that he was part of a large stream of people. Within the hall, there was a kind of stage with three or four seats on it, a podium, and fixed sitting space in elevated tiers with space for 250 people. Even though he was fifteen minutes early for what he thought was the beginning time for the meeting, Horse had that strange feeling that he was already late. The employees had come into their own and the place had been given a significant upgrade. It had to be a sizeable volunteer effort because, as Horse knew well, there were no funds.

He went up onto the newly decorated stage and spoke briefly with the committee members and sat down. There was a palpable sense of apprehension in the room that abated only when the chairman stood up to speak.

"We welcome all of the members of the American Observer Employee Stock Option Plan to this unusual meeting. A year ago, you elected me and your three colleagues, here with me on the podium, to constitute the ESOP committee and we have worked with Charles Bowditch, whom we all know as Horse, to prepare a plan for action in accordance with your instructions. This morning, we will report our progress to you. We will make a specific recommendation and we will ask for your support in a vote that will be formal and recorded.

"We all understand that much of what we're doing today has not been done before. We originally wanted to have a public vote, but to forestall any notion that any action was taken by this group pursuant to coercion, we decided to use the traditional secret ballot procedure. When the time comes for a vote, I'll ask you to stand up row by row as indicated by one of the wardens whom you can recognize from their blue uniforms, and to proceed to the teller's desk. There you'll be asked your name, which will be checked off against the official members' list, and you'll be given a ballot. You can proceed to the curtained alcoves in the back, mark your ballot, and put it in the box, after identifying yourself again to the verifying teller. That sounds very ominous, but it should sound important, because what we're doing today will have a great impact on the future lives of all of our families and on us. It may well set a pattern for all of American industry.

"I'm pleased to introduce Charles Bowditch, our trustee, the senior officer of the New York Safe Deposit & Trust Company. Horse has been more than trustee; he's been a friend. I've asked him to take whatever time he needs to fill you in on the background of your ESOP and to describe the action we recommend you take today. Horse?"

Horse had learned to be an effective speaker, and about employee ownership, he was evangelical.

"The bank for which I work has been trustee for all of the employee benefit plans created by the American Observer. I have been the officer responsible for all of these accounts for the last ten years. The company has long been committed to and has recently increased the size of employee plan ownership to 20 percent of the voting stock, which represents approximately 3 percent of the total capital of the enterprise.

"These have been sad times for the American Observer family. Stock prices have plummeted to the level of the initial public offering in 1990; revenues, earnings, cash flow, all have collapsed; management transitions have not worked; we all have friends who have lost fine jobs; and there is not a person in the company who is not concerned about his or her job.

"After last year's meeting, which, you will recall, turned into an occasion marked by forthright expression, your committee and I met to consider the various ways in which we could achieve your objectives. Everyone remembered the founders' pride in having a 'family company.' It was consistent with their vision that employees would have a large ownership in the venture. At the same time, they made dispositions in favor of some of the great charitable institutions in this country. What this means is that trustees are the majority owners of the stock of this company and they must run it so as to generate enough cash for the needs of the charities. The company continues to pay its dividend even though it hasn't been earned in five years. This deficit is balanced so to speak on the backs of the employees, many of whom have been discharged in recent years. Because the employee plans are substantial owners, free of debt, you asked us to explore the possibility of having direct representation on the board of directors."

Horse was encouraged, after so many months, to have the rapt attention of the membership. They had come a long way, organized and educated themselves and Horse saw them as so many hearts filled with hope for a better future. "I must be candid with you today. In trying to carry out what I continue to feel are your proper instructions, I am finding myself increasingly at odds with my own superiors at NYSD&T. When I told my immediate superior, the CEO of NYSD&T, that I intended to ask the CEO of American Observer to consider adding an employee/owner to the board, he...well, I guess the best way to put this is, he disagreed. You may wonder, now, why I am telling you all of this inside chatter. As I proceed with this history, it is important for you to appreciate my own role. I have taken great pride in being a trustee.

"I told my boss that the interests of the employee/owners had been subordinated to other considerations and that board representation was essential. He disapproved but did not order me to desist. I asked for a meeting with the CEO of AOM. The bank was embarrassed to tell their client that there was disagreement so they said simply that I wanted to talk with him about employee representation on the board. The CEO/Trustee apparently lost it and said something like: 'If we needed any help in deciding what comprises a proper board for this enterprise, we would know where to look.' He hung up. I did not get my meeting, but I did get an answer to your question, the answer was no."

There was an audible groan by several in the crowd.

"I have been consulting lawyers with increasing concern, both for myself and for you. Today, I am that trustee. Realistically, we must all understand that tomorrow there may be a different trustee. There is no bill of rights guaranteeing me the right to continue in my present position. You may be faced by a situation in which the trustee simply elects to follow the lead from those who control a majority of the voting stock of this company.

"There is good news and there is bad news. The bad news we have discussed. The stock is cheap. At the same time, the economy is booming and the banks are competing to find out who can loan the most money the fastest. We recommend buying more AOM B. We will ask you at the end of this meeting to confirm by ballot that we have acted in accordance with your wishes. We believe that this is the best way for AOM employee/owners to assure that their interests inform the direction of this enterprise.

"I should tell you that I have spent a great deal of time in Washington at the Pension and Welfare Benefits Agency of the Department of Labor. They have the responsibility for administering the ERISA statute, which governs our trusts. We have drafted a formal letter on your behalf to the Department of Labor asking them for clarification that we have the right to borrow money and to tender or purchase more AOM stock. The department will reply to this letter under a postmark this week and it will become part of the public record.

"I have kept my boss informed as to what we're planning and doing. Several weeks ago, I asked him for permission to go to our parent company bank in order to borrow the money. I have been trying, without success, to get a meeting with Vernon Stillman. As some of you know, I like to play golf. Vern likes me to play with him and I flew up on Saturday in the bank's GII to a course in Massachusetts with a new big customer. I cornered Vern and he agreed to a meeting, so that is where it is at."

The applause was warm for Horse but lackluster for their cause. When Horse finished speaking, an extremely harassed secretary summoned him to the back of the room to give him a message. "Horse, I can't figure some people out. This lady was so rude. She just said that Vern Stillman wants to see you in the worst possible way and to get your ass down to his office right away."

The meeting settled down, without Horse, to routine questions. Everyone followed the voting instructions calmly. There was little surprise that 88 percent of those voting approved the action of the committee and the trustee.

Horse had no intention of going to midtown New York, disaster or no disaster, so he dialed Vern's office. The CEO's personal assistant was right out of central casting; her boss was the most important person in the world and she was a close second. Horse asked to be put through to Vern; no way. Nobody gets through to Number One except her. That turned out to be pretty stupid as Horse simply said, "Look, this is a vacation day for me that I counted on to be with my family. I was working with the boss on Saturday, so I don't feel badly about having this half-day. I am working at a client's offices now. If you would be so kind as to give me a few minutes any time tomorrow, I will be there. Sorry I couldn't talk with the boss directly, it would have been much easier for both of us." She didn't get the hint, or, if she did, she wasn't going to budge.

"Drive, this is Scott Moffie. You should know that the former Mrs. Stillman, who uses her maiden name, Molly Munro, is now Assistant Secretary of Labor for the Pension and Welfare Benefits Agency."

"Great work, I'm sure, but what does that mean?"

"It means that she is in charge of administering all of the retirement plans in this country. Does that have anything to do with your deal?"

"I don't know yet. I have heard mention of an employee benefit plan that Horse is involved with, but they couldn't have heard what I am doing yet. On another matter, I need some time with you on arbitrageurs. I need one on my side. Any luck on looking into why those two guys quit the AOM board?"

"No leads yet. Nobody wants to talk. Rules of the club, don't you know? All I can tell you is that nobody leaves such a warm and cozy situation without a good reason."

"Well, I have to go for my interview with the *New York Times*, thank you very much."

"Be careful of those bastards, boss. Oops, sorry, I forgot what line of work you are in."

"Cheeky bastard..."

Drive walked down Forty-second Street, past the New York Public Library, through the gentrified zone, to the staid and timeless headquarters for the world's greatest newspaper. The public entry resembled something between a well-appointed government agency, and a place of correction done in fading Art Deco. There was a person behind a desk, who recognized him and led him to the waiting elevator. He was met, as the doors slid open, by an attractive woman who escorted him to the private office of one of the members of the family owners.

"Drive, it is so good of you to pay us a visit. My uncles and cousins regret being unable to greet you properly. We're as bad about summer vacations as the English are about their weekends. I gather you're here on professional business and my colleagues are looking forward to your interview. I hope this means we'll be seeing more of you on this Atlantic coast."

"As it happens, I am contemplating an acquisition here, but you'll read all about it first, in the *New York Times*. Unhappily, there's nothing of your quality available, you have cornered the market and you're not for sale."

"I'm intrigued. Maybe I can listen in on the interview?"

"You are the Massa here."

Journalists are a very different species from those who own the companies that employ journalists. They're usually suspicious, no one is spending time talking with them, except in aid of an ulterior motive. The question is, what's the real motive? And, is it something that we want to aid or to obstruct. These simple facts govern much of the length, futility, and ultimate rancor that characterize the relationships between journalists and their subjects. Drive had been interviewed many times and he had a simple technique. "My accent makes clear that I am a foreigner. That's both good and bad. Because I'm from elsewhere, people do not consider me a threat. It is a simple fact of nature, I don't want their job or their girlfriend; I am different." Occasionally, there is suspicion of foreigners just because they are foreign, but the *New York Times*'s quality correspondents do not suffer from that myopia.

As they walked across the floor to the interview room, a window-less cube populated by a square table, half a dozen chairs, three journalists, one representative from Joey's office, and the inevitable telephones and computer connections, Drive mused about the culture in the northeastern United States that seemed to require an air of overcrowdedness and shabbiness in the exclusive clubs and executive spaces of the best people. Entering the room, he repeated to himself the mantra, "talk about the voting stock."

Joey's guy was just repeating *his* mantra out loud. "This is all on hold until the close of business on Wednesday. Otherwise, whatever Drive says is on the record."

Drive realized these people knew who he was and the fact is, he was the senior executive of a world communications company and had been a major figure in the industry for half a century. He always spoke softly. Some people complained that this was a rather rude device requiring too much effort on the part of his listeners. But a quiet voice, a calm demeanor, and no sense of hurry created a persona that served him well.

"There are very few quality franchises in the communications business. One of these is the *American Observer* magazine. It's in a perilous position. All the reputation, subscriber lists, and worldwide recognition will not be sustaining assets unless management can reverse existing trends and find the keys to profitability. I believe that I can do so. I believe there are a number of possible synergies with operations that we control about the world."

A surprisingly rude interruption came from a baby-faced, over-weight youth, complete with vest. "I am sure you can, but one thing is plain. The *American Observer* isn't for sale. The Porters left control to a voting trust that's controlled by the management. They have made it clear, on a number of occasions, that the trustees consider themselves obligated to operate those businesses."

Drive had ignored more significant problems and continued unhurried. "You have brought us, very correctly, to the point. I hope to raise the question politely, but persistently, as to whether the affected constituencies feel that the existing arrangements are more to their liking than the prospect of my management."

The mosquito followed up. "This is not some kind of popularity contest. There's only one vote that counts and that's the trustees'. They are committed people, beyond financial inducements, who are life-long employees of American Observer. Why would they ever change their minds?"

Smile, thought Drive, *why are the youngest always the rudest?*

Still patient. "The Porters were very generous people. Aside from the two main trusts that hold a majority of the voting shares, they made very substantial specific gifts to some very prominent philan-thropic organizations, most of them located right in this city. The good news is the bad news, as they say." When Drive began to get homey, the experienced journalists started to pay special attention. "The Met-ropolitan Museum, Sloan-Kettering, Lincoln Center, and the others, received huge additions to their endowments and they were all deeply grateful to the donors of this largess. They adapted their lifestyles to this new level of wealth. All of a sudden, they need the 5 percent of the original capital level in order to meet their absolutely hard-core operating costs. Now, after ten years, the capital values are substantially reduced and the company has not, for five years, earned enough to cover its dividend. Where is the money for Sloan-Kettering's absolutely critical operating costs going to come from? I have looked down the list of trustees and donors to these wonderful institutions and I dare say there is virtually no one of "the great and the good" of Greater New York who is not at risk from the fragility of the Porter trusts. Look, if American Observer doesn't earn the money, sooner or later, the level of payments to these community jewels will be reduced and, ultimately, will be eliminated. You cannot get blood from a stone.

"I am not going to be critical of this management. I simply ask you to consider, based on my record, whether you would be inclined to feel that I could do better."

A new questioner, finally. "Have any trustees of these beneficiary organizations made public their concerns?"

"That's your business, not mine. I can simply pose a hypothesis of how reasonable and sensible individuals, bearing large responsibilities for community assets, would feel. There are other constituencies, the employees, for example. The Porters always spoke of the American Observer as a family company. They did not lay off employees in droves. You know the recent experience there. Let me ask you to consider a proposition. Was leaving that wonderful property in trust a mistake?"

Some eyebrows began to rise among the more senior journalists, and Joey's man just blinked and smiled.

"No, no, please, I'm not talking about the *New York Times*. It's absolutely critical that you continue to have family members intimately involved in the operations of this venture. And that's the difference. There are no Porter heirs.

"Look at the record. Employees are being laid off. We read in the recent financial press that they are demoralized and frightened about their jobs. Ask yourself, in whose interest is this venture being run? Who benefits from having such an arrangement? Must society stand by and watch all of these important constituencies be damaged, when an alternative exists? It is better to have a proven management for the business; it's better for the endowment funds of these critical institutions to be professionally invested in a diversified portfolio."

"It sounds like you are bringing a lawsuit rather than buying a company." The boy in the vest was persistent and Drive saw ruthlessness in his eyes. *How long till he heads his department?* Drive's mind wandered and came back with his canned speech. His pause gave everyone the impression he was seriously pondering the accusation.

"At a certain point, one has to wonder whether the appropriate authorities of the state of New York, the attorney general I believe it is, need to be concerned about the functioning of charitable organizations within their jurisdiction. I need to make clear to you one point. My offer on Wednesday will be only for the voting class of stock..."

"Wait a minute. What are all these crocodile tears about the charities? They don't own the voting stock. You are not helping them at all." *Is this little bastard the only one here? Pipe up, you sheep.*

A very cool Drive. "The proposition is a simple one. The two classes of common stock are exactly the same except with respect to the power to vote. If I am to become rich, so will the charities. If their circumstances do not improve, my own will be ruinous. I am agreeing to commit myself to make this company work. If it works well enough, they are perfectly free and able to sell their shares on the open market." *Take that, you shit*, thought Drive.

The host interjected, to break up the monopoly. "Do you think it's fair to get control of a company by buying only 20 percent of the total capital?"

Now you *want some? Stand back.* "I don't think that I heard that question in this building. Are there not two classes of stock for all the great American publishing companies, not only the *New York Times*, but the Bancrofts and Coxes in the *Wall Street Journal*, the Taylors in the *Boston Globe*, the Grahams in the *Washington Post*, the Chandlers in the *Los Angeles Times*? For reasons that appeal to the culture of the United States, you consistently divide an ownership class in journalistic enterprises between family and nonfamily owners. I associate myself with this tradition in making this offer to the voting shareholders of AOM. I think that is a good exit line unless anybody else has any questions."

And Drive rose up without waiting for any, but he did make a point of shaking everyone's hand. When he got to the mosquito, he recognized that the look of ruthlessness was gone and Drive knew from experience that he would be receiving a florid thank-you note and resume within the next forty-eight hours.

Because of the huge volume of paperwork and his own style, of personally doing all of the drafting work, Marty had asked Drive to meet again in his offices. Drive was startled by Marty's appearance. He reflected that the hours of work, pushing all those hours, grinding out pages and pages, while *he* had been on the golf course and lazing around a Manhattan Sunday with his wife, had been a twenty-hour, nonstop drafting marathon for Marty. A phrase passed through Drive's mind, "worked to death." He remembered the diamond miners, from his childhood. Skinny black men, bent and dragging like puppets. The already lean Marty looked sepulchral and his pale coloring had bluish hues. His usual staccato monotone was softened; and occasionally, there was evidence of a stutter. When Marty smiled, all Drive could think of were those medieval paintings of gaunt saints that filled the museums he was dragged around as a boy. Too much childhood came back all at once and his heart went out to his very expensive lawyer.

Drive began. His genuine concern for what this job had cost Marty elicited spontaneous openness that he had not intended. "I want you to have everything possible to help me get this job done. In fact, I do have a partner in this venture. She is an utterly unique human being with whom, I hope, I can spend the rest of my life. At this point, we want to keep her out of it as much as possible. Do you see this cellular? It is hardwired, with encryption and forwarding programs so that I, and only I, can reach her at any time. I don't know where she is, so I can't tell anybody what I don't know. If anything comes up, and we need special help, we will involve her in a minute."

Exhausted or not, Marty was persistent. "Listen, this can't be some kind of guessing game. You have to give me some idea what kind of help you and she can provide."

"OK. Over the years, I have kept a record of my involvement with leading figures. Some political contributions, some favorable articles. We have purchased a few biographies; we have commissioned and paid advances for many more that will never be written. Sometimes, an opportunity for timely investment crops up. Over the years, it is a very long list."

Nice, thought Marty, *tell me something I don't know*. So he asked.

"We may need some government help. At the state level, I would like to get the attorney general onto this case. On the federal level, we're going to get a lot of heat this week until we make the final offer for all of the stock. Do you have the resources to investigate quickly and discretely?"

"Yes, we have a number of private investigators on retainer."

"On this job, now?"

"All this is attorney/client privilege?"

"You bet."

"I have a long relationship with Scott Moffie."

"I knew it. I knew it. You had that son of a bitch checking on me, didn't you?"

Drive raised his eyebrows, in a Marty-like fashion, and began, "Well..."

"Hey, boss, I don't give a damn, I'd probably do the same thing, but one of the sweet things who makes my life worth living told me about this guy, it had to be Moffie, who was asking her all kinds of questions about me. Figures."

Marty laughed to himself, took a deep breath and continued. "OK. Now there are a couple of serious things that I have to go over with you. You need to understand how this deal is being put together. Your buddy Vern wants this put into a trust, with the bank, actually its subsidiary NYSD&T, to act as trustee. The trust receives the money, initially $600 million, then an additional $2.4 billion, from the pension funds. It uses these funds to purchase the outstanding stock of AOM. I have been adamant on two points, which you insist on. You and I have to be absolutely clear on these points, because they are costing you a great deal of money. The first is that you personally will not be liable in any way to anybody for the funds that are being invested in the trust. OK? So you can fly this plane into the Atlantic, if you want to. The second is that you will not agree to commit any particular portion of your personal time and energy to the venture. So you're the only one with a parachute, right? I gather that Vern himself put this to you on the golf course and you made him swallow 'trust me!'"

Drive nodded, pleased his conditions apparently were accepted.

"You have a colorful way with words but, yes, that's right. I agreed to serve as chairman of his foreign advisory board and thereby to screw up, utterly, the half-century relationships I've had with Citicorp. I said if he couldn't trust me, he'd made a mistake asking me to take on that job for him. I had him there, but obviously he is uncomfortable."

Marty's voice was going hoarse. "This is one of those things that has to be done at the boss level, because I could never get that past his legal team. Let me tell you what all this paper is about. Vern Stillman, as trustee, is going to tender for all of the stock of AOM in two tranches, the first on Wednesday, the second is presently scheduled to be announced Friday, the twenty-first. Only if we acquire at least a majority of the voting stock, the trust will hold the stock for your account. What is really important, and you have to hand it to this 'partner' of yours, is that you have gotten impossible financing. This money is being made available to you so that you have freedom to run the venture and, ultimately, to take all the profits. You have no personal liability with respect to the money and no enforceable obligations with respect to committing time to the venture. I never thought that I'd live so long. What gets into these bankers? Oy vey. That's the good news."

Marty seemed to gather energy from two complexities of the deal. "Now, the bad news. You are paying fees up the yin yang. Getting an impossible investment just costs more; it's the market at work. Here it comes. OK, first good ole Vern. Well, by putting it into trust form, he locks the bank into a 1 percent plus expenses management fee for the life of the trust. Of course, the bank is getting another 1 percent off the top in exchange for its 'investment banking' services in arranging the financing. Then, we have 1 percent for Mr. O'Neil, 1 percent for the arbs. And, less you forget, 1 percent for me. Let's do the math. Assume the $3-billion deal, 120 million off the top, 4 percent. The investors are glad to increase the amount of the loan to provide the cash for immediate payment. Then, you have the bank's ongoing thirty million a year for running the trust."

Drive knew the math well enough if the deal was successful. "Just one thing. Suppose the Porter trustees refuse to sell, who owes who what?"

"More good news. You have already paid me my five million, which I keep in any event. Frankly, I have had to spend about half of it already. The rest of the fees are entirely contingent on the deal closing, which means that you have at least a majority of the voting stock."

"Let's go back to O'Neil for a minute. Do I ever get to meet this guy who is rendering me such incredible services that are worth $30 million?"

"As your lawyer, I advise you that you do not want to meet O'Neil. You do not want to meet any arbs. You don't want to know where my two point five has gone. You want to treat the fees as being paid in the normal course of business. All transactions have fees. You are not on notice that anything unusual is taking place. You have attorney/client privilege to protect you against anything that I have told you. You're clean, leave it alone. Call it expensive deniability."

Drive knew he was off the hook, that's what lawyers are for, but he wanted to understand this thuggish new way of doing business. "I accept your advice. I am just curious, for sixty million bucks, will you indulge me?"

"Look, it ain't your money. The pension funds are putting it up, and if the investment doesn't work, you don't have to pay it back. I'll explain it to you, but to understand what is happening you must grasp, it is not your money. It's a long story, but I'm pretty well through your work and I have to tell you, I have never quite seen anything like this."

In another life, Marty would have been the greatest of rabbis. He seemed so wise and eager to teach. Drive never has to ask *him* twice.

"Whose money is it? It's legally owned by the trustees. They are the trustees of the defined benefit plan pension funds of America's finest companies. All that money that gets pulled out of everybody's checks in most organizations. All these guys have been heavily invested in stocks, rather than relying on bonds, which was the habit for years. The stock market has gone up like a rocket. OK. About four years ago, these accounts began to be overfunded. Today, many of them have twice as much in assets as the actuaries calculate are necessary to pay what they have promised to the employees."

Marty's eyes sparkled and his voice dropped to a whisper as he described every thief's dream: money for which there is no accountability, cloaked in legality.

"What legal rules tell you how to invest an overfunded plan? I suppose that they ought to buy annuities for everybody and then liquidate the plan and go home. Hey, nobody, but nobody, is going to do that. This overfunding is too much fun. The beneficiaries really don't own the money. If there is a fall in asset value, the company is responsible to make up the shortfall. And if that doesn't work, there is the Pension Benefit Guarantee Corporation that the government set up to protect the workers of bankrupt companies. The companies can't put the money in their pockets, which is what they used to do. This is a long story, I warned you. So they can use it pretty much any way they want to, which is why you could get this money so quickly."

Drive wondered, "Listen, it's a treat to get the inside view from an old master. With all this surplus money sloshing around, you would figure there had to be major theft. So this is how I get my deal on my terms?"

Marty nodded at Drive like a teacher to a good pupil. "Well, that's about the size of it. There's some protection against outright bank robbery in the big institutions because those guys can't afford to lose their license to work under ERISA, but this money is now being used to settle a lot of personal accounts. It gives the trustees some things to trade with the brokers. Look at our case; we need certain, very specialized services. It would be improper, if not illegal, for us to hire these services directly. When we start putting a hundred million dollars of fees into play, contingent on a successful outcome, we're unleashing a lot of creativity and aggression to make sure that the deal happens. Hey, it's the free market at work. Your deal is the best thing to hit fast-track Manhattan in a long time. A lot of markers are being picked up."

Drive waggled his head. The white knight strikes again. He felt a twinge of guilt about it all but he didn't know where to begin.

"Frankly, the O'Neil money, I really don't like that. You have to figure that some of that gets back to the trustees one way or another."

Marty confirmed Drive's theory. "You pay a custom's inspector ten dollars a year and you know, you have to *know*, that that man has no choice but to get his pay out of the traffic. That's part of the system. These lower-level pension guys are in the same situation. They control billions, they can make independent managers tens of millions, but they themselves are at the bottom end of the scale. Lots of ego stroking. Everybody thinks a guy who can decide to give you a contract worth millions tells the funniest jokes. There had to be an O'Neil sooner or later, but it isn't pretty. I understand that's just going to add a little leverage, a few more people who really have a lot riding on our deal getting done."

Marty was getting downright communicative. "The arb money. I don't even know how that's going to play. We're investing money in a firm that specializes in brokerage and the purchase and sale of communications industry properties. They have many connections in the arb community. With this amount of money, they ought to be able to print out a whole new series of stock certificates, if we can't win any other way. We may even make a profit. It's certain they will.

"The bank now has turned to a fee-driven, rather than loan-driven, institution. Notice, you're not borrowing a nickel from the bank. Lucky you aren't, as they'd absolutely *have* to have your personal signature, at least to the extent of the loan. There are no bank examiners for private pension assets.

"Between O'Neil, the arb money, and the bank fees, there's plenty of resources for putting the pressure on the Porter trustees; someone will know how to reach the trustees of the Met or Lincoln Center. Someone will know how to get the right articles in the right places, someone will know how to get the politicians stirred up."

"And here I thought that would be my job. It sounds pretty complicated. Can we just sit back and expect all this to happen at the right time and in the right way?"

"It's still your job, that's our edge. Frankly it's why I'm here. Between what I know and who you know, this impossible deal is possible. How do you think I earn my 1 percent?"

Marty walked straight down Lexington Avenue, bouncing like a ball. He knew he had blown Drive away. Straight As, 150 percent, top of the class, world-class. Another job well done, that only he could have done. He was cruising on pure adrenaline as he walked into a rather nondescript office building on the east side, took an elevator to the eighth floor, walked through doors proclaiming the tenancy of a small accounting firm, past the receptionist, down to the end of the hall to a door marked C.G.E. Wilson, Esq. Marty really didn't want to probe too far about the Esquire. *Lawyer-wise*, he reflected, *Hey, he says he's a lawyer, he's a lawyer*, and opened the door.

"How they hanging, little guy!" bellowed out from the great mass of hair and flesh sitting behind a rather messy desk, which with a phone and two chairs, comprised all the furniture in this rather small office.

"I'll have yours in the stew pot, Wilson, if you haven't gotten that work done."

"Listen, rabbi, you call me with the hots, give me about a dozen extremely difficult tasks and then I don't hear from you for days?" Charles Wilson resembled an overgrown schoolboy complete with three-piece suit, soup spills on the vest, and battered neckwear known as the old school tie.

"Don't give me that crap! Did the check clear?"

"Oh, yeah! So you are now addressing your most obedient servant! Let me give you a rundown on where we are."

"Wait a minute. Do you have a tape recorder in this place?" Wilson nodded as if to say, do you think I have gone soft in the head? "I want it on the record that this is a discussion subject to attorney/client privilege. I represent Cedric Rhodes and have engaged you to act as my co-counsel."

"Brother at the bar, may I proceed?" Wilson got up, although that hardly describes adequately the process of moving some 300 pounds, not all of which is fat, out of a chair and over to the door, which he opened, ceremoniously stared down the hall, shut the door, and then activated a supplementary security system. Wilson picked a small display easel off of the floor, which, in his grip, looked like a piece of paper in the hands of any ordinary mortal. He set it up, turned the cover page which revealed simply the words in outsize capital letters PUSH POLL and in oratorical tones, proceeded. "My assignment has been to gather information about the trustees of the various trusts created by Randy and Shelley Porter, two of which control pretty much all of the voting stock, which I call the Porter trusts, and seven are for the benefit of prominent local charities which I call the Seven Sisters, which own a substantial portion of the nonvoting stock of AOM. You asked me to devise a plan which will result in the trustees of the voting shares tendering them to an entity organized by our client."

As Wilson waxed on rather like a recording, Marty mused on this new species of lawyer. Wilson was a cutout. Drive would never know that he existed. Marty could not be held responsible for what he did. Everyone would invoke the attorney/client privilege. During the increasingly violent takeover battles of the 1980s, the principal lawyers became so successful that they did not want to risk their new wealth and reputation on the kind of aggressive tactics that had produced them. So, the new species was created, the undisclosed intermediate lawyer, who received his fee and orders from referring counsel and acted as principal in engaging those specialists necessary for the task. Lawyers finally condescended to learn something from the politicians. Many of the tactics used in winning elections were applicable to the corporate takeover situations because the problems were comparable. How do you persuade someone to do what you want them to do, particularly when somebody else wants them to do otherwise? Marty wondered, *Who is Charles Wilson? Is that his real name? Where did he go to law school? How did he come to provide this kind of service? He acts like an upper-class twit, but he has those pale blue eyes and a sense of hardly contained violence.* He stopped his musings as Wilson paused after asking, "Now, there is the question of budget. You know these political types have really inflated ideas of their worth."

Marty could never resist, "Hey, they should be so lucky, there is no election in August, as far as I know. It's all found money."

Wilson would not be goaded, "We're getting up to seven figures in U.S. dollars, seven figures to the left of the decimal point, with the polls, the push polls, the "investigation work," the special phone banks, and, last but not least, the legal opinions. Your instructions were not to go beyond that until I got your specific approval. I have now spent one million dollars of your money. Let me review with you the plan. Our primary target is the trustees of the Randy and Shelley Porter trusts. They are the legal owners of the voting stock. Without them, we have nothing. Our strategy is to destroy their bases of support. I won't bore both of us by reciting how they are totally protected legally in doing nothing and how no one is going to stand up in public and criticize them. We have compiled a list with the names, numbers, faxes, and e-mail addresses of all trustees of all trusts, their lawyers, everybody connected with the beneficiary organizations, the officers of AOM, their accountants, their wives, their adult children, their partners, which has resulted in the names of a thousand individuals, give or take, who are immediately affected by the way the Porter trusts are now functioning. Our friends from Washington have advanced the technology of the 'push poll' to a point that amazes even me."

Marty never really mastered the skill of admitting that he didn't know more about everything than whoever he was talking to, but "push poll" was off his radar screen. "Hey, talk English, what's with this push pull stuff?"

Wilson smiled; putting Marty in his place was an occasional fringe benefit. "It's like an ordinary poll. We will use a legitimate polling company. It has an address, real people, a record, a bank account and all that stuff. We're using specially trained callers. They are trained in the polite persistence of getting actual contact with the targeted person. They are further trained to ask inappropriate questions in a credible way. So, after we have introduced ourselves as the Capital Polling Group, working on behalf of a multinational communications conglomerate, we explain that we have been conducting surveys, of those individuals most sophisticated in communications matters, all over the world. This is the American portion of the study and we're particularly focused on the *American Observer*. Would they like to participate, blah, blah, blah. Nothing will be attributed, all confidential, we will be glad to send them a copy of the survey when it is finished. And so forth. You would be amazed. Nobody turns down the girls with the golden voices. They think *they're* going to secretly influence some public perception, the dirty sneaks. Then, there are questions about the *Observer*, all having to do with its outstanding characteristics, all the good news. Without warning, our interviewers purr, 'Some experts express doubt whether American Observer can survive in its present ownership pattern, what is your opinion?' We stay with this, kind of neutral for a few questions about the difficulty of the trust mode for running a business that must take risks. Depending on the answers, the questions escalate to 'Do you think those responsible should change to a more conventional form of ownership?' We then have a series of special questions for the trustees of the Porter trusts only. These raise the questions of conflict of interest, legal liability, and management failure. The special questions for the trustees of the Seven Sisters invite the conclusion that everybody would be better off if they could sell their AOM holdings and buy ordinary marketable securities. Push polling is a technique we use to place ideas in a lot of key people's minds with little immediate suspicion."

Marty said, almost in admiration, "I really like that. And you mean to say that people don't hang up?"

"Well, even if they do, then they call their immediate friends and complain. That gets the word around even further and faster. We're trying to create instant reality. We've done the work, we have the contact information, the best professionals have written the scripts and we have trained the top callers. So, we're ready to go on that one."

Marty felt better already. "What else are we doing?"

"A little change of pace, here." Marty could detect some elements of refinement here, a hint, almost, that Charles was well bred before whatever it was that brought him to his present state. "We went to each law firm which represents the Porter and the Seven Sister trusts. I made an appointment with the appropriate partner, wore my good suit, and actually carried a retainer check made out to each of them for $50,000. I explained to each of them that my client, a foreign company, was thinking of acquiring a U.S. company, the controlling stock of which was held by a trust, which authorized the continued holding of that controlling interest. I need their opinion that, notwithstanding directions in the instrument, the trustees can sell to my client. I was most tactful in saying that we had come to them because of their known involvement as counsel for one of the Seven Sisters, so we realized that they would have had to deal with our situation and would, therefore, have some special competency. Not one of those guys even blinked, not one of them mentioned conflict of interest, not one of them said 'We couldn't possibly give an opinion if the language is substantially the same as what we have in the Seven Sisters' documents.' Every one of them took the fifty thousand and promised immediate replies. When I got to the outside counsel for the Porter trustees, the people who have the power, the reception was correct but cool. I have followed up, but haven't yet gotten a reply as to whether their opinion will be forthcoming."

Marty thought to himself, *This is more fun than Chanukah.* There was a day when firms like those would have thrown Wilson out. Hell, they threw me out. It's all a matter of the overhead. Since they decided to become big businessmen and build huge staffs, they have to worry about paying the rent. "Charles, I wish I could have been with you. What else have you got for me?"

"Actually, you gave me access to some of the summer people at your own firm, so I had them do a law review article. They are frightfully clever and very anxious to demonstrate an ability to work at least twenty hours a day. Here are the proofs. Lovely aren't they?"

"Wait a minute, nobody will fall for that one. You can't just invent some law review name and expect any professional to pay it any credence?"

"My dear fellow." *My God,* thought Marty, *I have unleashed a monster. He is going to deliver a lecture on my naïveté. I love it.* "There are many esteemed law journals that have fallen on, shall we say, hard times, and many families of distinguished legal scholars who bequeathed more words than money. I happen to have kept track of several of these and you will be pleased to know that the *Piscataquis Law Journal* has published at least one scholarly paper in every year of this century. Their format is lovely; their reprints are precisely in the format of the best journals."

Marty picked up the long proof sheets and began to read, "...The law recognizes circumstances in which it is entirely proper for trustees to ignore the plainly expressed wishes of the settlor, if so doing is essential to preserve the corpus of the trust." Marty choked, "I'm not sure that I know what that means in English. What are we going to do with it?"

"My circulation list includes a number of government regulators, including the attorney general of the state of New York, and the full thousand names from the push poll list. I have also sent them to your Joey Jones. He wanted a hundred. I have no idea what he will do with them, but he seemed really thrilled."

"My God! Is there more? I know I shouldn't ask because it will ruin my leverage in bargaining for your fee, but you have weakened me." Marty almost sounded like a flesh and blood person.

Wilson said, "Now that you mention it, we're going to need more money, quite a lot of it. We do have our final poll and this is a legitimate one. Same people, but different side of the house, don't you know? We really are going to poll the present and past employees of the *Observer*. At some point, their attitude will be very important. We had a great stroke of luck. This shareholder activist group, LENS, who are working with us, published a whole series of ads in local newspapers near Tarrytown late in the spring, where they asked any present or former employees who were worried about the safety of their AOM holdings to contact them. The results were really startling. Over a hundred written answers and many long phone messages. We have picked up on these. I think we could manage a revolution, if it comes to that."

Marty, basking in the afterglow, pointed to the letterhead on the desk of his new hero. "Charles, what do all of those initials stand for?"

"Oh, when I was born, there were two Charles Wilsons in the business world, one heading General Electric known as 'Electric Charley' and the other heading General Motors known as 'Motors Charley.' My father never could stand General Motors; hence I go through life as Charles General Electric Wilson. OK?"

"Really? You goyim never cease to amaze me."

Drive was nursing a double scotch to celebrate getting this far, but deep down he wanted it for the call he was making. "The guy looks like death, but what a brain. He took me through what's really going to happen, what a trip! He was thrilled to know that there was a you. He paid you a great compliment about our timing. I explained to him that we wanted to keep you out of it as long as possible. He was OK about it. I've a feeling that you'll be needed."

"You're having luncheon with those trustees, the day after tomorrow." She could tell he was drinking. That wasn't a good sign. She knew he would be roused by a challenge. "That'll be a spectacle. The stock is still tanking. I've got us a very good position, a lot more shares than I thought we'd get without ruining the price. I can hardly believe they're letting you off without any commitment. It's so irresponsible. Don't you love it? You, the one responsible for so much money. That's going to make our lives a joy. Get over to the club, get a massage; we're going to reinvent your body."

Drive had spent his life always being responsible, but there wasn't time to have that conversation, even if she was interested. "It's hard to fathom. I never thought such a thing would ever be possible, but you're right. Marty has taught me a lot, too. Our friends have never been more important. Let me know tomorrow where we have a little leverage with this in Washington. We may need some help with the Labor Department."

"Nobody even knows where Labor is. That should be a cakewalk. That straw is not going to stir the soda, OK? I love you."

"This all seems to suit you. You've certainly come into your own. I do have an eye for talent. I'm off to the club to make myself more worthy of my bloodthirsty protégé."

"Drive, that seemed harsh, but I love what we're accomplishing together, all the same."

"And I love you too, my dear. Ta ta for now."

Drive wanted to ask what she thought they were creating? And, for the second time, Drive's favorite part of the day wasn't anymore, but he went to the club anyway because he'd nowhere else to go.

Chapter 15
Tuesday, August 11, 1998

When Vern arrived in his office at 8:00 a.m., none of the staff had arrived yet, but Horse was sitting patiently on the edge of the receptionist's desk.

"I wasn't able to get through to you yesterday, so I thought it best to come down and make arrangements for a time we can meet."

Vern was not at his best in the morning. He was not at all at his best when confronted with surprises, and the sight of Horse, at this particular moment, was so synchronistic, it caused him to gag, audibly. Just on leaving the elevator, in his mind he had been finishing a heated conversation with Horse, during which he fully expressed his resentments over the Society of the Cincinnati, Horse's golf skill, and his intimacies with Molly. The fact is that Horse haunted Vern. Vern had created such a successful persona for himself that he was horrified to discover the extent a single individual, with no apparent malice, could make him feel so inadequate. This was not a feeling that Vern knew how to deal with.

"Is there anything the matter? Can I get you a glass of water?"

Vern wasn't about to accept succor of any kind from Horse, but he couldn't bring himself to utter a syllable for several minutes. So they stood outside the office, Horse concerned, Vern grasping for vocal recovery. He waved them both in.

Finally, stimulated by his anger, Vern croaked, "We've got a lot to talk about. First off, would you mind telling me what you had in mind talking to Drive about the bank's clients?"

Horse reflected, as he had no clear recollection of what Vern was referring to. Then he remembered the "example" Drive had coaxed out of him, talking about employee benefit plans.

"That was a mistake. I hope it hasn't caused any embarrassment."

Vern wasn't used to such a direct admission of error so his intended line of interrogation had to be altered, another frustration. *I can't even hold my own with this guy even when he is plainly wrong*, he fumed to himself.

"Let's move on. There's a lot going on and it's essential that we all sing from the same hymnal." That was one of Vern's cozy trite expressions that he thought identified him as one of the elite.

"I can come back anytime today." Horse knew the bank president was stymied when people weren't afraid of him. He'd seen it before.

"This is important. Everything else can wait. I am working with Drive on the biggest deal this bank has ever done. Tomorrow, the announcement will go out over the wires that Drive is offering to buy the voting stock of the American Observer. I don't need to tell you that this is the culmination of years of my work trying to get this bank into the first tier. We've developed some imaginative financing. This is very important as a source of earnings for the bank. Drive has agreed to become chairman of our advisory board. You can understand how your comment about the American Observer employee plans raised some questions in Drive's mind."

"Congratulations, I know how hard you have been trying to create a major financial services company out of the old Universal Bank. I hope that my ill-considered anecdote did not cause any serious problems with Drive."

Vern was studying Horse now. The lowly trustee really was doing everything right. Butter would melt in his mouth. Golf wasn't all this boy was good for. Damn.

"In this deal, every problem is serious. Now, what is it that you have been trying to talk with me about these employee plans?"

Horse noticed Vern's Southern accent growing increasingly prominent.

"We've invested a great deal of time and effort with the employees over the years, hoping to devise a way for them to use their ownership interest to improve their situation. It's been bad for the last five years and it's getting worse. Maybe you'll remember last year, how I passed on the plan's request to add an employee to the board of directors?"

"Sweet Jesus. I remember. That was a mighty disaster. We almost lost the account on the spot. Look now, get on with what I have to know. This day might just be the death of me yet."

"Yesterday, the plan voted by an 88 percent majority to borrow money in order to buy more voting stock on the open market. We feel the price is low and the opportunity to add to our interest is attractive."

Vern made a face like Horse had just slapped him.

"Man, are you insane? The biggest deal that we've ever had involves our financing the acquisition of these shares by Drive, including the shares in the employee benefit plans." He wasn't gagging now, he was spitting, a lot. "He specifically wants to include those shares in his purchase. Not only that, but can you imagine what the Porter trustees and the American Observer management would have to say about your little scheme?"

"I'm no world-class financial executive. I'm a trust officer with a great deal of experience with employee benefit plans. I'm a fiduciary. I know that culture. I know what my responsibility is. It's clear I'm charged to consider exclusively the interest of the beneficiaries of the AOM plans. That means the trustee must act *independently* of any sister or parent organizations." Horse was cool and calm and it was driving Vern nuts. *Is he insulting me? I'm yelling at him, is he deaf?*

"Don't you get all up and sanctimonious with me about trust law. You are an employee of NYSD&T, all the stock of which is owned by Universal, of which, the last time I looked, I was still the CEO. You work for me, boy. I want you to stop this nonsense with the employee plans right now. You hear?"

Horse mused that if the CEO's accent went any further south, he'd start speaking Spanish.

"Vern, this isn't nonsense, it's the job you pay me to do and I'm doing it. I'm not trying to be sanctimonious, just clear about my position. At the time of the acquisition, there was a lot of concern about our cultures, whether they were compatible or not. That deal closed on the basis that you would respect our trust culture. I think you said there would be a Chinese wall protecting the fiduciary relationships."

"Charles, I am not going to debate the niceties of trust law with you. I just want to remind you of two things. First, every financial conglomerate in this country has conflicts of interest and they resolve them in favor of the guy who signs the checks. No one has ever been prosecuted for *failing to represent the beneficiaries' interest* under one of these plans. Your precious Department of Labor has prosecuted *no one* for the last twenty-five years for conflict of interest. Second, the American Observer can fire us; and I can replace you as the responsible officer in this plan without the slightest risk of illegality. That would be the end of this little problem, wouldn't it?"

"That's more your department than mine. I'm a simple person. I take pride in what I do. So long as it's my responsibility, I'll do what is legal and appears to be correct. My responsibility as trustee is to the beneficiaries of the plans."

Vern couldn't believe that he was having this conversation with a junior officer, not just any junior officer, but the one person in the world who was a reproach to his manhood, to his athleticism, and to his heritage. He knew that his rage would incline him to say stupid things and to make stupid decisions. Already, he had talked about replacing Horse, and suddenly started calling him Charles. *Why did I say "precious" Department of Labor? Time to stop before I do anything really dumb.*

"Horse, son, listen, this is something nobody could have dreamed up. Frankly, I don't know what to do. Drive's business is on a timetable to which we're bound. I want to work with you in the effort to accommodate the various interests here. I don't know how it will end up, but I promise to be available and I want you to promise to consult with me before taking any further steps."

Drive had spent the lion's share of the morning obsessing over the embassy bombings in Africa. It was a vice he recognized, born of the luxury of having any world paper at his fingers. He had sandwiches sent in. He was finishing one at his desk and he had absentmindedly started another by the table. Every flat surface was covered with newsprint from somewhere. He cross-referenced the local African papers, faxed to him at his request, with the European papers. In Europe the coverage was much more thorough, having a tradition of terrorism on its shores. The eyewitnesses saw trucks right before the bombs exploded. A two-million-dollar reward for any information. Once again, it appears the Yanks had fallen prey to their lack of vigilance in the face of increasing global privation. Tanzania is one thing but Kenya? Drive had vacationed with his children in Kenya several times, those days were among his happiest on earth. The entire world comes to Kenya on safari. It was clear the attacks had been coordinated. The naughty president stories were knocked down at last. Real news, real tragedy would be a wake-up call to the lazy American press.

Drive read the reports over and over again. Each nation had a theory, but they all agreed that the U.S. was culpable in its deafness to an increasingly hostile global climate. Sympathy was no longer what it had been for America during the days of the Cold War. This thought cut Drive to the quick. So much had changed since he first arrived in the land of the free and the home of the brave. *Would there be no sympathy for me any more? How foreign am I in this modern world?*

Like a saving grace, Drive's phone rang through before he could sink any deeper into treacherous personal reflection.

"Drive, Moffie here. Apparently, our boy has been spending a great deal of time at the Department of Labor during the last six months and with the assistant secretary."

"How do you find out stuff like this so quickly?"

"Easy, there's a sign-in system at most federal departments and agencies. Public record, but you have to send someone over to go through the documents. We found that Horse had been in PWBA about a dozen times, that means twice a week. I presume you've seen the opinion the agency sent out last week. It was made public today."

"What opinion?" Drive felt caught with his guard down. He should've called in today but consciously put it off. He remembered thinking to himself, *she'll keep.*

"Your friend Horse has asked for them to review the work he has done with the American Observer employee benefit plans and to approve of their plan to borrow money to buy a larger percentage of the voting shares. I'll fax a copy right over."

"Thank you, Scott, yes, right away." Drive felt vindicated in not calling. His team had gotten bigger then he originally planned. Still, he wasn't happy being filled in by his snoop when it was a matter of public record. Why hadn't she faxed it to him? But Moffie had more news.

"I have a good line on the two directors who resigned from AOM. No details yet, but I can confirm that one of them insisted the board authorize a valuation of the company. The board said no way. The valuation would mean specifying a price that a trustee could justifiably accept, in a sale situation. The first step down the slippery slope of sale. The board didn't even want to consider it, so this guy resigns. It's nice to know there's some honor among these freeloaders."

Drive couldn't help himself. "Quite right. Some companies aren't as lucky to have someone like me take them over."

Within minutes, Drive's private fax was humming. He pushed his sandwich away and crossed over to the machine, remembering the last trip he made to it, only a few days ago. It made him slightly sad. He wasn't sure what his dreamed-of future would hold, now that it seemed within his grasp. What would he find, once he opened his fist?

PENSION AND WELFARE BENEFITS AGENCY
Department of Labor
200 Constitution Avenue, NW
Washington, DC 20210

August 10, 1998

Charles H. Bowditch IV
Senior Vice President
New York Safe Deposit & Trust Company
748 Lexington Avenue
New York, NY 10022

Dear Mr. Bowditch,

You have asked the opinion of this department with respect to the operation of certain employee benefit plans of the American Observer Association for which New York Safe Deposit and Trust Company (the "trustee") acts as trustee. You have provided us with various corporate and trust materials having to do with the establishment of the plans and the appointment and service of the trustee. Based on these documents and the several conversations between you and our staff and our understanding of the Employee Retirement Income Security Act of 1974 (ERISA), it is our opinion:

- The plan has the right to enact rules respecting its conduct, the mode of securing consent of its members and a practice to record the votes of members who express no formal opinion.

- The plan has the authority to determine a strategy for the investment of its assets, subject to the provisions of ERISA and the consent of the trustee.

- To the extent it is consistent with the documents creating the plans and with ERISA, the trustee has the power to borrow money, to purchase AOM B shares, and to pledge the assets of the plan as collateral for the repayment of such loans.

Nothing in this opinion should be construed to limit the authority of the plan sponsor to appoint or change the trustees of employee benefit plans.

Very truly yours,
David Klebowitch
Deputy Assistant Secretary of Labor

Drive furrowed his brow. Who would fund them? They're a day late and 600 million short. There would be *no* arbs for the clock punchers. Looks like our war hero has got himself another no-win scenario. Drive wasn't cheered. The office, filled with papers, was evidence of his state of mind and less than productive day. Perhaps Marty would shed some light and lift Drive's spirits. He resolved to open with some good news of his own, as reached for his phone.

"Marty? Drive. Did you see the letter to the editors in the *Washington Post*? It came from one of our friends. It says that the AOM situation is destroying value for pensioners because federal law encourages it. We have a friend in a senior position on the Senate Committee on Government Ops. He is the chairman of the subcommittee having jurisdiction of all institutions of government. We plan to have him announce the intention to have hearings focused on the American Observer, the Internal Revenue Service, and the Pension and Welfare Benefits Agency of the Department of Labor."

Feeling interrupted, Marty was too tired for niceties. Marty had come down from his high of the day before and was more than overwhelmed with the amount of work left to do. "Any more surprises, Superman? Are you going to have the Pope declare an extra Easter this year? Listen, it really would be helpful if I could talk with your partner and get a real idea of what we can do, if we need it. Just tell me one thing now, any more surprises on the schedule?"

Drive was nonplused. Today was a bad day all around. He didn't want to bring up the Labor letter. Maybe the attorney general progress would assuage the surly, overworked lawyer. It was an idea Marty had liked, Drive recalled.

"Well, yes. The New York state attorney general's office is going to announce an investigation of the administration of certain charities, particularly those that own controlling stock interests in operating businesses."

"Think about it. You're paying me a lot of money to get this deal done. Houdini made a living out of doing it handcuffed, blindfolded, and underwater. I do better with all the facts, you know what I mean?"

"I'll get back to you." Drive hung up. Time to go home. The day was a wash. Time to rest, tomorrow was a big day. Tomorrow would be a better day. No time for newspapers.

To the dial tone Marty snarled, "You stupid jerk. I'm just trying to help."

Chapter 16
Wednesday, August 12, 1998

On Fifty-third Street, just off the east side of Park Avenue, nestled under the Citicorp tower, is the Brook, one of the country's most exclusive clubs. Clubs are rather anomalous in a society profoundly committed to democratic principles, but they have been in existence since the earliest days of the Republic. There is apt to be confusion between social and business clubs. The best clubs are those to which one accedes through inheritance, the fact that at some point some progenitor had to have made money is not discussed, and deny admission steadfastly to those who are considered to have become rich or famous too recently. Stockbrokers traditionally were the dominant energy in this kind of Manhattan social club. Up until the mid-1970s, most of the firms were still owned by the heirs of the founders, and communion with their counterparts in a club environment was arguably an essential part of their businesses. Like many other aspects of New York life, this seemingly immutable element of civilized life was battered by the realities of professionalism and new wealth in the marketplace during the last quarter of the twentieth century.

The Brook, in addition to the usual dining and drinking facilities, had several bedrooms that were particularly welcome for out-of-town grandees and for New Yorkers in the throes of divorce. The membership had a core of common interests: horses, shooting, yachts, country homes, and a continuing sense of its own superiority. The dirty little secret is that membership was bought, not on the crude auction block, but as an implicit condition of favorable business relationships. This is how some of the old-money semi-competents carried their weight in the new professional brokerage firms.

The Porter trustees were, if the truth be told, a bit impressed with the invitation to the Brook. If one has discretionary authority over the disposition of hundreds of millions of charitable dollars every year, plainly one will not want for fancy meal invitations. Indeed, most clubs will find a way to interest people in becoming members. That doesn't mean to say that one belongs, it's only the *money*, after all. This is why, in spite of themselves, and all of the Porters' money, they were impressed that Drive obviously belonged to the Brook.

Drive was one of the legendary figures in the global media pantheon, someone whose level none of the trustees, if the truth were out, could expect ever to attain. Clearly, he had something on his mind. They were frankly curious. Beyond that, he obviously had an idea, a proposal, involving AOM. And that was a subject on which their judgment was the final word. So they came with the expectation that this would be a particularly gratifying episode, confirming their utter dominion over the crown jewel, the *American Observer*, another triumph to brag about at cocktail parties.

Drive had reserved a private room on the second floor for his meeting with the Porter trustees, all five of whom, to his surprise, had accepted his short-notice invitation for luncheon. Habits have changed. Business lunches used to be preceded by a generous martini or two, particularly in the communications businesses, but the good-health mania from California had diluted that taste down to a glass of Chardonnay, or a sparkling water. Different countries have differing customs as to when, in the course of a business luncheon, it is good manners to begin the talk of business. In London, business is not discussed until the fruit course, but of course, the conversation *is* excellent. Drive, the gracious host, gave full license to all, ordered a martini, and started in.

"You will be wondering what occasions me to extend you the dubious pleasure of an invitation to midtown Manhattan in the heart of glorious summer."

Drive was pleased to note that everyone had ordered a cocktail. This might go better than he had hoped. "You gentlefolk," Drive was a bit uncomfortable with the nomenclature on political correctness, so he improvised, "certainly have one of the great responsibilities. The

American Observer Association properties have been one of the publishing wonders of the world. How would the Porters have responded to all the changes? I know in my own company, how difficult it has been to figure out what technologies we need and how to raise the finances. For the Porters and for myself, we at least had the comfort of knowing that if we made a mistake it was our own money." Drive paused and made deliberate eye contact all around. Corny, but it works. "I have vast sympathy for the position that you all are in. You are charged by law with conserving the property which, let's face it, can only be preserved through taking large chances. Very difficult, indeed."

This rather stylish monologue was appreciatively expanded upon, right up to the point where everyone had his second drink in hand. Drive guided them to the table that was laid in what he identified as club silver and club plate. Always the gracious host, he said, "I hope you don't mind indulging an old London habit of presuming on one's guests with a smoked salmon first course that gives the kitchen plenty of time to bring what is wanted from the menu for the main course and means that we don't have to wait." This provoked, it must be admitted, and the liquor helped, several war stories about catching Atlantic salmon. *My God*, thought Drive, *with some practice, some of these people could actually be club members!* The unfortunate conclusion of the stories usually boiled down to the cost per pound of landed fish. Iceland seemed the consensus champion, more fish but much more money. No, perhaps that membership possibility was a bit premature. The construction of a proper mouthful with capers, chopped white onions, and slices of lemon around extremely thin slices of dark bread strained the hand-to-eye coordination of the cocktailed guests. Drive excused himself and asked, "Does anyone else want their bread lightly toasted?" By this time, to use a perhaps unfortunate metaphor, he had them eating out of his hands and everybody raised their hands for toast. *There now*, thought Drive, *class has begun.*

Somehow, Drive had managed it so that he was finished with his salmon while the rest of them were still chasing errant capers and onion slices with the ill-suited heavy club knives. He began, "I have gotten to the age when I think a great deal about inheritance and how a property, such as I have put together, should be run when I am no longer active." *Maybe they think I'm putting them in my will*, mused Drive.

On cue, the now thoroughly domesticated trustees, some absolutely delicious cold Batard Montrachet having miraculously arrived in commodious club white wine glasses, almost shouted interruption, "Never. Your best years are yet to come" and more of the same.

Whatever they thought they were going to eat, ham was being served. Apparently moved by the accolade, Drive continued, "I really don't know that it would work very well for all of my children, and I must confess to having complicated the plot a bit with the odd marriage, don't you know," chuckles of appreciation for the Great Man's candor and a certain prurient insight into a fuller life than theirs, "my children who work in the business taking on responsibility for earning a return for those who are otherwise engaged. I can just imagine the conversation, in a year when the dividends are down, and, gentlefolk, I must confess to a real empathy with your recent situation." The trustees scowled in recollection of the misery of not generating enough returns, not only for those utterly ungracious charities, but to meet the requirements of the Internal Revenue Service. "And if it is felt that the business really needs a new mode of corporate transportation, I hesitate to mention the words Gv, as even today, it must be confessed, I suspect some days my putative heirs would deny even me that modest indulgence."

Murmurs of "Shame" accompanied the arrival of the main course, and, it must be admitted, some of the finest Chateau Haut Brion '77 outside of the cellars of the Dillon family.

At this point, a general breakdown was inevitable as everyone had a vineyard story. Drive, as usual, had the mot juste, "Actually, I imposed on the club to let us have some of my own wine, as, for a special occasion like this, they really didn't have anything suitable."

"I suppose," waxed Drive, who appeared to be able to process his food by osmosis, while everyone else was stuck with knife and fork, "that one must play with the hand one is dealt. When I contemplate how you must be torn between the need to pay dividends, the desire to continue the splendid relationship with the work force that has always been the pride of the American Observer, and the necessity of making constant expensive bets on new technology, I have to question the underlying sense of the scheme that has put you in such a dreadful place. Having had a bit of experience with this genre of property, I might be permitted to opine, this business really must have ownership. The money, the management, the editorial policies, the art, the advertising, the forward investment must all inform a consistent creative strategy. Trustees cannot accomplish this. While you have struggled to such purpose..." Drive paused and looked round the room, in a kind of reality check, to ascertain whether any of his guests detected a trace of irony in his comments. Nope, they were still nodding away, so "one cannot expect that your successors could possibly do so." Drive had to toe this line with exquisite care, so as not to seem obsequious, skillful. He got away with that, so onward. "At the risk of being presumptuous," Drive resumed, "it does appear to an outsider that it is best if this rather unfortunate situation were resolved by those most entitled and best able to do so." The waiters signaled Drive that the special fruit soufflés were ready, so he let his remarks slide and said, "Let's have it for the chefs" and the room literally exploded in gestures and voices of approval. While the lemon and raspberry and strawberry soufflés were being devoured, the last and smallest wine glasses were filled with Sancerre, the greatest of white wines, a rarity and expense beyond contemplation. *My God, he can't be serious*, thought the trustees. Drive raised the glass as if to toast the absent Porters, "Here is to hope that we're all worthy of what the Porters have given the world."

Having with those words made himself part of the solution, Drive proceeded to the hard part. "I am so pleased that you all have been able to get to know me a little and find out how much of what you have read is true. No, no, only the good things! I'm also pleased that you'll be able to understand the sense of humility with which I will announce this afternoon, what I think you will agree, is a generous offer to purchase all of the voting shares of the American Observer." Hardly a ruffle in the general sense of contentment could be felt as the last delicious flakes of the soufflé were washed down with the divine Sancerre. Drive quickly noticed that the chairman's face was getting particularly flushed, and added, "I understand, of course, that nothing can be done except when and as you gentlefolk decide that it is the right thing to do. I am content to abide by your judgment. I have left my various numbers in your offices and would only ask, if you have anything to say about my offer, that you do me the courtesy of saying it to me personally. I know that I have imposed outrageously on your time, but am delighted to linger as long as anyone would like to talk about my offer."

The trustees were stunned. They were the salmon and they had been smoked—charmed by the man, dazzled by the way he had controlled the conversation, immobilized by his ubiquitous hospitality. They nonetheless knew that they must respond in some way. The chairman spoke, perhaps more sharply than he intended, "I don't know what I expected when I accepted your invitation here, but I will say simply the voting stock of the American Observer is not for sale." He gathered back some of his dignity, "It will never be for sale. Thank you for your hospitality." Drive could see in the eyes of two of the trustees a glimmer of interest but as the chairman waffled, that glimmer faded. This was good to know. The chairman was not going to be an ally but they were not a uniform line of opposition either. *The meal had been worth it although it is always a shame to waste really good wine*, Drive concluded.

The trustees walked out of the club, crossed Park Avenue, and headed for the in-town American Observer offices. The air was cooling, but the mood was not. "Does that South African son of a bitch think he can sandbag us with a club dinner and a few sweet words?" It had been many years since the trustees had been placed in the position of having to respond to anyone. They had lifetime jobs, and within limits, the power to confer on themselves *any* financial advantage. The trust held a majority of the voting shares, so there was never a need to persuade anybody of anything. Of course, it's just this need to respond to the demands of a changing world that characterizes a successful business. The trustees were out of their depth. "We got snookered" was the cry, and the best way they could excuse their own incompetence. At some level of honesty, they knew this. They knew that Drive had skillfully handled them, and they were not confident they could handle him.

They strode across the marble entrance hall and into the elevator, which debouched at the formal reception area of the rather sterile, formal offices the company maintained in the city. The chairman barked at the receptionist as they strode past, en masse, into the conference area, "Get me our lawyers." While waiting, the chairman permitted himself some angry comments. "Who does he think he is? What is all that crap about understanding our problem and helping us to solve it? What a nerve."

Time passed and the titans of finance finally had to acknowledge that no contact had been made with the usually obsequious law firm. The junior trustee was signaled to find out what the problem was. The first problem was a tearful receptionist who hadn't the slightest idea who the company lawyers were or how to find out. Fortunately, this trustee had a reaction more constructive than anger. He reached for the phone book, looked up the number, gave it to the now-composed young lady and said, "Ask for Ms. Volpe. Say it is important and she is to be disturbed, whether on a call or in a meeting."

Back in the conference room, the intercom sounded, "Ms. Volpe is out of the office on holiday until August 21, but we can leave a message." The chairman took over, "Tell whoever is on the line that we, the AOM trustees, need to talk to a competent lawyer right now. Keep the line open." Minutes passed, the chairman's mood darkened as his sense of power was insulted yet again. What is the use of being powerful if you can't compel people's attentions? Someone once told him that the greatest joy in having a job in the White House is that everybody took your calls. Finally, a most apologetic voice came on line. "This is Alden Shucks. I am part of Ms. Volpe's team. Can I help you?"

"We certainly expect so. We have just been informed that Cedric Rhodes is going to make an offer this afternoon to purchase all of the voting shares of AOM. We want to stop it. I have all the trustees with me here in this room and we are all agreed. We want to stop it right now, before it gets started." Before realizing that he was beginning to sound hysterical, the chairman vented a bit, "Finally, we're going to get some of our money's worth out of that retainer we have been paying that firm of yours all these years."

Shucks didn't know much about the firm, but he did know that it was an article of faith, no work counted against the retainer and that this problem would be a bonanza of legal charges that could help his career if he played it right. He knew enough not to interrupt.

"Look, Shucks, I want you to get the top people in the firm on this right away."

Shucks made a career-threatening mistake. "This time of year is really tough, everybody's away."

"Listen, young man, what is it...Shucks, you just listen to me. The reason why we pay those goddamn outrageous fees is so that you will be there when we need you. Do you want me to call Ms. Volpe or can I count on you to get her in touch with us here, right away? *We are waiting.*"

"I know Ms. Volpe will be in touch immediately."

Shucks called the vacation house number. No answer. Christ, a degree from Yale should include some practical knowledge. Her secretary was on vacation, so he went to her office and looked through the Rolodex. He saw something in her diary about a yacht trip. He came up with the name of a club in the same Long Island town where she had a home. He called the club; it turned out to be a yacht club. Yes, they knew Ms. Volpe. Yes, she had been there that day. No, she could not come to the phone for the simple reason that she had taken her yacht out for a sail. No, they had no idea when she would be back. Maybe today, maybe not. Big boat, always provisioned. There were several people on board in addition to her professional crew. "Glad to be of help." OK, so Shucks decided, this was getting to be deep water.

He went up to the fiftieth floor where the managing partners' offices were. He approached the secretary for Caesar, the nickname the firm's rainmaker had been assigned by the peons at his level. In this firm, the secretaries were preponderantly men. This guy was decent and sensible. He heard the story. He said, "Damage control, that's what we need...give me the number of that boardroom."

Shucks was getting some idea how the law firm really worked when Caesar's man Friday dialed directly and said, "This is Charles Hildreth. The senior partner has directed me to contact you on his behalf to assure you of the commitment of the full resources of this firm for every minute of every day that it takes to settle this outrageous offer." Shucks watched while the man Friday continued to spin out the combination of concern, flattery, and common sense that was, after all, the only thing that the chairman wanted. It was agreed that nothing could be done until the offer was made public and that the full law firm resources would be committed to immediate and effective response.

All Shucks could say was, "I don't know what they pay you here, but it isn't enough." Friday allowed as how, "All I can tell you, it's a hell of a lot more than you get paid. Now stick around. I may need you. Where did you say that Volpe cow is? What time did she leave? What's the name of the yacht? Well, get the name and the call number. Yeah, I'm going to get the Coast Guard to call her in. Now I have to get some worker bees."

"Pardon, oh fearless leader?" Alden Shucks had made it upstairs, after seven months of trying to be noticed, and he was in no hurry to go back down. He was in way over his head. Humor was all he had going for him, in the present circumstance. Charles Hildreth did laugh. He had just saved a lot of bacon for everybody. He was proud of himself and felt a little magnanimous. "Oh, you don't know, we've got the ropers and the skinners. The ropers, and that includes Volpe, use their fastidious education to do anything to attract and keep the customers. The ropers, right? Then, we've got the skinners, they actually practice law and we need the best right now. I don't know who's here, but I can get the best we've got. There are going to be a lot of unhappy campers around here, this looks like the end of a lot of family holidays."

"Too bad," Alden proffered.

"Agreed," snickered his new best friend.

Drive was caught off guard as his cell phone buzzed next to him in the limo. Rose didn't give him time to speak.

"Hey, where's my call. How did it go? What happened? Are they still there eating out of your hand?"

"I'm floating off to the Racquet Club for a little steam and a massage before the press conference after the market closes."

"How did it go? Any blood?"

"Sometimes, I'm not too, too proud of myself, but this time I managed to get through the whole script without a break. I kept a straight face as I told them how I could help with 'our' problem. I'm not sure it makes any difference, but I think they'll respect me as something quite different. They'll have that little bit of worry I'll come up with something their advisers haven't thought of."

"That's all there is. Plus, your ease in confronting a whole bunch of them all by yourself." She knew what he liked to do, play the charming prince.

"If that's a hint, I couldn't do this without you."

"When I give a hint, you'll know it, because pain will be flying to your brain. Speaking of which, tell those guys at the Racquet to get the juniper out of your breath before the press conference. I think we're going to need just a little bit of help with the attorney general thing and the shareholder suit."

"We've got good lawyers, Marty is world class, and dying to pull out all your stops."

"Maybe we had best work with Marty now that he has most of the tender offer work behind him."

"Give him a call about those two matters. Hey, I'm already at the club, see ya." Drive was ebullient, but he knew there was a hollowness to this conversation, as he bent over to put his shoes back on.

The Racquet Club was ideally equipped for the one and a half hour recovery from a bibulous luncheon. Massage, the plunge pool, three levels of dry heat and wet steam were the precursor to a complete barbering. Drive was virtually horizontal in the barber chair with towels covering his lathered face and re-tinted hair, when he caught the nasal upperclass, "Come on down to the Waldorf, we can hear how this South African bastard plans to buy up the rest of the country." With that thought ringing in his ears, Drive stepped out into Park Avenue for the block and a half walk to the press conference. It was raining. *My God, the hair dye will run all over my shirt.* Not an auspicious beginning.

Having dragooned a club steward with a huge red and blue umbrella, a freshly coifed and relaxed Cedric Rhodes stood up on a dais in the beautiful small conference room on the left-hand side of the graceful stair to the Park Avenue exit from the Waldorf Astoria hotel.

Joey, looking nervous, stood beside him. "Hey, Drive, quite a crowd for an August afternoon. With no bombs, no broads, you're lucky to get anybody." Several more people entered the room and there was a palpable tension. A sense of respect, almost.

"Nice to see a friendly face, Joseph. Do us justice. Don't let them eat me." Drive was eager to charm.

Joey laughed, "Not on my watch," and rapped on the microphone to get the attention of the some forty people in the room. "The young ladies by the door have press releases. Now that the markets are closed for the day, you are free to use all the information they contain. Mr. Cedric Rhodes, the world-famous publisher, broadcaster, and entrepreneur, has today offered to purchase the voting stock of the American Observer Association. He's here to answer your questions."

"Mr. Rhodes, why are you offering to buy only the voting stock? Is that fair to the other shareholders?" This from a young woman, who was affiliated with the *Wall Street Journal*, if he heard Joey's whisper clearly.

"Randy and Shelley Porter created the capital structure of their company. That's the way their trustees have continued to operate. I have to take the cards that are dealt. I don't feel that there's any unfairness here. Nobody purchasing nonvoting stock was misled."

"Follow up: Isn't this just a way of taking advantage of some leverage in order to get back the nonvoting stock at some later time at a lower price?"

"Is that a question or an accusation? What I'm trying to suggest is that I have no intention of taking advantage of anybody. Simply, I don't understand how my present offer has that effect. I *am* listening. I have run a company with minority shareholders according to the laws of this country and the listing requirements of the New York Stock Exchange for more than forty years. I am aware of my responsibilities and am prepared to be judged by how I discharge them in this situation in the future."

"Listen, Mr. Rhodes," this from a young woman identified as *Daily Record*, "this just sounds un-American. You know what I mean."

"I must say that I have often been critical of my mother for staying in South Africa for my birth, but I have spent the best part of thirty years here and two of my children were born here. I have satisfied the Federal Communications Commission that my family trusts are American. I realize that I talk funny," he paused for a weak titter of laughter. He thought, *I'll have to try harder.* "But seriously, there are public trading markets in the nonvoting stock of the *New York Times*, the *Washington Post*, the *Los Angeles Times* before being bought by the *Chicago Tribune*, and the Dow Jones Publishing Company. Before the *Times* bought 'em, the Taylors had two classes of stock in the *Boston Globe*. If all these publishing companies already have two classes of stock, one that votes, one that doesn't, what's the problem with my just continuing the existing pattern at AOM?"

Someone from *Business Week*, "Mr. Rhodes, what are your plans for the *American Observer*? Obviously, you aren't buying this just to let it die?"

"Thanks for that question. It's a great franchise and a great name. Think out a dozen years. We will have worldwide communications with content available to each individual at their choice. My present company, World Publications, has substantial communications capability, a number of different kinds of outlets. The *Observer* complements us at two extremes; the largest number of individual customer records in the world and substantial content available for immediate distribution in several languages.

"Follow up: Why, Mr. Rhodes are you not buying this venture for World Publications and Broadcasting?

"Good question. WPB has so many challenges along the lines of our main businesses; we need to raise so much money to acquire cable and wireless capability that it is difficult to commit the company even more widely. Also, I am, as I like to think it, a young sixty-seven; that is a good age for a CEO, but I like to think that we have great depth in management in WPB and that my focusing on an ancillary venture will allow it to mature. I will continue of course as nonexecutive chairman."

"Let me get back to this fairness question," said a *Financial Times* type. "There has been a great deal of talk that many of the charities, beneficiaries of trusts owning AOM, are very concerned about the integrity of their endowments. How will your offer affect them?"

"Remember, the two classes of stock are identical except for voting. If I make any money out of this deal, so will the other shareholders. I feel justified by my record to suggest that the prospects for the charities are a great deal better tonight than they were yesterday."

"Do you think the trustees of the Porter trusts will consider your offer favorably?"

"You'll have to ask them."

"Have you had any conversations with the trustees?"

"Yes, I have fully acquainted them with my plans."

"What was their reaction?"

"I think it is more appropriate for them to give it to you directly."

"Where are you getting the money for this? You aren't just going to write a personal check...?" A good-natured laughter rippled throughout the room as Drive cocked his head as if considering doing just that and Drive knew he had them.

"Universal Bank is our financier. I have a feeling I'll be seeing a lot of you guys over the next few weeks."

Joey stepped up to relieve Drive and found himself shaking his client's hand.

"Nice job, boss."

"Always leave them laughing." Drive waved him to follow him to the curb outside. Drive wanted to talk.

"Joseph, did you tell any of those guys to call the Porter trustees?"

"Yeah, I did, and you know what they said? 'We told that upstart that AOM is not for sale, not now, not ever. Period.'"

"Their lawyers are not going to like that one. Listen, Joey, remember to pass along to one of our friends that these trustees seem to forget that they are acting on behalf of beneficiaries. They cannot just prejudge every possible offer. This makes them look very bad. One for us. Let's use it."

"Way ahead of you, boss. I just wish we'd caught him on tape!"

"Yes. That is a shame. As always, thanks for your help." Drive said, as he stepped into a cab.

"Well, you did all the heavy lifting," said Joey, confused by his client's kindness.

The door closed and Drive waved as the cab pulled into traffic. Joey wondered how lonely this captain of industry might really be. It didn't make any sense, this guy had it all and then some. It must be something else, and he ran inside to make sure his people had pushed a press kit into every empty hand.

It was late. The sun had come up and gone down and Marty hadn't been outside for two days. He got up for his regular stretching break, every forty-five minutes, no matter what. Standing next to his disheveled desk, he breathed deeply. Back in his California days, he'd learned how valuable basic yoga was to maintaining a balanced existence. The price was right and it made all the difference in the world. He was about to try and clear his mind briefly when the phone rang.

"Shit." It nagged for a few rings while he finished his stretches. Then he punched the speaker-phone button. "Yeah?"

"Lawyer Marty? I'm Rhodes's brains." The voice was alarmingly female.

"Ooo," he scooped up the handset and sat down, "Hey, lady, how'd you get this number, anyway?"

"If you have to ask, don't..."

A lady with balls. Nice, Drive, nice, Marty marveled.

"You need some help, huh! Come to Daddy. Hey, what am I going to call you?"

"Call me Brain and I'll call you Brawn."

"You aren't far wrong. If only you could see the real article."

"Stop selling. There'll be a package delivered to the lobby of your apartment at 6:00 a.m. tomorrow. I'll call you."

"Hey, how do I call you?"

"You don't."

How Marty loved a challenge. After all these days of being the only person in the conversation, he was glad for any relevant contact with another human, especially a woman with some moxie. This was going to be fun.

Chapter 17
Thursday, August 13, 1998

The next day, Marty was still at work but he had showered, in his private bath next to his office, right before the business day started at his firm. He catnapped every couple of hours through the night. He liked looking fresh when they showed up in the morning and knew he hadn't left. It freaked them out. Truth was, Marty freaked them out in general, but he was a boss to be proud of, even if he was crazy. They knew they were flying with an eagle and that made up for a lot.

His phone rang. He hoped it was the call he was waiting for.

"Did you receive the package delivered this morning?"

"Yeah, yeah, I got it." *Make her beg*, Marty thought.

"What's this? A contest to see who speaks first? You're our specialist. We need your judgment. We haven't got much time. Is this arrangement with the attorney general going to work? What do you think of the draft complaint?"

"Okay, okay, one at a time. The thing with the attorney general. Let me get this right. Someone has worked out an understanding with the attorney general that he is going to publicly issue a statement about the trustee situation at American Observer?"

"That's less than half of it. We also have an understanding with his Democratic opponent that he will endorse the same statement a day later."

"Someone has worked out that the attorney general's office, irrespective of political party, will express itself formally about the mess in Tarrytown?"

"That's it. Figured it would make the trustees a bit more attentive. They can't do nothing, or can they?" Rose was no lawyer but she knew there was always an out.

"I have to tell you, before being involved with you guys, I thought that I was a big-city lawyer. Not only do you deliver packages through locked doors, you get opponents in an election to do something politicians never do, and agree. These guys are taking on real power. You know, the fact that both of them are doing it kind of reduces the risks. I gotta hand it to you."

"We've been around a long time. Drive keeps score. We called in a few. It works out to everybody's advantage. Our kind of deal."

"Listen, we gotta make some changes. The trustees must understand their necks are on the line and feel there's a real chance they'll be forced to resign or, worse, get caught holding the bag. "

"Right. We've got to get the attorney general to take a position that gives the trustees room to back down to where we want them. You've got a road trip to Albany at some point."

"Usually, I get mileage, but for you, I'll throw it in. We have to be up front and yet sound like CYA politicians: 'The problematic aspect of the governing structure is it appears to create a tension...' Then we can keep the stuff you have in there about the attorney general being the protector of the public's interest in all charities, blah, blah. Yeah, keep the stuff about extensive investigation. Then, something like: 'Parties close to the transaction expect an agreement imminently.' That's to be a little surprise. The trustees have to understand that there's real money involved here. Conflicts of interest are just a legal nicety until somebody starts to lose money. Now we've gotta give them a road map: 'The attorney general's office confirms that discussions are taking place with trustees and their counsel.' We need something more. We have to show them that doing it our way is better than any other way. How about: 'The attorney general's office was unwilling at this time to opine that the interests of present and future charitable beneficiaries could best be served if the trust were invested in a diversified portfolio of traditional marketable securities.' Yeah, let's try that."

She knew not to squeeze a thing too tightly, something Drive might never learn.

"Have we left the trustees wiggle room? If we push too hard, they can hire lawyers to complain that political pressure is being brought to bear in order to do violence to the clear wishes of Randy and Shelley Porter. We have to stay out of that."

"Good point. We'll put that in the release. How about: 'Sources close to the attorney general deny that investigators have concluded the existence of misconduct in the paid professional relationships of trustees to the American Observer Association.'"

"You've a way with words." Rose never met a legal eagle that didn't, at this level of excellence. "Can we move on to the shareholders' complaint? You know we've invested a lot of time and care developing this case."

"This one is a fine piece of legal work. He has attached affidavits from a wide variety of sources, the flavor of damage is overpowering. The combination of understatement and repetition is devastating. Good solid work. A nice threat. Somehow, you think after reading this *somebody's* done something wrong and has to pay for it."

"The trustees should be staring at a very plausible argument that their handling of the trust asset has lost a lot of people a lot of money."

"Hey, ask me, 'What's the most important thing here?'" *Too easy*, thought Marty.

Rose played along. "Okay, what's the most..."

"Timing."

"Oof! I stepped into that," she laughed.

She laughed, thought Marty, but kept going on to make his point.

"We need to add some language or file an additional motion. The plaintiffs should allege that the risk of continued losses is at crisis level. Panic. The drop in the stock over the last thirty days from $28 to $18 is evidence enough, the market has no faith in this management. We should add on a request for a temporary restraining order, from this point forward to be referred to as a TRO."

"Thank you, counselor."

"You're welcome. Ask a judge to empower someone, like maybe the attorney general of the state of New York, yeah, to appoint a temporary trustee for all the Porter trusts to take control of this situation before there is complete destruction of values. It's 'Ladybug, Ladybug' time. The last time someone granted a TRO like this Boss Tweed owned the courts. Hey, have you guys got some judges on that list?" Marty felt giddy with a sense of mischief, "This is fun."

"Too crude. What kind of judge and in what court are we talking about? Yes, it's life and death, but it is fun."

"Ouch! Out west they like the state courts, but here it is almost always the Federal District Court. Sorry, Brains."

"That's tougher. That's why you're the brawn. Can't remember if we've gone that route before. We can certainly get some press urging some judge or other to do something before these charities are done out of their endowments. But that's not much. What do we really need, minimum?"

"Minimum, we need to have the federal judge at least consider it. Some time for the trustees to stew. We don't need to win; we need to have a forum for the arguments to be raised. Let 'em sweat."

"Can you find out what judge and what court?"

"Lady, with your information-getting skills, I wouldn't trust myself to find a phone number in the Yellow Pages if I could ask you first. They assign these guys by rotation and most anybody in the clerk's office can give an educated guess."

"I am not optimistic. For some reason, we've steered clear of federal judges unless we knew them before."

"Look at the Book of Genesis. On the seventh day, you, too, can rest."

"A comedian no less. We'll talk later."

"Yes, please. Ciao, baby." This was shaping up nicely. Marty felt some new energy and that was what he lived for, if he ever stopped running long enough to think about it.

FORBES
A Second Coming?
by Robert Gwirtzman

In an unusual move, World Publications and Broadcasting czar Cedric "Drive" Rhodes announced today a personal tender offer for all of the voting shares of the American Observer Association. Rhodes's half-century record of growth and adding value is so clearly established that there will be much speculation not so much why he is interested in AOM as why he chooses to make the acquisition outside of his colossal global communications company.

The *American Observer* is an important property. It is a property in decline. It is a property that would benefit from the quality of management represented by Rhodes. But, it is not a property for sale. The chairman of the trustees of the Porter trusts said yesterday, "AOM is not for sale; it will never be for sale, and you can print that." Whether this is a prudent statement for a fiduciary to make is not a matter to be pursued further here. There is no shortage of local companies and entrepreneurs who would be delighted to purchase AOM, which is currently selling at $18 a share, the lowest price since it was offered to the public in 1990. What does Rhodes know that the Porter trustees don't? He is not a man of quixotic gestures.

We will not have long to wait. The chairman of the Porter trustees said there would be a formal meeting on Monday at which the Rhodes offer would be the sole item of business and will presumably be rejected. We can expect an imaginative and, perhaps, surprising response from Cedric Rhodes; that is his established fifty-year trademark.

Joey was ecstatic. The business press reported the tender utterly differently than one might have expected from the questions at the press conference. This meant that Joey's behind-the-scenes work had been effective. There was one steady drumbeat: this is an effort by a foreigner to steal a treasured American property. The effort to buy property by offering for 20 percent of the equity is blatantly unfair. The offer was compared with the Mitsubishi purchase of Rockefeller Center as an indication of foreign insensitivity to American icons. The bombings had made it an easy argument to seed and push. The articles were strewn with comments from "persons close to the trust" who echoed a consistent wail: If anybody is going to get cashed out of this disaster they had better take out the charitable trusts, too. There was no logic or fairness in these comments. They simply reflected an opinion held by many people in positions of authority in the life of New York City that the decay of AOM represented an intolerable risk to the continued provision of essential services to the community. Implicit was anger that Rhodes might be able to make a good deal for himself without having any obligation to deal with the problem of the prominent charities. No one seemed to accept his statement that the only way he could make money would be by making money for all the shareholders. The surprising theme in the stories about Rhodes's offer was the general community agreement that something needed to be done and soon about AOM.

The trustees' prompt statement that the company was not for sale was recorded starkly. It was expected, but stated so bluntly there was a strong sense that this would not be the end of the story. One article focused on the reaction of the attorney general's office to the concern over charitable control over the decaying venture. Rather than the expected "no comment," the attorney general's spokesperson issued a formal statement: "The attorney general is responsible for monitoring public charities within the state of New York. His office has conducted an extensive investigation into the state of affairs at the American Observer. A formal statement will be forthcoming within twenty-four hours."

Joey shook his head. How did Drive get that to happen? Sweet. Just the right touch, just a hint. Like a whisper, it'll get the most attention.

Marty walked down from his office on Third Avenue and crossed over at Forty-third Street to enter the Chrysler Building. As a city native who had lived away for a time, Marty relished particular walks and particular views in the city he considered beautiful. When he was a child, Art Deco was the coming thing. Until the Lever Building went up on Park Avenue in the early 1950s, there was nothing that bespoke the modern world more dramatically than the lobby of the Chrysler Building.

He was immediately ushered into Drive's office by a most improbable combination of English accent, fine French limbs, and German bust. Marty's "Where do you find 'em?" was dismissed by a wave. The great man was pouring over what looked like *Who's Who in America*.

"Who is this guy Anthony Williamson, anyway?"

"We're going out the door of this building in half an hour, walk two blocks, go up to the twenty-first century and pay court on King Tony. You know that his Shark Management is the largest shareholder outside of the Porter trusts of both the A and the B stock of AOM."

Impatiently Drive closed the book and looked at Marty, "I know all that and I can make nice when I have to, but what's going on? I thought that I had heard of all the big investors. I can't believe that the guy is so important that you feel it's worth your time."

"The world has changed. You and I got into the wrong lines of work. Powerful people have always needed someone like me to make it work for them; there are always builders and owners like you. Now we have the new world of paper ownership. The richest guys don't own the businesses anymore. The richest guys own the firms that manage the pieces of paper. Tony Williamson is a lucky guy. He spent twenty years in one of those self-proclaimed gentlemen's brokerage firms, like Kidder Peabody, managing money. Not a top-level job, not a top-level firm. But, he was in the right place. He found out about the consultants. This paper revolution started about twenty-five years ago when somebody figured out that most of the savings in the country would move out of banks and into pension trusts. Even a low-level Kidder guy figured that being just one of the managers for the New

York Telephone pension plan produced more revenue than the whole moth-eaten investment banking department. Money management is close to the perpetual motion machine in the list of man's greatest creations. No heavy lifting, no going out of doors in the cold, no bar exam, just great fees, no incremental costs, and this is the good part, no performance requirement to speak of."

"Wait a minute. Who manages our pension fund?" Drive winced at how the rules of the game had changed, right under his nose.

"The King has floors full of dweebs, just like he used to be, and they have the answer to your question, and they've analyzed it and modeled it and thrown darts at it." The teacher was speaking and Drive was taking notes. "You see, that's the magic of it. The real money game is being played in a different world than we grew up in. Look into it and I'll predict something. The trustee and the manager of your pension fund will turn out to be clients of your old buddy Spencer Sherman. The pension money is the grease that keeps this great city prosperous."

"Well, how did some low-level twerp in middle age get this kind of power?"

"Hey, I'm getting there. This is a win/win game if nobody complains. The only possible problem is when these well-paid managers actually lose money or underperform. Well, that's where the consultants come in. First, the law. The law says the trustees are not responsible for the fund's performance; they are only responsible for having acted reasonably in picking the managers. And who decides what is reasonable? You guessed it, the consultants. So, Anthony, never Tony to his face, lucked out, and began referring business to one of the local consultants and the merry-go-round got started. A consultant recommends Tony and Tony invests some of the pension fund into specialized investment baskets invented by guess who? The consultant. A couple of more clever ideas and the money really began to flow. Listen, we better get out of here. The King doesn't tolerate lateness..."

They crossed Forty-second Street still deep in conversation, passed the old Mobil building, and turned down Park Avenue next to the

Grand Central viaduct before turning left to the entrance of a new building obliquely sited on the lot. Drive couldn't believe that he was going to yet one more meeting to ingratiate himself with yet one more egomaniac. He was getting upset over how difficult it was to keep Marty on his right side as they crossed the streets. He didn't want to miss a word. "Marty, you aren't along just for the ride."

"You bet I'm not. Tony's gonna want something. As long as I am there, he knows the message has been received. There is no point in your going alone."

"What are you talking about?"

"Just enjoy the view; we'll talk about it later." The elevators streaked up in their clear plastic tubes; the doors opened with a huge swoosh from above, depositing the passengers into a several-story, light-filled dome. Drive understood now why the building was constructed at an angle to the street, to optimize its exposure to the sun's passage. He marveled at the combination of shades and tints that seemed in constant harmony to provide for optimal illumination. It was almost an anticlimax to stare out at the Empire State Building and the incredible semicircle of open office space with room dividers, a cunning contrivance of clear plastic and wiring that made museum-quality statuary appear to be suspended in space.

There was no receptionist, but a tall blond young man, with the kind of intelligent physical confidence that advertised he had played major league baseball at the same time as going to Harvard, moved up to greet them. "Anthony's been held up with a conference call from China. The Prime Minister insisted on a follow-up from our visit last weekend. He asked me to get started." Jim escorted them to a jewel-like space, suspended on the westerly side, literally a glass cube with an opaque floor hung on spun-glass cables. He bounded up the three risers and advised, "This space can be moved around this entire open area as Anthony feels comfortable." There was a round table and four Lucite chairs. The cube was lifted silently. Jim began pompously, "We've an identity device in the downstairs lobby and elevators so we've some notice about who is visiting us; it allows us to have that clean-space feeling when you arrive. I don't know what you know about Shark Management, but it is entirely the creation of Anthony Williamson. We pick securities from all over the world. We bet that they're going to go up or go down. We leverage the bet and, for the last half dozen years, have produced great results for our clients, who include most of the big institutions of the world. Anthony no longer has a need to work; he enjoys creating beautiful spaces like this office and acting as mentor to employees like myself."

At this point, Drive couldn't figure out how the King was going to make his entrance. Somehow without his noticing it, the conference space had been lowered and turned so that a short, rather florid, gnome of a man, clad in the most improbable Donegal tweeds, strode into the space and took his seat at the end of the table. "Well, gentlemen, welcome, I trust Jim has given you the honors of the place. You are as busy as I, so no apologies in order. Let's get to it. My business is to provide something extra for my investors. In a distress situation like AOM, usually I am part of the solution to the problem and I expect to be paid for my value added." He smiled at Marty in departing, "I can leave it to you gentlemen to figure out the details. Maybe something with World."

Marty cautioned Drive not to say a word in the elevator or downstairs lobby. When they got to the street, Drive could stand it no longer. "That little chiseler is going to be no partner of mine. He is ridiculous. Absurd." They strode back towards the Chrysler Building in silence. Marty just waited. They settled in at Drive's office, in the comfy chairs by the view. Drive looked expectantly at Marty. The lawyer took a deep, calming yoga breath and began.

"Tony has gotten to the point that he can afford a few whims. His numbers are great this year. AOM is not a big holding out of his $20 billion currently under management. He gets his kicks from having us pay respect. The word will be out all over town that you came by to get his advice. You're the deal of the year and his chubby fingers are all over it. Now we have to figure out how to give him something, so that he doesn't dissent, threaten lawsuits, or solicit votes against us.

It gets complicated because we have to give him something he can boast about so he can extract even more from the next deal. So no secret deals. The trick here is to make this his deal; then the word gets around town that King Tony has forced yet another management to accommodate him. If you can forget the personal side, we should be so lucky as to have this guy in the AOM stock."

Drive asked, "I hate giving that poofy toad a nickel. Have I got the math right? One percent of $20 billion, that's $200 million. And if they outperform whatever index it is, by say 2 percent, that's another 20 percent or $50 million!"

"You're getting there. Add on the brokerage fees they control, maybe another $200 million, and all the expenses of the fund: custodian, accounting, legal, you name it. This money has a way of getting around. Now you understand who the really rich guys are in today's world. Great business has always been done by the middlemen. The King just found a new middle in the new technology boom. The stakes are in his favor. He got there first and he's got us coming and going. There's no losing for the King right now."

"I feel like a pauper. So, if the fees are big enough, any deal can be done."

Marty concluded, "That's how our impossible deal gets done, in the end. You know, money or no money, the guy was really nervous. He called me yesterday and rehearsed a whole pile of stuff about SASSOL (South African Synthetic Oil), just so he could let you know that he knew more than you do about South African business. Then he shows up in that suit. Some tailor probably told him it was just the thing for a meeting with an Oxford man. He spent so many years at Kidder in the back room. When the real people showed up, Al Campbell and Ralph DeGuglio took 'em out. Poor guy. Never learned any social graces. Now, all the money in the world won't buy 'em."

Drive was amused, "Hey, I didn't realize that I had a social critic and a psychologist helping me."

"I'll tell you something else. Being with a guy like that makes you think. Lawyers are guys who did well at school, but have no brains.

Our clients have all the money and control our lives. We make landlords rich, we make our clients rich, and we aren't even smart enough, like the accountants, to sell stock in ourselves to let the public make us rich."

Drive couldn't resist, "Ah, pity the poor lawyers, a touch of midlife crisis!"

The trustees met back at company headquarters in Tarrytown in order to review the situation. The city could prove treacherous. Everyone was horrified by the prominence given the chairman's hasty comment that the trustees would *never* sell AOM. A pall hung over the meeting in the absence of the chairman facing up to his mistake and encouraging a forthright assessment of their alternatives.

Their law firm had struggled to mount what appeared to be a coherent competence to deal with the Rhodes threat. Calls had rained in to everyone at late hours, long after the trustees were accustomed to being responsive to anybody. The chairman's account of his late-night phone call with a hysterical general counsel, their great legal diva, La Volpe, was the topic at hand. Nothing would do, apparently, short of a stroke-by-stroke account of how every imaginable device had been set in motion by La Volpe. She would be in immediate command of any problems and how all of these provisions would be totally reliable, but apparently had in fact failed. The notion of the chairman, at midnight, having to respond to his lawyer's plight, why she couldn't do what her best client could reasonably have expected, brought smiles to some of the faces around the table. Ms. Volpe was apparently in full voice and required an immediate account of every step that had been taken in her absence. By this point, the chairman knew that he was beaten. He was back in the hands of the professionals and he had no choice but to sit back and do what he was told. The upshot was that they were now in attendance of Volpe's arrival.

The chairman teed off on the morning press. "What an infernal outrage that no one pointed out the simple and obvious fact that Randy and Shelley Porter wanted us to continue to own and run AOM.

Simple as that. What is this nonsense about the charitable beneficiaries? Those people with the fancy names running those charities have
never raised nickel one. How they ever got so lucky as to get the attention of the Porters, who really, if the truth be known, didn't give a hoot
for those particular charities, that's a real story. What a nerve they
have. They are lucky to have anything."

While the chairman continued to inveigh against the moon and
the stars for not instantly aligning with the interests of the trustees
of the Porter trusts, the unmistakable noise of a helicopter descend-
ing filled the room. There hadn't been much helicopter presence
around here lately. It struck a really bad note when so many personnel
had been laid off. Trust the lawyer. The blades had not come to rest
when the exit ramp was set and an elaborately dressed middle-aged
woman led a procession of young men toward the front door. It was
noteworthy that she was the only one who didn't duck as they passed
under the spinning blades.

La Volpe was all business, no tireless rendition of how she had
gotten from yacht to land to clothes to office to documents to
helicopter. That story would be someone else's punishment, no doubt.
"This is straightforward. From a legal point of view, there is very
limited exposure. None, I might say if," and she permitted herself a
glance at the chairman, "we can be disciplined about public statements. I do not like the situation. Too many things are happening that
I cannot account for. What is happening with the attorney general's
office? They never stick their necks out when a prominent local company is involved, this close to an election. And what is happening
with all those wonderful people who are trustees of the Met, the Ballet,
the Hospital? What's got into them? First things first, we've got a lot
of friends. It's time to call in some favors. Who handles the public relations here?"

The chairman bumbled through an explanation that combined
regret that there really wasn't any need for the department so the personnel had been dismissed, and anxiety, in that the decision had, in
the present circumstances, been proved to be wrong.

"Who's in charge of handling this crisis?"

The fact that La Volpe had to ask the question was its own answer. The chairman had already blotted his copybook and did not want to risk repeating the experience. It was the Romans hiring the barbarians to protect them all over again. The Porter trustees were going to have to rely on the hired help. To her credit, Volpe took over with a vengeance. She had one young man after another scurrying to phones, drawing up lists, assigning tasks, and periodically grabbing an instrument to deliver the instructions personally. Morning passed, sandwiches were brought in, and still the trustees sat around in semi-stupor. By mid-afternoon, Ms. Volpe was prepared to report.

"Number one. We have hired Nick Denton & Company to do our public relations. They are expensive but we can't afford not to have them. Nick, of course, is on vacation. This is, after all, August. Leave it to a foreigner. I talked with Nick and he assures me that he will keep in personal charge. Here's the plan: we'll get our friends in the press to give a retrospective on the positive impact that the American Observer Association has had on this community for many years; the number of people and institutions whose lives have benefited, the wisdom of the Porters, the volatility of business, and the desirability of encouraging continuance of what has been a very good thing. Then we move to the attack. Not those beneficiaries, who are stabbing us in the back, but Rhodes. We will do this subtly. What is some foreigner doing meddling with one of America's crown jewels? Why doesn't he pay attention to his own company, which, by the way, hasn't been making anybody much money lately? What is a bank like Universal doing financing a project like this? They have a responsibility to the community to protect its pillars. Several of the directors will be getting personal calls from the right people. Doesn't one of their subsidiaries have a relationship with our employee benefit plans? We ought to think about firing them, quickly. Finally, we've organized a delegation from the Bar Association Committee on nonprofit organizations to make an official call on the attorney general in aid of the proposition that his monitoring responsibilities must be discharged in a discrete manner, remote from apparent political considerations. There may be a couple of articles suggesting the current attorney general is over-reaching in light of a tough election. Now we have to get organized for a proper trustees meeting. Everything has to be by the book, so we need the notice period. I think Monday's the right time; we'll organize a little press conference afterwards, have the meeting here. That's a statement to show that we possess the property."

The chairman saved the last word, "That goddamned bank. No loyalty anywhere. But, I think we better not fire them from the ESOP. The old New York Safe Deposit & Trust Company goes back a long way with the employees here, and we're having enough trouble on that front." Volpe agreed and added, "Indeed, we should send a letter to the officers of the ESOP, urging them to act for the exclusive benefit of the members. They might just come in useful somehow."

At this same time in another part of the Tarrytown complex, quite a different meeting was taking place. Horse has come directly from home to meet with the ESOP committee, and Drive Rhodes.

Drive had probably gone alone to several hundred confrontational meetings over the last forty years. During this time he had come to understand that angry gatherings need to vent their frustrations before anybody can hear what anyone else is saying. He had learned that his unobtrusive manner and quiet speaking tones were ultimately very useful. While angry meetings start with a roar, they usually end with a unanimous murmur.

When Drive entered the small conference room, the angry members of the ESOP committee were subdued by the fact that he was alone and that he very politely introduced himself to each one of them separately. When Drive began to talk about his empathy for the ESOP, no one really knew whether they could indulge in the luxury of believing him. He moved on to lay out so clearly that with all the best will in the world the Porters had bequeathed a nightmare. With an exquisite skill, Drive directed the meeting's anger towards the sustained poor performance of the trustees and the management. He said, very modestly, that his own record of creating valuable properties and well-paying jobs was a matter of public record. By this time, the mood of the meeting had changed.

When it was time to respond to Drive, Louis Skapinsky spoke slowly and patiently, "Excuse me, sir, I don't think you understand us, Mr. Rhodes. We're the people who make this business here, and we think we ought to own this company. We have nothing against you, but you're a coming late to our party, and uninvited."

Drive was eager to get this meeting over with; he felt he was merely being polite in talking to them at all. "I don't want to say anything that could be understood as being disrespectful. I believe in employee ownership. That's why I've always put all my money in companies where I work. I would simply suggest to you that the global competitive pressures on all publishing companies are today so different than they were when the Porters were alive, that a continuation of past practices may not be enough for success. I am not a magician and I don't promise you any certain success but I can sincerely ask you to consider my record and whether you might not be able to credit that I could build greater value and better jobs here." Drive felt flustered, and embarrassed by his last convolution. *Maybe I'm under the weather*, he thought. It had been a stressful time. He continued, "I really think that's all I have to say. I can understand if you don't agree with me, but I hope that you will ultimately feel my offer represents the best route for all of us."

"Mr. Rhodes, look, say we don't tender, you can still get control of our company, the American Observer, yes? And if we do tender and..." Skapinsky waived dismissively in the direction of the helicopter parked next to the executive building across the lawn, "they don't, they don't do a lot of things, you know, and you still don't get control of our company. Please tell us why are we important to you?"

Drive was utterly at a loss to respond to these unexpectedly moderate words. He was feeling feverish. The room was warm and all these people. He waffled, "All the stock...accounting...taxes...minority problems under Bermuda law."

It was getting worse. A second questioner said calmly, "Would it be fair to conclude that you want to be free to organize this company's future without having to deal with its employees as significant owners?" Horse couldn't help but smile at that shot, boom, right between the eyes.

Drive's continued discomfiture was an elegant answer. The parties simply looked at each other and shuffled their feet until Drive, with a polite wave, simply walked out to his waiting car. Horse, who had been silent throughout the meeting, walked with Drive and they exchanged pleasantries. The air was cooler. Drive began to recompose himself.

"You've built yourself a sharp little team, Horse, if I may call you that?"

"You may. Mr. Rhodes, they did it all themselves."

"Make it Drive," Drive said as he offered his hand. "It's to your credit all the same and now I'll bid you a good day. I look forward to our next day on the green."

"Me, too." And with that Drive closed the door on the limo and drove away, haunted by his miserable performance.

Horse returned to the meeting and was asked, "What are we going to do about this?"

Horse was decisive. "One thing's for sure. We need to have an official meeting of the ESOP and formally decline Rhodes's offer. We can do that on Monday. OK, so much for that. Let me tell you what I know. Vern finally talked with me on Tuesday. He said that the bank is financing Rhodes's offer, and it's the biggest deal of his career and we simply have to get out of the way. I told him plainly that so long as I am the trustee of the ESOP, I feel constrained to express the interests of the beneficiaries without reference to any other considerations the bank may have. He took this in bad grace, but seemed to understand that either the company would have to discharge the bank as trustee or the bank would have to fire me as its representative. Nobody in the bank is willing to talk with me about lending us money. I have made some calls around town and the word is out, don't deal with us! I have some more calls to make, but it is beginning to look as if the system is going to shut down in our faces, no money."

"I can't believe they can simply dispose of this company over the dead bodies of the employees. Don't we have any legal rights?"

"Right after our vote on Monday, I'm off to the Department of Labor in Washington. They'll have the last word on our rights in this situation. I know the law but I don't know this administration's commitment to enforcing it. Once we know that, we will know our next steps."

FRIDAY, AUGUST 14, 1998

Vern and Drive talked briefly on the phone. Vern was confident, or at least hoping to appear so. His job was to never disappoint the client and having the finger on Horse's button would be his last resort. He'd push it if he had to, frankly he wouldn't mind in the least.

"It is all going according to plan. I have had a few apologetic calls from my directors who acknowledge some kind of past indebtedness to the Porter trusts, but nothing serious. They just have to say something for the record. It's funny but nobody likes that situation out there. There are just too many connections for anybody but you to raise the issue, that's the definition of good business. Opportunity seen and developed."

Drive was still cautious. "I'm glad you're so upbeat today. I'm feeling pretty good, too. I have one television interview for an end-of-week summary. Are you confident that you have that ESOP situation under control? It worries me. I met with those guys in Tarrytown yesterday. There's no meeting of the minds there."

Upbeat Vern replied, "I talked with Charles directly. Frankly, I think we have them stymied. They can't get financing in time to pose a problem. I don't think that we can fire him right now in view of his prominence in the industry. The AOM management is mad as hatters with us, but they've got the performance problem and the unhappy charities. They don't want to take on their employees too, right now. I agree with you, it is uncomfortable, but I can't see how they can stop this deal."

Drive carried on as if that issue had been resolved. "I am beginning to worry about your Molly Munro. What I hear is that she has a lot of discretion in cases like this. I don't know what it means, but I don't like it. I think that you can expect a formal announcement from the New York State Attorney General's office. There is a little spin there that will amuse you. We have a couple more things set up for next week, but I am spending my time being sure that my friends are prepared to move quickly as we may need them."

At the Department of Labor, Molly was having her end-of-day meeting with Levin and Klebowitch.

"I talked with Charles Bowditch today. A strange situation. We've given them our opinion, they can borrow money. Now they find that no one will loan it to them, Charles says that the town is shut down. The word's gone out. We haven't got authority to force banks to make loans, do we?"

Klebowitch shifted uneasily in his chair. "You know. There are so many conflicts of interest in all of these situations that if we could get the right facts, we might be able to loosen everything up. I don't have anything specific in mind yet, but I am going to think about it. Bowditch is coming down next week to talk with us. Maybe we'll come up with something."

Molly looked at the floor in disgust. "You know, it's just sickening to go through all these legal procedures, create rights so that policies can be implemented only to find out in the real world, the beat goes on and nothing changes."

Levin observes, "Hold on Boss. It's a fight for sure but it's still an early round. We've got plenty of blood and ink to spill if it comes to that."

OFFICE OF ATTORNEY GENERAL
STATE OF NEW YORK

August 14, 1998

The Attorney General of the State of New York today confirmed reports that his office has conducted extensive investigation of the administration of the trusts created by the late Randy and Shelley Porter holding controlling interests in the stock of the American Observer Association. The attorney general is highly confident that ongoing discussion with the trustees and other interested parties will result in a resolution that will protect the affected vital interests. It is recognized that a structure appropriate for one time may not be appropriate for another. There is no indication of misconduct or negligence.

Drive's interview on the "Week's Business Review" hour-long broadcast at 6:00 p.m. had been taped at noon, so that everyone could get to the beach ahead of the traffic. There was, therefore, no reference to the action of the attorney general and his political opponent. The interview followed the style of television, a lot of softballs wrapped up in showmanship.

Drive was asked one surprisingly intrusive question.

"Are you not concerned, sir, that one of the shareholders of World Publications and Broadcasting will take the position that you are making use of that corporation's assets in order to make a personal profit for yourself?"

He answered platitudinously about the years of effort he had devoted to creating his supreme corporation until interrupted by the questioner.

"Sir, excuse me, I've asked a very specific question, you've acquired vast influence and power as the chief executive of WPB. Is it unreasonable that people who bought stock in that venture depend on your continued fidelity to the enterprise?"

"I am not sure that I appreciate your choice of words. Faithful I am and always will be." Drive had to regroup. *Slow down, slow down, Big Boy*, he told himself. "My relationship with WPB is defined by a contract that is in the public domain. It might be felt that at age sixty-seven, I had earned the right to some time of my own."

For the second time in this pursuit, Drive realized that he was blowing it. He hadn't got it right with the ESOP and he was not coherent on the expectations of his lifelong partners in WPB. He needed some downtime. He left the broadcast studio, returned home to the Sherry Netherland, collected his wife, and headed out for a weekend in Southampton at the splendid estate of longtime friends.

The frantic Ms. Volpe had the attorney general's press release read to her over the cell phone on her yacht to which she had repaired in an effort to salvage at least a weekend of the long-planned holiday.

"Mother of Jesus, what is going on around here? Since when do politicians attack mothers, babies, and apple pie?" She remembered the old saying: When you are in a poker game and you don't know who the fool is, he's the one holding your cards. That's how she felt now and she had no idea what to do. But notwithstanding, client control demanded yet another call. Billable time and everyone knows everything, even when there was nothing to know, then they just know that you still care.

"Mr. Chairman." There was no need to tell him that she was calling from the yacht. "About the latest developments?" That was a tactic straight out of Client Control 101. Always make them feel they're on the outside looking in. It makes them more dependent.

As it happened, the chairman had gone home early and was desperately trying to escape from any thoughts of the past horrible week. Deeply into his third Chivas of the evening, he felt like being gracious. He was sick, though, of the little tricks. "I suppose you want me to ask, what developments? Cut the crap and tell me what I need to know."

La Volpe had gone too far; pretty soon, he would figure out his twenty-four-hour-a-day protector was, in fact, far away on her yacht. She had best shut up. "The attorney general issued a brief release talking of an investigation of the Porter trusts and their relationship with AOM, and was confident that an amicable rearrangement could be made. What do you know about all this?"

"I just know that they've been around for months. My secretary called around five o'clock and said there was a registered letter from the attorney general's office for me. I told her I'd pick it up on Monday."

"My advice is to get that letter now and to let me know what's in it. I haven't gotten to the good part. The attorney general is a Republican. Guess what? His Democratic opponent issued a press release in which he associated himself with the actions taken, saying AOM was too important an asset to get caught up in partisan wrangling. I've never heard of such a thing. What is going on? Have we *no* influence?"

The chairman was dumbfounded. The one constant in his life had been the venality of all politicians and their willingness to do anything for AOM and the Porter Trusts, in the hope of grants or gifts. Nobody had ever attacked Santa Claus before this damn offer. The unhappy consequence was that the organization, from the chairman down, had no survival skills. This probably meant they had the wrong lawyer, the wrong PR person, and the wrong strategy. Playing catch-up ball, they were doomed to fail. The chairman still couldn't figure out how Rhodes was going to succeed, because no matter what else happened, no matter how embarrassing the dialogue or how damaging the disclosures, nothing could happen unless he personally permitted it. He could not imagine what on earth would make him do so.

We have influence, but who are we fighting? And what is the battlefield? he thought out loud in his lonely study, decorated with trophies from a lifetime ago.

Chapter 18
Sunday, August 16, 1998

When they connected, Drive's family kept together with weekend calls, so he was not surprised to hear from his younger son. Everyone understood, that barring emergencies, the week was usually just too frantic to be able to hold his attention, so no one ever tried.

"Hey, Da, it sure is great to see the old genes conquering new kingdoms, and in the middle of the summer, too! Didn't they tell you nothing gets done in August?"

"Yeah, you're right, Trip. I should've talked with you before you read about it in the papers, I know, I know."

"Oh no, Da, that's fine. I'm not nagging you. I'm sure you know what you're doing." His son was actually enjoying one of the few times in their relationship when he had the old man on the run, so, cunningly enough, he kept quiet.

Drive understood that he was going to have to say something. "I've been trying for a long time to figure out a way to get out of the way of you kids, give you a chance to grow, and, at the same time, do something for myself." Drive didn't usually give much in conversations with his son, but he felt a particular need to explain because of the stupidity of having talked with no one before launching this scheme. How could he have forgotten? *Thoughtless old fool*, he thought. "I like the challenge of trying to rebuild a great business using someone else's money. It'll give me a focal point; it'll make me less restless."

"Dad, you can do whatever you want, but, believe me, buying a new business is *not*, repeat *not*, going to do anything for your restlessness. You don't need the money. We don't need the money. I know you'll tell me what you want me to know, but I just hope you aren't digging in too deep."

Drive thought to himself, *I hope so, too.* He changed the subject. "Have you talked to your uncle lately?"

"Sure, I talk to him all the time. He has no idea what you're doing, but he always says you've done so much for us, he prays you'll find some peace for yourself."

"That does sound nice, all we can do is hope, I guess. I am looking forward to some quiet time after the storm."

The weekend passed without any public developments beyond an article in the *New York Times*. Joey was very impressed. It read like one of his press releases. He had to hand it to Drive, he sure knew what to feed them to attain the desired result.

> The decline of the American Observer Association has been a matter of profound regret for the many people in this community who have benefited from its bounty. At this point, we need to raise fundamental questions. When an attorney general publicly discloses the need for his office to monitor the affairs of a prominent organization, that is a matter for concern. When his opponent in an upcoming election associates himself with the incumbent's effort, that is a matter for wonder. What is going on that is so serious as to merit this extraordinary behavior? We have considered the scholarly concern with the propriety of conducting business corporations within the framework of ownership by charitable enterprises. There are serious questions that need to be answered. We hope and expect that those answers will be forthcoming shortly.

Drive began to feel that something was going on that he couldn't quite put his finger on when his oldest daughter, the American Rhodes herself, made a surprise call as well.

"Come on, Daddy, give me a break. What's going on? You always tell us to buy the future and here you are, buying something that Queen Victoria would have loved. Daddy, do I detect a little restlessness?"

Drive was flattered that his daughter still thought of him as a person, a male person with the usual needs, but he didn't want to cross that bridge yet, so he said lightly, "You know the old man, Sis. I'll be buying and selling on my deathbed."

"Uncle John hopes that one day you are finally going to feel free, free to do something for yourself. He says that you are a deeply spiritual man and that business is just a distraction, something you do because it comes easy, and we should understand this business with the American Observer as a step toward your freedom."

"My brother is a very wise man. I believe this is exactly that. I'm trying to make this thing come together so I can have something of my own to tinker with. I should've called but, you know, there's so much to do and I'm working with new people. We're doing something that's never been done before and many people believed was impossible. This is all a little heavy, my dear. I'm just a businessman." Drive felt tired, trying to explain it all. He felt like he was auditioning again.

"Not in my books, Daddy. I know a lot of businessmen now, and there's more going on in your head than anyone else I know."

"Thanks for that. I'll call you when things settle down, in a few weeks. Give my best to your mother."

Chapter 19

Monday, August 17, 1998

The board of trustees of the Randy and Shelley Porter trusts convened in their meeting room in New York City at 9:00 a.m. Also present were Ms. Volpe and several attendants from the law firm. Before the chairman could call the meeting to order, Ms. Volpe inquired, "So, what did all of you think of that statement by the attorney general?" There were blank and confused faces all around the table. Silence. Even La Volpe, who was not noted for sensitivity to the feelings of others, was reluctant to pierce the silence. Finally, the chairman angrily shouted, "There wasn't anybody around on Friday afternoon to help me circulate the material to anybody else." He was a person who was not used to arguing, so if he must make a point, he took on anger.

This was a trigger for expressions of rage and frustration from the long-silent trustees. The chairman's iron hand was instantly a thing of the past. One of the members asked their lawyer, "My colleagues and I would be grateful if you could tell us what this is all about."

Magdalena Maria Volpe, who had an acute sense of who in a client organization has to be pleased, detected a distinct sea change in the room. Rather than deferring to the chairman, who had retreated to a silent scowl, she said simply, "That is a very good question. I *have* read the attorney general's letter, and my firm has studied it with exquisite care, and we cannot answer your simple and essential question. The attorney general, who is joined in his opinion by his Democratic opponent for election in November, says that he is confident the problems between the trustees, yourselves, and the company AOM and the state of New York can be amicably worked out without criminal or civil liability for anybody."

Each trustee looked stricken and their chairman was now concentrating on a bit of lint he had noticed on his sleeve. Suddenly,

Volpe was bombarded by questions from everyone. "What problems do we have with the attorney general's office?" "What is this about liability?" "What investigation?" It's unmistakable that the chairman had considered the yearlong involvement with the state of New York to be an affront personally and professionally, and he didn't deem it appropriate to share with his colleagues.

The tenor of the meeting changed utterly by the time La Volpe finally managed to raise the only piece of business on the agenda; the trusts' response to Rhodes's tender. She felt that power has shifted sufficiently and decisively for her to establish control. "No one should ever say that this trust would *never* consider an offer to sell any assets that the trusts may hold." She insisted on plowing ahead pedantically in further effort to cement the primacy of the law firm in the trusts' affairs. "The trustees are under a sacred and inveterate obligation to manage the affairs of the trusts for the benefit of the designated charities. This means that you must consider all possibilities in the effort to optimize values. You can't reject anything out of hand." With the chairman's authority destroyed, it was not surprising that one of the trustees asked plaintively, "Well, what should we do?"

Ms. Volpe, who had more to lose out of this situation than most, being counsel to the prestigious trusts was fine, but the bulk of legal fees came from the company. She retreated into legal caution. "The trustees will have to consider seriously any offer. This offer, $30 per share, represents a 60 percent premium over the price at the close of the market on Friday. However, the stock has traded near this level within the last nine months."

The trustees were emboldened. "Before we get all caught up in due diligence chatter, please tell us what we should do about the discomfort of the designated trust beneficiaries. Purportedly, the word is they're thinking their interests would better be served by an endowment of diversified marketable securities. Is this something we ought to consider?"

Volpe, newly respectful, saw the chairman fit to burst, but no one else seemed to care. "That's another difficult and important question.

Of course, the two big trusts, holding the voting stock, don't have named beneficiaries. You have the discretion to decide to whom to make payments. This is where the attorney general comes in."

"Are we violating the terms of the trusts, if we accept an offer to sell the AOM voting stock? My impression was the Porters were very clear in wanting to make permanent provision for control of the publication."

"Nothing at the end of their lives is as clear as we would like. I can tell you the law is unlikely to enforce any provision that is plainly contrary to the interests of the various beneficiaries. Our firm feels that you'll have to exercise your discretion in considering offers of sale."

One of the silent trustees spoke up. "We need to have confidence in each other. I need to know, have any of the trustees or our counsel actually been in contact with the charitable beneficiaries of the Porter trusts?"

La Volpe spoke up. "You know how lawyers are. I can simply tell you that my firm *has* had informal contact with several law firms who've raised the question as to whether the trusts would be agreeable to a policy of diversifying the portfolios. Everybody is apprehensive with the decline of cash flow and the fall of the stock price."

The tone in the room had grown somber. No one was sure what should be done about Grandma. But it was not really that altruistic because these were practical people, even if they were woefully out of touch with their own responsibilities. "What is this mention in the attorney general's report about there being no consideration of liability?"

Volpe frowned. "I have to tell you I've never seen anything like this. It sounds more like a sleazy PR person than a law enforcement officer. We are protesting to the attorney general in the firmest possible manner, but I have to tell you, the harm is done. The public now has the taste of liability, and that changes the way people will consider the matter."

Another silent trustee nervously spoke out, "What possible liability could there be?"

"To the extent that my firm has been informed of the facts, we advise you that there is no basis for personal liability in the various relationships that each of you have with the trust and AOM itself."

"Yeah, but what? Come on, you sound like some law-spouting machine. What's the problem?"

"Frankly, the problem is in having trustees who are also paid for being officers of the company and providers of professional services. The allegation would be that the trustees abuse their discretion to feather their own nests rather than exclusively run the trust for the benefit of the charities."

"We've all done that since the beginning of the trust. I am sure it's specifically permitted."

"You're correct. I only wish that the legal system were always predictable. You know the old country saying, What you see depends on where you sit. Someone looking at this trust today will see declining values on the watch of well-compensated trustees. You have to figure that we're getting a nudge from the attorney general."

After two hours of deliberation one thing was clear. This was not the same board of trustees who had entered the meeting. The dynamics had dramatically shifted away from a regal denial to instructions to their formerly demonized lawyer to issue a legally appropriate declination, which made clear the trustees' continuing willingness to consider new offers.

In Tarrytown at 9:00 a.m. the full membership of the ESOP assembled raucously to shout down any thought of accepting Drive's offer. Charles Bowditch was repeatedly interrupted as he calmly explained his utter failure to get either response or financing from the parent company. The meeting became angry when he reported the word on the street that nobody was going to even consider lending the ESOP money for its own tender.

Horse explained the basis for his belief that the Department of Labor might be able to help find a way out of the mess. He was headed to Washington as soon as the meeting adjourned.

Drive got a call in his Chrysler Building office around 11 a.m. and learned that the AOM ESOP, at a full public meeting of the members, has voted *not* to tender its shares. This triggered the ultimate danger signal in his mind, perhaps because of his own culpability, or maybe a sense of reversal, in his heart or in the way the wind was blowing. He wasn't afraid of the clock punchers, they didn't have a chance, he was afraid that his restlessness had returned too soon. His passion was compromised. He picked up the phone and called Marty.

"We've got a real problem with the ESOP. We're just going to have to turn that one around. I do not trust many people, but I trust you. Have you got a pencil? Write down this list of eighteen numbers and you will be connected directly and securely to Rose. I don't need to tell you not to give this number to anyone under any circumstances."

Marty thought to himself, so *don't* tell me, but he kept his mouth shut because he was a smart man. He wrote the numbers down very carefully. And thought, *Rose?*

Drive hung up with Marty and started to call his lifeline.

"I've given Marty the code. We need to pull out all the stops; I feel I can trust him and we need his genius. Tell him anything, but, quaint American custom, be sure everything is said subject to attorney/client privilege." But Drive wasn't certain what he was doing.

Marty literally vibrated with satisfaction. "Now that I have the imperial permission to get in direct contact with you, we no longer have a one-way relationship; this is much more intimate so we need new names. Drive called you Rose. I don't suppose Rose is your real name, but it sounds fine, so why don't you call me 'Thorn,' OK? Now that the fat is in the fire, the client finally calls in the first string."

"Thorn it is. I've never spoken to anyone other than Drive on this phone, so it will take me a bit to get comfortable. Tell me what we need."

"What are you anyway, the Easter Bunny? Are you the answer to all young men's prayers? Can you answer any problem we have?"

"I'll have to be careful with you. What I meant is, what are we missing to make this deal work? Are there individuals or governmental bodies whose support we need?"

"What do we know beyond that the membership voted this morning not to accept Drive's tender offer?"

"Quite a lot. From a business point of view, we know Bowditch represents an AOM ESOP, holding 20 percent of the voting stock of AOM, that has carefully worked with the U.S. Department of Labor, created operating procedures, and authorized the borrowing of money to make their own tender for the balance of AOM voting stock. From a personal point of view, we know Bowditch has been the intimate friend of the Assistant Secretary of Labor with jurisdiction in this matter, the fact of which Drive acquainted his pal Vern."

"That guy. Sure gets around. You know they call him Horse?" Marty realized she was all business today. Maybe she's not a morning person. He went back to work, "Can Bowditch get the money any other place?"

"The community has been advised hands off, but for how long? It's a lot of money within a short time frame at a lousy time of year to try and conclude a complicated transaction."

"Business is business. It didn't stop us. But OK, agreed. So, what happens if we replace Bowditch?"

"We get delay. A new trustee would need time and all the rest. This is too high profile to put in some stiff who'd say no. What's the problem with a Bowditch who can't raise any money? The only place he can get it from is Universal and Universal can't be compelled to lend, can they?"

"You get to a place in deals like this where you don't know if the other guy is so smart that you're missing something obvious or if he is so stupid he doesn't understand he hasn't a prayer."

"Tell me." She was begging. Marty loved it.

"The U.S. Department of Labor, Bowditch's old girlfriend. What do we know about her anyway? We had best find out what is going on at the agency. Do you guys have the contacts to get that information?"

"I think so, yes."

"Oh, yeah, that shit Scott Moffie. Oy vey, he ruined my sex life when you guys sicced him on me."

"I have to believe the Moff gets us the real stuff, even about you; it wasn't very much. I know they call him Horse and I know why. I'll get Moffie on to this right away."

"Listen. We need to know whether there are any letters, any meetings, and any proceedings. Anything at all, going on about this AOM situation. Do you guys have any other miracles to pull out at this critical moment?"

Rose took a deep breath and began, "Tomorrow, there'll be a press conference. We talked the other day about the shareholder suit. Your brother at the bar, Bill Pomerantz, will announce the mother and father of a class-action lawsuit against the trustees of the Porter Trusts, as controlling shareholders of AOM. He'll claim that the whole class of public shareholders has been defrauded because the trustees have never run the venture in the mode of a public company but rather one for the perpetuation of the trust arrangements for noncommercial purposes."

"My hat's off to you. Bill's a winner and he's good ink. The trustees can't ignore this. I like our basic idea. How do you get these guys to do what you ask them to? I understand money and power, but I have never seen a Rolodex where the other guy always answers and does what he is supposed to do."

"One of these days, we may have that little talk." She wanted to tantalize him.

"Why did I work so hard for a living for so long?"

"So long for now, Thorny."

"Thorny? That's a spelling error."

"Whatever."

At Molly's usual close of business meeting with Levin and Klebowitch, she asked, "What's going on with the American Observer?

Levin said, "Both the Porter trustees and the ESOP have announced that they do not accept Rhodes's tender offer. Offhand, I'd say that just about kills it."

Molly asked, "Does this put the ESOP in a better condition to make its own offer?"

"Bowditch tells me the word has been put out on the street that this deal is poison and nobody will consider giving them financing," Klebowitch said.

Levin speculated, "We'd never be able to prove that. But I am beginning to get an idea as to how we might enable the ESOP to pull this one off."

As eager as Molly was to help her friend, she would need everyone in the room to agree that justice was being done before she exercised any of her department's authority. It was late, so she ended their meeting. "Charles tells me that he's coming to town tonight and will meet with the two of you tomorrow. Keep me in the loop."

Chapter 20

Tuesday, August 18, 1998

Nobody was paying attention to anything other than the Clinton spectacle. All of the people crowded into the Wall Street conference rooms of the Pomerantz firm were talking about one aspect or another of the latest twist. "It is simple," said a gray-haired man. "They left the shame gene out of him." With some difficulty the packed audience quieted down to hear the noted west coast attorney William Pomerantz. He announced the filing that morning of a class-action lawsuit involving the American Observer Association. The suit was brought on behalf of all the holders of Class A voting stock and alleges that the trustees of the Randy and Shelley Porter trusts, holding a majority of the outstanding shares, have failed to perform their fiduciary duties and have injured those who have bought shares over the last three years. The trustees, through their control of the board of directors of AOM, have participated in the repeated publication of unrealistic and false projections of future performance. Buyers of stock, reasonably believing these management statements, have been injured. The suit was also brought against the board of directors of AOM with similar allegations. There were paragraphs relating in detail the precise financial arrangements that each trustee had with AOM over a full decade.

Mr. Pomerantz explained that the complaint, comprising almost 300 pages, had been updated to include the refusal of the trustees and the board to consider the recent offer of Cedric Rhodes to buy shares at $30, a price some 60 percent above the current market. He went on to explain that his clients sought appropriate relief. The only way in which their damage could be effectively addressed would be through replacing the current board of trustees with a temporary board consisting of individuals without conflicting interests. Because the situation of AOM was deteriorating rapidly, Pomerantz has asked the

Federal Court to issue a temporary restraining order on the trustees until the merits of his argument for equitable relief could be heard.

The financial press is very conscious of the usually successful efforts of the more flamboyant corporate litigators to manipulate, so the questions were cautious. The barrage of recent information about AOM in the midst of the usual August lethargy impressed everyone as being out of the ordinary. Pomerantz's complaint, three hundred pages of detailed allegations supported in many instances by affidavits, clearly had been long in the preparation, but there was a certain discomfort with the unveiling of so many seemingly unconnected acts focusing on AOM. The atmosphere of disbelief was tense, but no reporter could bring himself to ask directly, "Are you part of the Cedric Rhodes scheme?" Joey, who had choreographed the press conference, was asked by some of the more cynical reporters, "Hey, what circus have you got for us tomorrow?" This level of suspicion notwithstanding, the lawsuit filing got full coverage.

A planted question, that garnered a few snickers, was asked, "Do you plan to bring suit against the trustees, personally?" No unequivocal answer, "We will use every mechanism provided by law to investigate that possibility, including depositions." There was the headline. Most of the people in the know left the conference at this point, everyone racing back to their televisions.

Marty's suite of offices had a television in the conference room and it was packed. Lawyers, secretaries, paralegals, and messengers were all in attendance at some point. Every network ran the same clips, over and over. There was Clinton himself, confirming everyone's suspicions. "I did have a relationship with Miss Lewinsky that was not appropriate. In fact, it was wrong." The scandal was all played out and people could not get enough of it. The networks played his January denial in rotation. "I want to say one thing to the American people. I want you to listen to me. I'm going to say this again: I did not have sexual relations with that woman, Miss Lewinsky." It was a car wreck that no one could avoid turning to see.

Marty was glued to his phone like the rest of his staff was glued to the television in the conference room. He would see to that later, but he was busy now.

"So Moffie came through....Gimme!" Marty barked.

"You had better believe it." Listening carefully, Marty believed her accent was changing from light, phony British to the local vernacular. Was her choice of words less international and more Manhattan? "Apparently, there have been phone calls, visits from Bowditch to the staff, and draft memoranda of law relating to the whole question of Universal's obligations to the AOM ESOP to make financing available on the same basis it makes it available to a third party."

"Shit! This is brand new." Marty was incensed. "They've never done this before. No reason to think they have to start now. Goddamn Feds. There ought to be a law. Now we've got to figure out how to persuade the assistant secretary to let this matter drop."

Rose said, "It won't work with mere persuasion. This is her baby."

"So I've been told. I presume everyone in this government works for somebody. Who does she work for?"

"The president, the secretary of Labor, and the oversight committees of the Senate and particularly the House of Representatives."

"I don't want to sound naïve, but I'm sure that you've got ways of getting the attention of all of those worthies?" Marty had faith in her magic powers.

"Frankly, the president is out of pocket at the moment, but otherwise yes."

"Schmuck should've spent a little more time in pocket, he's wasting the entire nation's time with his office poaching. The lowest, what a cad. So, tell me good and kind mistress, how do we work down from the president?"

"Right now, I've a lot of calls to make; it'll take forever to find some of these people. I'm going to push for next Friday, the twenty-eighth, as Assistant Secretary Molly Munro's Reality Day." Marty heard real relish in her voice. "Wouldn't you know it, with the president on the run, all of these prima donnas are God knows where, but we'll get 'em."

"Let's think for a minute. What kind of personal pressure can we bring to bear on little Ms. Molly? The usual questions, family, career, pocketbook."

"Your old friend Moffie has outdone himself on that score. Do you want the net net?" Since she was comfortable talking this way, Marty was sure she was a local girl.

"Let me guess. She's a Rockefeller, taken sacred vows to enter an unspeaking religious order after leaving government service."

"Not bad for a lawyer! Aside from being married to Vern Stillman, worth high eight figures, maybe nine. Her New York law firm would hire her back whether they lose every client we can finger or not. The only clubs she belongs to, her mother belonged to. Her present husband's a sculptor, devoted to her and she to him. We can rattle the cage, give her some grief, but I'm not optimistic. No favors here."

"Tell me something. Is this the kind of favor where these guys can call back and say 'Sorry about that, but I did my best' or is this the scene in the movie where somebody makes an offer she can't refuse?"

"Never. Drive would personally snap the neck of anyone who suggested such a thing. He is a profoundly decent man when it comes to fair play. Look, there are favors and there are favors. I guess I can answer your question by saying, a little bit of both. We own some people, other people owe us something, and with some it's just a courtesy. In this case, we need to have the muscle."

"I don't want you to break *Omerta* but it would help a lot if you could tell me exactly how you're going to get her government bosses to turn this one around."

"Drive told me to share, so I'll give it to you straight, I'll just have to make a speech, get comfortable. The president? Easy..."

"Apparently," Marty interjected.

"Agreed. Now back to my point. We've all kinds of debts there. Own significant communications properties, and you've got a million ways of helping people in office. You help their friends. Create favors and make them look good. Cash. Everybody knows somebody who needs a job. Vernon Jordan hired the First Musician's whore Monica before he knew whether she could type. With a business like ours, we always need people somewhere."

"Ha, ha. I get it. Whore Monica. That's rich. I thought he only played the saxophone." Marty was delighted. She had a sense of humor and wasn't all work and no play. These were all prime requisites, but was it too early to speak of requisition? Marty refocused and listened carefully as she continued.

"We're close to the biggest investment banks. With the purchase and sale of communications property, the issuance of new licenses and worldwide auctions of new wavelengths, there's been a huge amount of money raising."

Marty thought to himself, *What a chatty little fox. I think she likes me.*

"Initial public offerings have been the rage. We should be allocated a good portion of all these IPOs. It's in everyone's interest for us to direct these allocations where they will do the most good. What happens to the profits as the IPO stocks go, in a matter of days, from 10 to $100? Answer? It's legal, it's cash, they all sell on day two or three, and you go from no net worth to a nice piece of change. The guys who get this stuff, we own those guys."

The accent, underneath, pure Brooklyn, Marty thought.

"There's art in the process. That's my problem here. I have to make it a win/win for a very hungry congressional chairman. Not only will there be IPO allocations, but the papers, the network will pick up the incredible vigilance of his oversight committee and flattering accounts of the chairman's conscientiousness, all to be published in his district. The challenge is to end up with stronger credit than you started with. Relationships should be on our balance sheet as assets."

Marty was dazed. "Glad I asked. That's something that I haven't said to another human being since my bar mitzvah. Has anyone ever told you that you are special?"

"Not twice, hotshot. Let's stick to business."

"I hate to think how much money you make out of this. Can I assume that the New York Attorney General thing is receiving your incomparable asset-building attention?"

"Yeah, that meeting is set up for first thing Thursday morning in Albany."

"I'm going to haul my tired carcass up the Hudson to meet with a guy who has an office in Manhattan?"

"This is a respect thing. Our guy is so vulnerable. A one-term attorney general, first Republican since Teddy Roosevelt was governor. You can't be just another Manhattan wise guy looking at an investment. We're asking him to reach, and we can be valuable to him and he needs us badly, but that AOM network is a lot to confront."

"It's a privilege to do business with you. Can I ask an impertinent question...?"

"*No.* Call me directly from Albany on Thursday."

"Well, if you're going to insist." Marty liked trying to be infuriating.

Bernie Levin was talking to Charles Bowditch from his office on the fifth floor of the Frances Perkins Building at the end of a long afternoon of reading documents and pondering solutions. "I am beginning to feel as if we have something here. Frankly, I can't believe it. When we issue opinions, we always make them subject to the facts and circumstances of a given case. In this situation, we know the facts and circumstances and they're unbelievable. It's so incredible that I have to think about it overnight and talk with David about it. If you come in around eleven, we'll have our act together, but before you go, let me review a few facts."

"Let's do it," Horse said hopefully.

"First, Universal Bank owns 100 percent of the stock of New York Safe Deposit & Trust Company," Levin said and Horse nodded in agreement.

"Second, NYSD&T is the trustee of the American Observer ESOP. Third, Universal entered into a contract to provide financing to a partnership of which Cedric Rhodes is the general partner to purchase common stock of AOM. Fourth, the financing agreement between Rhodes and Universal provides the following: Rhodes will have no personal responsibility for the borrowing. The bank can look only to the collateral, which is to be the common stock of AOM. Rhodes is not committed to devote any specific time to the management of the partnership's business."

Horse's nodding was picking up speed to keep up with Levin's queries. They did seem to lead to an inevitable absurdity that begged redress, and for the last time today, Mr. Levin, public servant, couldn't help but relish it.

"What this means is that the AOM ESOP, which owns 20 percent of the outstanding stock and has no indebtedness, can be shown to be a better credit risk than Rhodes's partnership. It's beyond dispute; a lender to the ESOP will have 20 percent of the stock as extra margin. This brings us, in my opinion, to a very rare place. We can ask, is there a breach of trust when a bank refuses to loan money, on *more favorable* terms, to an employee benefit plan for which it, or its wholly owned subsidiary, acts as trustee, than those on which it is committed to make funds available to an outside party? I've been here since the passage of ERISA in 1974 and I've never seen a fact situation that permits an exact comparison. Tonight, I believe that we can give the opinion of breach of trust."

Horse had never known Levin to be so excited. Highly intelligent desk-types just don't giggle this much, in Horse's experience. It was as if his statute was a living organism and, examining it for the millionth time, he had detected a new and exquisite feature. Horse was embarrassed, like someone unconfirmed at the communion rail, to ask, "What does this mean for us?"

Levin came down from Mount Olympus with statesmanlike eloquence, "The AOM ESOP will be able to compel Universal to make financing available. If you want to acquire control, there is no way that Rhodes can outbid you unless he gets backing somewhere else."

The last question in the Friday press conference had reverberated across the Atlantic Ocean to London and to Cape Town. One could expect shareholder reaction to the apparent distractions of the company founder, chairman, and suspected "driving" influence. What Drive had utterly failed to take into account was the reaction of his own family's most senior member. Leaning back in his desk chair at the end of the long business day, Drive awaited the arrival of the one person on earth he truly and fully loved, his older brother, John.

John had solidified the family's preeminence in the life of South Africa. He had married young and happily and sired six children. He had provided for both of their parents and carried on his father's life-long struggle for a fair society in South Africa. Drive himself had four children by his three wives. This fourth generation was educated in Europe and America. All of them worked in one branch or another of the family businesses. The family wealth was divided equally among the ten members of this generation. It was a source of pride for Drive that he had provided the great bulk of the economic value to the family, of which his children would receive less than half. Because Drive was neither uxorious nor paternal, his own offspring considered Cape Town their home and John's family as their own. The substance of the patriarch's dream had been fulfilled, but in a way he couldn't have anticipated.

Now in his seventy-first year and in vigorous good health, John had given up business and was one of the most diligent participants in the work of the Reconciliation Commission. He took every effort to make South Africa the real home that all men ultimately seek. His normally sweet nature had undergone the trauma of intense exposure to the brutishness of humankind. "To understand all is to forgive all," but to forget nothing. He had lost the naïve appearance of the fortunate and his body and face had taken on the cast of an El Greco saint.

The Rhodes brothers lived half a world apart and lived lives about as different as possible. John could discern, from the family rumors and from a clip on CNN of Drive's Friday press conference, that something really important was going on with his little brother. On the gut level, something was up. It wasn't the deal, it was the look in Drive's eyes. Was he distracted? Confused? John needed to see him to know for sure. Little mistakes, like not letting the family know, meant Drive was not his old fastidious self. There was no sense that he owed the family anything, Drive was the family benefactor. He was, to his brother's loving observation, a little more at sea than usual.

On this Tuesday, the lean ascetic John Rhodes walked into his brother's office and embraced the pomaded, massaged, and dieted exemplar of a U.S. senior corporate executive, because their intimacy was the strongest element in their lives. Other than physical features, they were very different people, with only a childhood in common. The brothers held each other at arm's length and looked at each other, communicating the love and concern they had for one another. It was plain that John's toil on the commission had aged him; there was spirit in his eyes but there was tiredness as well. He spoke directly, "Cedric, I admire your youthful energy, but I didn't think I'd see the day when I would be watching a press conference on TV to find out that you're going into a new business by yourself."

John's kindness was palpable. Behind the suffering, John's appearance imparted personal concern. He listened with love as his younger brother explained his compulsion for the American Observer acquisition. Drive warmed to the occasion and assumed his mien as supreme salesman as he took his brother through all of the negotiations, his ultimate accomplishment of getting it all for nothing, and his brilliant new partner, a younger woman eager to be his future mate. "John, I've been feeling empty, my vitality ebbing away, like never before. I needed to test myself, to prove...that I am still alive, that there remain challenges; that life has savor."

With care and some sadness, John said, "The saddest truth that I've personally had to come to grips with is that there is no guarantee of wisdom with my old age. And we *are* old men and I know I'm still making many mistakes, every day. You make life sound like a magic show, a search for just the trick that makes it all worthwhile. I'm a bit confused. In the past, you've sought wealth as a means to an end, not as a game. Is it the same thing with women? You're on your third wife. Lily is a very fine person. Do you really think a single 'magic' woman will make life all worthwhile?"

"All I can tell you is the pursuit of a woman, of a bold new business, is what makes life work for me."

John held up his hand to interrupt, "Why, pray tell, have you gone to all this trouble with American Observer only to insist that you'll personally have no responsibility for the outcome? I don't understand. Is it that you want to perform a feat? You want a gold medal for the Deal of the Century? Why would you acquire the company and decline personal or financial responsibility?" He threw up both hands to indicate incomprehension. A man who had spent years witnessing and reconciling the most horrible manifestations of human violence could not comprehend the vagaries of the person he'd known the longest.

Drive was fazed, "What can I say? It's just the way I am, I guess." He knew as he said it, that it was a paltry excuse. He was the baby brother, all over again.

John's face morphed into a mask that was hard to read, as he articulated a feeling that insisted on expression. "I'm going to say something that may hurt you, but it is too late for either of us now. Your restlessness and dissatisfaction with life reminds me strongly of our mother." He looked up to see the mixture of shock and anger break like a wave on Drive's lined face. He paused to make sure Drive really heard what he was saying and then continued, "She dealt with this anxiety in a very self-destructive way; are you repeating this pattern?"

This was probably the first time that Drive had thought of his mother in many years. He had never, ever, thought or felt that anything to do with her had anything to do with him. And yet John could not be ignored, he had traveled halfway round the world out of concern. *He cares for me. He is the only person in the world who could have any idea what being that woman's child means.* Drive needed to perform this catechism of feelings in order to cope with what his brother had said. He couldn't begin to process the idea that he was like his mother in any way. He was horrified that he could have done anything in life that was as hurtful to anyone as she had been to him.

"My God, John, I just don't know. I do feel confused and conflicted. Am I being as absurd and ridiculous as Clinton? I do wonder if the chase is just a variation on the same unsatisfying theme. It's an awful thought, but I have to face up to contradictions in what I am doing."

The brothers embraced and John left with, "You have done everything anybody ever asked of you. You must forgive Mother. And in forgiving, you will forgive yourself. It's probably time for you to come home." John walked out the door. He paused to wonder on flying halfway around the world just for a ten-minute conversation. He took a step forward, reflecting that while he was in almost constant psychic connection with his brother, this was a time when he had to physically be part of communicating his unwelcome insight.

"Home," Drive said it as he realized he wished he could beg his brother not to go. Abandoned in a room full of ghosts, Drive couldn't go after his brother, *they* wouldn't let him.

Drive's lifestyle accorded with his nickname. Work harder, work smarter, drive to excellence. Take bigger chances and delight in disaster avoided. He never thought of himself in emotional terms; he certainly had never conceived of forgiving, to say nothing of being forgiven. John's conviction was so palpable that Drive could actually feel the flavor of forgiveness. His body language indicated an understanding and a tentative acceptance that he could not articulate in words. Consciously, he resolved to push forward on the AOM takeover with greater focus and commitment, but he sat for an hour, watching from his window as the daylight faded from his office and never acknowledged that he would carry a profoundly changed consciousness into the future.

Rose spoke first. "You know, this phone feels differently now that Marty has the number. It used to be intimate. Now I switch it on and it's someone else. I know, we'll do something different when this deal is done. What is it? Another two weeks. How are we doing?" Drive thought he was listening to himself for a moment.

"Everything is on track, but there's no way to get a status report. Expect some heavy going the rest of this week. Those guys may get their act together enough to put some pressure on. Talk to you soon." He didn't want to talk any more, he wanted to punish her, he knew he was being childish but he felt her trying to reach out.

Chapter 21

Every newspaper, every television news broadcast, and every trade association had something good to say about American Observer and something bad to say about Cedric Rhodes and his tender offer. It was there, behind pages and pages of post-presidential confessional turmoil. The national soap opera distracted the general public from anything else. But for those who cared to look, Drive had a great opera of his own making for the financial pages. It didn't require very much skill or sophistication to conclude there was a sameness to the content of the various sources. Well-orchestrated and harmonious, the campaign was predigested and the media gobbled it up, grateful for the free programming and column content. It was effortless on their part; Drive and Joey made it so. The wheels turned and news churned and the dragon was left to sleep. The "hormonica" music played on.

Vern spoke to Drive on the phone in whispers, as if he were in awe.

"I've never seen anything like this. The word on the street is that all of the charitable organizations' trustees are determined to take advantage of your offer. They're calling us to plead that we make available the funds so you can extend your tender and take them out."

Drive took this in stride, "Pretty sensible people." Vern only needed to know so much. Drive liked listening to the pushy banker's fascination, his naïveté.

Vern simply was fixated, "No, it goes beyond that. There's superb organization somewhere. Normally it would take a month for these people even to agree on a date for a talk. This is August, for God's sake. Someone with a good Rolodex has been working hard. I can't imagine how they've organized so many calls."

Horse met with Bernie Levin and David Klebowitch in a conference room way in the back of the working slums of their building.

"Look, Charles, David and I have thought about this and consulted with our people. We think we can write you the letter that we discussed yesterday."

"What do we do now?" asked Horse, too concerned about what was next to really enjoy the moment.

"You'll write us a letter. Indeed, I've taken the liberty of summarizing what you told me last night and what I gleaned from the SEC filings, to prepare this draft note on blank 8 1/2 x 11 paper. If you want to fax that letter to your office, have it retyped with your letterhead; the department will issue a formal reply. Today is Wednesday. If we officially receive your request today, I think we can have a draft response on the assistant secretary's desk on Friday."

David interpolated. "We really would like to post this correspondence in the Federal Register, maybe on Monday, not because it has legal significance but because it's going to be controversial and, in this town, a lot depends on how respectfully you treat your brothers in government. So we propose to publish on Monday. Our thought is that the assistant secretary would sign the letter on Monday the thirty-first."

Horse was speechless. "Done," but Horse couldn't contain himself. He had a strategy and an objective, these guys had thought of everything. "What can I say? After all these months, you guys have given me a reason to believe in government."

Bernie said , with a nice touch, "Hey, you pay your taxes, don't you?"

La Volpe talked to the Porter trustees by conference phone. It had been decided, at the conclusion of the previous meeting, that the board should act as a whole and the practice of acting through a chairman was discontinued. She reported proudly on the number of news inches and minutes that the counterattack had yielded. This body count had about as much importance as its Vietnam counterpart years earlier, but it also had the merit of pleasing while misleading the clients.

Ms. Volpe then volunteered something truly disturbing. "I want to return to a question that you asked at our last meeting. You asked whether any of the beneficiaries of the charitable foundations had been in touch with my office or me. Since we last talked, I must inform you, that we have received, from first-class law firms, formal letters representing the trustees of each of the named beneficiary trusts holding class A stock. The timing is extraordinary. This can't be a coincidence. But, we must recognize it's one thing to get in touch with a lot of people in August. It is quite another to motivate them to get in touch with counsel. I have to tell you, we have a long-term problem with these people. Going forward, we're dealing with people who have no personal loyalty to the Porters, to AOM, or to us. We have to recognize that they feel a *need* for sustained and increased annual distributions. What I know about our business makes that a very tough proposition indeed." She did not mention a phone call from Martin van Buren Beal in which he made it clear (or did he?), that change in the outside counsel of AOM might not be necessary if the proposed takeover went through.

One of the trustees asked, "What is the upshot of this? What are you suggesting we do?"

"I'm your lawyer. I do what you tell me and report back."

Emboldened by the physical remove, another trustee piped up, "Cut it out and tell us what you think."

Volpe very sweetly contented herself. "I think you should consider your alternatives."

"Like what?"

"Spend a few minutes talking among yourselves as to the impact on you of being the trustees of a $1.5 billion foundation invested in diversified marketable securities. Just think about it...OK?"

The stygian chore of drafting behind him, Marty was well rested and ready for more. Now he was concerned about Drive's stamina as they spoke on the phone.

"Have you seen what the arbs have done?

"Arbs what? What are you talking about?" Drive had been hiding in his papers, letting himself get angry at the sorry state of national politics with the tabloid presidency, and when he got angry, he got tired.

"Have you seen the stock price for AOM? Voting stock is now trading at $30. Not a bad move!"

"I haven't checked lately. What does that mean? It's sounding expensive."

Marty was surprised. *How could he not be checking?*

"No, not really. That means, to this city, that the smart money thinks your deal is going to succeed and you'll have to up the ante a little. Now everybody climbs onto your bandwagon. Watch. The press, all those guys, every fence-sitting fickle prick under every rock; nobody wants to be on the side of the losers. In this country, at this time, the market makes the winners and you look like you're taking home the gold, my friend."

"Do you think this has anything to do with that arrangement we were talking about the other day?"

"What arrangement? Listen, the market is king and the market has spoken. This deal is a go!"

"Even if the King is the market and he's doing the speaking?"

"It's not just him. He's just the biggest chunk in the avalanche. In the battle of perception, you, my nephew, and our mutual lady friend have made the impossible seem possible to a lot of people."

"Momentum has always been good to me. How can we make the most of this? What about Horse and his federal girlfriend?" Drive was happy for Marty but he wasn't ready to relax yet.

"We've come so far, so fast, I don't see how anyone can catch up to us now."

Sitting in the midst of his papers, he waited for her to speak.

"We don't talk as much as we used to. It's not the same."

"I'd think you'd be happy. Everything we've worked on is coming up just roses. All your planning. Did you know that the arbs have already given this deal the go-ahead?"

"Yeah, Thorn told me."

"Is that his name? How often do you talk with Marty anyway?"

"I have this phone, right, you gave him my number. When the phone rings, I answer it. I'm like one of those Pavlovian dogs. I think it might be you, so I answer it."

"That's turning out to be not such a good idea."

"It's too early to say, but I have to tell you we've worked out some excellent schemes to keep this deal on track"

"Terrific."

Later, Drive had to pause after putting down the phone. *It's too early to say...what?* He had called originally to mention his brother's visit, oddly enough, but now he felt it wasn't anything he could share with Rose and was glad that he hadn't. These calls had been feeling like an obligation for quite a while. Drive was getting itchy. At least his wife left him alone and didn't nag him about going to the club. Drive was unable to see the irony of his situation, but his brother's words stood right next to him, palpable, like a stranger in an elevator you can't bring yourself to look at. He was, spiritually, staring at his feet.

Chapter 22

Thursday, August 20, 1998

Charles "Horse" Bowditch discovered something surprising. He was actually enjoying meeting with the AOM ESOP trustees at eight-thirty in the morning. He was never a morning person but today was a magical day. The bagels, donuts, and coffee, the buzz in the room; Horse had leaked some of the news to Skapinsky. That guy was a sieve, and good news was so rare these days, the sooner they heard, the sooner they could mobilize. Horse knew the happiest people are the people with a sense of mission and they had their work cut out for them now. They would have to go from zero to sixty, and he knew they could. Horse stood up, everyone was waiting for him to say it. He couldn't get the foolish grin off his face. He tried. He was too happy. The room was chuckling before the words were out of his mouth.

"This letter from the DOL says in plain English that Universal has got to make financing available to us on the same terms it has offered to Rhodes. *Period.*"

A chorus of voices to the effect "Cut it out; this is unreal; no government agency ever says anything clearly; none of them ever act until it is too late; this is an aberration; they will change their minds; nothing will happen at the end."

Unfazed, the Horse plowed on, "Nothing is going to change this."

Skapinsky stood up, and tried to dull the roar. "Wait a goddamned minute, before everybody becomes drunk like sailors. Do you mean to tell me, Mr. Chairman, all those fancy trustees and their son-of-a-bitch lawyers and consultants, they are going to sit still and watch us while we buy control of this company, this company they think is only theirs, and then we kick their expensive asses out of here? Come on, give me some of whatever you're smoking." That was a big, nervous laugh for everyone.

Horse had led men in battle before. He knew about ambushes. "I understand the process. I know who has to do what to whom. I stand by my statement; the bank will have to make the financing available to us."

From the floor, there was a raised hand. Horse pointed and a non-descript member rose to speak. "I don't want to rain on the parade, but come on, Rhodes can promise those people television time forever." *That wasn't true*, thought Horse. *He* could *buy the whole bunch of them and he wants this deal. He's taking it personally. He knows more ways to influence public officials than any of us ever dreamed of.* But Horse had been in much tougher places. This would be their test, not his. He was only their leader.

"He'll pull out the heavy guns. I know that, but I know the professionals in the Department of Labor, I know the assistant secretary, and I know the law governing this procedure. I'm telling you, this is going to work. So we have a lot to do I have to see our lawyers, make sure we can move fast, and get our tender offer updated. You have to figure out how you want to run this place. We need a business plan. We need a timetable. We need to define some benchmarks. Who's going to do what to whom by when? I won't leave here until those responsibilities have names on them."

It had become perfectly clear to everyone in the room, except of course the man himself, that there was only one possible candidate for leader of the new AOM. But this wasn't the time or the place for coronations. Events would take their course. In the meantime, there were practical problems.

Horse continued, "We have to figure the odds are I'll get kicked out of the position I'm now in. We need a strategy. Here's how it goes. The Porter Trustees can cause the company to simply change the trustee of the ESOP. They don't need a reason. I have no right to a particular piece of business and, if they are sufficiently pissed off, they may just fire me. Period. If that happens, I'm well provided for, so don't worry."

"What do you think is going to happen? Will they really do it?" The usually ferocious Skapinsky sounded genuinely worried.

"I don't think they'll do anything, frankly. I have a date with Stillman this afternoon. I wish it were otherwise, but he's struggling not to strangle me with his bare hands. We have some history. Our Vern thinks of himself as a class guy. It's simple for me; I know that a class guy wouldn't change anything in this situation."

"Listen, Horse, we always call you that, and we always will. We're really grateful to you for being a stand-up guy. We understand we're way down at the end of the food chain. But we're grateful for you always treating us as if we're important. If they fire you, I cannot give any guarantees as to how the employees of this company will react."

Horse was touched. "I really appreciate that, but don't worry. I know the ground. I've been in firefights and I'm going to walk out of this one, no purple hearts this time."

It's rare when one can drive into New York City and enjoy the experience. The beauty of this late August day had persuaded everyone to stay at home so there was only light traffic. There had been a lot of rain this summer so the trees and shrubs retained their early refulgence. Horse arrived in midtown Manhattan around 1 p.m., availed himself of the rare privilege of executive parking in the building, and went directly to Vern's office, where he had been told to wait for an available appointment.

The special anteroom where he presented himself was all done up in somebody's idea of the small library in an English country estate. The receptionist, with a matching English accent, recognized him and told him to sit down and wait. Mr. Stillman was still at lunch but there would be a good chance for a few minutes when he got out. Horse didn't sit down. He looked briefly at the superb Sixteenth Edition set of *Encyclopedia Britannica* and noticed to his horror that they only had the even-numbered volumes. Maybe they couldn't fit all the volumes into the shelves. Instead of lingering on philosophical questions of the phony and the real, Horse turned and said to Her Highness, "I'm famished. Do you think someone could get a sandwich and some fruit for me from the kitchen? I'll be waiting in the sanctum, to which Horse repaired without further comment. Even the new Horse, *maitre de soi-même et de l'univers*, might have paused had he realized that the sanctum was associated forever in Vern's consciousness with the revelation of Horse's intimacy with Molly.

Surprisingly, edible sandwiches arrived with a peach and a pot of coffee only minutes before the great man himself. Vern, to his great credit, ignored the multiple offenses to his dignity and proceeded directly. "Horse, how the hell do we stand on this ESOP tender business?"

Horse pulled no punches. "The ESOP has been unable to get financing for its tender. I've talked with the officials at the Department of Labor and asked for their instructions how to proceed. Here's a copy of the letter I sent yesterday."

Vern scanned the letter quickly. "Look here, you and I understand each other. I'm the boss and you work here, right?" Horse did not deign to react. Vern continued, "I've told you not to obstruct the bank's critical interest in financing Cedric Rhodes's tender. This letter just raises questions that I *do not* want raised. Is there *any* reason why I shouldn't consider this insubordination?"

Horse had been through this whole scene many times in his reveries. "I respect you as CEO of this bank and I expect you to respect me as a trust officer of NYSD&T. The law and the lore plainly impose responsibilities onto a trust officer. So long as my bank is trustee and I'm its officer, I am compelled by loyalty to the highest law to behave as I am behaving. You always have the right to disagree with me. You always have the capacity to cause me to be discharged."

Vern listened and realized this was the longest time he'd listened to a bank officer since becoming CEO. Horse was right. One hires principled people and lets them do their jobs. Personal pique was getting in his way. "What kind of answer do you think the department will give to this letter and when do you think they will give it?"

"I can't know the answer to that. You and I are working here under very difficult personal circumstances. I respect your restraint. Thank you. You, in turn, can count on me to be straight with you. You know as well as I do, that without any reference to you, me, or the American

Observer, Molly's great professional passion is in aid of employee ownership. I expect, and, as your employee I want to be clear in advising you, she will do whatever she can to empower the AOM ESOP."

"OK, Charles. Goddamn it. Every time I think I'm going to lose it, I go back to calling you Charles. Horse, Horse, my kingdom for a horse. Ha, ha! That's a funny one." Horse wondered if Vern was capable of having a breakdown, but he seemed to regroup, take a breath, and continue. "Of course, I'm not going to fire you. Also, I'm not getting near the Porter trustees. What I hear on the street is that all of the professional leadership of New York, who donate their time and skill to our most important charities, are grabbing at Rhodes as the deliverer from this hopeless trust situation. The Porter trustees have plenty on their plate without worrying about this. Keep me in touch and leave word where I can reach you."

The world was changing and Vern's mind was spinning. He simply couldn't believe the incredible feat of creating this successful tender offer could be stopped in its tracks by a bunch of disgruntled employees. *There ought to be a law*, he thought.

Drive was picking through his newspapers, Starr was demanding DNA evidence from the girl's stained dress. It was all so squalid. He thought to himself, *men can be so utterly ridiculous*. He was relieved when the phone rang. Marty exhibited a new level of excitement. "Have you seen the stock? Those arbs have done it again. This time it is important."

Marty's enthusiasm was a daily ritual with Drive, but truth be told, he liked him better when he was drafting. "Tell me."

"Not only have they bid up the price for the voting stock to your offer of $30, they have now bid up the price of the nonvoting to $29."

"Interpret this for a poor old newspaper man."

"The arbs are telling the world that they are confident you will expand the offer to all shareholders."

Drive insisted, "They're just guessing. The world knows that sometimes they're right and sometimes they're wrong."

"Not this time, sport. This time, the word is it's a sure thing. There are commitments here. This is a tight little world. Not all deals are tight like this. Now the reality is you're going to succeed in buying all of the stock of AOM at $30 a share. You don't have to advertise or struggle. If they've any hopes of keeping the status quo, they're going to have to come out with something a lot better than that pathetic hatchet job in the press yesterday."

Drive was never comfortable relying on good luck. "Wait a minute, just because a few guys in the know, lubricated with my money, buy up a pathetic few shares in a very thin market doesn't change whether the sun rises tomorrow morning or the earth changes its direction of rotation. What gives us the right to think that this will persuade any intelligent people of anything other than we have fixed the market?" *Jesus*, thought Marty, *who broke this guy's spirit?*

"I'm glad you have me as a lawyer. Welcome to the U.S. of A., where the market is king. Those trustees are toast. The street has turned on them. The guys who amount to anything in this city are involved in those charities and they want out of AOM. They have an offer from you. Is anybody else offering? Usually guys are jumping into deals like this the minute some poor sucker like you opens the doors. Where are they? What do you think the Attorney General of New York is going to think? What do you think he is going to do after the November election if the stock price is back at yesterday's $18? He's taken a big chance, speaking out publicly in the midst of an election. If you have two choices and one involves a personal guarantee and the other doesn't, what choice do you take? See what I mean?"

"So right now, it looks like we might win this one!" Drive was finally infected by Marty's enthusiasm.

"It isn't over until it's over, but until we take another hit, we have the ball and the route to the goal is clear."

Drive was still cautious. "I have to tell you, I'm worried about the ESOP and the Labor Department."

"Me too. We're trying to be sure we persuade that assistant secretary not to get in the way."

"Wait a minute; you were up in Albany today. How did it go with the attorney general?"

"I would've mentioned it, but those guys have really got religion. I just got off the phone to tell them the same story of the arbs that I told you. They get the message. They feel good being out in front in a winning cause like this. They look very good taking on the interests before an election. Win/win."

"That's a good note for tonight. Incidentally, how are things going with my assistant?"

"She's better than both of us. Boy, thank you for that introduction. It has been an education and a pleasure. We're doing a good job for you. If you hadn't let us communicate, we would've missed out on a lot."

Drive had acquired, surprising to those who thought of him as a business mogul, sensitivity to the vibrations occurring during what could crudely be called, the boy-girl thing. He wasn't a stupid man and he knew well how to interpret the first loquacious and generous thoughts his lawyer had expressed about anything or anybody. Fine.

Drive didn't feel like chatting with Marty anymore so he proceeded to conference in Vern, and together they agreed that because of the rise of the nonvoting stock in yesterday's market, they would advance the announcement of tender number two to the opening of the markets on Friday.

Chapter 23
Friday, August 21, 1998

Once again, Drive awoke from a troubled sleep, now filled with dreams of his African childhood. Since John's visit, Drive remembered the dreams that he hadn't been recalling in recent months, as August, the target month, approached. It wasn't long before he realized the president had once again upstaged him. The headline by his mandatory fruit plate stopped him in his tracks: U.S. CRUISE MISSILES STRIKE SUDAN AND AFGHAN TARGETS TIED TO TERRORIST NETWORK. The payback for the bombing of the embassies certainly seemed like the perfect presidential distraction. The paper said as much. WASHINGTON, August 20—"'The danger here,' said Senator Dan Coats, Republican of Indiana, 'is that once a president loses credibility with the Congress, as this president has through months of lies and deceit and manipulations, stonewalling, it raises into doubt everything he does and everything he says and maybe even everything he doesn't do and doesn't say.'" Not quite seventy-two hours earlier Senator Coats had called for President Clinton's resignation over the Monica Lewinsky issue. Drive was disgusted with what his beloved host country had been reduced to.

"Mr. Cedric Rhodes announces the expansion of his tender offer to include all of the shares of the American Observer Association, both voting and nonvoting. The appropriate documents have been filed at the Securities and Exchange Commission effective 9:30 a.m. Friday, August 21, 1998. Mr. Rhodes is glad to make clear by this offer, his pleasure in the possibility of acquiring the entire equity interest of the company."

Short, sweet, to the point. The arbs were delirious. They had locked in one of the fastest two-day profits in the history of the business. The only remaining obstacle was the presumed obduracy of the trustees of the Porter trusts. The financial and fiduciary community rose as one, a spontaneous outpouring of phone calls, faxes, and e-mails erupted. All the trustees, their spouses, their lawyers, their known associates were barraged with an increasingly insistent chorus pleading, and demanding, they not be obstacles to a resolution wanted by everyone.

La Volpe had received a late call the night before with the news of the proposed expanded tender. She arranged a conference call with the trustees for 10 a.m.

"I hope that you've had a chance to think about the scenario that I left you with yesterday."

The trustees had almost adapted themselves to a world where everyone didn't scurry to accommodate their every wish, but the traces of absolute power never disappeared entirely. "Have we lost our minds? The Porters were entitled to make whatever arrangements they chose with their properties. Nobody alleges that we've failed to carry out that mandate. Why is everybody thinking that we should change?" Volpe wanted to let the question remain in the atmosphere until one of the other trustees felt impelled to break the silence.

And so, one of his colleagues blurted, "Grow up, Jack. We had our chance. The company hasn't done well by anybody's measure. In my view, we're fortunate to be able to look forward to running the foundation with a portfolio of stocks. Let this wonder boy try and adapt America's sweetheart of the '30s to the twenty-first century. Are you really interested in being any more liable to these ingrates? Screw that."

That statement of patent disloyalty to the myth of *American Observer* magazine's universal and everlasting appeal proved the catalyst for remarkably rapid approval by the whole board. The chairman had been so defeated by his personal demotion that it was unclear what his position was. Nobody cared.

Ms. Volpe wisely counseled, "The tender offer period is thirty days. We need to be seen to reflect very carefully about all this. Let's agree to schedule a formal meeting for a week from today in the New York offices at this same time. In the meantime, we should all be circumspect." No psychologist of group behavior would fail to predict what happened next. To put it mildly, the confidentiality agreement leaked like a sieve. By noon the word was out that the trustees had folded and AOM was a done deal for Cedric Rhodes.

Once in the office, Drive put in a call to Moffie, picked through his papers, and began following the bombing fallout around the world. The consensus was the cruise missiles were aimed at the Starr investigation. It was received as either a happy coincidence at best or, more cynically, a presidential ploy. Moffie called in, relieving Drive's increasing aggravation with national affairs.

"Charles Bowditch? You wanted to know if he's vulnerable? I've got some dope for you, but first, my operative at Labor has really come through. I'm faxing you a copy of the letter that the department will publish Monday in the Federal Register in answer to the AOM ESOP's questions about Universal Bank. This is just plain dynamite. They're saying the bank must loan money to the ESOP on the same terms as they've agreed to loan to you."

Drive's reaction was so physical his presence could be felt through the telephone. "Can they do that?" This bomb blast shattered every other distraction Drive might have been nurturing.

"Boss, I'm just the messenger boy. All I can tell you is when they start things like publishing in the Federal Register, it usually means that someone is doing a number on somebody. Now about Bowditch."

"Forget about Bowditch, I've got to get going on this."

It was 2 p.m. in Vern's conference room, exactly fifty minutes since Moffie's call to Drive. Vern, Drive, Marty, and the representatives of Universal's legal department were all present and accounted for. Vern was running the meeting. "Let's take this one from the top. General counsel, tell us in plain English what the situation is."

"Vern, the Department of Labor, actually its Pension and Welfare Benefits Agency, is the federal agency authorized to interpret and monitor the Employee Retirement..."

Vern couldn't stand it. "Sweet *Jesus*, get on with it. We don't want the whole federal catechism."

"Assistant Secretary Munro *has* the authority to write this letter. We haven't finished our investigation, but on a preliminary basis, I have to advise you that her opinion would not necessarily be reversed in court."

"Come on, in English?"

"Ms. Munro's letter is probably going to bind us."

"Fuck!" Marty couldn't help himself but it looked like no one noticed. They all thought they had said it.

Vern politely explained, "But first, look, let's get it out on the table, if any of you don't know it, hear it from me. Molly Munro was my wife for twenty years. We aren't in close touch. Indeed, I didn't even know what her job really was until a week or so ago. But, she wouldn't use her government authority to spite me. Of that, I'm certain. I'm also sure, general counsel, that you'll tell us that starting when Molly became assistant secretary, there is an impeccable record of development and definition of this aspect of retirement law?"

"Just so, Vern. In July, definitive regulations became final. Last week, PWBA issued a letter to the AOM ESOP confirming their authority to borrow against the collateral of the stock they now hold. With this newly proposed letter, there is a legally impeccable record. What can we do about it? We can write the strongest possible letter objecting to the assistant secretary's interpretation."

"But, you just told us that the courts wouldn't back us up."

"You never know and you asked me what we *can* do."

Vern persisted, "Well, damn it, that ain't much. Let me start again. What can we do that stands a good chance of success?"

"Boss, we'll have to take that one under advisement. I'll get back to you before the close of business."

The legal department exited, leaving Vern, Marty and Drive.

Drive, a bit peevish, said, "Now, I've seen everything. We've just succeeded in making the most secure trustees in the history of writing, roll over and sell us their company, only to find some *woman* writing a one-page letter and stopping us in our tracks."

Vern looked like somebody had taken away his lollipop. "How do you think I feel? Frankly, this financing will be a Harvard Business School case study. Nobody could have done this..."

Marty was Marty. "Hey, guys, this is big boy time. It's as simple as this. Nobody could make Ms. Munro write this letter. Ms. Munro is writing this letter and using the Federal Register because she wants to do it. This is her personal agenda. It's not a government priority. The U.S. government isn't going to collapse because the assistant secretary of Labor takes a month or two to answer a letter. By that time, we can have the deal done. Let them try to unscramble it. Some things happen because the person in authority wants them to happen. But they don't have to happen. We just have to persuade the assistant secretary that she wants to change her mind."

Vern was back to being chairman of the bank again. "I'm neither sticking up for my former wife nor taking advantage of this occasion to vent some anger, I'm just telling you that she is a careful person, who likes to think of herself as principled. She has all the money in the world; our children are independent and will support us both. What are you gonna do?"

Marty was tenacious. "Look, the answer is right there. This is a principled person. She has chosen, as a matter of personal prerogative, to issue a letter in this situation that has vast impact. This kind of turnaround time is not illegal, but it is highly unusual. Would a principled, appointed official use every bit of permitted legal leverage to advance what has to be considered a personal agenda? That's where she's vulnerable. The question is, who can make that argument persuasively to her?"

"Well, I'm out of that race," Vern contributed.

Drive asked, "Listen. Isn't there anything we can do through government channels? After all, she works for people. Tell her not to follow through with this. She may not like it, but doesn't she have to do what she is told?"

"Yeah, she does. She could probably stonewall the secretary of Labor. The only person for whom she indisputably works is the president. Can we get his attention on this one?"

Drive was getting reconciled to the new game. "The kind of month he's had, this can't make it much worse. Well, we know what the challenge is, we'll pull out all the stops."

Vern was increasingly uncomfortable as the minutes passed. This was his weekend of weekends, annual member-guest golf at Piping Rock. Sure, it looked like his bragging rights were crushed but still; his wife, the limo, the clubs, everything was waiting to get out of town ahead of the Friday-night rush. Vern had been looking forward to this tournament all year, ever since he had found a closet professional to play as his partner and was sure nobody would find him out, as they had, so embarrassingly, a couple of years ago. Indeed, it really wasn't wrong for Vern to leave at this moment. When bankers get too far away from lending money and getting it paid back, they quickly get out of their depth. When a deal of this kind goes sour, there's nothing that a traditional banker can do to save it. So Vern's apologetic departure scarcely registered, it confirmed what was already known. Marty watched him go and just thought to himself, *what a lightweight*.

Drive and Marty repaired to Drive's office. They hardly noticed where they were walking, so great was their misery and preoccupation. They connected with Rose on the conference phone. Nobody could take it in, that his or her hard-earned victory has been snatched away.

"Everybody wants something," pontificated Marty. "It's just a question of price." Addressing himself to Drive, "Did you ever meet anybody who couldn't be persuaded, sooner or later, to accommodate to a different view of priorities? Listen, we just have to focus on this. It's simple. What does this lady want more than signing this letter now? She can sign a slightly different letter now or she can sign this letter later. That's not too unreasonable, is it?"

Rose interjected, "You're just blowing smoke, you don't understand this lady."

"You better believe I don't understand Ms. Munro, but I understand human nature, which will maybe give me a little insight into the lady herself."

Drive got off of a call on his cell phone, "The White House says she can have anything she wants, short of the Supreme Court or the vice presidency. There's a guy, right there with the president, who told me to work directly with him. Nobody ever handed me a blank check like that before. He'll see me on Tuesday when he gets back from the Vineyard."

Marty hadn't come down from the high of actually completing his biggest deal ever. He couldn't absorb that it was disappearing in front of his eyes. So Drive picked up the silence. "OK. Listen, we've a week to get this lady to change her mind. I'm going to focus on the high road. What can we get for her that will compensate for bending a little on this one? I will get Joey to get us some of the right kind of press. Marty, I want you to work with Scott Moffie and come up with some leverage that we can use. I count on you, Rose, to be there for all of us. Right now we need to focus on getting the right kind of weekend and weekly press confirming that we've won and the trustees will tender. They tell me that the Department of Labor is posting a copy of their proposed letter in the Federal Register on Monday."

"We haven't got the answer yet," was Rose's answer.

Drive was energized. He always felt a bit compromised having to accommodate the temperament of his professional advisors. Now that he had a direct contact in the White House, he could do what he enjoyed the most and did best, discovering the other person's price and figuring out how to pay the least. The possibility of defeat had not yet entered his consciousness.

Marty could always be counted on to get things back to reality, "How do we get, what does she call him, the Big Creep, to roll Ms. Fancy Pants in the Department of Labor?"

Laughing, more grateful than ever to have Marty on *his* side, Drive had to add, "Hey, counselor, you might have missed insulting somebody. Do you want to try again?"

"OK, guys, things are rough. We have the usual structure: chief of staff, internal affairs, external affairs, national security advisor. They run the shop. They can't help us. All we have to do is be sure that they know we're trying to do something, that's all, they don't want to know but they don't want to be surprised either. Marty, I've got to think out loud with the boss about this. There's no point going the big contributor route, you're already off the chart. Can we do, First Friend, all dozen of them, let's think about that. Do any of these guys want to cash that big a chip for us? They're all thinking Supreme Court, trustee of the library, that kind of thing; no, they want something for themselves that only he can give them. How about the spinmeisters, who get up every day and spread the daily lie? These guys are so into their own thing, they couldn't even pronounce our name when it came time to make the sale. The First Lady's side is a strikeout."

Marty had to get practical. "No, this is pure commerce. If we want to get something done, we have to do it the old-fashioned way. We hire a former White House counsel. These guys are in business to sell their entrée. There's no question what they are, it's just a matter of price. I'm told that's why some guys prefer the pros. You know what you're getting."

"And they know when to leave. Look, we get straight answers from people who're going to want to do business with us in the future. The president really is not available. Period. He is driving himself crazy. The American people will never believe that he had every reason to send the missiles; we aren't on the agenda."

Gradually, it became clear that Drive wasn't a participant in the conversation. He actually got up to stretch, looked out the window, and picked up a newspaper. Sometimes, a relationship is as slender as a single symbolic act. Marty didn't notice.

Drive was listening after all, but in a way that indicated he hadn't heard. "It's hard to believe after all these years when I've had excellent access to everyone that I can't get through to the most accessible and needy president when I need it. We've a plan. Let's get going with it. Let me talk with the special counsel, I may have figured out something irresistible." So Drive broke up the meeting, by walking out.

It had been a very long day for Drive and it was late. Thank God for speed dial was his foremost thought as he personally placed some fifty calls. He shook the tree hard. Everyone he could imagine, with any pull of any sort, was contacted. There was very little small talk but anyone who knew Drive understood. Anyone would love to be the person who helped him out. Hopefully, something might come out of his effort. He had one more call to make but he'd have to use his special phone. It would be just strictly business.

"As our friend Marty would say, 'Welcome to the Bigs.' We now have the challenge of getting to a president on vacation with his mind on other things."

Rose had plenty to report. "We have a lot of lines out now. I'm one person away from someone who's supposed to play golf with him tomorrow. But with this missile thing, and the assumption that some kind of national crisis is involved, he may stay in Washington.

"I've worked out a deal with the chairman of the Congressional Pension Labor Committee. A contingent arrangement; 1,000 percent bonus if he succeeds in getting the letter withdrawn. He'll be back in Washington on Friday the twenty-eighth and has summoned her to a meeting. He can taste the money. The secretary of Labor is a woman, now the custom. Picked by the First Lady, and it gets worse. Did you know that Ms. Munro was one of the original backers of the president? This president has proven he can do a lot of things that nobody thought a president of the United States could and still stay president, but I am worried about us on this one.

"That Marty is something else. Do you know what he suggested? The Supreme Court. Do we think she would go for that? Can we deliver it? This is the deal of deals. We've worked the impossible with all the problems that we could think of in advance. Everything worked and then...none of the above. That is the story of life. How are you feeling?"

"A little confused, but I've got the bit in my teeth. We'll get this one on track." But in the tiniest recess in the back of his battered brain, Drive had a thought he'd never repeat to a living soul, *I've done this too many times before.* The deal? The relationship? Both. He just wanted to go home and sleep, too tired to care.

Chapter 24

August 21, p.m.

Marty lurched into Wilson's office, out of breath, his impeccable coiffure in danger of coming unstuck. Wilson was emboldened. "Hey, rabbi, has the world come to an end? I've never seen..."

"Listen, Wilson, we've got one week, just one week, to persuade one junior federal official that she wants to do things our way. That's where we're at."

"When I got your call, I thought you wanted to congratulate me on the incredible response we generated from the program. It looks like we won big. So what's the new job?"

"The assistant secretary of Labor has decided that she will issue an opinion that takes the deal away from our guy and gives it to the employees."

"She can do that?"

"Yeah, she can do that. The question is, is she going to want to do it? We have a week to change her mind."

"Shit! Doesn't she have a boss? Doesn't he want to eat? Don't we have a court system? This is America. Hey, isn't this what *you* guys get paid big bucks to solve?"

"We've got people working on all sides of this. Right now, we need to find some vulnerability. We've got some legit articles coming out in the business press. We have this big-time investigator, Scott Moffie, on the payroll. You can use him all you need."

"I went to school with the Moffster. Funny place to meet again. Had her background checked?"

"Yeah. It's like trying to get your fingers around a blob of mercury. Nothing to hold onto, money, job, family. She even disclosed an affair with the guy on the other side of this deal when she took the job. We had her personnel records."

"You haven't broken into her *psychiatrist's* office yet, have you?"

"Hey, wise guy, we got a real problem."

"Exactly what do you want me to do? And the meter has started to run again, you know."

Marty started to look mean, real mean, $30-million-lawyer mean. "Wilson, you're pissing me off. No, I'm pissed off because I won this thing fair and square, one great piece of work and now, I don't know what to do and I don't like not knowing what to do."

"Calm down, Superman, and join the human race. We can agree, I take it, that there are limits to what your client is prepared to do? We're talking Marquis of Queensbury Manhattan '98 Rules?" Marty nodded, only half joking, "Afraid so." Wilson wondered, *Are there any limits to what these guys will do?* but continued, "Let's think about this carefully. Somebody else is in charge of telling the lady all the nice things that can happen to her if she goes along with this, right? What we have to find out is who she respects and focus our best case, by whatever means, on those people." Life was flowing back into the exhausted system of Marty Beal.

"Yeah, there's got to be somebody."

The big guy went for an end run. "Wait a minute. Before we get the answer, we need to understand what the question is. What's this lady supposed to have done that is wrong, she seems to be going out of her way to promote some other group? Who are those guys anyway?"

"It's the employees. It's motherhood, apple pie, and war heroes, all rolled into one."

"Huh?"

"Forget it."

"OK, false lead. How could she be criticized?"

Marty wasn't used to answering another lawyer's questions.

"You can *always* criticize a public servant for acting too precipitously."

Wilson's wheels started turning. "She's helping a close friend, she's acting too fast! What else? That's not going to win anything. Maybe, we're making this too complicated. Maybe she can't be reached, but somebody she respects can be. Think about it, an old law school teacher, mentor for all the ladies, a federal judgeship. Marty, we aren't getting anywhere. Here's what I suggest. I've still got my push pollers on the string. We should work the list that Moffie has come up with."

Looking at his watch for the time, Wilson looked like a conventional chief executive officer. "We can still get some of my good diggers to verify names and numbers. Everybody who knows Molly Munro should get a very polite call. Some will say they are writing a magazine article about the assistant secretary; others can talk of background work for a biography; maybe we can mention a forthcoming public television documentary on women in government leadership positions, whatever. I've got great people. Everybody gets a call. That'll take a few days. The calls are different, but they're all the same: Is there anything in your experience with Ms. Munro that would provide some explanation for a certain stubbornness, a headstrong commitment to something, a lack of loyalty, maybe? Let's see what we can catch. We start now, maybe by Tuesday, we'll know something new."

Marty just smiled, "You know, I don't know anything about you, Wilson, or even about your ole buddy, the Moffster. I don't know where you guys went to school, but I am figuring out how the British Empire dominated the world for two centuries."

"Well, thank you, my Hebrew brother, it's that goyim magic."

The weekend financial press contained surprisingly substantive accounts of the rumored acquiescence by the Porter Trustees of Drive's tender offer. There was much speculation as to the future direction of American Observer under the dynamic leadership of Cedric Rhodes. Although there was no mention of the AOM ESOP, one journalist presciently concluded, "The fat lady has yet to sing." On such obvious insights are the greatest reputations built in the world of contemporary journalism.

MONDAY, AUGUST 24, 1998

Marty van Buren Beal was a good lawyer. Sitting in his office early Monday morning, he carefully read the faxed copy of the assistant secretary's letter to be published later that day in the Federal Register. At moments like this, witnesses could feel the palpable workings of his intellect. The office knew to leave him alone. Talking to himself, Marty said, "OK, OK, guys," addressing himself to the professional staff of the Department of Labor, "you're right because the bank is offering financing on specific terms to an outsider, it can't decline financing on a better deal to its own subsidiary. Now, change the terms. Somebody offers $31 a share. The bank is not obligated to Drive, and, therefore, it cannot be compelled to extend this new financing to the ESOP. We need someone else to make a bid. This opinion is only binding with this precise financing."

Marty was also a gifted dealmaker. All weekend, thinking, thinking, who could help save the deal, and, incidentally, his big contingent fee? He reached Patrick O'Neil by phone late Sunday night, talked about the turn the deal had taken, asked him to be in his office first thing in the morning, as if O'Neil could sleep on hearing that news! Marty went out to the reception area and saw this prototypical Irish choirboy. As the Irish worked their post–World War II ascent from the mailroom to the boardrooms of Wall Street, their appearance and garb remained the same—pink cheeks, hair sleekly brushed, three-piece blue suit, white shirt, and innocuous striped tie. Without bothering to introduce himself, Marty indicated that O'Neil should follow. Marty wasn't one for coffee, sweet rolls, or any kind of nicety, so he left it to O'Neil to sit wherever he chose. "Hey, we've lost a lot of money." A surprisingly high-pitched voice with a touch of a lilt caused Marty to stare more closely at his visitor. "For this kind of money, we'll just have to kill somebody." Visions of Irish terrorism flashed across Marty's consciousness, so he quickly turned in more conventional directions.

"It's as simple as this. We've got to get those pension funds to back another bid, here. Another bid, the ESOP will be stuck without competitive financing and we're back in the fee business."

O'Neil pointed out, "I think we got a problem. It doesn't look like the bank's going to be comfortable financing any other deal here, so we got to find a new trustee. How's that gonna make our friend Mr. Stillman feel? He'll drop a few fees on that one. Is Drive gonna go for a deal which cuts out Stillman? Who are we gonna get at this late hour to stand up and act as trustee?"

For the first time, Marty looked at O'Neil as if he was in the same room with a sentient functional human being. Suddenly O'Neil began to laugh. "I don't know why we're sitting here, all gloomy, I just have to think of all the yachts, new houses, new girlfriends, and fancy trips, all going down the drain with this one, and the funny thing is, they don't know it yet. This fee was going to fill a lot of cups and create a lot of happiness. This was one of the big deals of all time. A lot of people were gonna get healthy on this one. Some of these guys may be able to help us."

Marty was looking for permission to believe. "We haven't got much time and I need to make some more calls. Can you get on to your people right now and get back to me by close of business today with any progress? OK, we'll meet here again at five."

There was an air of unreality as Horse met at the ESOP offices in Tarrytown with the executive committee. The whole world thinks Drive has won; only these few think otherwise.

"Vern and I had a very straightforward talk. I'm not going to be fired or taken off of the account. They're in a very ticklish position with the Porter trustees, because they stand to win very big if the Rhodes tender goes through. So there's no communication on that front. The word is that the trustees have decided to take Rhodes's way out."

Skapinsky, the practical, "What's our timing, Horse? Tell us what must be done?"

"Molly's office, PWBA at the Department of Labor, has published the proposed letter to us in the Federal Register today. They'll pick up a lot of comments. Presumably, Universal's legal staff and outside counsel will outdo themselves in filing objections, but there's nothing they can do. You have to understand. The assistant secretary, who has the authority to interpret the statute, has reviewed the circumstances of our situation and has concluded that a breach of trust exists. People can disagree with her but the facts are clear. She can't be proven wrong. The great thing is, where people think we're weak, we're the strongest. Molly doesn't have to do this; she is making this choice as a matter of the deepest personal conviction."

"What do we do?"

"Hold our ground. Wait for the letter to issue, *formally*. Then I'll present myself to Mr. Stillman and *formally* request he make available the appropriate financing to the ESOP."

In tones that suggested he'd achieved a lifelong goal, Skapinsky said, "Look, Horse, you should know. We've polled the membership and there'll be a unanimous vote for you to become the CEO of the American Observer ESOP. Nice to know, yes?"

Horse looked surprised and everyone present was afraid he was coming up with objections, and then very slowly he broke into a smile, normally reserved for the golf course. "Believe me, I've never thought of that, but now that I do, I like it. I'll do a good job."

Marty was utterly frustrated by a whole day with no new ideas, so he called Charles General Electric Wilson, "Meet me in my office as soon as you can waddle up there."

"I've got a rule. If you're rude, it'll cost you."

"Just get your ass up to my office."

"Ten-four, my rabbi!"

Marty got back to his paper-strewn quarters only about five minutes ahead of a surprisingly cool, well-dressed Charles Wilson, who improved on the occasion. "What, if I may ask, is the excuse for all of this?" and his hand waved in a magisterial way across the entire mess of the room which included, of course, its patron and occupant, the now thoroughly bedraggled Marty.

"OK, I owe you an apology. I apologize. But, listen to me..."

"I've never seen you like this, Marty. What's really bothering you? After what we have been through, this lady obviously wants something. Don't they all?"

"Her family and friends are tight. She can have any job she wants. Short of kidnapping her and applying some electrodes, I don't know what we're going to do."

"Hey, boss, you're kidding about the electrodes?" The big guy was intrigued.

"Yeah, I'm just overwrought. I thought I got to the finish line. Except, now it turns out, it's the starting line. What do you think?"

"We've started on the calls. Nothing yet. How about her authority?"

"You know," Marty ruminated, "as a lawyer, I started with that. I got the best guys in my firm to comb through the whole issue of ERISA regulations, and interpretive letters, conflicts of interest. All I can tell you is, that branch of the Department of Labor has first-class administrators and lawyers. They've done everything right. Bastards. No hurry, public hearings, public notice. You name it. It makes a lawyer want to puke; there is nothing for us to grab on to."

Wilson tried to cheer his cash-paying client, "We can give her a hard time. Believe me. Somebody will break, but the only sure solution here is in the chain of command, President of the United States, Secretary of Labor. I don't want to repeat myself, but I am not supposed..."

"Yeah, yeah, Drive is almost wild now. He has a confidential assistant, who, I must tell you, is the smartest person I have ever talked to. She keeps their ledger cards, who owes who, except their ledger cards look like a Swiss bank record of illegal deposits. I love this woman. She's way beyond anything I've ever encountered. They'll go to the limit on this. Our target is the Assistant Secretary of Labor, Ms. Molly Munro."

"Boss. You're telling me to do the sensible things?"

"Yeah, I guess so, but I don't feel good about it. I can't see that it's going to work. We have to try everything though. What a bitch this is. We performed the most incredible feat in the history of takeovers, and now we're trapped."

THE WALL STREET JOURNAL
Monday, August 24, 1998
American Observer Trustees to Tender
Rhodes's Bid to Be Accepted
A series of weekend meetings, following Cedric Rhodes's revised Friday offer, has resulted in the surprising decision by the trustees of the Randy and Shelley Porter Trusts to tender their shares to the South African, according to sources close to the transaction. The trusts own a majority of the voting interest in the famous American Observer Company, so control over this especially American institution will pass to the World Publications czar.

Trust officials, on a not-for-attribution basis, spoke of the intensity of the consideration given by the trustees and their professional advisors. It was reported that the trust felt itself in a powerful bind, between highly respected charitable organizations owning substantial nonvoting shares that were concerned with the stability of their annual distributions and the demands of public shareholders, who expected the management to invest in the company's future. Counsel for the trustees is reported to have advised that it would not be imprudent to take steps that would at the same time assure future payments to the charities and to place the famous company in the hands of one of the world's great publishers. A spokesperson for "King Tony" Williamson from the Shark Fund answered "No comment" to repeated questions as to whether their influence as the largest outside shareholder had been critical in yet another profitable transaction involving corporate change.

The street loves this deal. From beginning to end, it consumed only part of the month of August, a time when people's principal attentions were elsewhere—from vacation, to scandal, to war—and it is rumored that the imaginative financing provided by Universal Bank will place that institution in the top tier as CEO Stillman leads it into the twenty-first century. The arbitrageur community bet big on this one and they won. There continues to be some question as to the situation prevailing with the American Observer ESOP, which owns 20 percent of the outstanding voting stock. The trustees of the ESOP have recently indicated a disinclination to tender to Mr. Rhodes and a determination to make a tender offer for the balance of the voting stock for their own account. Sources indicate that the ESOP has not been successful in securing financing for its plans, so, while the denouement is not yet clear, it seems unlikely that Mr. Cedric Rhodes's efforts to acquire control of American Observer will be thwarted.

Marty knew he would pay a price for calling King Tony, but maybe it would be worth it.

"Hey, Anthony, where are you anyway? I can hear wind and waves."

"Listen, Beal, I keep this special hookup for real people and making money. Say something or get off the line." The King had a way with his subjects.

"OK, here it is, that American Observer deal. We've hit a snag. Department of Labor is going to require the bank to finance an employee buyout. I know, I know, but it's a problem we can solve. Do you want to organize a syndicate and take the lead here? We have the pension-fund financing. It's just a question of a nominal price increase."

At this point it sounded on Marty's end of the call like a huge wave had engulfed the conversation. Finally, he could glean, "Hey, Beal, you're a smart lawyer, and you know why you're a lawyer and I'm a client? I'll tell you why. At $30 a share, I'm a seller. Get that Beal, a seller. I'm not a buyer at $31, I am not a buyer at $30. That, my friend, is the difference between rich and poor. There's more to money than making a deal, it's knowing whether to buy or sell." The call simply ended on that note.

And the horse you rode in on, you putz! thought Marty.

Marty called his friend and colleague, Big Jack Piaseki, CEO of Diverse Enterprises International, for whom he had acted as counsel for over thirty years. "Hey, Jack, who'd be interested in a little jewel of a publishing company? American Observer. Three-billion-dollar deal, financing is in place, need fast action."

"Marty, publishing companies aren't my thing. We're into pipes and valves and that kind of real stuff. But, listen, don't I remember. There was a lot of talk of a merger with Time, Inc., some years ago. Yeah, I remember now. It didn't work. What did that poet say that you guys quote all the time, 'There was no there, there.' Sorry about that. See you at the next board meeting."

"I'm sinking here, people!" Marty said out loud to no one in particular.

At 5 p.m., Pat O'Neil and Marty met in the reception area. O'Neil said in that calm, squeaky voice, "I talked with my people in the pension funds. They like the deal, but they, like, are doing it as a payback for this guy Stillman. I never figured that guy could do favors that would earn this level of payback, but live and learn. We gotta keep him in the deal and there's not a lot of interest in going up in price." Marty just nodded, and the six-foot leprechaun continued stomping on his heart, "Except for guys like us, trying to protect our fees, there's no appetite for this baby at more than $30 a share. Without somebody feeling like putting a lot of fast money in their pocket, we're not going to have the necessary leadership to make this thing happen." Marty was silent, staring straight ahead. O'Neil went on, "Maybe we can figure out a way to fix this assistant secretary. My people really want this deal to go, if you know what I mean."

"Yeah, I know, we're working on it. If you have any special insight, I'd be glad to have it." But all Marty got was the unblinking big baby blues, swimming in the sea of pink Irishman. "God, what have I done to have come to this?" he asked out loud.

Marty walked right into Drive's office as there were no formalities at seven o'clock in the morning. Drive hooked up Rose on the conference phone for a progress report. There was something different about Drive, apparent even to the usually all-business, insensitive Marty. No Italian clothes, that's it. He looks just like a British gent today. Dark suit, cuff links, club tie. Dark mood with a phony air of cheerfulness, too, like bad frosting on a worse cake.

"How is everybody on this famous day? Yeltsin's having the same kind of luck we are. He's dismissed the Russian government. Sounds like a sweet trick. And today, the Egyptians captured the Jackal himself, Abu Nidal, the most famous terrorist in the world, dirty bugger. This August is definitely one for the history books." Nobody spoke up, as it wasn't yet possible to know where the boss was going and the other two were still a bit groggy. Drive was determined to be the life of the party.

"OK, let me tell you about the favor factory they're running down there on Pennsylvania Avenue. I'm getting old or something. I don't know what I expected, but I was genuinely shocked."

Marty was not interested in political theory. He was barely capable of civility on his best days. Today was particularly bad. Not only did he have to face up to hours of insomnia and the conclusion that he had lost his greatest ever deal, but he also had to face up to his complete inability to figure out how to fix things. "Boss, hey, boss, is there anything in this honey pot that is going to do us any good?"

"OK. I went down to D.C. on Monday and met with 'the guy.' He told me he has full authority from the president to commit. We went through a book called the Plum Book with every high appointment listed and described. In the end, we had three thoughts: first, an ambassadorship; second, a cabinet office; third, an appointment to a high federal court. We're talking about a serious lady. This is an administration that takes serious ladies pretty seriously. Senate approval, that's where I can help. Wellborn ladies tend to have friends on the Republican side of the aisle, so we can work that."

Rose spoke to the point, "The critical thing is...who makes the pitch? When do they make it?"

Drive receded more and more into the persona of a typical elderly chairman of a fine old company. "Folks, this was handled by me personally from the White House on Monday. Before lunch, we agreed and my friend Charlie picked up the phone, asked the White House operator to get Molly Munro. Four minutes later, there's Molly Munro on the other end. 'Hello, Charlie,' she says, 'how did I get so famous that I warrant a call from the vault?' They call Charlie's office the vault because that's where the treasures are kept." Marty couldn't stand it another minute; Drive had disintegrated into some tourist who was so overwhelmed by the White House he'd lost his ability to lead. He got up and grabbed the door for Drive's executive bathroom. Then he thought, *Oh, shit, can mere mortals use these facilities? How much more can I lose; here goes.* Meanwhile, Drive was talking away in the empty room for quite a while until Marty slouched back into his chair; he hadn't really noticed he was gone, or gotten to the point yet. "All right, my guy Charlie goes through this whole routine. He's got Molly on the conference line, but he hasn't told her that anybody else is in the room. I guess in D.C. you just assume there are listeners in the room, on the tapes, and over the airwaves, so everybody is careful. Molly interrupts him, honest to God, here the guy is warming up to offer her every girl's dream, and she can't even let the guy finish. 'Charlie, I really am grateful for the Administration's approval. As you know, I loved working with you at 1600. The only reason I left was for the only job I ever wanted in government. I want to finish this job and then go back to the private sector.' Charlie's got a routine for that one, too. 'All the best ones won't take the jobs. It's part of a day's work for us. But, I have to warn you; they're going to be all over you about this one. They really want you, so heads up, girl.' Charlie hangs up and takes me to lunch, not just to the White House mess, but to the little room off to the side which is kind of saved for the vice president, except he's not in town, so we use it; has its own match books even." Marty wondered if Drive had had a stroke. His billionaire had gone boring on him.

Rose began, "OK, so we're not getting anywhere with a better government position. I've worked out a pretty tough piece. The question of political appointees advancing personal agendas without adequate time for political consideration of the underlying issues. This will give a hook if the president wants to grab it. She doesn't seem to want to be a college president; certainly won't want our legal business. I don't think we can do this one with carrots."

Marty didn't know whether he was relieved or depressed that the others had done as badly as he had. He described, with no names, the efforts to mount a telephone information campaign. His work on finding new financing he kept to himself because that was, at the end of the day, mostly about fees. He concluded simply, "The kind of people whom she respects and hangs out with are just as happy if you don't buy American Observer. We're not getting any traction there."

Chapter 25
Friday, August 28, 1998

Drive had taken to walking around his office and staring out the windows. Every day he followed each developing news story to distract himself. The longest-serving American weapons inspector in Iraq resigned yesterday, charging that the United Nations Secretary General, the Security Council, and the Clinton Administration had stymied the inspectors on the doorstep of uncovering Iraq's hidden weapons programs. And today the Russian economic situation was playing havoc with the world markets. This was a boom time and the Dow and NASDAQ were making record lows. This was earmarked to be the worst trading day of the year. But all the news in the world still hadn't made this week pass any easier. In the last few days, he had spoken to everyone he had ever known and still felt no connection, with anyone or anything. His dream was evaporating and he wasn't sure what to do about it. His sleep was filled with disturbing dreams and his restlessness had come back in the worst way.

He called Vern once or twice a day, but neither had very much to say to the other. Vern had his problems, but he'd come through with what he promised. He'd like to help, but, what could he do? He's only a banker and that's all he wants to be. It's as if somebody had died and everybody's waiting for the funeral. Well, it's not over. There is still the president.

Marty showed up in his jogging clothes promptly at 7:00 a.m. Drive was torn between disgust for those hairy pipe-stem legs and envy for the cardiovascular system that would carry his counsel for decades to come. "OK, it's game time." They connected with Rose.

Rose had plenty to report. "Here's where we're at. We've got a big day for our Miss Molly today. Chairman will demand her presence first thing this morning. That means ten o'clock in D.C. She'll have some upset phone calls and we've got one of the most persuasive and influential lobbyists in the country prepared to offer her eternal happiness. We're keeping close to the president. He knows what's going on. We're just going to have to hang in there and hope we get a clear shot. And the right answer. We've got Judge going in to see her on Monday morning. It would help if either or both of you would talk to him. Frankly, we're not going to get the best results if a person of that stature takes his orders from me. He's our best chance. He won't lie and she'll know that he can speak for the president."

Marty was really speaking to her while he was looking at Drive. "Guys, I've given it a lot of thought and this is our best move. Drive, you definitely call him. We're just trying to save a company, a national treasure that deserves the best. This isn't some ESOP test balloon; we're offering a guaranteed, proven model for success. He's Judge, for Christ's sake. He's the most prestigious individual in government. At this point, he's got a whole lot more credibility than the Big Creep himself. She's a believer, and Judge represents everything she believes in. No way she'll refuse him."

Molly knew that it was going to be a horror of a day from the moment she turned to park her car in the Frances Perkins Building. There was only room for one car at a time to pass through the two-way alley. In exasperation she used her car phone to call her secretary, Barbara, to come sit in the car until the way cleared. Not the kind of job any secretary wants to do on a typical Washington August day, when venturing out of doors was the equivalent of plunging into an odoriferous Turkish bath. As she walked up the public entry off Constitution Avenue, only one of the four indicated double doors actually provided access and this through a particularly shabbily constructed security check turned irritation into rage. The elevator lobbies were crowded, so she walked up to the nob's floor. For the one-hundredth time, she cursed the government architects who placed the magnificent public offices half a mile from where the staffs actually did the work. For a hands-on manager, this was a nightmare. Molly cursed again as she turned into her office suite.

Government offices at the level of the political appointees have two in-boxes, the regular mail and the "Congressional"; traditionally, for her department, the House of Representatives' pension committee, having oversight of PWBA, acted like her bosses. Both the majority and the minority staff had long tenure and an exaggerated view of their own importance, so it was with no pleasure that Molly saw the phone slip with the crimson flag, a code for emergencies, from Don Meyer, the minority chief of staff. She knew the price of not returning such a call immediately was too high. The day had started itself.

"Don, this is Molly Munro, to what do I owe the honor of communication from my lord and master?"

The light touch didn't pass the first contact. "I just wish that you had been there when I called. The chairman himself was on the line and he wants to meet with you right now."

Molly had been around long enough to not even think of mentioning the traffic or trying any humor. "What's this all about, Don?"

"I get paid to do what the chairman asks, not to read his mind. The only thing I can tell you is, this is the first time that I've ever gotten a phone call from him before noon. It's also the first time I can recall him demanding an unscheduled, immediate appointment."

"I don't mean to be obtuse, but, like you, I am unfamiliar with the protocol here. Immediate means like, right now, cancel the other appointments and come, right now?"

Back to being a bureaucrat, Don simpered, "I wouldn't presume... but the man..."

"OK, OK. Where is Janet? It isn't like you, running errands for the Democrats."

"He wanted to know that, too, so listen, give us a break and let's get this over with."

"It's 8:45 a.m. I can get a car and a driver and be up there, say 10:00 a.m. OK?"

Molly put the phone down, went into the outer office to discover that her secretary had not yet arrived. She couldn't find anybody else who knew how to reserve one of the department cars for her trip to the Hill, so she ended up walking halfway around the building and putting herself at the mercy of the deputy secretary's assistant. He dialed the three digits, said a dozen words, and raised his right hand in the universal signal that all was well. As it happened, that about used up Molly's luck for the day.

Back in her own office, the phone rang. It was her secretary's voice. Before Molly could apologize for the dreadful assignment or vent some discomfort herself, the message was, "It's your brother, Dr. Phillip, on three."

"Hi, Phillip. What a terrible day this is turning out to be. How are you and yours, anyway? It's nice to get your call."

"Everyone is fine. Little Sister, I wish I could say it's nice but it isn't. I have to pass some drivel on to you. A bunch of people around here called and asked me to talk directly with you. This bunch included the chairman of the board of trustees of this hospital. I don't know what you're doing, but they want you to stop it. Before I told them to perform an indecent act on themselves, I figured I'd give you a heads up. Good lord, Little Sister, what is this public service all about?"

"I guess after all these years, I'm finding out what it's like to play ball in the big leagues. Do you remember that work of Ancestor's?"

"Oh yeah, your old Communism kick," he teased.

"You shut up, Flip! I'll have the Secret Service come over and break your golf clubs. Look, I'm sorry for the hassle. The deal is I've been working to make it easier for the development of employee ownership. In doing this, I have, for reasons I don't fully yet understand, gotten in the way of some major power and influence. I've just gotten summoned to the Capitol. The next thing you know, my friends in the White House will want to pass a little word to me. Thanks for the call, Big Brother. You know me, pretty soon, they'll get tired, but keep your line open, I want to find out about some of those indecent acts."

All the lights on her console were blinking. Molly ignored them and buzzed for her secretary, who came storming through the connecting door. Molly said as nicely as she could, "Could you shut the door and come and sit down for just a quiet minute? It looks as if this is going to be quite a day. Thank you for taking care of the car. It looks like we're playing Alamo." Now that the struggle was engaged, Molly had gotten back her humor and her balance. She didn't yet have a feel for the scope of the assault, but it was clear that major energies had been enlisted across the power spectrum to make it unattractive for her to continue with the American Observer ruling letter. Government secretaries are at their best when under attack, because, among other things, they know that there's nothing that anybody can do to disturb their position. Molly was very popular with both the men and women on the staff. Her coming directly from a White House position to this relatively obscure agency gave everyone a jolt of pride. People profoundly appreciated her knowledge of the field and her commitment to improving the professional status of the agency. The battle strategy began.

"Molly, seeing as how you are going to be on the Hill, we don't have to accept anybody insisting you come to see them."

"Nice one, Babs. Good thinking. Maybe the White House..."

"Just who in the White House? Certainly not everybody."

"As I look at the papers, the Boss and Boss Lady have plenty on their minds, but I've got to be accessible to them if necessary. I guess the chief of staff and the domestic policy chief. You know the drill. I hope to get back here in one piece. Listen, they may be hanging out in the lobby to waylay me. I am going to take my personal cell phone. You know that private elevator up from the garage that lets out by that big conference room?" Molly got up and moved to the doorway. "If I call, can you go out to it, down the hall? Look and see if the coast is clear. If it is, get a couple of other people to stand by the doors to block for me when I get out."

And with that she was out of her office and on her way.

Molly reflected on the beauty of the crêpe myrtle shrubs that embellish the Capitol at the bottom of the summer. She had never known of their existence before moving to Washington. *Such beautiful things*, she thought, *in the occasionally sordid world*. She smiled and thought that Chairman Chevrolet was a handsome man with a fine smile and a great sense of humor. He resembled nobody as much as Robert Redford. On the times that she had met him in his office, he had the disconcerting habit of reaching into a lower desk drawer and pulling out an unlabeled bottle that he would periodically tilt and pour a colorless liquid impeccably down his throat. His eyes would roll for an instant and then he was back at full attention. A hard read, he seemed to depend a lot on his staff.

When she arrived at the committee rooms, Molly was ushered directly into the chairman's office where both an abashed Janet and Don were at quivering attention. There was no funny-man stuff today. "Assistant Secretary Munro, I do not know how you have done this. I have felt, and I must confess that I like the feeling, that I have come to a point in life where I could not simply be jerked around like a fish on a strong line. I have been naïve and I don't like that. Ms. Munro, I cannot imagine how anything that our polite, conscientious, people-oriented little agency could do that would get the attention of a few of the only people in the world in a position to say to me "Jump." I got one of those phone calls very late last night. I hope, Ms. Munro, that I have your attention and that we will be able to count on your cooperation and ingenuity to work out our little problem."

Molly's experience with government officials, particularly those senior to herself, and especially those whose mandate flowed directly from the vote of the people, was that they preferred to come to the point in their own time and to frame the issues in a personal way. Chevrolet was a master of congressional circumlocution. One side of her regretted not having a tape recorder to inscribe the full nuance of the genius's communication, another side was terrified because she had a pretty good idea what the problem was, what he was going to ask her to do, and she had no idea how she was going to get out of that room...alive.

"It'd be a shame if any of you were to have a mis-impression. The chairman of this subcommittee has never inferred, never implied, and certainly never suggested that an executive branch official should do otherwise than to observe her oath of office and to perform her duties as she and her God think. Right?" At this point, the left hand went down to the desk drawer, up came the bottle, out came the stream of liquid, not a drop was spilled, the eyes rolled, and not a syllable was missed. "I am actually uncomfortable even being in the room when the details of specific items of the agency's business are discussed. Janet, my dear, now that you have finally gotten here, could you give me some comfort in this?'

The flustered Janet Black, being, if the truth were told, a bit over-weight, was not at her best in humid summer Washington. Nothing seemed dry and perspiration came easily even in air-conditioned rooms. She was so uncomfortable that she started to excuse her late-ness. The chairman was having none of it. "Janet, I need your full attention on this matter, right now."

"Mr. Chairman. It's always the prerogative of the oversight com-mittee to review the operations of the agency with whatever depth of scrutiny may be necessary to discharge the legislature's responsibilities."

"Janet, goddamn it, stop talking like a congressional guidebook. I need to know exactly what's going on here and I don't want to find myself holding on to a bundle of shit when some wise guy decides that my attention is inappropriate, out of the ordinary, and explainable only in terms of purchased interest. Janet?"

"Oh, OK, Mr. Chairman. I believe that if Don and I take up the matter with Assistant Secretary Munro, that the record will show that you were at that same time engaged on the phone in other committee business, out of the room for much of the time, and otherwise not able to follow the conversation. When and if Don and I feel that you need to be informed of a particular situation, we'll call it to your attention."

"Now that's what I call creative thinking. Deniability, that's what we have here." The chairman's presence was largely the energy of his personality rather than physical. Having set the stage the way he wanted it, he seemed virtually to disappear. In looking back on the next hour, Molly really could not remember whether the chairman actually was participating at any given time. That is real deniability!

Molly had long ago learned that most meetings involve people with very strong, if unexplored, emotional commitments to particular aspects of the subject matter. Nothing could be accomplished by way of an orderly agenda until these emotional imperatives had surfaced and been confronted. Janet and Don hated to acknowledge how vulnerable they were to the chairman's moods. Somebody had to pay for their discomfort. Molly was to hand. It took a while but finally Don blurted out, "This is all about the new regulation on ESOPs." Calmly, patiently, the three of them traced the history of this interpretive bulletin right back to the passage of the Employee Retirement Income Security Act of 1974 (ERISA).

Forty-five minutes passed and the chairman was still in a state of suspended consciousness. The bureaucrats, and that included Molly at this point, were a bit bewildered. They'd moved through anger to calm acceptance of the finality of a proper procedure in which they'd all participated. From the perspective of the world that they shared, this was the whole story; there was nothing else to be said. They'd forgotten what they must do in order to alleviate the chairman's problem. An embarrassed silence elicited a genteel cough from the vicinity of the desk. As they turned toward the chairman, he crooked the index finger of his right hand to summon Janet to come closer so that he might speak to her in confidence. Janet lurched out of the sofa, approached the chairman, and bent over solicitously to hear every murmur. As seconds became minutes, Don and Molly became more and more uncomfortable. If anything good was happening, it was not evidenced in Janet's body language. Her initially awkward posture has deteriorated into acute discomfort that she could do nothing about so long as the chairman continued to demand her attention. Finally, ashen-faced from stress; she straightened up and rejoined the others.

"This is not a time for a history lesson," reported Janet for the chairman. "His people want to buy American Observer. The only obstacle is the employees' stock option group. They're organized and they'll make a competitive bid. Congress has given ESOPs so many tax breaks they'll always be able to pay a higher price. Also, his people can't stand the public relations label of beating the employees, it sounds un-American and, to boot, his people are not Americans. We have to find some way of stopping the ESOP. Surely, they've done something illegal and the department should intervene."

"We're very familiar with the American Observer ESOP. Indeed, they're one of the lead groups with whom we've developed the regulations. We've known of their wishes to acquire more AOM voting stock and we've encouraged them. The agency is in the process of issuing a letter opinion confirming our earlier advice that their borrowing and tendering for additional stock is in accordance with the law. My senior staff is meeting with their representatives...." Molly paused to look at her watch, "Hmm, the meeting may already be over."

"The chairman understands there's a close relationship with the AOM group. He wanted me to stress to you, Molly, that he and his people are acutely aware of the close relationship here. It may be necessary for you to recuse yourself in this matter."

There were three Molly Munros struggling to find the right response to this barely muffled threat. There was the well-bred polite Molly abashed to have her private affair a matter of public discussion. There was wealthy, accomplished lawyer Molly itching to show this prurient corporate whore some limits to congressional indecency and, finally, there was the Molly who'd acquired specialized and sophisticated political skills in two years of warfare between the west and the east wings of the White House.

"I just wish it were that simple," she cooed sweetly. "Always wishing to avoid the appearance of impropriety, several years ago I disclosed in writing the entire history of my relationship with the American Observer ESOP and with bank officer Bowditch to the conflicts officer in the Labor Department and have received from the Solicitor of Labor his written opinion that my involvement is entirely appropriate. With no circumstances in my own position having changed, the timing of a recusal, at this precise moment, would certainly raise questions. The department has been proud of our work in this area and in the current edition of the *Labor Department Journal* there is an extensive article detailing exactly how we have carried out the congressional intent in this area."

A dry, clear, almost disembodied voice said, "Very funny, little lady; just remember one thing, this isn't the end of this matter."

With that whiff of grapeshot in her nostrils, Molly exited the Rayburn Building and eventually found her car and driver. It only took a little longer than the walk back to the Frances Perkins Building itself. She reached for her cell phone. As the car turned down Pennsylvania Avenue, she connected to her secretary who couldn't restrain herself from saying, "Thank God it's you, we couldn't imagine what was taking so long."

"I'll tell you about it. What's the situation there?"

"Definitely the private elevator. I'll get the 'blocking staff' into the hall."

As the car pulled neatly into the Labor Department's executive garage, Molly looked again at her watch, only eleven-ten. What else could happen today? There was the usual delay waiting for the little private elevator. When the doors opened at the second floor, Molly was conscious of a lot of people and a lot of voices in a place that was usually sepulchral. She didn't pause to reflect but plunged behind her protecting staff into the opening that allowed her quick access to her own office, and safety, for the moment. In passing, she said to her secretary, "I need a few minutes to myself."

It was definitely time to take charge of the day. Simply tearing around town to get beaten up by a succession of people like the chairman, who were entitled to believe they had the right to command her attention, was inevitably going to lead to mistakes. Indeed, Molly acknowledged that she had made a permanent enemy in Chevrolet and that relationships with Janet and Don would be close to impossible in the future. One thing was in her favor. The White House, what with the Grand Jury, the August 18 presidential broadcast admitting "misleading statements," the bombing, and the interrupted Martha's Vineyard vacation, was not in a position to react to anything other than the day-to-day survival of the principals, as individuals and as a married couple. There was no one on the staff who could be confident that the First Lady would not aggressively and effectively take her confidant and friend Molly's side in any dispute. What this meant, Molly mused, is that she could "outbluff" the White House staff long enough for AOM to be a done deal. All of this made Molly wonder why she was doing this. What was so important in this whole situation? Why did she care? Why didn't she just do what Chevrolet wanted? As an experienced executive, Molly realized that she would have to shut down this line of thought if she had any hope of getting through the day. She would come back to it. A buzz for her secretary.

"All I can tell you is that it was awful. Chevrolet has made this personal. I can't get away with some smart talk and good intentions. I'm just lucky that the president has got other things on his mind right now."

"How do you want to handle this? Do you want me to hold on to all the messages and just pass on the ones that I feel you absolutely have to know about or do you want the whole picture?"

Molly reflected for a minute. *I can't make judgments unless I know what I'm up against, but I really do need to get some advice from people I trust. One more incident like the one with Chevrolet and I might as well resign.*

"Barbara, can you get David and Bernie to come down here? I'd like them to hear everything so I can understand what I must do to protect the Agency. But first, I need fifteen minutes to make a couple of personal calls."

Molly picked up her cellular and placed a call to Horse's.

Horse excused himself from the rather tense meeting he was having with the loan staff at Universal to hear Molly. "If you're getting anything like what is going on down here, you'll be toast by lunch."

"Nobody seems to know what to do. Vern wants me to disappear, but he can't actually fire me. The bank guys seem to understand that I'm a leper. They're all getting phone calls from journalists wanting to know what kind of guy this C.H. Bowditch is. The AOM guys figure they're all going to lose their jobs. They're on a wartime footing. Otherwise, life is great."

"I'm out of my depth. I really need some time to go over all of this with you. Judd is away this weekend and if I stay here the press, and God knows whom, will barrage me with questions. I know you're planning to be down here this week, can you fix me a place to stay?"

"Not a problem. It's a great place. We'll have some quiet time together. When you leave work, just turn north for a few blocks until you hit Massachusetts Avenue, turn west, go up to and around Dupont Circle and then continue on Mass as you pass the Ritz on your left. Right next door is this big ornate structure. You can drive your car right into the courtyard. They'll take care of it. This time of year, there's nobody there, so we won't be bothered. They'll know who you are and that you are my guest. I'll have two bedrooms and a connecting living room."

"I'll be coming from Georgetown, but I'll figure it out. I'll be there close to seven."

Molly's next call was through the department phone system. There were some calls she wanted there to be a record of. This call was to the senior partner of the New York law firm where she had practiced for so many years. He not only was a personal friend but he was a very wise man. Fortunately, he was in the office and could take the call.

"My dear, it sounds as if you had your guns trained on Fort Sumter. I can never understand what goes on down there, and in the middle of a perfectly pleasant summer at that."

"What has come to your attention?"

"Half the financial press, many of our brethren at the bar, and several clients."

"Oh, God, has it come to that?"

"Molly, do not be concerned. There is nothing we can't deal with. I have complete faith in you and there is nothing anyone can take away from me that would cause me to change my mind."

"You are dear, to know that I need that right now. My own priorities have somehow gotten in the way of some of the most powerful people in the capitalist world. They want American Observer and the ESOP is in the way. They want me somehow to destroy the ESOP's legitimacy. To make it worse, my friendship with Charles Bowditch gives them something to gnaw on. Have you any advice?"

"Molly, these are cruel times. The virtues of the free market have been adduced to excuse many developments that historians will deplore. You've always had good judgment. You have all the money in the world, a fine husband, splendid daughters, a job here, if you want it, anytime. Don't do anything of which you might be ashamed."

"It's wonderful to hear you say that. I am truly sorry to be the cause of any trouble for the firm."

"Dear, dear girl, you're paying a much higher price than we are, attempting to preserve a measure of civility and pride in our system. We're grateful for the chance to contribute a little." Molly knew she needed to hear this as she got a little misty.

Back to the real world. Klebowitch, Levin, and her secretary responded to the buzzer.

"I really appreciate your destroying your schedules. I need your help. I had a rotten morning with Janet, Don, and Chevrolet. As I think back on it, I never should've gone up there without getting your advice first. The chairman wants us to dis-something, -qualify, -eligibilize the American Observer ESOP. It's gotten in the way of some significant constituents. 'No' is a career-destroying option. Tell me, what other lions are at the gate?"

"Well..." her secretary timidly began, "the entire executive branch of government has decided that they need to see you right away."

"Does that mean the president and the First Lady?"

"Not yet. Here's the list: chief of staff, domestic policy advisor, head of the office of management and budget, everybody in the press office and two legal advisors to the president. Maybe I've missed a couple. Oh, there's our very own secretary of Labor. She, like any sane person, is on holiday, but she wants to talk with you, and the deputy secretary has personally put his head in the door here every fifteen minutes to wonder where you were and when he can expect the pleasure of your company. Then, there's the press. Thank God it's summertime. Seems like a lot of fuss for a magazine you only read in a dentist's waiting room."

"Funny," Molly deadpanned. "OK, friends, what do you think? David?"

"We believe in you and are grateful for the expertise and the enthusiasm that you have brought to the agency." Molly was moved by the praise. "We believe in the ESOP regs. I've reviewed all of our procedures carefully, and I'll let Bernie talk in detail to this, but there's no question, the ESOP regs are the law of the land. This is America. They say 'This is a country of laws and not of men.' For me, I want to be sure you take care of yourself. You need to talk with the secretary. You even need to meet with the deputy. The way things are, they'd be embarrassed if it appeared you're less than punctilious, and there's no need for that kind of trouble. Bernie?"

"You have a judgment call. Bowditch has encountered a situation that, in our opinion, is covered in our regs, but, frankly, it's such an outrageous occurrence that we didn't cover it specifically. He's now asking us to issue a clarifying letter to deal with what clearly is behavior violating the law. As your counsel, I advise you that executing this letter is entirely proper under the circumstances. As your friends, David and I just want to caution you. They'll never forgive you if you issue this letter, they'll hound you out of public life. We don't want to tell you what to do, but we do not want you to have any illusions. We don't want to lose you, either. It sort of sucks."

Molly laughed at his touching personal, unprofessional lapse. She wanted to hear it out loud, one last time. "Let me understand the clarifying letter in one sentence?"

"We're asked a focused question: Can Universal refuse to make this same financing available to the AOM ESOP when the credit is no worse, indeed it's substantially better, than the Rhodes offer?"

"David and Bernie, you're wonderful friends for me. I appreciate it. I'll have to make this decision over the weekend. Could you leave Barbara with phone numbers in case of emergency? And, Barbara, will you make me a list of calls divided among government, press, and personal in order of importance while I present myself to the deputy secretary?"

Molly walked down the corridor, turned into the secretary's suite, and asked the receptionist if the deputy was available to meet with her. Usually, this intra-departmental meeting at the secretarial level had to be arranged in advance to preserve the illusion that everybody was busy. Today, no problem, just raised eyebrows as Molly walked right into Deputy Secretary Dodge's office. The deputy secretary was not asleep, but he was horizontal on the generous sofa provided by the government to officials of his rank. He didn't bother to rise, but contented himself to lift his head and rest it on a sofa arm to contemplate Molly.

"What may, I ask, has God's gift to the Labor Department been up to that has created such a brouhaha?" The deputy secretary's qualifications for his job were slender, it must be confessed. Indeed, allowing for the fact that the job had no particular requirements, the job of functional assistant to the secretary being performed by the undersecretary, one would conclude that being the husband of one of the president's private secretaries was a perfect credential. Nor did the deputy scruple to put a good face on things. He was required to put in a few hours every day and he did so. His involvement with Molly was simply bad luck, bad luck for both of them. Everybody else was out of town. He didn't appreciate disturbance, but, by virtue of his wife's job at the highest rank, the secretary depended on him to be a reliable conduit to the White House. The secretary, like most of official Washington, had confidently vacated the town knowing that the First Family would be on Martha's Vineyard. She couldn't know that Monica and missile firings would change this calculus, nor that Cedric Rhodes's acquisitiveness would put an otherwise obscure agency of the Department of Labor right in the focus of executive branch attention. And yet, it all seemed so contrived that she couldn't bring herself to return from holiday. The price for this personal independence was the implication of confidence in and approval of the deputy secretary, who made no secret of his contempt for the better educated and more accomplished senior department officials.

Molly had no time for the deputy under the best of circumstances. She bit her lip to hold back whatever wisecrack she might have chosen; she had enough trouble without creating new enemies. So, she sat at the desk, shut her eyes, said her mantra, and waited. She was aware of shuffling noises and finally a voice from the sofa, "I must have had a call from every high-priced fixer in town. Look at these phone messages. I can't believe the people who've called. The office of the vice president, the Speaker of the House, the senate president, three more senior cabinet officers. What kind of power does this guy have? How can he get people at this level to intercede just to make a few bucks? It makes you wonder about our government. I've talked with the secretary almost hourly, she's apoplectic that her department is seen as being obtrusive to the wishes of people in high places."

"Tell me one thing. Does the president have a horse in this race?"

"You must be kidding. That guy is incapable of coexisting in a world in which races take place where he doesn't. At the moment, however, even his prodigious powers of compartmentalization haven't permitted any focus on whether another foreign billionaire makes a few more stateside."

"Well then, what's the problem?"

"I'm not the smartest guy in the world, but I know a few things. People at the top don't want to go on record as being interested in a private transaction unless the relationship means a great deal to them personally. I know that it isn't going to do me any good to be asked to fix something that concerns these people and to come up empty-handed. I've got to give them something. What's it going to be?"

"Tell them you've talked with me and that I've assured you I'll reconsider the agency's position in this matter."

"You don't get it, do you? Harvard degree and all, you don't understand, this guy Drive is calling in favors. He's calling in big favors. He's not stupid. He knows the difference between a brush-off and real results. He's paying for the real thing. These guys owe him, he's calling the debt, and they have to pay, or die in the attempt. What you're giving me isn't even perspiration. We've got to do better. I, at least, don't want to spend the rest of my life having pissed off the half of the Forbes 500 who own access to TV and the newspapers." The sound of his whining was grating on Molly's concentration.

"Is this the secretary's view?"

"Honey, you still don't get it. This is the view of every single breathing human organism who didn't inherit half of General Electric. Yeah, I know, it's bad manners for me to read through your financial reports, but there it is."

Molly wouldn't put anything past this reptile at this point, so she reverted to her legal training. "Apparently, I don't process information the same way you do, so let's be plain, are you asking for my resignation?"

"Oh, my gracious. No official in this department would make such a request. If you conclude that would be the right thing, I'm sure you can be counted on to do just that, do the right thing."

"Let me use one of your offices to call the secretary so that I can check back with you right after talking with her. Can you ask your secretary to place the call?"

Molly fumed as she waited for the call to be connected. Everybody in the food chain was nervous. They didn't know how to find nutrition, so a sacrifice, of somebody else, seemed the right idea. She could play that game. None of them were up to a direct confrontation.

Molly started at full speed. "I'm sorry I wasn't available for your earlier calls, I was summoned up to the Hill by our favorite chairman and I've just finished talking with the deputy. Let me be clear about one thing: Would you be more comfortable if I were to submit my resignation? If that's the case, we can save a lot of time and anxiety in this phone conversation."

The secretary's warm supportive reply was so welcome on this dreadful day. "What has that unspeakable jerk been saying to you? It's out of the question for you to resign. If you resign, I would feel obliged to resign as well. You are considered the outstanding female appointment by this administration. As a responsible public servant, I could not abide such a result. As a woman, I'd rather die."

Molly mused, *Well, so much for confrontation. Now, where did that idea originate? My White House people would have told me straight out. Where is Mme. Secretary going to find the hostage money to keep all these powerful people from being embarrassed?* "I am very grateful to you. I don't mind saying, this is a very rough experience. I feel like the person who didn't get a chair when the music stopped. With the president out of pocket, who's going to decide whether we just roll with the punches or not?"

The secretary went on, "There is no word at all from the usual channels. All I know is powerful people, whom I haven't really known well or seen for many years, have found my number on vacation and have called to make sure that I understand their personal desire that Rhodes's bid be accommodated. I've never experienced anything like this. I've talked with the Solicitor of Labor. He's painstakingly reviewed the ESOP regulation and assures me that it is now as much a part of the law of the land as the Constitution. Molly, it may just be that I'm here, out of the flow, but I think this is a situation in which we act exactly the way we undertook when we took the oath of office. Do what you have to do so that people in the future looking back will say that this was an occasion when the American people got the government they deserve."

"I'm lucky to have a boss who backs me up. Thanks." Molly hung up, turned on her heel and walked into the deputy's office where he was making an effort to conceal the obvious fact that he'd eavesdropped on the conversation. "Well, how have my two ladies decided we're going to extract ourselves from this one?"

"Just what you suggested. We're going to do the right thing," was what she said but Molly walked out thinking, *You worm.*

Molly headed back to her office and suddenly remembered it had been a long time since breakfast. She had an inspiration, probably stimulated by the secretary's decency; the country wouldn't expire if the assistant secretary took a few minutes for lunch. One of the few redeeming characteristics of the Frances Perkins Building was its location across Constitution Avenue from the National Gallery of Art. In the artfully skylighted subterranean passageways, between museum buildings, was a cafeteria where simple food was available cheap and quick, giving time to pause and admire some of the museum treasures. Molly managed to get across the crowded avenue and to find a seat near a splendidly engineered watercourse. A few minutes for a pizza and a glass of Chianti improved the outlook for the day. She knew what painting she wanted to see. Upstairs in the old museum building, she went into the gallery of nineteenth-century American art and admired again, like a very dear friend of long standing, John Singer Sargent's painting of Ellen Crowninshield Endicott, the wife of President Grover Cleveland's Secretary of War. Her wonderful posture and regal demeanor communicated a sense of confidence in the values and society in which she lived.

Nourished in body and spirit, Molly took her time walking back to the office. She tried to admire the new Canadian Embassy building and reflected that Washington was a hardship post for the diplomatic corps in the pre-air-conditioning days. Barbara's list took up about three pages. Molly felt the important political calls had been made and she didn't intend to talk to the press, so she turned to the personal list. There was a name to contend with. Maybe it was the recent impact of Sargent's wondrous evocation of a Yankee lady, but Molly couldn't resist directly dialing Mrs. William Schermerhorn, one of her mother's greatest friends, descended from the original Dutch settlers.

The voice answering the phone did not sound old, nor was it tentative, "Speak up, who is it? Molly Munro, girl, what are you doing down there in Washington? Up here at the Adirondack League Club, last night I heard nothing but Molly Munro this and Molly Munro that. And it wasn't the usual twits who were talking. For what it's worth, it was the people who actually work for a living and, hence, have some idea as to what's going on in the world. Finally, I had had enough, so I summoned one of the younger ones over and said pleasantly enough, 'My dear man, it's not the custom in this club to discuss the private affairs of members in public. I would be grateful if you would accord that courtesy to myself and to Ms. Munro.' You might have thought that I had hit him with a squash. He was obviously abashed to be caught out in such dreadful bad manners. But more than that, he looked me straight in the eye and said, 'I do apologize. I think fondly on Molly Munro and, if ever you are talking to her, please ask her to be careful.' Whatever did he mean? Molly, neither your mother nor I've ever given a tinker's damn for what anybody else thought of us, but neither of us made our way in the world the way you have. I hope you will take care. We love you." The call ended with assurances of mutual affection.

Whenever Molly thought she was too old to cry, an incident like Mrs. Schermerhorn's call would reduce her again to childhood. It was unbearably touching of the old lady. She would be careful. She was getting angry. *Who are these people who can reach all around me and find every lever, pull them, and make a lot of decent people uncomfortable?* She was in no frame of mind to be tactful to a bunch of political hacks or prurient press types. Barbara had arranged phone calls to Molly's daughters and it was joy to spend twenty minutes with each of them. Sometimes Molly felt that she had pushed the girls out too fast. She was so conscious of coming from a family background where ancestral expectations cloyed and threatened self-development. The best family experiences she had shared with both daughters were trips to Georgia and visits with their grandparents, Vern's parents. Vern was always too busy to come, but daughter-in-law and granddaughters found in the quiet holiness of the Scottish clerical home a serenity and a peace, which, if it did not make churchgoers out of them, made them respectful for the life within the human soul. Maybe, from their two grandmothers and herself, these young women had acquired a breadth of experience and wisdom that would reduce the ignorance that is the fate of human beings and allow them to continue to be contributing members of the species.

There *are* personages who *must* be seen by government officials in Washington, D.C. These characters, who in former times might have been referred to as lobbyists, are now former chairmen of this party or that party, current fund-raisers for half the Senate, and the committee chairs in the House. Their minimum retainer is $100,000. Their clients are the usual suspects plus every company or industry that is in particular need. They refer to virtually every powerful person in the land as "my close personal friend" and with most leaders they say "we go back a long ways." Molly had to reflect on the distaste, no, disgust, with which she contemplated her last formal meeting of this horrible day. As a well-brought-up lady, she didn't like to find elements of the snob in herself, but the fact is, fat-faced Southerners with thighs too big for even their fancy tailor-made pants and voices like corn syrup made her wish that General Sherman had gone straight south and finished the job. A large flushed man with a manner that combined impatience, self-importance, and proximity to power, the former Chairman of the Republican National Committee, Clarence Hershey, had no time for niceties.

"I don't know what you think you're doing, but you can't act like this in this town..." There followed a torrent all in aid of accommodating Drive Rhodes's wishes.

The realignment of parties in the United States had culminated in the seizure of power in the Republican Party by Southern, anti-Semitic, anti-black, antiwomen, anti-you name it white males. Notwithstanding a Democrat in the White House, these handmaidens of the business community acted as if their power was permanent, reclaiming their rightful places in elected power was, at worst, inconvenient, and just a matter of time. The way the incumbent has been destroying himself, they really didn't want to be in too much of a hurry. Molly's nonresponse triggered the lobbyist's impatience and resentment over having to come back to sweaty Washington from his moneyed retreat on the shores of the Gulf. What pushed him over the edge was the realization that he could be jerked around so much, and end up asking a favor from some snotty, rich, Yankee bitch friend of the president's wife.

"You're finished in this town if you keep on stepping out of line..."

Molly reached for the intercom button on her phone, "Would you please come in and escort Mr. Hershey out of our offices?"

Hershey couldn't believe his bad luck. What had he said? He really did have too much to drink last night. Had the bitch recorded him? He had to backpedal fast.

"Madame Secretary," that was the second time that Molly had been promoted in the last hour. Power may not be rated highly enough! "I've misspoken and I apologize." Molly waved Barbara back out of the office and waited. There was no point marching this specimen through the niceties of the Administrative Procedures Act.

Molly played the D.C. grovel-to-power card. "I appreciate what an inconvenience this matter must be for you. We greatly respect the extent of your concern and are grateful to have your opinion to help us in the process. Of course, I cannot hope, personally, to meet everyone who has a legitimate and strong interest in this matter. I hope that your client can be informed that I've left open a final decision until after having the opportunity to meet with you." Molly felt like a talking doll whose string had been pulled.

The pitchman was taken aback. *This wasn't going to be easy, the bitch knows the game. She gave me something; it has value, not enough, but too much for me to discard carelessly. Also, she didn't give me the speech, this is the government, it's not me, you have to respect that. Let's see if we can get something real.* Underneath that perspiring fat-lipped bonhomie resided a considerable talent for persuading others and a real genius at discerning what a person valued, so that bargaining could be effective. Hershey knew that she didn't want the usual things.

"In every administration there are senior officials who perform their responsibilities in such an evenhanded way as to earn universal respect. Why, I remember when Jack Kennedy appointed old Douglas Dillon, he was young then, to be Secretary of the Treasury and Jimmy Carter put that fellow," he couldn't be civil about a northern Brahmin Republican, "Richard something to run the Law of the Sea." As fishing ventures go, this was a long cast with a very dry fly. It floated on the water and sank. "You know, on a hot day like this, I always envy those people who get appointed ambassador to nice countries."

Molly decided to help him out. "I really have no plans after this administration. I'm one of the lucky ones who got a position doing something I know about and about which I care. That brings us back to matter at hand."

Hershey was now back to full voice and baying. "Lucky, you are. I like to think that I do what is right. I don't for a minute want to suggest that you do not. Let me give you my take at what is involved, why I would leave my holiday to come up here today. There are a few very creative people in this world, they're the people who create jobs, products, new technology, and wealth. A country prospers when it can make itself attractive to these folks. When I think of a great American property like American Observer and I consider how badly it has slipped since the Porters got old, I yearn for proven executive competency to save this asset for America. For our children, it makes a huge difference if there is an *American Observer* magazine. This has been the voice of what's best in America since it was founded, what, seventy years ago. It has the largest subscription database in the world. I'd like to see that used. Mr. Rhodes has a lifelong record of creativity in the communications businesses. Frankly, I feel lucky that he wants to commit himself in a major way to a U.S. situation, particularly one that is troubled. I appreciate completely the importance and integrity of employee ownership. Just my being here today should tell you that I'm an employee and I understand where they're coming from. But, are these the folks who're going to revitalize this great American institution? Where did they get this new experience? Have they been hiding somewhere? I have to ask you to consider the national interest."

Impatient and unimpressed, Molly crossed to the doorway and outstretched her hand and carefully recited the rote. "I care deeply about the vitality of life in America and will consider carefully the facts that you've brought to my attention. I appreciate deeply the courtesy that you show to this office." As the crestfallen mercenary lumbered out, Molly thought, *That was as bad as they come. Lose/lose. Nothing for either of us. I'd best get out of here before I cause some real damage.*

Molly shut the door and felt in need of nothing so much as a bath. Apparently, creatures like this come with democracies. She hated being a snob. These reflections inclined Molly toward her own source of solace. One of the government's benefits provided for assistant secretaries was a private bathroom, where Molly kept her athletic clothes. She put on her tights and jersey and then pulled on a dress over them and ducked down the stairs to the garage as if her greatest problem in life was her sartorial appearance.

"Drive? Marty? Are you both on the line? OK, bad news and good news. The chairman promises that Congress will not appropriate one more penny for that agency so long as that lady is employed there. That doesn't do us any good, but it makes him feel better. Our lobbyist frankly admits that he blew it. It sounds, though, as if she is getting a little frayed."

"What's the good news?" said both Drive and Marty in the same breath.

"Judge really appreciated your call. That man is such a professional that he prepares every assignment with the greatest care. He's confident he can take it right down to the wire. Either she will defy the president, which he doubts, or she is still open to persuasion. As of this minute, our advice is the president won't commit himself and order Molly not to issue the letter. He's agreeable, however, to having Judge create the impression of his approval. So there it is. Enjoy the weekend!"

Drive had to ask, "Do you think it would help if I went personally to see the president?"

Marty replied, "Look, I hope I've made clear I really have enjoyed working for you. I like you. I respect you. So understand my recommendation not to go. All you'll do is screw up any future relationship. He's going to do what he feels he has to do. Period. Guys like that never say 'No.' No matter what, he won't turn you down to your face. But, somehow, something will happen and you'll run out of time. Know what I mean? It'll just be embarrassing and it'll be harder for you to make the next deal."

Drive just couldn't let this deal go without his own personal hands-on involvement. He insisted, as his last chance for personally turning this deal around. "I think that if I could talk directly with Molly Munro, I might be able to make this thing go. I have to back my hunch. I'll get back to D.C. this weekend and have a quiet and informal talk with her. I know that both of you think this is a bad idea, but you've got to give the old man a little leeway here." Drive turned to his secretary and asked her to begin the process of making him a weekend appointment with Molly Munro.

Chapter 26

August 28, Afternoon

The offices of the American Observer Association's headquarters in New York City were a beehive, like never before. The national spotlight, however fleeting, had brought the moribund business to life. The ambitious Ms. Volpe was keenly aware that she was the big loser out of the month's peregrinations at American Observer. She had some hope to believe that Marty's whisper could be translated into retaining much of the legal business. She had no optimism about her standing with the employees' stock ownership plan, many of whose members had memorable complaints about their treatment by her firm, which was on management's side.

The deal had echoed the choreography of President Clinton's disgrace: uncertainty, denial, obfuscation, and capitulation. Yeltsin's troubles had taken over the front pages this week. In like manner, the deal, which had dominated, violently dominated, everybody's life for days, was quiescent with only the occasional murmur to remind that there was anything else to react to.

The meeting room carried bad memories for everyone as the physical situs of their incompetence and impotence following Drive's lunch at the Brook. The natural order of the trustees had broken down. The sense of their mission was shattered. No new vision was yet evident. The phoning and polling efforts had successfully reached right into their lives and reminded them that the violence associated with maintenance of wealth at the highest levels involved a personal price that they were unable and unwilling to continue to pay. There was now a kind of empty affluence, power without impact, after a period of most of a decade, during which what each of them did was important to many people. One thing was clear: There was no appetite for conflict.

The trustees just wanted the whole matter closed, out of reach of public controversy.

La Volpe may well have been the only human being in the whole world who actually read the Monday Federal Register publication of the Pension and Welfare Benefit Agency's proposed letter to New York Safe Deposit & Trust Company, as trustee for the AOM ESOP. The iron logic of the situation was reflected in the letter. The bank had overreached. Drive had pushed so hard to eliminate ambiguities that he had managed to create a certainty that alone could have caused this extraordinary result. The ESOP had behaved impeccably and the assistant secretary was a person who knew her mind and ran her agency with integrity and skill. Somebody had changed the rules. Ms. Magdalena Volpe, Esquire, had the contacts and the clients, she had the "power" to control the situation, and now, after only a few weeks, they were all reduced to cowering in this room and seeking whatever refuge saved face the best.

La Volpe's depression was slightly relieved when one of the trustees kindly remembered, "You cautioned us to be very respectful of the ESOP. That was good advice. We'll be sure those people realize your personal intervention made it possible for them to get this deal." She felt a little better about keeping the client.

The formal act of accepting the tender was an anticlimax. Nor was anyone particularly careful whether the approval covered only Drive's tender or the anticipated ESOP tender or a tender from any *other* party. The vote was to get $30 a share and run. Volpe put a good face on it, "You should all be proud of carrying out the intent of the Porters and assuring their wish for employee ownership be fully implemented and that foreign ownership be rebuffed." And she packed her Vuitton briefcase and started shaking hands as the prelude to her grand exit.

The Friday late afternoon summer traffic was light as Molly turned off of Constitution onto Virginia Avenue and to its intersection with Rock Creek Parkway and the parking area for Thompson's Boathouse where she stored her Vespoli Matrix 24 rowing shell. Most of the local rowers waited until the summer sun was down and for the dissipation of the day's heat so there was quite a crowd on the "hard" as Molly easily trundled her superb racing shell and oars down to the edge of the dock. Oarsmen are not impressed by much, but the sight of this tall shapely woman expertly opening the locks, lowering in the oars, fixing her feet in the straps and, in one smooth motion, pushing off from the dock, settling into her seat, and pulling authoritatively on the oars caused several involuntarily to stop what they were doing and gape. At age fifty-two, Molly Munro was still someone in the rowing world. Molly rewarded them by setting off immediately with those long strokes, that seemingly effortlessly propelled her past Roosevelt Island, under the Route 66 Bridge and quickly out of sight to the south. The magic of rowing is the rhythm. Like dancers, rowers must build and maintain their bodies like pieces of machinery to practice their art. Once physical competency is attained, the "art" is in the mind; how much can one ask of oneself? Molly decided on a long row. The river at this point is quite wide, with the runways of the newly christened Reagan Airport about a mile from Potomac Park. As she emerged from under the Fourteenth Street Bridge, Molly realized that she was at the start of what had often been used as a 2,000-meter racecourse, keeping to the District shore following the Potomac down to Haynes Point and the memorable statue of *Awakening* in the ground at the confluence with the Anacostia River. This never failed to stimulate her competitive instincts. She increased the rate of striking and prepared her will for that blend of pain and euphoria that is the oarsman's challenge.

Tears began rolling down her cheeks. Molly was so caught up in the exertions of rowing that she didn't really notice until her frame began to shake convulsively with the compelling expression of grief. She stopped rowing and endured the spasms that seemed to last for an eternity. *What's happening to me?* There poured out of her unconscious not just the frustrations of the day but the insistent questions: *What am I doing? Who am I anyway?* She turned the boat around and intermittently paddled back up river, all the time reflecting on some ugly realities. *Why do I have such an unquestioning view of life? Why did I get married so stupidly? Why did I stay married so unquestioningly? Why am I so content with an unquestioned life? It has always been nice, being me, but who am I supposed to be now?*

This middle-aged woman had some practice with introspection, but as she glided the shell past the boathouse, past the architect's conceit called Washington Harbor, and up under the Georgetown Bridge where the river narrowed and she had to pay attention to rocks, her willingness to directly confront unpleasantness began to indicate some answers. She didn't care a damn about being beaten up by *le tout* Washington. Indeed, in a perverse way, she delighted in being above it. What she couldn't stand was having to react to someone else's reality. She shuddered at the realization that if she hadn't actually seen Vern's arm on that beautiful stewardess they probably would still be married. That one incident transported her outside of herself. *Am I just a cliché?* She became aware of her own sexuality. *Is that what I am, an oversexed, middle-aged, rich, lady? I want this transaction to go through. It's important to use my position to advance the reality of employee ownership. Decide what's important and then do everything I can to make it happen.* This humble epiphany brought Molly to the beginning of the rest of her life: an informed, courageous, energetic person believing that what she did was important.

There was still light on the top of the westerly oriented trees beside the George Washington Parkway, but down on the river, it had become dark. Molly was barely conscious of rowing back to Thompson's and storing the boat and oars. She drove the few blocks home to Dunbarton Street. Nobody was there. Judd was away for a few days with a sculpture dealer, showing some of his work in one of the galleries in the Hamptons. She showered, pulled on a summer dress, pulled her hair back, and drove across Rock Creek Park following Horse's directions to Anderson House, the headquarters of the Society of Cincinnati, and pulled in with the last light. The society that calls itself America's oldest patriotic organization was formed in 1783 by soon-to-be-demobilized Revolutionary officers and named after the humble but martial Roman farmer-warrior Lucius Quinctius Cincinnatus. Membership is limited to descendents, generally only first sons, of Revolutionary War officers. Horse had told her to drive in, leave the car, and make herself known at the desk. Molly was used to rich people but the impact of the marble parquet floors, thirty-foot ceilings, sculpted balusters, and carved wall panels that Lars Anderson and his wife Isabel Weld Perkins had assembled caused her to gawk like a tourist. An impeccably white-tied attendant's "Madame" brought her back to the present. Her room was splendidly late Victorian and had an interconnecting door. *Why is it that times of special need in my life seem to coincide with the physical presence of Charles Bowditch?* Horse had left a note that she should meet him in the bar whenever she arrived, so, because it was late, even by sophisticates' time, she went right downstairs.

Drinks and dinner were so perfect, the old friends were unaware of the passage of time. The club didn't disclose the names of members or their guests who were in residence; they really needed this time and privacy. They spoke intimately, sharing their deepest thoughts with the fearlessness of true friendship. Horse had increasingly committed his career to the development of employee ownership. Now that he was actually close to having put together the necessary ingredients for employees to acquire control of a major international communications business, he needed perspective. Of course, a development that affected so many people and so much money, as much as an employee takeover, was creating problems he hadn't anticipated and wasn't at all prepared or capable of dealing with. Horse felt comfortable with what he knew. He had absolutely no idea of what he did not know and that was the problem.

Molly "owned" the concept of employee ownership of vast corporations. Whether in family conversations, college thesis, or professional work, she had stuck quite closely to this particular range of ideas. Maybe that is why uncontrolled grief seized her in the middle of the Potomac River. Her life seemed to be a continuum of unexamined steps. Her inner compass pointed only in one direction at a time and her disposition, good fortune, and wealth had deprived her of that sense of danger that day-to-day life imposes on most people. She had talked with her personal lawyers and with her daughters. All the women in the family were proud of being brought up to be inner directed. At times like this, though, she missed having someone to share with. She and Judd had the kind of fine relationship of two sexually attracted middle-aged people with largely independent lives. *Maybe, this is what growing up is. For once, I'll deal with a situation with my own interest paramount and I'll let other people react. I'll do some things my mother wouldn't have done, no more going along with everybody else's reality.*

"Charles, I wonder about myself. Have I simply set this whole crisis up just to have a real hurdle to jump, not just another social passage enabled by my money and family?"

"You know, I feel you're doing what you think is right. Simple as that."

Horse and Molly were so lost in their own thoughts that they failed to appreciate the subtle dimming of the lights, discrete coughs, and other well-bred indications that it was time to let the staff go home. They looked at each other in bemused recognition, got out of the chairs, and took the elevator to the apartment floor.

In the fourteen years since they first met in the Gotham Hotel, Horse and Molly had become unmistakably middle-aged. Molly would have been a grandmother had either of her independent daughters gotten married and Horse had two preteen sons. No time, no place, no thing was capable of diluting the remembrance of shared pleasure. The past improved on the reality of their present. On these two the gods had smiled, nothing impaired their capacity to give each other a true love, born of a spiritual kinship even though the physical glories were in times past. Molly, alone in her own room, ready to sleep at last, sat on the bed, looked down at the scar on her right index finger, and smiled.

Chapter 27

August 28, Evening

Drive took great pride in the utter predictability that his personal involvement was essential to the consummation of the company's greatest deals. There was almost a rhythm to these transactions. Advisors of all stripes would be summoned and given great latitude; and, then, at the last minute when the recurring nonrecurring problem predictably arose, Drive himself would do the necessary. The newly introspective Drive had begun to wonder whether he set up the deals and his advisers with this idea in mind. Marty was smart, but maybe too smart, too Manhattan; Moffie was not a strategist, he was a good gofer; Vern was a conventionally successful banker, enough said; and Rose never took the lead, she always deferred to Drive. Drive occasionally felt that pride would be his undoing. He knew that the photographs of himself and the newly elected in front of 10 Downing Street and the White House the day after elections were an affront, but he consoled himself that it was a little conceit he was entitled to.

Late Friday afternoon Drive organized his pilots and the reservation at the Ritz. His wife preferred to stay in New York. On the drive to Teterboro, he had raised Moffie. "Find out where I can find Molly Munro either on Saturday or Sunday. When you find out, please call my secretary directly so that she can arrange a meeting. Do whatever you have to do, but find her."

Marty gave the predictable advice of the lawyer in the face of irrefutable evidence that he is not indispensable, "Hey, any legal problems are hers. She probably needs to have some Agency guy with her if she agrees to a meeting. But, I got to tell you, the notion that a federal official can be rolled at the last minute by the person most affected by their act is pure poison. OK! OK! You're the boss."

The first calls started coming in on the short flight to Reagan Airport.

From Moffie, "She left the Department of Labor around 5 p.m. They think she's gone for a row on the Potomac." Half an hour later, "She's finished the row and she's not at home. I've got someone parked near her house and it looks as if no one's there."

From his secretary, "I haven't been able to raise any answer from Ms. Munro's office or home."

On the limo ride to the Ritz, Drive called Rose, "Nobody seems able to find this lady."

"According to the people I talk with, she has very regular habits, office, home, or theatre. Has anybody thought about her husband? He ought to know where his wife is."

"We can't find him either. Moffie's people have talked to someone at the place where he does his sculpture and they said he is delivering a piece to some client in Canada this weekend. They don't know where."

"Drive, I may have a dirty mind, but has anyone checked where Horse is."

"Oh, my God, you've got it." By this time, the limo was exiting Dupont Circle and about to enter the slender turnoff to the hotel entrance. Drive leapt out of the car, vaulted past the assembled array of hotel dignitaries who were accustomed to greet him, and demanded that an astonished hotel manager immediately take him to his suite. No pleasantries, once the door was opened, Drive was on the phone to Moffie, "Did you guys ever think of finding out where Horse is?"

An abashed Moffie admitted, "Jesus. OK, we're on it."

Drive was so near and yet so far. Not one hundred yards from where he was resting on the sofa with a hand nervously cradling a silent phone, Molly and Horse were enjoying the finest dinner the city provided and were about to repair together for the night to a suite, albeit to separate rooms. Drive was still trying to figure out what he was going to say when, not if, his people were successful in chasing Molly down.

Moffie again, "OK, nobody is home at the Bowditchs. The neighbors say the Mrs. and the boys are in Europe at a tennis tournament in Gstaad, Switzerland."

"I know where the place is, for God's sakes. Call her up and find out where she thinks her husband is."

"Boss, we're ahead of you, the lady couldn't be nicer. She said that her husband had some very important business on Monday in Washington and was preparing there over the weekend."

"Good work. Well, you've got someone watching her house. Let me know when your people discover what hotel he's at, and I can take it from there."

An hour later, the obviously disappointed Moffie advised, "There is no Bowditch and nobody looking like our Horse staying tonight in a D.C. hotel. My people have checked out 20,000 rooms in the D.C. area. They've probably got a private place. We'll keep someone watching her house. Sorry about this, boss." So was Drive and it was a measure of his perturbation that he took no effort to make Moffie understand he appreciated all this effort on no notice at the end of the usual business week.

Was it the prospect of failure? Was it the thought that his hasty and dramatic act had turned out to be expensive, almost hysterical, two trips to D.C. in a week foolishness? Or, was it the realization that he really had nothing to say to Molly Munro? She didn't want to be a movie star. She couldn't care less about having a column in a big newspaper or even having airtime on a TV station. At the end of the day, it was all about money and power. She wanted something. The magic had always worked in the past, but he couldn't figure out, as he drifted in and out of a fitful sleep, exactly what it was he was trying to accomplish. All he really knew was that he was depressed.

During the restless hours of his tormented night a familiar dream wove in and out of Drive's consciousness. The site was always the plains of Kruger National Park in the northeast corner of South Africa. The theme familiar, he and his brother standing in the back of a Land Rover with his father and a guide in front driving through the last light, come on the familiar sight of a bunch of hyenas feasting on the remains of a zebra. As the headlights illuminate the scene, the hyenas, threatened by this intrusion, smeared with blood, horrible gnashing teeth and iridescent eyes in the headlight beams, as always, slinked away, invisible in the darkness. At this point Drive awoke, because the dream departed from its time-honed course. Invariably in the past, lions would emerge from where they had been driven to finish off the feast of their kill. Large and powerful, they lumbered out, the kings of his childhood fantasies. When the car lights had passed, the process would reverse, and again the hyenas would drive off the lions. Except this dream had no lions. Drive had never spent time trying to understand his dreams, but he couldn't ignore the absence of the lions. The dream and its horror was an old friend now, after the many months of reoccurrence, but today it held a new terror. Drive couldn't remember if it had ever *really* happened. Was it a memory? Or a nightmare? Was it phantoms or Freudian symbols or simply a poignant moment from childhood? His mind was like a sieve these days.

SATURDAY, AUGUST 29, 1998

Saturday morning was a little better. Moffie continued to report no sightings. When Drive took a short stroll across Massachusetts Avenue over to the Cosmopolitan Club, it was fickle fate that he didn't bump into either Horse, who he knew well by sight, or Molly, who he'd never met. Was this a worse result than meeting Molly and proving beyond doubt that the consuming energy in his life was simply to acquire more, and that he really had nothing to say beyond..."I want"?

In the early afternoon, he took *Blue Wave* back to New York, waiting for the final inning. He told himself that he had every right to be optimistic. The president wanted to help him. The most skilled conflict resolver in the world was well prepared to bring Molly Munro to the place where she would yield. Why did he have a pervasive sense that somehow he was pushing very hard, but not in the right direction?

Saturday started with a late brunch. Molly was clear in what she was going to do. If the president or his wife asked Molly not to issue the supplemental letter in the AOM matter, she would obey this order. In the absence of such an intimation, and she had a friend and a phone number to call in Martha's Vineyard, with the secretary's blessing, she was entitled, indeed obligated, as a public official to use her own best judgment. Molly decided that the supplemental letter was essential in order to give the commercial world unmistakable assurance that the Department of Labor would strictly enforce the conflicts of interest laws as they protected the beneficiaries of employee benefit plans.

Horse was at his best on a battlefield. He had an excellent sense of danger. He had walked through the shadow of the Valley of Death more frequently than most people. He knew that he could be killed, but he had faced that prospect so many times that he felt a power beyond his control or knowledge would make that decision and there was nothing he could do about it. He didn't even think about his career, about his employability, about a life of endless litigation. The battlefield imperatives shaped his mind: get the guy with the machine gun, first. With Molly's letter in hand, he had immediate access to the press. Universal could stall him, lawyer him, and kill the deal, but would the bank, would Vernon Stillman, want to be known as the incarnation of a Wall Street that preferred a foreign predator over a company's own employees as owner of a treasured venture? Vern was the key and the language was simple, laughingly simple: win/win. Vern would have to make up with Drive however he could, and there'd be chance aplenty for that; Drive could be counted on to create the opportunity. Otherwise, Universal became the bank supporting employee ownership. They collect a big fee for putting the deal together, although much reduced; they collect big management fees for administering the pension fund private equity.

The problem was how to get to Vern before he got sidetracked into a needless orgy of retaliation. Vern had to see the situation as not being the ultimate and most humiliating macho test between Horse and himself. How to get Drive to call off his dogs? They could cause real pain.

In late afternoon, Horse and Molly decided to take a long walk across the mall down to a seafood restaurant on Maine Avenue. The beauty of the city is apparent to walkers. There is greenery everywhere. The height limitations have served to preserve a sense of openness. As they crossed Virginia Avenue by the Federal Reserve Building, Horse realized that he'd never seen the Vietnam Veterans Memorial. Molly had never actually visited the memorial but she felt confident she could locate it near the Lincoln Monument. They recognized the statue of three soldiers as marking a war memorial site, but they were utterly unprepared for the physical impact of the embedded sheets of stone inscribed chronologically with the names of those who had died. Horse found the years and traced with his finger the names of those he had known, for several of whom he had been responsible. This experience gave him some needed perspective on their present problems and Molly felt a wave of gratitude for a life so very rich and complex. The tears she saw on the face of the friend she cared for so, and the emotions she could share that day, made her wonder, what would have happened if he had never returned like his friends? And very slowly, Molly began to understand that in a nation that reveres the sacrifices of the thousands of individuals in the ongoing war to preserve liberty, there is the occasion that "the sacrifice will be me." Association of her personal plight with the noblest traditions of the country, rather than in self-gratification, calmed the raging that had confounded her. She didn't look forward to the destruction of her career; she approached it with sadness, but in this sacred place, Molly was consoled by a bittersweet gratitude that it might advance the causes in which she believed and to which she had dedicated so much of her life.

Sunday, August 30, 1998

Sunday Horse had to go back to New York to organize the agenda for the most important week of his life. Molly, for the only time she could remember during her residence in Washington, had a completely free day. She called her closest friend on the First Lady's staff and asked if there was any intimation that she should reconsider her position in the AOM matter, "Honey, I wish I could help, but I have to tell you that subject is so far off the radar screen around here that I couldn't get the lowest-ranking official here even to put it on his agenda. They aren't even taking phone calls from their relatives; forget anybody who is trying to collect political favors right now. You'll just have to run with it."

Chapter 28

Molly came into the office on Monday with a steely reserve. For the department, the agency, and herself, there were people who simply had to be given the opportunity to present arguments. At this time in August with POTUS (the Secret Service acronym for the President of the United States) and the Congress out of town, no lawyer or lobbyist was in town by coincidence. There had to be a compelling reason.

The modest demeanor of her visitor surprised her. Here was one of the legendary Senate Majority leaders, known universally as Judge, one minor title to which he was entitled, who was credited with having brought down a president of the other political party. Many times considered for the Supreme Court and the tireless arbitrator of international conflicts that seemed to yield only to his decency and persuasiveness, he was such a formidable person Molly wondered if she would be able to maintain her own position. She reminded herself that the tobacco companies hire him. He puts 'em on one leg at a time. She had prepared carefully for such meetings.

"I thought it would help, Judge, if I were to give you some of the background of this agency's involvement in the question of ESOPs and our recent activities."

"That would, indeed, be most helpful. First, I want to thank you for your courtesy in giving me time on such short notice. I hope this hasn't disturbed your vacation arrangements."

Molly proceeded for a full half hour to explicate the Employee Retirement Income Security Act of 1974 and its ESOP regulations.

"Let me move on to the situation with the American Observer Employee Stock Ownership Plan. We have been working with this plan for several years. In the first place, the founders of the company indicated a great interest in the concept of employee ownership, and

transferred 20 percent of the equity to a trust for this purpose. The
AOM ESOP, following the effective date of our regulation, decided to
borrow money to finance a tender offer for control of the company,
using its existing shares as collateral. At this point, I can only report
what I know. Apparently, Mr. Cedric Rhodes entered into a relationship with Universal Bank, of which the ESOP trustee is a wholly
owned subsidiary, by which Universal would provide the financing
necessary for him to acquire, ultimately, all of the outstanding shares.
This private equity financing was raised from pension funds, the pro-
priety of whose participation is not at issue, in the form of a trust that
would be administered by Universal. The terms of the trust are of
critical importance in three regards: first, Mr. Rhodes has undertaken
no personal commitment with respect to the loans; second, all of the
AOM stock is collateral for the loans and is the sole recourse in the
event of default; and third, Mr. Rhodes has made no personal obligation with respect to management of the enterprise. This loan has been
approved by Universal's loan committee and, indeed, by its full board
of directors.

"As near as I can determine, the executives of Universal were igno-
rant of the activity of their subsidiary as trustee of the AOM ESOP.
The trustee's executive, acting as the administrator of the AOM ESOP,
brought to the Universal loan department a request for financing of
the proposed tender offer. At some point, the chief executive of Universal, to whom, in the interests of full disclosure I must tell you, I
was once married, became aware of the two parties, each with an interest in tender, each with an interest in financing the tender through his
bank. At this point, I have no confidence that I know what has happened beyond having received a formal letter request on Friday from
the plan administrator requesting that this agency rule that Universal is obligated to extend to it the same credit that it has approved for
Mr. Rhodes.

"What is apparent on the face of this request is that the ESOP
request is based on credit at least as good as that offered by Mr.
Rhodes. The value of Mr. Rhodes's personal participation in the future

of AOM is not at issue, because he has refused to commit himself to any time or role. Mr. Rhodes has invested only nominal capital in the new venture, so the credit is based entirely on the company's capacity to repay it.

"I realize that I'm taxing your patience, but it's essential for this department, this agency, and for me professionally that our procedures be understood and that they be understood as meeting our statutory responsibilities. You'll bear with me when I conclude simply that I've decided, subject to being persuaded otherwise by yourself, as the official charged with responsibility in the matter that I'll issue the letter requested by the plan administrator. I believe due to the notoriety of this situation the department has an obligation to make unmistakably clear our commitment to the principles of our newly effective regulation. To fail to take action would, in my opinion, damage the cause of employee ownership to which this government has been committed for over thirty years."

Judge had been a splendid listener, attentive and reactive. Like an Olympic swimmer making his turn, he effortlessly and powerfully began to talk. "I'm grateful for your candor. I'm appreciative of the time, talent, and integrity that the department and you personally have invested in the development of this important code. I'm grateful for your rendition of the statute's history, which comports with my own understanding; and I am respectful of the process right up to your last sentence. I do not understand why this agency feels that it must immediately interpose itself, as a matter of first impression, into an admittedly fractious and confusing situation. Respectfully, I suggest that time is needed for the relevant facts to become clear. One worries that damage to the department's credibility could result from a decision seen as taken in needless haste. There is no question of bad faith here; there is no allegation of irreparable injury. Why, therefore, isn't the public good best served by a deliberate review of the issues, a forum in which all parties are given the opportunity to present their view of the matter and in which all parties have equal opportunity to dispute the view of others? Why must we have this rush? I haven't analyzed the history of this agency with care, but I wonder whether there's another example of a request involving issues of great moment and economic significance being received on a Friday necessitating a reply on the following Monday."

Molly knew there would be heat, but she was confident. "I have carefully considered the issues which you raise, although I must say that I can't do it as clearly and persuasively as do you. In my prepared remarks, I tried to convey some of the culture of this matter. At the risk of being repetitive, I want you to realize that we've spent two full years patiently developing the modern interpretation of a centuries-old trust doctrine. There are no issues relevant to my formal opinion that are in doubt. They are as I've just summarized them. I'm confronted with two financing alternatives that differ only in three quantifiable respects that make possible a precise comparison. That being the case, for the reasons I have cited, I'm of a mind to issue this formal letter."

Judge paused, as if uncertain how to organize his next assault: "Yes, yes, indeed....There is always the question...of 'one government.' The left hand and the right hand. Cabinet officers really carry out White House policy..."

Molly knew where this conversation was leading. Rather than attacking the implied question head on, as was normally her style, she waited patiently to find out more of what she didn't know.

"This administration," no names or titles, that's significant she was careful to notice, "has had a very compatible relationship with Mr. Rhodes and I'm sure there's a strong desire not to inflict damage in that direction needlessly." *All very tentative*, she thought, as she watched the Great Man dance.

Molly continued in silence.

"Someone of your stature would, I know, be most sensitive to important relationships..." He stumbled. Perhaps he had danced too long.

The thoughts whirled around in Molly's head. *Does he have authority from the White House? From whom? How specific is it? I know the president owes him a lot. He should've been in the Cab-*

inet. He could've been on the Supreme Court. If he asked for this as a favor, I can't think they wouldn't give it to him. But has he asked? I won't let him bluff me just because he knows people in high places, but I don't want to back him into a corner and needlessly create another powerful enemy.

Molly decided on candor. Let the chips fall. "I'm very clear on the chain of command in the Executive Branch and, to my knowledge," leaving open the possibility that he had better information than she did, "my proposed acts are in compliance with administration policy."

Molly was getting more comfortable. *Either he has clear authority and will order me, or he doesn't have authority and will bluff me, confident that he can retroactively get confirmation. Or else he'll play it straight. Does he know I spent several years in the White House working for the family? How much does it cost to get a man like this to perform this kind of task, to spend his own political capital?*

Molly continued, helpfully, "Things are obviously confused at 1600. My former colleagues in the East Wing don't feel they can get specific consideration of this matter at this time, and the information that I've received is I'm to proceed in accordance with my own convictions. It's important that I not make a mistake about this. I've a number to call that will put me through to an aide who has physical access to the president. Should we make a call right now?" There it is, if he has an ace to play, play it; or let's see the bluff.

Judge, for the first time, looked a bit uncomfortable, as if he were calculating whether it was worth it to risk this kind of political capital on this matter, at this time. *Molly has played this one straight, she reminded me, very politely, of something I'd forgotten or, perhaps I never knew; she's a confidant of the First Lady. She didn't let me embarrass myself. I don't find myself in that position too often, but the game is over unless I do something.* "Why don't we make the call?"

Judge quickly calculated Molly was playing this straight. *So what do I get from the call?* As Molly was punching the numbers into her conference phone, he waved his hand to indicate she should stop. She raised her finger and then disconnected. Judge went on as if nothing had happened. "I don't really feel comfortable adding to the burdens the man is dealing with at this time. The chief of staff has assured me, as recently as this morning, the president wants everything possible to be done by this administration to accommodate the interests of Mr. Rhodes."

Molly said, "I know of this general policy, but I'm not specifically sure the president won't direct me to do otherwise than I feel appropriate in this matter. There's only one way to be sure," and she started punching the phone buttons again.

When he heard this, Judge realized that he wouldn't be successful in pushing this bluff further. He didn't want to risk mismanaging the affair and extract a negative. He waved his hand again to facilitate what he found hard actually to say, "I personally, Madame Secretary, am very satisfied with your conduct here. I might just add, I've had a certain amount of experience in government. I've always been grateful for caution in situations where I'm conscious my personal, rather than purely professional, sensitivities are involved."

Molly was profoundly comfortable that in the final process of making a decision she had taken the measure of this "great man": "I'm sure, Judge, that you've found sometimes your most important decisions have been in areas where personal and professional considerations are congruent."

It was now close to lunchtime and Molly needed a few minutes with Klebowitch and Levin.

"OK, you guys, it's show time. What do we have to do now?"

They looked at each other. This was a very different Molly from the dispirited lady who had dragged out of the building on Friday.

Levin was sad at the moment of victory because he knew the price. "As a legal matter, we've complied with all necessary procedures. When you sign and issue the order, it becomes official. We can publish it in the Federal Record and on the Internet."

Klebowitch was exhausted leading his agency through its unaccustomed day in the sun. "Every lobbying and public relations group in the country is bombarding us. I've put in extra extensions to cover the calls. Nothing new. Same stuff. We're getting calls from lawyers who say they are close to the situation, but who don't answer when we ask who they represent. They smell something. I don't think these people are going to try and block this through the legal route."

"There's some nastiness in the press. One paper says that you're power mad. Another says frankly that you're doing a favor for an old boyfriend. There's a contrived nature to all of this, it's as if the PR people are being paid to produce a result, but they haven't got the smell of blood. Mercenaries. This doesn't appear to be more than a one-day story. What else is new? Rich guy wants a favor from the government. Government official has another idea. Rich guy hires the usual lawyers, investigators, and journalists to dig for mud, to separate the wheat from the chaff, to publish the chaff, and see what happens. Nothing has happened. For the next ten years, when anybody runs a search on your name, they will come up with the damnedest collection of libelous material. In this great country of ours, public officials are deemed to have consented to having their reputations besmirched."

Molly asked, "Is there anyone else I need to consult before signing this letter? I've asked the White House, I've talked with the secretary, I've gotten a limp handshake from OMB, Congress is not in session, but I've endured the chairman. OK, well, call in the cameras and we'll have our own little ceremony."

It was now twelve-fifteen on Monday, August 31, 1998. Molly was sitting at her desk flanked by Levin and Klebowitch. Klebowitch handed her a document, the cameras rolled; she placed the document on her desk and signed it with a wistful glance at the scar on her finger. More cameras, she passed the document to Levin, who, lawyer to the end, blotted it. Levin passed the document to Barbara; photocopy machines, e-mails, fax machines whirred, and the letter was now the official policy of the U.S. Government.

Quite a good beginning to the week.

Epilogue

In his office, Drive was on the phone with Judge. "You told her that she should be a team player and she said that, as far as she knew, she was carrying out administration policy. She offered you a phone call directly to the president..."

"Yeah, she played it straight. Her instructions were that no orders would be forthcoming and she should use her own discretion. Then she explained why she chose to sign the letter now."

"OK. Do you think the president would take a call directly from me? I know, I know you would've cashed any chips you had. OK. I can't get anything you couldn't get for me better. They're just not letting any calls get through to the president. Well, they never ring a bell to tell you when it's over, but I don't see how we can outbid the fully financed company employees who already have a 20 percent position. Thanks, I appreciate your effort."

Vern and Drive just looked blankly at each other as the click sounded on the conference phone signaling the end of Judge's call.

Drive shook his head. "If I ever teach any of my children anything, it'll be it's the unintended consequences, of the best plans, that are decisive. We won the war. We broke the trustees. We had the shareholders swarming to tender us their stock and then my own blindness hangs me. It wasn't life or death for me to have explicit contractual freedom to work for the new company. I could've lived with a reasonable provision. And it's only because I *insisted*, that the Department of Labor was able to measure the credit, the ESOP's, and mine exactly against each other. You just have to figure that this deal didn't want to happen. How could you figure that the president at the end of the day would not want to risk further offending his wife?"

Drive recovered from his maudlin musing. "Who's that singer who said that life boils down to knowing when to hold 'em and when to fold 'em?"

Vern wasn't used to disaster on this scale and wouldn't have known a pop culture icon if he sat in his lap. Drive pushed his intercom, "Send him in. Thank you." Vern looked toward the door as Joey entered with an oversized envelope in his hand.

"Hey, Drive, Vern. I heard, I'm so sorry." The three shook hands.

Drive went on with the classical references, bred into those with a traditional British education, "Do you remember 'Those whom the Gods despise, they give them what they ask for?' I wanted the perfect financing and you got it for me," Drive smiled and pointed at Vern, "and in its perfection, the only way I could be thwarted. Your ex-wife, and, a first for me, world events, prevented me from getting through to someone I've bought before and will buy again. If I'm not careful, I'll turn into a philosopher and a monk. This isn't a game I can win. There'll be another day, old friend."

Ever-practical Vern chirped, "Well, at least we both made some money, your own profit on tendering. I feel good we loaned you the money; it'll be a bit of reward for a month's work and we should end up with something from somebody."

Drive reflected. "A lot of the guys in this on spec aren't going to believe their bad luck. The arbs will come out all right, but some of those 'facilitators' will have little luck finding anyone to pay them. Having backed down the trustees, they're probably still celebrating and already spent the money. We need to be a little careful with how the story is handled. As the great Yogi put it, 'It ain't over till it's over.' Why don't your people work with Joey here and his team and prepare a press release, something like 'Cedric Rhodes, having established the feasibility of acquiring ownership of AOM, concedes to the superior bid of the company's ESOP out of respect for Randy and Shelley Porter's final legacy to their employees.' That's the idea, graciousness but nothing that exposes us to liability from the slime. This'll be a one-day story. Blink and you'll miss it. I'm going on to the next one. I leave town today." Drive stood up.

As Vern stood up to leave, he screwed up his nerve to ask, "I hope you still feel good about chairing our advisory board."

Drive managed a terse, "Just don't count on any meetings for a while." Vern was content with that, all things considered, and he shook Drive's hand as he slipped out. Joey stood, not ready to leave, and Drive nodded, "Joseph, if you've got a minute?"

"Sure," Joey sat, "Thanks. So you're gone?"

"Yes. I'm off to recharge and meditate on my mistakes and get ready for my next one."

"Nice, that sounds like a plan."

"It does. See here, I asked you over to say goodbye and to say goodbye to your uncle *for* me." Joey was confused and looked it.

"I hope things are OK with you guys?" Now Joey looked worried, "He's the hardest working man I've ever met. I'm sure..."

"Joey, things are great between us. Your uncle fought hard to save me from myself and I still wouldn't listen. He's a fine man and I'm now more indebted to him than I can say." That sounded extreme and Joey looked confused all over again.

"You were hired because of family and your uncle was right to recommend you. You impressed me and I've been doing this," and he waved at his big office, "for a while." Joey was a little embarrassed and was about to say something but Drive cut him off. "I know what family means and so now I want you to understand that this is a 'family' favor I'm asking."

Joey wasn't any more comfortable than Drive at that moment but he nodded at Drive, to show he understood. Drive continued, "Family is a funny thing, people get older, they move on, and sometimes if they're lucky, they grow up too. Some people you work with and they become like family, but they have to move on, and dreams change, and the love you feel for people...evolves into a different kind of..."

Joey couldn't stand watching this old man struggle at describing something that was clearly so difficult to share with someone else. He could bully presidents, blow billion-dollar deals, and not blink, but his own feelings were an intangible mystery. Joey cut him off and just spit it out.

"You mean about Marty and your press lady in the CNN building?" He said it light and boyishly as if he didn't really understand who was who. He knew he'd done the right thing because Drive looked relieved.

"Oh. Oh, yes. So he's *met* her?" Drive was curious, but mostly relieved.

"Not yet," Joey looked at his watch, "they're supposed to meet for the *first time* this afternoon."

Drive smiled to himself, and then spoke thoughtfully, like a father, "They're kindred spirits. I wish them all the best. That's my message for your uncle, that I wish them well."

"I'm sure he knows that."

"I hope he does. I hope they both do." Drive stood up, refreshed as after a brisk walk. Joey stood too and remembered his envelope and handed it to Drive. Drive opened it and pulled out an artist's caricature of Drive as a white knight, in the center of the fray, protecting urchins and peasants labeled "Charities and Shareholders" from a fiendish hoard of serpents and baboons labeled "Everyone Else." Drive laughed with delight.

"The white knight! Who told you?"

"I just came up with it, you know, it was the best spin, once the deal actually went down. I thought it would make a nice cover for the newsstands. I thought you might like to have it. The kid who did it is really quite good."

Drive was touched and put it back in the envelope.

"The best spin. Spin we did. It's marvelous and I will cherish it." Drive spontaneously put a hardy grip on the back of the young man's neck, like a caress and gave him a big smile as he followed him to the door.

"No 'runner stumbles' for you, see to it."

"Marty told you that?" Joey felt a little naked, hearing the rule for their family business outside of the family.

Drive turned back to his desk, "Your uncle told me a lot of things."

In walking back to the Sherry Netherland, Drive decided to go by way of Park Avenue and crossed in front of St. Bartholomew's Church. When he glanced at the placard in front of the church all he could see were the recent words in the *New York Times* about the president's trip to Russia, "Disagreed on what he should say...or even whether he should go at all." And wondered if they applied to him. Events have a way of creating their own reality. He didn't feel any younger but he did feel lighter. He was relieved, at last.

When he got back to the apartment, he called out.

"Lily, do you think we can get ready to leave this afternoon?"

"Where are we going?"

"I need to go home."

"Home? Goodness, Drive," as she obediently turned to go pack, "which one?"

Drive had to laugh.

"It's good to hear you laugh, dear," Lily said from the bedroom.

Vern was still staring out the window of his dining area where he had morosely been eating alone with his trusty calculator when Horse came in. He turned and said, "You look different. Do I look different? This has been a hell of a business."

Horse sat down without affectation or invitation. Everything had changed. "For the first time since I left the Army, I feel I've been doing something worthwhile." Vern was a little shocked but he was too tired to react. Horse was a fine golf partner, and a decent enough guy. Horse continued, "We'll never be real friends, you and I, but I want you to know that I have affection for you. I can't help you, but I appreciate you. I have to resign. You have my letter. It's nothing to talk about. It's necessity. I'll be the 'shareholder' of AOM, the CEO of the Employees' Benefit Plan. I'll do a good job. You can either continue to be the trustee or be our banker, but not both. Please resign as trustee. The DOL people won't permit a continuing conflict of interest, and I *want* to do business with you. You deserve to be paid a fair fee for arranging the financing and for administering the trust, but we have to get DOL approval on account of the related parties problem. No fairness opinions, no funny fees. We can be good customers and good references. This won't work out as well as you hoped, but there'll be fees and ongoing business. All worth your commitment. They'll be a welcome addition to the bank's earnings. Shake hands with a new customer!"

Poor Vern had no idea how to respond. Was he being buffaloed? New business? He almost reached for his calculator. The concept of friendship was not within his ken. The assurance he would continue to be in a business relationship and there would be immediate fees out of a situation he feared to be a complete failure was joy itself. Somehow, he realized Horse had moved beyond him, that there "are things in heaven and earth that are not dreamt of in thy philosophy." He could cope with this. "I'm glad to think of a future with you as a customer. Now, I can sign up for all those member-guest golf tournaments with a guest who is a customer. We can use the big plane. May I ask a personal favor? I've always admired that little pin you wear, as a souvenir?...You know..."

Vern always had his eye on the important things. Horse realized this was as far as Vern could go and there was nothing more to be said. He pulled his Cincinnati rosette out of his lapel and handed it to Vern. This would have to be the epitaph for a transaction and their relationship.

Vern returned to his office and called in his secretary. She hung on his every word, a prerequisite for this particular job. Vern said, "We've wonderful news for the next board meeting, the prospect of immediate fees from the AOM financing and leadership in one of the great future businesses of America. We're the world's leader in financing employee ownership of great companies. I'll be terribly busy communicating with the board members this great news personally. Could you call Mrs. Stillman and let her know our ship has come in, after all. We'll have the company jet for next weekend in Paris. Tell her to invite friends.'"

When she walked out of his office, Vern realized that he was really alone. He would have to live inside his own skin. And so he mused, *this might be a good time to take up with the dean that professorship they've been wanting me to endow at Harvard. The Vernon Stillman Professorship. Sounds damn pretty, yes, sir.*

Horse took a train to Pleasantville and met with the ESOP executive committee in the AOM main directors' room. Everybody was too excited to listen. Finally, Horse was able to make clear that the ESOP would shortly be in the position to tender for all of the outstanding stock of AOM.

He said very wisely, "I'll be Chairman of the ESOP, the owner of the company, and I'll carefully monitor the management, but you should all appreciate where I'm coming from. Not everybody will get all they want, I'll have to make decisions that none of you will like. What I understand is it is my responsibility to make this business flourish. That'll require many hard choices. I'll do the best I can. This thing isn't going to work unless we can agree that the tough decisions must be made."

At this point, Horse could have had them agreeing to anything. What was essential was their understanding that he could do nothing that diluted his own integrity.

Molly took out another sheet of writing paper and tried yet another draft of her letter of resignation. While it was clear that civil servants were entitled, indeed, required, to use their own best judgment in making policy decisions, it was also clear that the permanent government, the lobbyists, the committee chairs, the fund-raisers, would make life impossible for the official and their agency who flaunted an important request. While Molly could be protected by the First Couple, this would cost everyone more than it was worth. The only course was to be a step ahead of the guillotine blade. With the elections coming up in November, Molly felt she could finish vital agency business by the time the new Congress came into session, so she timed her retirement for year's end. It was hardly worth her enemies while to cause her grief in those few months.

Molly didn't want a life where she acceded to other's expectations and timetables. She wanted to invest her considerable resources into a force that would effectively promote the cause. Under the name of Munro, Young, and Company, she planned on creating an investment banking firm that would counsel and finance employee groups wishing to exercise effective ownership roles within public companies. She looked forward to confrontation with the CEO-dominated system, because now she had a rep. She'd stood up to the best and she was still standing.

It was a magic time of day. Shadows were long and everyone was happier to be going home. The day wasn't the hottest and in the shade you could almost feel a breeze. Nothing beat summer in the city. And this was the summer to beat all summers. Marty Beal, splendid in a three-piece gray Armani with scarlet handkerchief and matching accoutrements, including a garment bag, checked his watch for the third time. He was early and impatient. The cloak-and-dagger stuff had gotten old. Let's get it on, Lady, he thought as he scanned the hundreds of faces leaving the building at the end of the day, everyone hurrying to some place they'd rather be. He only had eyes for one person; a young woman, a striking redhead, simply clad, who looked as if she'd stepped out of a biblical painting. She was tall, taller than he, in her heels. He approached the woman he had known only as Rose and said, "You must be Ruth. Rose, I get it. Where's your luggage, I thought we're flying off somewhere."

She said, "Who said anything about flying?" and pointed to the limousine waiting at curbside. "I figured if we're proposing to get married that I'd better take you to Borough Park to meet my parents and find out if you can pass muster in the *real* world."

Marty didn't feel like he'd been hit by a bus, but he looked it. All that red hair, and the palest blue eyes. Where did she put all those brains in that skinny frame? Tall. Tall is good. Freckles, like a schoolgirl. He knew this day would come. The pit was before him. Goodbye, single life. That was fun, but this was better. Marty opened his heart and he leapt.

"Brooklyn, I can do Brooklyn." *Where'd that posh accent go?* he wondered.

"You've got a good start by getting the name right." She looked at him carefully and decided out loud, "There must be children." For the rest of his life, Marty was proud that he hadn't missed a beat.

"Sure. Why not? We can all play basketball together."

Acknowledgments

I acknowledge the unique help of those to whom I dedicated this book: my great grandfather, George Augustus Gardner, my "ancestor" who provided a context for a free life; my cousin, George Gardner Herrick, whose sensitivity to the difference between sacred and profane has illumined our lives; and my nephew, George Gardner Monks, who encouraged, improved, and collaborated on this venture.

It is, indeed, courageous of Jim Pannell to encourage a first novelist in his seventieth year and I thank him for his faith and support. Debra Hudak asked all the questions I prayed nobody would and edited with acuity. Barbara Sleasman has made everything in my life better for the last twenty years. I particularly appreciate her generation of draft after draft of this work that has been a long time in the making.

Nobody should see themselves in any of the characters in the book, but I hope the great joy I have had in our interaction is obvious to all with whom I have worked over the last fifty years. Milly, with whom I have shared this life, gave attention and improvement beyond human limits. Thank you.